Melvyn McHugh was born in 1953 in a small rural village in Essex. From the age of five, his journey to school passed by a garden centre, an army camp, several fruit orchards and a small village shop. While most boys of his age played football and fighting games, Melvyn would invent stories and then, most often, act them out as the hero or main character.

His after-school activities included collecting lizards, snakes, climbing trees, scrumping, and occasionally catching the odd chickens.

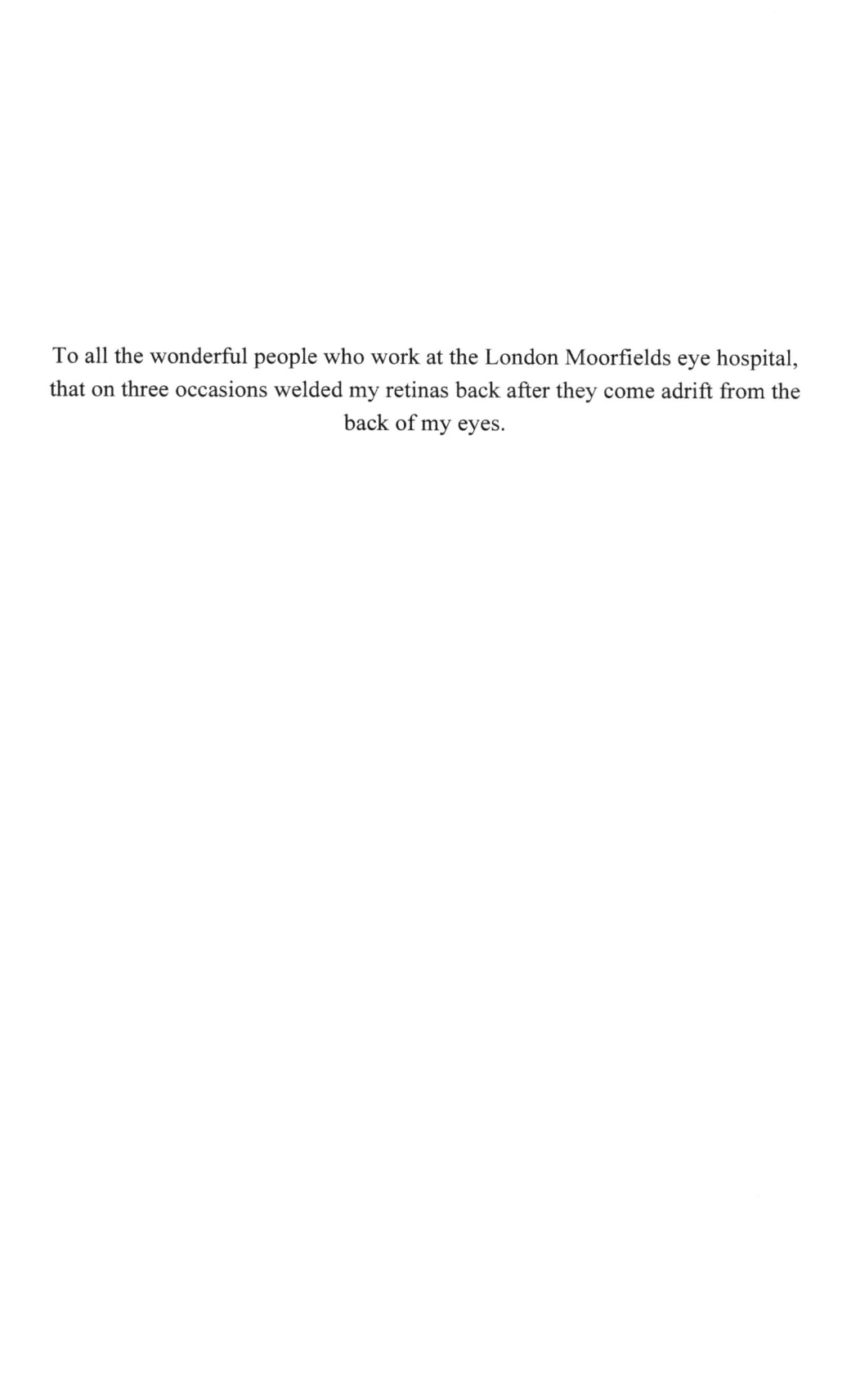

To all the wonderful people who work at the London Moorfields eye hospital, that on three occasions welded my retinas back after they come adrift from the back of my eyes.

Melvyn McHugh

BYE-BYE, INGLATERRA

Austin Macauley Publishers

LONDON * CAMBRIDGE * NEW YORK * SHARJAH

Copyright © Melvyn McHugh 2023

The right of Melvyn McHugh to be identified as author of this work has been asserted by the author in accordance with sections 77 and 78 of the Copyright, Designs and Patents Act 1988.

All rights reserved. No part of this publication may be reproduced, stored in a retrieval system, or transmitted in any form or by any means, electronic, mechanical, photocopying, recording, or otherwise, without the prior permission of the publishers.

Any person who commits any unauthorised act in relation to this publication may be liable to criminal prosecution and civil claims for damages.

This is a work of fiction. Names, characters, businesses, places, events, locales, and incidents are either the products of the author's imagination or used in a fictitious manner. Any resemblance to actual persons, living or dead, or actual events is purely coincidental.

A CIP catalogue record for this title is available from the British Library.

ISBN 9781398487789 (Paperback)
ISBN 9781398487796 (ePub e-book)

www.austinmacauley.com

First Published 2023
Austin Macauley Publishers Ltd®
1 Canada Square
Canary Wharf
London
E14 5AA

To all the crazy people that I have met along the way that have given me the incentive to create and write my stories.

And to all my family who obviously think I am crazy but up to this point haven't abandoned me.

Table of Contents

Chapter 1	11
Chapter 2	15
Chapter 3	25
Chapter 4	30
Chapter 5	36
Chapter 6	44
Chapter 7	50
Chapter 8	58
Chapter 9	71
Chapter 10	81
Chapter 11	95
Chapter 12	110
Chapter 13	119
Chapter 14	129
Chapter 15	140
Chapter 16	147
Chapter 17	153
Chapter 18	163
Chapter 19	172
Chapter 20	185

Chapter 21	194
Chapter 22	205
Chapter 23	214
Chapter 24	222
Chapter 25	231
Chapter 26	239
Chapter 27	254
Chapter 28	267
Chapter 29	277
Chapter 30	285
Chapter 31	294

Chapter 1

Horace Dankworth stood in the centre of his perfectly designed bay window, gazing out down Victoria Avenue, wearing his almost brand-new Calvin Klein cotton stretch trunks.

"Please don't stand there just wearing your pants, darling, people can see you," his wife Delia asked very politely from her position sitting on the edge of the sofa so she wouldn't crumple her new black skirt suit.

"This is our house and our bay window and these are my pants and besides there is no one out there," Horace replied, half turning his head and speaking over his right shoulder.

Delia looked at her husband standing in the bright early July sunlight, wishing she hadn't thrown out Horace's old white Y-fronts and that she hadn't bought the new black stretch Calvin Klein modern look pants.

When Horace had stood in the window wearing his old white Y-fronts, he just looked like a regular old guy in his late fifties. But in the new stretch black ones with the high white waistband, he looked ridiculous.

His bottom had taken up some weird shape that almost made her vomit, luckily for Delia from behind she couldn't see the front and the weird lumps that seem to be lurking inside that stuck out in every direction, Horace looked nothing like the young male model on the front of the packet.

Delia had realised right from the very first day when Horace had first worn them that they were totally wrong and that she had made a terrible mistake.

Delia hadn't bought the pants so that Horace could look sporty or trendy, she had bought them because she had noticed that in the last year or so, Horace forever had an unsightly yellow stain around the front opening that stood out like her bright yellow marker pen that she used to highlight the errors in the school children's homework.

Her very good friend from her old school days, and later coincidentally, university, Doctor Carolina Banks had suggested changing the colour of

Horace's pants to black after Delia had discussed the nasty little recurring stain problem with her.

Doctor Banks had reassured Delia that it was normal for a man of Horace's age to be a little damp around the front of the pants area and that the colour of yellow that Delia had described sounded to be of quite a healthy nature by its appearance.

"Dickhead!" Horace suddenly blurted out from his position in the bay window. "What a dickhead!"

Delia took her gaze and thoughts away from Horace's weird shaped arse. "Horace," she cried, "what language, we have to maintain standards."

"Dickhead," Horace repeated but this time with a bit more venom and spitting slightly onto the crystal-clear glass of the bay window.

"Who is a dickhead?" Delia asked, feeling quite uncomfortable using such language.

"Why would you park your car outside the front of your house? Especially on a day like today?"

"His wife Julia says he has a mild form of OCD and since he has retired, it seems to have gotten a lot worse," Delia said, standing up from the sofa and brushing the creases from her suit.

"AWYA. More like it," Horace said, not moving from his position inside the bay window.

"AWYA? What is AWYA?" Delia asked glancing down the road at the next-door neighbour but one.

"Always watching your arse," Horace chuckled.

"Don't be so ridiculous!" Delia snapped.

"For someone who is the headmistress of a junior school, you're not very streetwise," Horace chuckled again, "you must have noticed. When you go out into the front garden, he is out there seconds later, polishing his car and staring at your arse."

"The cars should be here soon," Delia said, glancing at her watch and moving back to the sofa and sitting down. "Horace darling, you're OK, aren't you? This whole business has been a terrible shock for everyone."

"I don't think any of us will ever be the same again," Horace said. "Who would have thought that our next-door neighbour was building a space rocket in the shed at the bottom of the garden."

"Can you imagine the damage it would have done if it had been closer to the houses," Delia said.

"Well, it completely buggered our conifers," Horace said, "they will never grow back, and all the bits of metal on our roof, some of them look quite sharp and dangerous."

"And the embarrassment for poor Hilary," Delia said shaking her head in disbelieve, "all those girlie magazines, charred and scorched all over the neighbour's gardens, with disgusting pictures of lady parts!"

"He was such a nice guy, he was the only decent one there at the office nothing like all the other backbiting bastards," Horace said and then spitting a little more onto the window.

"All those boxes and parcels that used to arrive at his house," Delia said, "we even signed for some and kept them in the hallway!"

"They could have been anything," Horace said. "Rocket launchers, sex toys, pictured of naked women, and nobody had a clue to what was going on and what he was building in that shed."

"Why would a man of his years want to look at pictures of naked women?" Delia said, "and locked away in that shed at the bottom of the garden for hours upon hours."

"Judging by the number of pages that are still blowing around all over the place, there must have been hundreds of magazines!"

"I feel so embarrassed for poor Hilary," Delia continued, "OK, a space rocket but sitting in that shed night after night reading all those filthy disgusting magazines, the poor woman. You haven't got any magazines, Horace, have you?"

Horace swung around, "Why would I want to look at stupid girlie magazines, and anyway where would I hide them, our shed is just about big enough for the petrol mower and a box of slug pellets! What about you! Have you got pictures of naked men or scantily dressed firemen hidden away in your school locker?"

"Don't be so stupid!" Delia snapped. "I haven't got a school locker and besides, I prefer policemen!" Delia began to laugh hysterically.

Horace couldn't help himself, Delia never ever made jokes, or laughed but to see his wife laughing hysterically and rolling around on the sofa, set him off laughing until the tears were rolling down his cheeks.

"That was a hell of a bang though, wasn't it, poor old Trever," laughed Horace. "I wonder what went wrong and why the rocket exploded like that?"

"That's what happens when you buy a rocket on the Internet from North Korea!" Delia laughed hysterically and wiped the tears from her face with a tissue.

"I wonder how big it was?" Horace said, sitting alongside his wife on the sofa. "Was it big enough for space travel? Was Trever planning on launching himself off to another planet? Or was it like one of those scaled models that he was planning to launch in the local park, just for fun?"

"The police didn't seem to be bothered much either," Delia said, she had now gathered her composure and was now sounding more like her normal self.

"Yes, very strange," Horace said. "They had a quick look around the garden, kicked a few metal fragments from the rocket around and left."

"The two young police constables seemed to be more interested in the girlie magazines than anything else, one of them kept picking up different pages and showing them to the other one and sniggering," Delia said, standing up from the sofa. "Accidental death, or death by misadventure, case closed, according to his wife, Hilary."

"Well," Horace said, "nothing is going to bring poor old Trevor back and the cars will be here at ten o'clock sharp so I am going into the bedroom to put my suit on and get myself ready."

Chapter 2

Horace emerged from the bedroom wearing his brand-new black suit, a pale blue shirt, black tie and brand-new black shoes. He had greased and carefully moulded what was left of his ginger and grey hair tightly to the top of his head.

Delia gave him the quick onceover as he made his way across the room to see if the cars were arriving from his lookout post from inside the bay window.

"You look very smart, my darling," she commented.

"I will claim it all back through my personal expenses," Horace said. "One of the perks of being an accountant. What in the hell of Mothering Sundays is happening here!" Horace blurted out. "That crazy guy from the home delivery service is coming up the road at about two hundred miles an hour!"

Delia suddenly heard the sound of screeching brakes and the slamming of a van door.

"Incredible!" Horace said. "He has double parked next to Richard's car and is unloading all the stuff from the van in middle of the road."

"Julia said he is very good; he carries everything into the house and puts it all away for her in all the correct cupboards," Delia said rising from the sofa and joining her very smartly dressed husband at the window.

"Yes," Horace said, "and he is most probably robbing her blind at the same time."

Just as the crazy delivery guy was walking towards Richard and Julia's door, balancing a pile of plastic trays loaded with food, the sombre shapes of the black funeral cars appeared, and were slowly heading up Victoria Avenue towards them.

The first car was a very long car with large rear windows so the coffin that it was carrying could be easily seen along with a beautiful tribute made from bright yellow roses which read, devoted husband, father and grandfather.

The driver was obviously confused by the fact that there was a huge white van blocking the road and a number of plastic trays full of what looked like white iced sticky buns. The black funeral car stopped behind the white van and the brightly polished Jaguar that belonged to Richard, the next door but one neighbour.

Just to add to the confusion, the four other black cars that had been following stopped in the middle of the road also.

Some people came out from next door and began to walk down the road towards the parked cars.

"The two men walking side by side are Trevor's and Hilary's sons," Delia said. "I suppose we should go out there now."

Horace pulled the front door shut and the handle sharply up, then turned the key, triple locking the front door and then following Delia along the garden path and out into the street.

One of Trevor's sons was telling the driver of the first car that he had to move the car closer to the house so they could load up all the flowers, that had been delivered to the house over the past few days.

Then Horace and Delia heard the other son saying to the driver, "I think you can squeeze past if you drive one side of the car up on the kerb and along the grass verge."

The driver, without questioning Trever's son's judgment, turned the steering wheel to the left and slowly applied the gas and mounted the kerb and then began to drive the long black vehicle, carrying Trevor's coffin along the edge of the grass verge.

Trevor's son by that time was walking backwards and beckoning the driver forward, paying particular attention only to the right side of the vehicle as it slowly passed the beautiful flowering lime trees.

The left side of car however passed quite easily over one of the plastic trays full of white sticky glazed buns; the driver had no idea and didn't even feel the slightest of bumps.

The rest of the cars followed in procession, and by the time they had parked outside Trevor's house, the recently deceased, there was white icing sugar and bright red glace cherries, stuck to all the tyres and all over the road, everywhere!

Nobody noticed the trail of squashed sticky buns until the driver suddenly appeared from Richard and Julia's house carrying his empty plastic delivery trays.

The delivery driver seemed to be totally unaware of what was actually going on in the street and not showing even the slightest hint of respect, he started to shout and scream in a foreign language at the driver of the leading hearse.

Meanwhile, Richard Heed, accompanied by his wife Julia, casually left their house, walked across to funeral car number three and made themselves comfortable in the backseat, completely unaware that all the carnage had been caused by him parking his very flashy, over-polished Jaguar car in the street right outside the front of his house.

"I thought you said he was a nice guy?" Horace turned to Delia, whispering into her ear. "He doesn't even seem to be able to talk using the Queen's English."

"He's just probably upset about all his ruined sticky buns," Delia replied naively.

Horace walked over to where the delivery guy was standing, very carefully avoiding the squashed sticky buns not wanting to get white sticky goo all over his brand new black shiny shoes.

Horace politely tapped the delivery guy on the shoulder with one hand and taking out his wallet with the other offered him a twenty-pound note.

The man snatched the twenty-pounds from Horace's hand, said something in a foreign language what could have come from anywhere in northern Europe, picked up his trays jumped into his van and sped away.

"That was very nice and thoughtful of you, darling," Delia said after Horace had made it safely back through the minefield of sticky buns.

"Don't worry," Horace smiled, "I will claim it all back from my personal expenses."

By the time all of the five drivers from the funeral cars had loaded all the flowers into the first car, both of Trevor's sons had organised everyone and had them all seated in the four other cars.

Then Trevor's sons went back into the house and reappeared with their mother, walking on either side, both holding her by the hand and then helping her into the first car.

Delia reached across and held Horace's hand as the cars began the slow journey up and along Victoria Avenue. Horace and Delia were both surprised by the amount of people that were gathered in the church by the time that they had arrived. Horace glanced around, he could see most off the men and women from squirrel and squirrel the large firm of accountancy that he had worked for, during the last twenty-five years or so.

But apart from that he didn't seem to recognise hardly anyone else, just a few neighbours and the guy from the bar at the golf club.

"All these people," Delia said.

"Yes," Horace whispered, "it appears that Trever had a lot of family and friends, but we never ever see anyone visit them or hardly anyone ever go to their house, or socialise."

For Horace the service passed by very quickly they sang a few hymns, a young man from Trever's relatives read a poem and then it was all over.

Everyone slowly made their way out of the old eighteenth century church along a very narrow pathway along the side, and then across the cemetery to where Trevor's body was finally being laid to rest.

And then later, exactly after two and a half hours had passed, at twelve midday, Horace and Delia were being dropped off in the large gravel car park of the Belvedere golf and country club.

"I must say, everything has been very well organised," Delia said as she held on to Horace as they walked up the white marble steps of the grand old country manor that had been tastefully converted into a club house with function suites, surrounded by an eighteen-hole golf course.

"Yes," replied Horace, "considering poor old Trever only blew himself up just three weeks ago, but something even stranger than that, our company are actually paying for everything, the food and the bar!"

As Horace and Delia passed through the large entrance doors and into the large reception hall, they were greeted by a huge staggered row of sandwich boards and large brightly printed posters stuck to the walls, all reading, *Come to Spain! Don't waste all your hard-earned cash, don't leave it all to your children!*

Wake up every morning to the smell of freshly squeezed oranges.

You can own your own villa in the sun and eat freshly caught sardines every day.

"Really!" Delia puffed, looking around at all the display board and posters in dismay. "One would have thought that they might have waited until the funeral was over."

"I suppose all this stuff was organised well in advance," Horace said. "We were very lucky to get the function suite at such short notice."

Horace and Delia carefully negotiated the very tricky pathway between the large Wooden framed signs that had been carefully placed to cause an obvious obstruction so they would receive the most attention.

Horace quickly glanced around the function suite once they passed though the large opening between the large wooden and crushed velvet double doors.

On the right-hand side standing on the polished wooden flooring surrounding by his usual crowd of bum lickers was Cyril Squirrel senior partner of Squirrel and Squirrel. And then to the left surrounded by the normal crowd of back stabbers, was the other senior partner, Cedrick. Beyond and straight down the middle and seated at the back of the room, Horace could see Trevor's wife Hilary.

"I am going over to talk to Hilary," Delia said, "she appears to be sitting over there all alone." In a split of a second, she was gone, wandering off, leaving Horace standing there all alone in the doorway. Delia made her way across the wooden dance floor towards the thick spongy area that had been laid down with dark blue patterned Axminster carpet.

Both groups of men, the bum lickers and the back stabbers, watched her as she passed them by, Horace could see them eyeing Delia up and down and then turned their gaze in his direction, Freddie Tidmarsh the biggest and the best of the bum lickers said something to the rest of the group and they all laughed.

Then instinctively, both groups turned their backs on Horace, making it clear that he wasn't welcome. Horace looked around the room for a friendly face, normally in the past at Christmas time or other functions, Horace would have found and spoken to Trevor, but he wasn't there anymore; Trevor had gone forever and he was never coming back.

Horace felt alone and awkward not knowing what to do or what direction to take, he could see Richard and his wife Julia his next door but one neighbours sitting alone on two very comfortable chairs on the right-hand side of the room, but Horace would rather burn in hell than to talk to that dick head.

Horace made a snap decision and spun around and went back out of the doors and turned left, skipped down the four steps, passed the toilets on the left-hand side and went into the club bar.

Frank the bartender who Horace and recognised at the church earlier had changed out of his black suit and was now looking smart but casual. Like Trevor, Frank was a good guy, always very easy to talk to.

Horace glanced around; the bar was unusually empty.

"Hi Horace!" Frank smiled. "Come and take the weight of and stop me talking to myself."

Horace shuffled alongside one of the light brown leather bar stools and manoeuvred himself up onto the round spongy seat.

"What can I get you? Orange and club soda?"

Horace looked anxiously at all the different types of drinks that were lined up on the shelves behind the bar.

"No," Horace said, "I need to break the no drinking in the daytime rule, I feel like shit and alcohol might make me feel better."

"What's it going to be? Whisky, Rum, Gin?" Frank teased, knowing that Horace was a lightweight and from past experience, Horace had gotten himself pissed on two small Irish coffees. Frank looked at Horace; he could see he wasn't his normal self. "What about one of these new spritzers?"

Frank waved his open hand in the direction of some brightly coloured fruity drinks and then towards the large cardboard cut-out at the end of the bar.

Horace looked at the new cardboard display of a very large breasted woman, holding a bottle of spritzer, wearing a bikini and at least five litres of fake tanning lotion, with the caption reading, whip off the top and shake it out.

Horace, shock his head in disbelief and then examined the row of brightly coloured fruity drinks.

"I will try an orange-flavoured spritzer, please Frank."

Frank picked up one of the brightly coloured orange drinks and gave it a good shake before whipping off the top and pouring it into a glass.

Horace slid his hand inside his jacket to get his wallet from the inside pocket.

"That OK," Frank said, "your company is paying for everything."

"What, even in this bar?" Horace said, genuinely concerned.

"Yes, no problem; I will keep a tab and then ring it up on the till next door."

"Well in that case, Frank have one yourself," Horace smiled, he was feeling much better already.

Frank poured himself a double fine malt whisky and then took a small sip and put in on the bar next to Horace's bright orange fruity drink.

Horace then picked up his drink and downed it in one go. "Tastes just like freshly squeezed orange juice," he said wiping his lips with his brand-new silk hanky. "Give us another."

Frank looked at Horace, he wasn't sure if that was a good idea, the drinks had a good shot of vodka in them. But it had been an awful morning and besides, it was his job to sell as many drinks as possible.

Horace grabbed the drink directly from Frank's hand and downed it in one go. "And another!" Horace said.

"Slow down a bit, Horace me old mate, it is only one o-clock in the afternoon!"

Horace ran his gaze along the shelf loaded full of drinks. "I will try a passion fruit this time."

Frank poured the passion fruit spritzer into a fresh glass. "Now promise me, Horace, that you won't drink this one all in one go, they have got a lot of vodka in them you know."

Horace took a small lady like sip from the glass. "These really are good, really fruity."

"Terrible business," Frank said, "poor old Trevor!"

Horace took a slightly bigger sip from his glass. "Yes, poor old Trever, such a nice intelligent guy."

"Did you know anything about the rocket that he was building in his garden shed?" Frank asked.

"No, nothing," Horace said. "The first Delia and I knew about it was the really loud bang at two o clock in the morning. We were nearly tossed out of our bed and then the roof of the house was peppered with pieces of hot flying metal. And the next morning, Trevor's shed had disappeared along with all our conifer trees that were neatly planted at the bottom of our garden."

Horace gulped down the passion fruit spritzer. "I suppose you heard about all the magazines?"

"Funny business," Frank said. "The last person in the world, that you would think of who would be looking at and reading all that kind of mucky stuff."

"Give us another, please Frank, I think I will try a blackcurrant this time, and pour yourself another."

"I bet it feels a bit strange at the office now, doesn't it?" Frank said as he poured the almost black-coloured blackcurrant spritzer into yet another clean glass. "Will it be hard to find a replacement for poor old Trever?" Frank asked, placing the almost black fruity drink on the bar top.

"That's the strangest thing about it," Horace said, "I haven't heard his name mentioned at all in the office since the explosion and the two bosses don't seem to be bothered in the slightest."

"Well, it was a terrible shock to everyone here at the golf club," Frank said sadly, "and we will all miss him," then Frank put his glass to his lips and downed his second double malt whiskey.

Horace picked up his glass and downed the very fruity blackcurrant drink, "Let's go on a bender," Horace smiled, banging the empty glass down on the beautifully polished oak bar top.

Frank laughed; he had never ever been asked to go on a bender before in all the years that he had been working in the bar at the golf club.

"I will have one more whiskey," Frank smiled, "and that's the last, and besides the Queen Elisabeth suite next door is only booked up until three."

Horace glanced at the large clock up on the wall above all the shelves of different types of alcohol, "We have a good hour and a half left," Horace said, "and I need to try the rest of the flavours of your very fine fruity spritzers, Frank, my old mate."

Frank poured himself one more fine double malt whiskey and placed it on the bar top, "so what's it going to be this time, Horace?"

"What's that one?" Horace pointed to a bright pink bottle.

Frank picked up the brightly coloured pink bottle, he had to squint his eyes a little to read the small print on the label, the very fine malt whiskey was beginning to affect his eyesight.

"Baby pink grapefruit, I think," Frank poured the brightly coloured thick sugary liquid into a clean glass.

"To Trevor!" Horace raised his voice and his glass at the same time.

"To Trever!" Frank said, "God rest his soul and may he rest in peace!"

Horace tilted his head back slightly, hoping the much thicker than the other liquid would slide down his throat.

"That's disgusting," Horace gagged. "Quick, give us one of them light blue ones to wash it down."

Frank squinted his eyes, "Ice cool Blueberry!"

"Give it," Horace croaked, "give it!"

Horace downed the Ice cool Blueberry drink in one go, it was much thinner than the last and seemed to wash down all the sugar that felt like it had glued itself to the back of his throat and his tonsils.

"Well," Horace said, "I must say, I much prefer the blackcurrant one much more, so I will have one more of those and then I will go and find my lovely wife Delia."

"That sounds like a good idea," Frank said as he poured the final fruity mix of sugar and vodka into yet another clean glass. "And I might just have one more myself, just for medicinal purposes."

Horace raised the glass to his lips and took a large slug. "Frank," Horace said. "I think I need to go to the bathroom, something weird is going on in my lower half."

Horace quickly slid off from his barstool and walked as quick as his legs would able, out through the door and sharply right into the men's toilet. Horace crashed through the half open door of the toilet cubicle, quickly pulling down his trousers and then cursing at the tight waistband of his new Calvin Klein pants.

Horace sat down onto the toilet seat, kicking off his trousers and pants just as the express train shot through platform poo, poo. After the train had passed, Horace felt much better and tried to push the toilet door shut with his left foot, being very careful to keep his bottom in the centre of the toilet seat, fearing that another train may be arriving at any moment.

After a few more trains had come and gone and a lot of disgusting noises from his bottom, Horace began to feel very, very drunk. Horace lent forward and picked up his trousers and then tucked them inside his new stretch Calvin Klein pants making a pillow. Then holding the pillow up to his right side of his head he lent against the wall of the cubicle and shut his eyes.

Suddenly, Horace was aware of voices, somewhere in the distance, on the other side of consciousness, what sounded like golfers returning from a morning round of golf.

He opened his eyes, luckily the toilet door was still pushed shut, his head started to spin and he quickly closed his eyes again, He could hear the sound of running water and the light conversation as the golfers went about their business and then the banging shut of the blue cushioned light oak toilet main door and then silence.

Then after another hour had passed and what seemed like in the distance, he could hear the voice of one of his bosses, talking.

"How much?" Cedrick asked, as his brother came into the toilet and stood facing the urinal and doing a very long wee.

"One thousand seven hundred forty-three pounds and sixty-seven pence," Cyril replied.

"That's a lot cheaper than what it would have cost us for his redundancy pay-out."

"Yes," Cedrick said coldly, "he's done us a huge favour by blowing himself up, now we don't have to think of an excuse to sack Spankworth we can offer him some sort of redundancy package, instead."

Even though Horace felt very drunk and his brain was only functioning at about thirty per cent, he was still shocked and very surprised that his bosses referred to him as Spankworth.

"Yes," Laughed Cyril. "Christmas has come early for Squirrel and Squirrel partners, we have buyers for the company and at a good price, and now we don't have the extra cost of redundancy."

"Yes, just one more little obstacle to overcome, Spankworth!"

The toilet door slammed shut once again and Horace was left all alone once again, feeling very, very drunk, and now very, very confused.

Chapter 3

Delia glanced around the Queen Elisabeth suite, her eyes searching for Horace, the function room had emptied considerably, with just a few pockets of people here and there.

Delia reached across and held Trevor's wife Hilary by the hand, "I must go and find Horace, he seems to have disappeared." Delia quickly glanced around the room shifting her eyes from side to side one last time before passing out through the door and turning left down the few steps and into the club bar.

Delia could see that Horace wasn't there, just a few golfers and Frank the barman propping up the bar.

"Have you seen Horace?" Delia said loud enough so everyone in the bar could hear.

"The last time I saw him he was rushing off to the toilet," Frank said trying to hide his guilt and thinking by now that Horace should be totally pissed out of his brains.

A large man stood up and turned to Delia, "I need to go to the little boy's room. I will see if he is still in there."

What only seemed like a split of a second later the man was shouting from the doorway, "Somebody call an Ambulance! he's had a heart attack, his tongue is hanging out and it's all blue!"

Frank quickly rang for an ambulance and everyone else rushed out of the bar and into the gent's toilets.

It wasn't pretty, Horace had slipped off from his perch and was now lying on the toilet floor with his head to one side and his tongue hanging out. Everyone stared at Horace's black tongue and then at the bright ginger pubic hair that covered his testicles. One of the golfers lent across and flushed the toilet after taking a deep breath and putting his hand over his mouth.

Delia pushed herself forward past the group of male bodies and retrieved Horace's make shift pillow fabricated from his trousers stuffed inside his pants, from down the side of the toilet. She then pulled the trousers out from the inside of the pants and then one leg at a time put them over Horace's feet and slid them upwards covering the clump of bright orange pubic hair.

Meanwhile, Freddie Tidmarsh, the champion bum licker at Squirrel and Squirrel, had snaked his way into the toilet. Searching for the two bosses and then stayed just long enough to gather sufficient information about Horace's black tongue and his heart attack before rushing off to report back to both bosses all the valuable information that he had successfully gathered.

Then, suddenly the main toilet door burst open, and two paramedics appeared carrying a stretcher closely followed by Frank the barman. One of the two paramedics, unfazed, politely squeezed passed everyone and dropped down onto her knees quickly feeling Horace's body for a sign of a pulse. Then she carefully rolled him onto his back and then shone a torch into both his eyes while gently pulling up Horace's eyelids with her thumb.

"Good news, everyone!" she said, "he's not dead, he's just drunk, totally immobilised by the effects of a little too much alcohol."

"What about his black tongue?" the man asked who had originally raised the alarm.

"That's probably the effects of the blackcurrant spritzers that he may have drunk earlier," Frank confessed from his position standing in the main toilet doorway.

"He's as drunk as a cricket that has fell into a bucket of cider!" one of the golfers interjected.

Some of the crowd chuckled approvingly while others turned away in disgust.

"Well, we need to get him out of here," the other paramedic said as he pushed his way forward into the toilet carrying the stretcher.

Then using all their skills and expertise they loaded Horace's limp and intoxicated body onto the stretcher.

"We need to get him outside and into the ambulance and hook him up to a drip, he must be very dehydrated by now."

After Delia and the two paramedics had been sitting in the back of the ambulance, patiently, for around fifteen minutes, Horace suddenly opened one eye and gargled two words, "Sick bowl!"

The female paramedic very skilfully intercepted the huge gush of vomit that was shooting towards Delia and her brand new black trouser suit.

"Thank you so much!" Delia said, she felt so awkward and embarrassed and confused, "Horace had never ever acted in this way before. I don't know what could have made him act this way," she said, looking down at the few splashes of vomit that had caught her new black shiny shoes.

"Don't worry, we have been waiting for that to happen, just the effects of the drip." The male paramedic smiled.

Horace opened his other eye after spitting a huge lump of green phlegm into the bowl being held by the female paramedic. He glanced around the ambulance and then at Delia and then fell backwards onto the bed, unconscious once again.

The paramedic stood up and disposed of the sick bowl. "Right, I think he's ready to go home now." She handed Delia a fresh sick bowl, "you will probably need this, but don't worry he will be fine after a good night's sleep, indicating that Horace would be totally out of it for the rest of the afternoon and most probably all night."

After sleeping all that evening and all night, Horace awoke very early the next morning to the sound of his heart thumping and his head banging like a drum, the birds were singing a chirpy dawn chorus in the distance.

Delia was sleeping in a chair opposite still holding the sick bowl with her head slumped forward.

Horace lifted the bed covers and glanced down at his very white naked body.

"How the hell did I get here?" he whispered to himself.

Horace leapt out from the bed and crashed into the en-suite, covering the blushing pink and white marble effect toilet with a torrent of multi-coloured vomit.

Horace had never ever suffered from the ill effects of alcohol before, but in the past had never ever drunk to that extreme before. Even at his wedding and the stage night before, he had only drunk three and a half pints of bitter Shandy.

He held onto the blushing pink and white marble effect pedestal sink and sploshed some warm water over his sweaty face and then gargled a little water around the inside of his mouth. Horace suddenly got the feeling of a mega bomb or something about to explode in his stomach. Needing the toilet, he dumped his bottom onto the vomit-covered toilet seat, his head was banging and he could feel his blood rushing around his body not to mention whatever was squirting out from the inside of his bottom.

After spending what felt like the worst ten minutes of his life, Horace felt confident enough to get up from the toilet and pushed down both buttons on top of the system to make a big flush with maximum water, and then stepped into the shower.

After a good scrub with lemon and honey dew soap, Horace then lent his head forward, holding onto the moulded blushing pink soap tray with both hands and let the warm water fall onto his throbbing head. After a further ten minutes, Horace felt confident enough to leave the shower, he dabbed at his white body with a bath towel and then quickly pulled on a clean pair of pyjamas.

Then with the damp bath towel, he did his best to clean the toilet and mop up the vomit off from the floor, he then opened the large bathroom window and tossed the sick bomb out, thinking it would land somewhere in the rear garden below. Then once back in the bed, he coiled himself up like an unborn baby and went back to sleep.

Horace slowly awoke around two hours later to the familiar sound of Delia taking her morning shower. He very carefully opened one eye and looked at the bedside clock and then at the bathroom door that was slightly ajar and the smell of Delia's Peach and Honey shower gel wafting through.

Horace closed his eye and curled his body even more, how was he going to face Delia? Should he pretend to be asleep, seriously ill or possibly dead?

Through one squinty eye he watched Delia as she entered the bedroom wearing her white bathrobe and rubbing her hair vigorously with a small white hand towel. Then from the other side of the bed Delia lent across and kissed Horace on the side of the face like a mother may possibly kiss her baby first thing in the morning while still sleeping.

Horace couldn't believe his luck, whatever had happened the day and night before, Delia still loved him but he had to be very careful with what he did next and how he responded.

Horace watched Delia through one half closed squinty eye as she slipped out of her bathrobe and pulled up her plain white knickers that She normally wore to work and then fasten her bra at the front before twisting it around and slipping her breasts into the cups.

"What happened?" Horace suddenly cried out with his best shaky voice, sensing now was the right time to test the water.

Delia turned and faced Horace and then surprisingly smiled, "Finally, you're awake!"

Horace looked at Delia doing his best to imitate somebody who was very sick, possibly delirious.

"I have called your bosses and told them that you won't be going in today, I left a message on their answerphone."

"Thank you, darling," Horace warbled, once again using his best shaky voice. "I feel like I am slipping away it must be Chinese flu or something."

"Or possibly all those spritzers that you drank at Trevor's funeral," Delia smiled as she took out her blue and white summer dress from the wardrobe. "Anyway," Delia said, as she sat on the side of the bed so Horace could do up the zip at the back of her dress. "Trevor was negotiating his redundancy; did you know anything about that? And furthermore, your company is being taken over by another firm of chartered accountants, and your two bosses are retiring."

Suddenly, the tide of memories started to ebb back to Horace, of him being half unconscious in the toilet and overhearing his two bosses talking.

"And who is Spankworth?" Delia continued, "apparently he's also on his way out."

Horace didn't know whether to laugh or cry; his wife Delia was a very intelligent woman, but was hopeless at putting two and two together.

"And Hilary overheard some of those men from your office talking about his wife saying they would all like to do her from behind."

Horace pulled the bedcovers up over his head, he had an awful headache and a lot to think about, but for now he needed a little more sleep.

Chapter 4

When Delia arrived back at the house that evening, the very first thing that she noticed was the huge wreath propped up against the front door. Delia picked up the wreath and turned around and began to walk back towards Trevor's house assuming that someone had made a mistake, and had left it at the wrong house.

And then she suddenly noticed the card addressed to Mrs Delia Dankworth. Delia swiftly leaned the large wreath up against the side of her car and opened the envelope.

To Mrs Delia Dankworth, please accept our deepest feelings for your sense of loss and our condolences from everyone a Squirrel and Squirrel.

Delia read the card again and then looked at the wreath, "Please accept our deepest feelings for your sense of loss and our condolences?"

Suddenly, Delia threw down the card and raced back towards the house "Horace!"

Delia fumbled the keys into the lock and raced up the stairs and crashed into the bedroom, expecting to find Horace lying there dead.

Horace looked to be in the finest of health especially for a dead man. He had somehow managed to move the television from the spare bedroom and from the mess on the bed covers he had obviously been binging on potato crisps and chocolate chip cookies. There were three empty tea mugs on the bedside cabinet along with an apple core and a banana skin and three or four empty yogurt pots.

Delia turned around and ran back down the stairs and back into the street, swiftly picking up the huge wreath and the card and raced back towards the house.

"What's this?" Delia panted, throwing the wreath onto the bed.

"Looks like somebody has just died," Horace said, smiling, now feeling much better.

"Yes!" said Delia, "and that somebody appears to be you!" Delia flicked the sympathy card at Horace.

Horace did exactly the same as Delia.

"Please accept our deepest feelings for your sense of loss and our condolences."

"Must be some kind of mistake," Horace said looking just as puzzled as Delia, after starring at the card for at least a few more minutes.

Delia sat on the side of the bed being careful to avoid all the lose debris, mostly biscuit crumbs and small chips of chocolate. "Why would everyone in your office think that you are dead?" Delia suddenly sprang up off from the bed. "Yesterday, when I was looking for you, some man checked the toilets and then came rushing into the bar shouting that you had had a heart attack!"

Delia began to pace up and down the bedroom as a detective would or a courtroom barrister. "Somebody from your office must have heard all the kafuffle and assumed that you had a fatal heart attack in the toilets and must have assumed that you were dead!"

"Life insurance!" Horace bleated out, "we all have life insurance through the company, this is an ideal opportunity, now we can really screw the backstabbing bastards! I wonder if the life insurance is worth more than the redundancy?"

"What redundancy?" Delia said looking confused. "I thought they were trying to get rid of somebody called Spankworth?"

Horace looked at Delia, "Have I ever spoke about anyone new joining the company who went by the name of Spankworth?"

Delia stopped pacing up and down the bedroom and stared at Horace while thinking.

Horace continued, "Now Delia, try and think of someone's name at the office that may possible rhyme with Spankworth?"

"O my God!" Delia said, "all those nasty sweaty fat-bellied men from your office all want to do me from behind!"

Horace looked at Delia standing at the end of the bed and smiled, she still was a very attractive woman and any man would grab at the opportunity to take her from behind, but besides all that, in spite of everything she still loved him.

"How did I get here back in my own bed?" Horace suddenly remembered being in the toilet at the golf club and the conversation that he had overheard that his bosses had, had.

Making jokes and saying how relieved they were that Trever had killed himself and all the money that they had saved, not having to pay him out with his agreed redundancy package.

"Two very nice young paramedics," Delia said, "they first took you out to their ambulance on a stretcher and flushed you out and then they bought you home."

"I am sorry, Darling," Horace said, turning on the shaky voice once more.

"The last three or so weeks have been very unsettling for everyone," Delia continued, "and besides, I never realised that you worked with such a group of horrible disgusting men." Delia walked around to the side of the bed where Horace was, and sat down beside him. "Would you mind if I pop out tonight?" she said. "I was invited to the special Spanish evening at the golf club and Carolina also wants to go."

Horace reached across and held Delia's hand, "Thank you darling."

"For what?" Delia smiled.

Horace was suddenly filled with emotion, his life was a mess, His neighbour Trevor was dead and the company that they had both worked for didn't want either of them and he had made a fool of himself at the golf club.

Suddenly Delia's mobile sounded. "It's Carolina, she is outside in the car, I must go. Sort yourself out, Horace!" Delia shouted as she went down the stairs, "take a shower and tidy yourself up, and sort the bed out!"

Horace was sitting downstairs watching television when he heard the sound of Dr Carolina Bank's high-powered Mercedes pull up outside. The sound of two car doors slamming meant that Carolina was also on her way in.

Horace quickly turned off the television and straightened his hair in the mirror and squirted some men's cologne behind his ears before grabbing the financial times and then sitting back down again.

The door burst open and Delia and Carolina came in side by side, singing, "We're off to sunny Spain, a viva Espana!"

Delia was wearing a very cheaply made paper sombrero and Dr Carolina looked like she had applied some fake tan on her face.

"We are off to sunny Spain!" Delia threw herself into one of the armchairs, "we have had a lovely time. Just what the doctor ordered," she said laughing and pointing to Carolina while kicking off her shoes.

To Horace it was quite obvious that Delia had been drinking but under the circumstances thought it best to pretend that he hadn't noticed.

"I only wish I could come with you," Carolina sighed.

Horace quickly put down the newspaper and looked at Delia expecting an explanation.

"We're off to sunny Spain!" Delia repeated. "Viva Espana!"

Carolina suddenly jumped up from her chair and went back out into the hallway and then outside to the Mercedes.

"Almost forgot," she smiled as she came back into the room holding two bottles of wine. "These are for you Horace, two bottles of complementary Spanish vino!"

Horace quickly scrambled from his armchair, now feeling very anxious at what was happening.

Carolina pushed the two bottles of Spanish plonk into Horace's hands, "you and your beautiful wife are off to sunny Spain!"

Horace turned to Delia, he could feel his heart rate changing up through the gears and beginning to pump harder and faster.

"We, my darling, we are both off to sunny Spain and it isn't going to cost you a penny!"

Delia reached into her small clutch bag and pulled out two airline tickets, waving them around and smiling.

"I can't go to Spain!" Horace said, his voice this time genuinely shaky. "I have ginger hair, look at my skin, its whiter than white and I'm full of freckles, I'll die! I will be baked alive, just like poor old Trevor!"

"Don't be silly," Delia said, putting the paper sombrero onto Horace's head, "you can wear a hat!"

"And some of this!" Carolina laughed rubbing some fake tan onto Horace's very white but highly stressed-out face.

"Well," Carolina said, "now I have to love you and leave you, I have surgery tomorrow and you, my darling, have got a school to run."

Delia came back into the room after waving Carolina off, the wine she had drunk earlier had made her feel very happy.

Horace was standing in the bay window studying the plane tickets, "These tickets already have our names printed on them and they are for the day after tomorrow?" He said, overcome by panic.

"Yes, Horace my darling, it will be nice to get away for a few days, we don't have to go out in the sun We can stay in our room and watch the sun go down from the balcony."

"What about work?" Horace said, "I just can't go off to Spain willy nilly!"

"Yes," Delia replied, "what about work, and what sort of company or business sends a wreath and a message of condolence to the wife of an employee at the drop of a hat? No one has rung or tried to contact us, we have heard nothing, to send a wreath without having all the facts, it's ridiculous, barbaric even. You have worked for that firm of accountants for twenty-five years and they repay you by plotting behind your back to get rid of you!"

"It could quite possibly be a sick joke from some of the guys in the office," Horace said. "Some of them are very unsympathetic, especially Colin the carver."

Delia starred at Horace in disbelief, "are you sure you work for a firm of accountants, Darling, and not a wholesale butcher?"

"I must admit in recent years it has felt that way," Horace sighed. "Trevor and I were put under enormous pressure from the bosses to shave the accounts. Nowadays we just have the accounts from religious or charity organisations to work on. All the big businesses and the big money boys are dealt with by Colin the carver or Nigel the Knife."

"That's terrible," Delia said, the feeling of happiness had quickly left her body and now she felt full of disbelief and uncertainty and that whole world was full of bad people. "Horace, why haven't you mentioned this before? The whole setup sounds illegal or in the least fraudulent."

"It didn't just happen overnight," Horace said, "I didn't turn up for work on a Monday morning and the bosses just came out with it, like, listen up everyone from this day forward we want everyone to screw the tax man as much as possible. Slowly, little by little, the firm changed its direction so they could attract more accounts, especially the big foreign ones and by doing so make more money."

"Well," Delia said, very assertively, using the voice she always used in her capacity as a headmistress, "tomorrow is Thursday the last day of term and on Friday, Horace my darling, we are off to Sunny Spain."

Horace held up the plane tickets, trying to read the small print under the heading terms and conditions of use.

"So why have we got two plane tickets for free, and where are we staying once, we get there?"

Delia produced a piece of very crumpled A4 size paper from her clutch bag and ironed it out the best she could with the palm of her hand, smoothing it up and down across the top of the glass coffee table. "We have six nights booked at the Hotel Golf and Mountain Resort, Buena Vista."

"But why us?" Horace said, "why have we got a free holiday? Nothing is for free, not in this world."

"It was a special holiday promotion that they had at the golf club and I won the raffle and this is the prize. We don't even have to worry about getting to the airport," Delia continued, "they are sending a taxi for us at eight thirty Friday morning."

"Well, it all sounds a bit dodgy to me," Horace said, "Much too good to be true."

After all what had happened in Victoria Avenue during the past few weeks, Thursday passed by relatively smoothly.

Delia had gone off to school a little earlier than usual that morning, as it was the last day of summer term, and then at lunch time she had popped out and around to the medical centre to pick up a certificate for Horace that allowed him two weeks off from work due to the fact that he was suffering from vertigo.

Horace had spent most of the day working in the back garden, he had pruned what was left of the scorched conifer trees the best he could and had fed all the charred branches into the garden shredder.

Then he had set about picking up all the small pieces of debris that still littered the garden from Trever's exploded Space Rocket, and tipped out the shredded mulch and worked it into the ground around the most affected areas that had been scorched by Trevor's rocket fuel with a garden spade.

Trever's wife Hilary, had gone to stay at one of her son's houses in the new Forest, Horace straddled the waist high black coloured plastic-coated metal fencing and pulled out some of the nasty sharp objects that had lodged themselves between the gaps on the other side.

Working in the garden for the best part of the day had made him feel a lot better, maybe a holiday in Spain wasn't such a bad idea after all.

Around three o clock, Horace drove the car around to the local council recycling plant and dumped all the bags off rubbish, just before they had closed.

The school closed for summer recess later that afternoon without any problems and Delia arrived back at the house around four thirty to find Horace still working in the garden.

Chapter 5

Friday morning and the first day of the school summer holidays, Horace was back standing inside the bay window wearing his Calvin Klein cotton stretch trunks, gazing down Victoria Avenue.

The weather had changed dramatically overnight and it was absolutely tipping it down, small streams of water were rushing by before disappearing down the nearest drain.

Delia was back in her normal position with her bottom just resting on the edge of the sofa, earlier she had been wearing a pretty printed summer dress but had swapped it for a trouser suite once her legs had begun to feel the cold.

"Why don't you get dressed, darling, are you not feeling the cold, just standing there in your pants?"

Horace was staring down the road, waiting to see if Richard, the next door but one would still be parking his car outside his house on such a dreadful morning. Something else had caught his eye, some of the remains of a sticky bun was being shunted along by the fast flowing rain water.

Horace watched the misshaped bun edge even closer to the drain, but suddenly it stopped something else was stuck in the kerbside but Horace couldn't make out what it was.

Then Horace's interest in the bun was interrupted with the sound of Richard's Jaguar slowly nosing it way out from his driveway.

Horace half turned and spoke to Delia over his right shoulder, "Even on a day like today, that knob head still has to park his car right outside the front of his house."

"Why don't you get dressed, darling, the taxi will be here in ten minutes."

Horace turned to Delia. "I am not sure what to wear, we have never ever been to a hot country before and it's too late to get a tailor-made asbestos suit. We have been fell and fen walking," Horace continued, "hill and dale walking, we have been to remote Cottages in the Scottish Highlands, not forgetting all the skiing trips over the years."

Delia stood up and instinctively checked her trousers for creases, "You must have something, Horace."

Horace followed Delia into the bedroom and Delia slide open the door on Horace's side of the mirror wardrobe. Delia quickly shuffled the hangers from one side to the other, Horace had plenty of suits and shirts and ties which he always wore to work, but not much in the way of leisure wear.

"Well," Delia said, "you have two choices. Ski suits or waterproofs?"

"What's inside the suitcase?" Horace said, grabbing the handle and lifting it up off from the bed.

"Mostly my stuff," Delia chuckled, "you have pants and socks and some thin shorts and casual trousers, mostly all the clothes that you wear when you go to the golf club."

Just then the doorbell rang, "O my god!" Delia flapped. "Quick Horace, put something on, that must be the taxi!"

Delia rushed out of the bedroom and opened the front door.

Horace could hear the conversation between Delia and the taxi driver, Horace snatched at the bright mauve and lilac ski suit from the inside of the wardrobe and put it on, grabbed the suitcase and rushed out into the hallway. The taxi driver was already back in the street standing next to his cab with the boot and passenger doors open.

Horace grabbed the front door handle and pulled it sharply up treble locking and turning the key at the same time.

The taxi driver met Horace halfway and promptly took the suitcase and put it into the boot. Horace quickly slid along the back seat next to Delia pulling the door shut just as the taxi sped away.

"Passports!" Horace suddenly shouted out.

"Don't worry I have them here," Delia patted her handbag. "And we also have around one hundred euros in cash, left over from the skiing holiday last year."

"So," the taxi driver said, "where are you off to?"

"Spain! Skiing!" Delia and Horace shouted out from the back seat simultaneously.

"Water skiing!" Horace shouted; he could see the taxi driver looking very strangely at him in the rear-view mirror. Horace suddenly felt a bit silly, the ski suit seemed to be much brighter in the taxi than it had appeared from inside the darkness of the mirror wardrobe.

"I feel a bit like a member of a boy band from the eighties," Horace whispered to Delia.

"You could have worn something a little less conspicuous," Delia said as she reached across and held Horace's hand.

"Do you remember darling," Horace said, "this ski suit is from our very first skiing holiday together, we booked that ski lodge and ski lessons in Switzerland. They asked us to wear something bright just in case we got lost or buried alive on the slopes."

Delia squeezed Horace's hand, "I suppose you're very lucky it still fits you, most men your age would have fatty globules, bulging out around their waistline and buttocks, preventing them from putting it on by now."

The journey to the airport in the taxi passed by quite smoothly considering the weather, the driver had commented about the amount of water lying on the approach road to the airport and had said to Horace that he didn't need to go to Spain to water ski. He could do it outside and around the taxi.

Horace had followed Delia across the huge departure lounge and joined the back of the check in queue at the global holiday desk.

"Once inside the departure lounge Horace had felt more at home and not feeling out of place wearing his bright ski suit. There were all sorts of people wearing all sorts of things, large groups of people were wearing ski suits, also a large number of hen party's with very inappropriate attire and in some cases very rude slogans, that had been printed onto balloons and banners."

The biggest inconvenience had occurred when Delia and Horace had boarded the plane.

There had been some kind of mix up with seat numbers and the seat number next to Delia, Twelve A was already occupied by a very large lady with obvious breathing problems.

Horace had been ushered very quickly to the back of the plane by a very slim attractive stewardess and found himself squeezed into the middle seat, twenty-two B, in-between two very young women from a hen party that Horace had noticed in the departure lounge earlier.

Both the young women at first seemed to be taken back by the fact that a much older man had been plonked in-between them both.

Then the one nearest to the window suddenly stood up and shouted to the rest of her party, "aye, aye, the stripper has arrived."

Horace could hear young women giggling all around him, he suddenly felt like a goldfish, swimming helplessly around in a goldfish bowl surrounded by crazy wailing cats. Then suddenly the plane was moving forward, the seat light sign buzzed on from the overhead display panel and the cabin crew were in their positions, quickly running through the safety procedure.

Then the cabin crew done a swift passing check to make sure everyone had their seat belts fastened correctly and then quickly returned to their own seats and strapping themselves in. Then just a few minutes later the plane had passed through the wide band of heavy rain and the thick grey and black cloud and was setting a course high above, in the pale blue sky and the brilliant sunshine.

The *please fasten your seatbelt* sign was switched off, just as something black and rubbery landed in Horace's lap that seemed to arrive from behind with a sudden shrill of laughter. Then three white plastic cups also appeared that had been passed through the gap from the seats behind, followed by a bottle of pink gin.

Before Horace had time to react the black rubbery thing had been thrown back and he was holding a plastic cup with the pink gin being rapidly poured in.

"Say when?" The young women smiled.

Before Horace got the chance to say anything the white plastic cup was full of the pink alcohol and the young blonde women to his left said bottoms up and downed her drink in one go.

Horace could see the back of Delia's head; she appeared to be reading and probably had no idea that Horace was about to embark on his second heavy drinking session of his entire life.

Horace took a sip from the plastic cup; it didn't taste too bad, a bit plasticky and not as enjoyable as the fruity spritzers that he had binged on at the golf club.

"What's your name?" the young women that was sitting to the left, had undone her seatbelt and had turned her body almost ninety degrees in her seat, with her right leg raised with half of her foot on Horace's seat, her toes sliding under his left leg.

Horace felt embarrassed. "Horace," he said and then taking a quick sip of his drink.

"Well Horace, if you're going to sit with us you have to keep up with the drinking otherwise, you're going to get us all busted!"

Horace drunk as much as he could from the plastic cup and then lowered it down onto his lap.

"I'm Trudi," the young women held out her hand, "you're probably about the same age as my dad."

Horace quickly changed hands with the cup so he could shake the young woman's hand.

"I am getting married next Saturday, to Kevin."

Horace quickly finished the rest of the drink, he felt slightly embarrassed and awkward, he wasn't used to being in the company of beautiful young women.

Then the black rubbery thing suddenly hit Trudi on the head before falling into Horace's lap, but this time it had been switched on and it was squirming around and vibrating through Horace's brightly coloured ski pants in and around his numb, dormant, hibernating man parts.

Trudi very skilfully grabbed the black rubbery merchandise and lobbed it back over her head with no particular interest to where it was heading or who it might hit. The young woman that had been sitting in the aisle seat and to the right had disappeared without any formal introduction, then suddenly a different young lady appeared, holding a fresh bottle of pink gin.

Trudi grabbed the both empty cups from the small drop-down table in front of them and held them out, one in each hand while her friend swiftly filled them up to the top.

"Hi I'm Alice, you must be Horace, well, drink up Horace, we have sixteen bottles of this, we all bought one each from the duty-free shop."

Horace being an accountant and very good at number crunching didn't need a calculator to work out that if the girls drank all the gin that they had purchased it would equate to a whole bottle of gin to each girl. Horace didn't know very much about alcohol especially about the effect it might have on a very young woman after consuming a whole bottle of gin.

Horace suddenly felt overwhelmed with emotion Trudi had already compared him to her dad and with parenthood came a lot of responsibilities, like stepping in front of a bullet or donating a kidney, or drinking as much Gin as possible to stop her from killing herself before she got the chance to celebrate her wedding night.

Horace could see the back of Delia's head, and that was going to be the object of his focus, as soon as her head became blurry, he would ease off with the pink gin.

"Can you drive, Horace?" Trudi gave him a little nudge with her right foot.

"Yes, but I don't drive much, mostly at weekends, I normally walk to work, weather permitting."

"We need a driver," Trudi continued, "our Goalkeeper was going to drive the minibus for us, she is much older than us and doesn't drink but she had a big bust up with her husband and went back to live with her mother in Scotland."

"This is a double celebration," Alice said, "Trudi is getting married and our football team won the local women's league."

"We have been planning this trip for ages, we are going scuba diving, paragliding, windsurfing wine tasting and we are going to sunbath on the nudist beach so we will all have a nice suntan for Trudi's wedding photos."

Horace finished off his drink and then focused on the back of Delia's head, it didn't appear to be blurry, and tried to put the thought of sixteen naked women running around the nudist beach to the back of his mind.

"I am sorry but I would love to drive the minibus but I am staying in a hotel up in the mountains with my wife Delia for a week and I don't think my skin would allow me to sunbath, especially naked."

"You're funny, Horace, much funnier than my dad. Let's have some more Gin!" Alice said, springing up from her seat and opening one of the overhead lockers.

Alice quickly grabbed a plastic bag from the locker and threw it to Trudi, Trudi took a quick glance up and down the plane to check that none of the cabin crew were watching before opening the new bottle.

"Hold your cup out, Horace, and get ready for another splash of giggle water," Trudi smiled and tipped the bottle up filling Horace's cup to the brim.

Alice then furtively sneaked from her seat with the bottle, and then with the blink of an eye, another young woman was sitting next to Horace.

"Hi I'm Gemma and I already feel really, really pissed."

Horace glanced at Gemma and smiled and then down the plane to where Delia was sitting, quickly checking his vision.

"I have got the bag of lipsticks," Gemma said opening a plastic bag and offering it in the direction of Trudi.

Trudi reached inside the bag and pulled out a tube of traffic light red, then using her phone as a mirror applied a nice thick heavy layer to both her lips.

"What do you think?"

"Not bad," Gemma said, "not sure how it will look once you have a suntan."

"What do you think, Horace?"

Horace took a large swig of pink gin. "I think Kevin is a very lucky young man and I think he will want to marry you with or without the lipstick."

Trudi let her right foot slide down from the seat and at the same time reached forward and planted a huge kiss onto Horace's left cheek. Trudi laughed. "The colour looks nice on you Horace; you have bright red kiss marks on your cheek."

Without any warning Gemma kissed Horace's other cheek with freshly applied dark and mysterious chocolate brown.

Horace finished off his drink. He could see one of the female cabin crew walking down the plane towards him, she was looking directly at him, Horace knew that he was in trouble.

"Would you mind following me to the front of the plane, please sir?"

Horace done his best to follow the young woman towards the front of the plane, his legs didn't seem to be working to well and it felt like he was walking up the side of a very steep hill.

At the end of the aisle the stewardess turned right and backed herself into the small alcove along with two other colleges.

"We have had several complaints from some of the other passengers," the young woman began as soon as Horace arrived, "most of the women in your party appear to be very drunk and are throwing sex toys around."

There had not been enough space in the alcove for Horace, so he found himself totally exposed and out in the open, standing in the aisle, he glanced back down the plane, everyone appeared to be watching him.

Delia was staring straight at him, she had a very strange look on her face, a mix of disbelief and is that really the man that I married thirty-five years ago?

Even the very large women sitting next to Delia was looking at him and appeared to be talking to Delia through the side of her mouth.

"I am very sorry," Horace began, "there seems to be some confusion." Horace could see all three-cabin members staring at his face. "I am sitting in the wrong seat; I should be sitting next to my wife but somehow I ended up at the back with those young women."

"You really shouldn't be sitting in a different seat, sir," the male steward interjected, "if something happened like for instance we crashed into the sea, it would make it very difficult for the crash site investigators to identify your body."

Horace looked once again down the plane; he could see the young women who had moved him in the first place preparing the snack trolley.

Horace turned his attention back to the steward, he was probably about the same age as the young women travelling with the hen party, his face was very white and spotty and his hair was styled with mousse with a huge moulded quiff pointing up towards the sky. Horace realised it would be much better for everyone concerned just to say what they wanted to hear.

Horace raised both his hands in the air, gesturing that he was surrendering, "OK I will talk to them, I am very sorry for the inconvenience."

Horace turned around and began to walk back down the plane's fuselage, Delia quickly put her head down, pretending to read her book, the rather large woman sitting next to her gave him a look of total disgust and then took a quick squirt and inhalation of her puffer.

Chapter 6

Luckily for everyone on the plane and especially for Horace, there had not been any mid-air disasters and the plane had successfully touched down at Malaga airport with the very slightest of bumps. All the young women seated around Horace let out a shrill of delight and then cheered and then clapped and some whistled.

Horace glanced out of the cabin window and for the very first time he could see the dry sun scorched landscape of Spain rushing past at around one hundred and seventy miles an hour. The plane slowed rapidly, and then seemed to taxi for what seemed like an eternity. Eventually, the plane bumped to a halt, Horace glanced out of the window, the plane seemed to be in the middle of nowhere.

"Let's go, Horace," Trudi pulled herself out from her seat while holding on to the headrest of the seat in front.

Horace barely managed to squeeze himself out into the aisle, he could see Delia trapped in her seat unable to move and the lady next to her sucking on her inhaler.

Horace's newly adopted family of sixteen young women were all pushing and shoving, trying to retrieve all their possessions from the overhead lockers.

Suddenly there was a stream of bright light and a rush of very hot air rushing into the cabin from both ends of the plane.

"Come on Horace, we are out of here!" Trudi shouted, all the passengers in front of Horace began to move towards the open doorway at the rear of the plane.

Horace felt himself being shoved along from all the people behind, all very keen to get off the plane and begin their holiday. Horace passed through the open doorway and into what felt like a very large oven or possibly hell. He couldn't see anything; the sun was shining directly into his eyes and it felt like his head was going to explode with the intense heat.

Horace could sense the people behind him getting inpatient, he put out his left hand in front of him and grabbed hold of the hand rail and slowly made his way down the steps the best he could. Horace then stepped onto the red-hot tarmac surface, what felt like a bed of hot coals, then through squinty eyes he could see Trudi and the rest of the girls walking across the tarmac in front of him.

Horace held up his right hand, trying to make a sunshade, with the palm of his hand facing down, and the side of his hand firmly pressed against his forehead.

Trudi had glanced over her shoulder and see that Horace was shuffling along on the tarmac similar to her grandfather after he had suffered from a major stroke.

"Are you OK, Horace?"

"I can't see anything; I think the sun may have lasered out my eyes!"

"You are funny, Horace," Trudi took off her bright pink heptagonal sunglasses and carefully placed them onto Horace's face.

By that time some of the other girls had come back, one of them, placing a large pink sunhat on his head, "come on we have to take the bus to the terminal," she said.

Then instinctively, all the young women surrounded Horace like worker ants carrying an egg away from danger and ushered him up the steps and onto the shuttle bus.

Everyone from the rear of the plane squashed themselves into the bus, Horace found himself being nudged towards the back and into the far corner. Most of the bus had been designed for standing only with just a few drop-down seats here and there.

Horace grabbed hold of a stainless-steel pole that went from the floor to the ceiling, all the girls were now all squashed around and up against him, Trudi lent forward and took her sunglasses off from Horace's face.

Horace could see much better now from the inside of the bus, looking out through the tinted windows, now that the sun wasn't shining directly into his eyes.

All the people from the rear end of the plane were now all squashed into the second bus, Horace watched the trail of people walking across the tarmac from the front of the plane and towards the first bus, that was parked just a little way up in front.

He couldn't see Delia; she was either already on the bus in front or possibly still on the plane.

The bus was very hot inside; Horace normally wasn't a very sweaty person but he could feel the sweat running down his whole body on the inside of his ski suit. Suddenly, all around him, all the young women were very skilfully wriggling free from their top layers of clothing.

Horace felt like a parent at a swimming pool party as all the girls dumped their jumpers and tracksuit tops onto him, freeing up their hand to struggle with their trainers before sliding out from their trouser bottoms.

Horace turned his attention back to the plane, finally he could see Delia, she was slowly coming down the steps behind the rather large lady that she had been sitting next to on the plane, some of the cabin crew seemed to be assisting with her decent.

Then as the rather large lady moved closer towards the first bus, her and Delia went out of view. By that time all the girls had unloaded all their excess clothing taking it back from Horace and had squeezed it into their plastic duty-free bags, along with their empty pink gin bottles.

Horace was suddenly aware that most of the people on the bus were now staring at him, the girls, now looking like some kind of dance troop of partially dressed young women, and him being the manager, dressed in his brightly coloured nylon ski suit, or worst some kind of middle-aged scheming, manipulating pimp, herding a young group of innocent girls across Spain and possibly into Morocco.

Then just at that moment and without any warning what so ever, the bus suddenly jerked forward to start the beginning of its journey back to the airport terminal. The bus gathered speed very quickly and in a very short space of time most of the people on the bus were panicking and fearing for their lives.

Luckily for everyone on the bus, they were all packed in so tightly everyone swayed to the left and to the right without any serious injury as the driver made no attempt to slow down while zig zagging in-between all the different buildings.

Some of the people closest to the sides often gave out gasps of pain as the human mass shoved them briefly and squashing them against the side before a quick change of direction and the people on the other side copped it.

Then just as quickly as it had started, the bus journey ended abruptly with the whole body mass of very hot and sticky people squirming forward as the bus braked like an emergency stop on a driving test. The front and back doors opened simultaneously with a loud puff of air from the hydraulic workings and everyone scrambled from the bus as if their lives depended on it.

Horace followed the line of people past the first bus that had stopped a few metres in front, he could just about see Delia through one of the large side windows, struggling, trying to help her newfound friend out from one of the small drop-down seats.

Horace quickly made his way across the tarmac, out and away from the bright sunlight, towards a small entrance door in the main terminal building and then along a brightly painted corridor that had thick blue carpet on the floor.

It was much cooler inside, Horace now felt more relaxed and his thoughts turned to Delia. For the very first time since exiting the plane Horace could now see properly, He followed the other passengers along to the end of the corridor and then through some glass doors and up some escalators, Horace turned his body around and looked back down the corridor, there was still no sign of Delia.

Horace waited around for a few minutes at the top of the escalators, watching the stream of people coming through the glass doors below and up the escalators towards him. Horace then looked around and at the various signs, buses and trains straight ahead, toilets to the left and baggage reclaim and car hire down another set of escalators.

Horace turned his attention back to looking for Delia and then just like magic, Delia was there, coming up the escalators towards him and smiling.

"Have you seen your face?" Delia began, "you have lipstick plastered all over it!"

"Where is your new friend?" Horace smiled back at Delia, "On hindsight, I think I got a better deal than you."

"She was a lovely person, a doctor and a scientist, she studies and works on new and highly contagious viruses."

"We need to go down to the lower floor to collect our case," Horace said pointing out the way to Delia.

Horace and Delia followed most of the people from their flight along another long corridor and back down another set of escalators, down to the lower floor and pushed their way through some solid wooden doors.

A sudden rush of very hot air hit them full on in the face, it seemed much hotter in the baggage reclaim area than it had been outside in the direct sunlight.

Delia took hold of Horace's hand as they made their way forward and towards the luggage conveyors, Delia stopped to look at one of the large information screens, to check what number conveyor they needed against their flight number, just at the same time Horace could see his friendly hen party standing in and around conveyor number six.

Horace gave Delia a little tug by her hand, "come on, that's got to be ours over there."

Most of the people from their flight had already positioned themselves around the conveyor waiting for their cases to appear through the plastic curtains hanging down from the opening at one end.

Suddenly the conveyor began to move and the first of many cases slowly made their way around the conveyor belt.

Horace turned to Delia, "Can you remember what our case looks like?"

"Yes, it's the large brown one, the one we used last year."

Horace carefully scanned the conveyor, there were quite a few large brown cases travelling around on the conveyor belt.

Then a golf buggy type vehicle was slowly being driven towards them from the other side of the conveyor belt, it had a bright orange flashing light and was making a loud beeping sound, Horace and Delia instantly recognised the passenger. "That's Mrs Beatrice Wainwright's," Delia said.

The driver jumped out of the buggy and pushed his way through the line of people and positioned himself next to the conveyor, almost opposite Horace and Delia.

Acting on Mrs Wainwright's instructions, the driver of the buggy pulled a large brown suitcase from the conveyor, slung it onto the back of the buggy and slowly drove away through the crowded baggage reclaim area towards the exit.

Horace turned to Delia, "I think she has just driven off with our suitcase!"

Delia smiled, "She's a doctor and a scientist combating deadly viruses, I think she should be capable of recognising her own suitcase when she sees it."

Horace turned his attention back towards the conveyor, all the way around people were grabbing off their suitcases and scurrying away.

Suddenly, Trudi appeared on the other side of the conveyor, pulling a large brown suitcase along by the handle, "have a good holiday Horace, and if you change your mind about driving the minibus, you will find us at the hotel Tropicana!"

Horace gave Trudi a small polite wave of acknowledgment, "I think that's ours!" Delia shouted to Horace, pointing at a very lonely large brown suitcase that was slowly making its way towards them.

Horace took hold of the handle and with both hands dragged the large suitcase from the conveyor, then he quickly checked, looking up and down and then around the whole conveyor, by this time the conveyor was quite empty and there were no other larger brown suitcases.

Delia followed Horace towards the line of empty trolleys, Delia very helpfully backed one out from the others and Horace hoisted on the case, "what have you got in here?" Horace groaned, "it's really heavy."

"We should have a taxi waiting for us," Delia said, as they made their way passed the rest of the conveyors and then the car rental area.

The arrivals hall felt much cooler than the downstairs baggage reclaim area, once Horace had pushed the luggage trolley up a never-ending ramp and through yet another set of glass plate doors. The arrival hall was full of eager faces all staring at the glass doorway for their friends or loved ones to appear.

Delia spotted her man, he was a smartly dressed suntanned fairly short guy with dark brown hair with a receding hairline, he was holding a card with Mr and Mrs Dankworth that had been written with a black ink marker.

"Mrs Dankworth?"

"Si!" Delia replied confidently, having never ever been to Spain before and never had the opportunity to practice her O-level Spanish.

"Follow me please."

Delia and Horace followed the taxi driver across the arrival hall and out through the glass exit doors and towards a line of parked taxi cabs. Horace sat in the back alongside Delia, while the taxi driver put their suitcase into the boot.

Soon the taxi was passing through what appeared to be a small industrial area, passing by a San Miguel factory on the left and rows of buildings, advertising car hire on the right.

And then onto a motorway and open countryside with large built-up areas in the distance on both sides.

Delia turned to Horace, "I meant to get my make-up bag out from the case so I could clean the lipstick from your face, and my phrase book."

"I am starving," Horace replied. "It must be all the stress from travelling, and all this heat."

"You should have eaten some breakfast," Delia smiled, "instead of staring out of the window at the neighbours."

Chapter 7

After a two-hour journey the taxi stopped just outside from the main entrance of the Hotel Golf and Mountain Resort, Buena Vista.

Horace and Delia had fallen asleep along the way. Delia instinctively awoke as soon as the taxi had jerked to a halt. She glanced out of the taxi window at the large building and then to Horace. It wasn't pretty; Horace was still sleeping, his lower jaw had dropped and a line of dribble was coming out from the corner of his mouth.

"Horace darling, wake up, we are here!" Delia slid sideways across the seat of the taxi and opened the door.

The driver had already taken out their suitcase from the boot and had placed it on the pathway leading up to the main entrance.

Delia reached into her purse and pulled out a twenty euro note and handed it to the driver, "muchas gracias," she smiled.

"Thank you very much," the driver smiled back, before getting into his cab and speeding away.

"That was a bit extravagant, darling, wasn't it?"

"Well, it hadn't cost us anything up until now and besides, we don't know how long and how far we have travelled."

"That's the worrying thing about all this," Horace said, "there has to be a catch to all this, as I said before, nothing in this world for free, especially a week's holiday in Spain for two."

Horace grabbed the suitcase by the long brown handle and began to pull it along on its wheels towards the hotel main entrance, "come on I am starving, we have already missed breakfast and lunch."

Delia glanced at her watch, "It's four o'clock already, so it must be five here once we put our watches forward one hour."

Once inside the main door the whole place opened up into a wide-open space with a lot of light coming in through the roof and the large floor to ceiling windows. To the far left there was some kind of coffee lounge with people sitting around in comfy chairs.

Directly ahead, Horace and Delia could see what looked like the reception desk all made from opaque glass with LED lighting, brightly lighting up the whole front of the counter. There were huge palm trees growing out of the white and grey marble flooring each side of the reception area and just behind the palms to the left was a beautiful blue pool with water flowing down from a water fall, splashing down onto different coloured rocks.

Horace followed Delia over to the reception desk, "I don't think you will need your phrase book in this place," Horace whispered into Delia's ear.

"Good evening madam, how can I help you?" a young man in his thirties, dressed in white shirt and black trousers, greeted her.

"I believe we have a reservation?"

"Yes, we won it in a raffle," Horace joked sarcastically, as he whispered into Delia's ear.

Delia stepped forward and away from Horace and placed her handbag on the glass top.

The young man sat down in front of a computer, "And your name please, Madam?"

"Mr and Mrs Dankworth."

The young man quickly stood up from his position at the computer and took two key cards from a drawer, "Room number one hundred and fifty-four, on the fourth floor. We will need your passports, please Madam."

Delia took out the passports from her handbag and handed them over across the counter.

"The lifts are to your right-hand side madam, at the end of the reception hall, and if you need any information, you will find all the information you need in the information booklet in your room."

Horace followed Delia across the reception hall and over to the far-right corner Where there was a black sign hanging from the ceiling that read lifts, that was written in gold lettering. Delia pushed the large white button that was mounted on a stainless-steel panel and it instantaneously lit, that read the words lift coming.

"This place is really nice," Horace said, sounding very surprised, "it's nothing like I imagined Spain to be, all dusty and mangy dogs dying in the street."

"I think you're confusing Spain with spaghetti westerns, my darling, or possibly, Mexico." Delia smiled, just as the lift doors opened onto the fourth floor with a ping.

Horace found himself following Delia along a very pretty yellow and blue patterned tiled walkway with large green and blue ceramic pots that had beautiful bright pink geraniums growing out from them.

Delia stopped outside the door of number one hundred and fifty-four and slid the key card into the black box. A green light came on and the door opened with the sound of a click.

Horace followed Delia inside, "Wow, this is nice, a bit dark, but lovely and cool, too cool in fact."

Horace noticed small horizontal lines of light shining through the large white shutters that were closed on the outside of the patio doors. There was a control panel on the left-hand and right side of the bed with basic instructions all written in English.

Horace pushed a white button that had a black arrow pointing upwards towards the ceiling, the white shutter on the left-hand side silently moved upwards. Then Horace opened the middle shutter and then the one on the right, the whole room was filled with light and through the doors, opened up onto a white marble floor and glass front balcony.

Horace slid back the patio doors on either side and Delia followed him out onto the balcony. Horace and Delia stood there in silence, they were completely overwhelmed by the beautiful very green landscaped golf course that stretched as far as their one hundred- and eighty-degrees view allowed them.

Luckily for Horace, the afternoon sun was shining down from the other side of the hotel building, their balcony was shaded and at a reasonable temperature and a slight breeze, blowing from left to right.

Delia turned to Horace, taking hold of both his hands and kissed him very lightly on the lips, "I am going to get out of this trouser suit and take a nice long shower, and then, Horace my darling, we are going to find something to eat."

Delia went back into the room and opened the bathroom door, "Wow Horace, come and take a look at this."

Horace went over and looked into the bathroom from the open doorway.

The bathroom was well lit, with the sun shining down through a stainless-steel light tunnel, the walls were fully tiled in a soft grey and white, and the floor had been finished in a polished egg shell white marble. There was a large hand basin that appeared to be just floating without any kind of support, with highly polished gold-plated hot and cold taps.

In the corner was a large gold-plated shower head that was surrounded by beautiful clean crystal glass, and the tiled walls had inverted niches with small bottles of shower gels and shampoos placed inside. In the opposite corner to the large shower area was a white unit with gold button handles and two sets of fluffy white towels laid out on an eggshell white marble top.

"How much did you pay for those raffle tickets?" Horace said.

"Just one pound each, I bought a strip for five pounds."

Horace turned in the doorway. "I am going to open and check the case, we could possibly be carrying drugs or guns for the mafia, somebody somewhere has to be paying for all of this."

Horace threw the suitcase onto the bed and undid the buckle that secured the case with a thick leather strap.

Then he popped the two latches with either hand and opened up the zip, sliding it fully around the outside, as soon as Horace opened up the flap, he knew that the case that he was staring into wasn't theirs.

The inside of the case was beautifully lined with a plush red quilted material and a square of similar gold coloured material stitched to the inside of the lid with black letters that read, Mrs Beatrice Wainwright MD. DS.

Horace stood back, agog, staring into the case, everything with the holiday had gone very smoothly up until that point, the taxi from the house, the flight, and the taxi from the airport to the hotel, in his past experiences no holiday had passed by without a problem of some sort or two. So maybe this was that problem that every holiday had, and once they had sorted it out from then on, everything would be perfect.

Delia opened the bathroom door suddenly, wearing a very soft fluffy white towel around her body, with the top rolled over and fastened slightly above her breasts.

"Well," Horace said, "the good news is, there are no drugs or guns, the bad news is, there is bugger all else of any use to us in the inside of this case."

Delia looked at Horace, he had suddenly developed a weird sense of humour that was rarely a character quality of an accountant. Delia walked over to where Horace was standing and slightly bent forward as if she was about to take something out from the case.

"My God," Delia held up a very large pair of white silky French knickers. "These must belong to Beatrice."

Horace had to take a few steps backwards, for one, he was standing much too close to the enormous undergarments and couldn't appreciate how big they were, and for two, they were a little bit scary.

"What are we going to do? I don't have any clean underwear to put on," Delia said as she dropped the French knickers back into the case.

"And I have to wear this stupid ski suit for the whole holiday," Horace said, "if we can't track down our case. I need to take a shower darling," Horace said, "and then we have to have something to eat, we have been on the go since early this morning and we still haven't eaten."

By the time that Horace had remerged from the bathroom all clean and showered and wearing a fluffy white towel, Delia had emptied the top layer of contents from Mrs Beatrice Wainwright's case out onto the bed.

"I was hoping to find something like a telephone number, so we could call her."

"Let's go and eat," Horace said. "If I don't eat something very soon, I think that I am going to faint."

"I don't feel very comfortable going out to dinner without wearing any underwear, Delia said as she pulled up the trousers of her trouser suit."

"You are very lucky that you changed out of that very thin patterned summer dress this morning, Darling, that could have proven to be a little difficult with the rest of the hotel diners all staring at your arse. Don't worry, nobody is going to notice you while I am wearing this brightly coloured ski suit," Horace said, as he gingerly pushed his legs into the sweaty clammy ski suit bottoms that by now smelt a bit like a well-used deep-fat chip fryer.

Delia noticed the hotel information booklet on the bedside cabinet, she sat on the bed and reached across and grabbed it, quickly looking through the few pages.

"The hotel restaurant Buena Vista," Delia read out aloud, "that translates into the restaurant with a good view, it's on this floor at the other end of the passageway."

"Right," Horace said, "let's get there before the rush." Horace moved quickly towards the door and opened it.

Delia grabbed her handbag and the key card from the side and quickly passed Horace in the doorway and sped off in the direction of the restaurant and hopefully some good food.

Horace walked into the restaurant with Delia in his shadow, a few paces behind, very conscious of the fact that she wasn't wearing any underwear.

A waiter very quickly approached them just inside the doorway, "Good evening, sir, good evening, Madam, a table for two? By the window?"

The waiter didn't wait for Horace to answer, he just half turned and gestured with his outreached arm in what direction that they would be heading off in.

Horace followed the waiter over to their table and he then very politely held onto the back of Delia's chair and then very skilfully shoved her forward exactly the right distance from the table.

"My name is Javier spelt with a J," he smiled, "what can I get you to drink?"

"Just some water for now, please," Delia said, "we are very hungry, we haven't eaten all day."

The waiter fell hopelessly in love with Delia, her poise and her beautiful English accent, the way that she pronounced the letter W when she said the word water and the way she pronounced her T, with the word eaten.

"Would Madam care for fizzy or still?"

Delia looked at Horace she knew he wasn't a great lover of fizzy water. "Still please."

The waiter melted and swooned away.

"Blimey," Horace said, "how much is all this going to cost us?"

The waiter promptly returned, carrying a tray with two very posh light green-coloured glass bottles of still water and two very expensive looking long fluted drinking glasses.

After placing the water and the glasses onto the table top, the waiter produced two very posh brown leather menus with gold lettering, which he handed one to Delia first and then to Horace and then slightly bowed and backed away.

"These prices aren't too bad," Horace said. "Much cheaper than what I was expecting, it's a shame we didn't find this place years ago."

"I am going to have the grilled breast of chicken and vegetables," Delia said, closing the menu.

Horace quickly ran his eyes down the list of meat dishes, chicken was by far the cheapest, quite reasonably priced at twenty euros. "Why not, let's both go for the grilled chicken," he said.

Once Horace had taken on board several mouthfuls of very tender grilled chicken and some of the perfectly cooked vegetables and a few sips of the chilled still water, he could turn his attention to other things.

"That's a fantastic view," he said, "the colour brochure in our room doesn't lie."

Delia put down her knife and fork and turned her head to the right, the whole side of the restaurant, next to where they were sitting was completely constructed from glass that went from floor to ceiling.

Just like the view from their balcony the beautifully green landscape of the golf course stretched as far as their eyes could see and in the very far distance, mountains with dotted specs of white houses.

Horace could see someone about to tee off, about two hundred metres away, from the green nearest to where they were sitting, he watched the person strike the ball but had no idea to where it had gone, even at seven o clock in the evening everywhere was still too bright and sunny, still too bright for Horace's eyes to pick out the small white ball, traveling through the air.

Horace turned his gaze away from the window and back to Delia, sitting opposite. His vision felt blurry with red and black specks in front of his eyes. clouding Delia's face.

"I desperately need sunglasses," he blinked wildly. Slowly Delia's face come back into focus.

"I packed your sunglasses safely away between some clothes, darling," Delia said, "if we ever get our case back."

Suddenly the waiter arrived and offered Horace the wine list, "Would sir, madam, care for some wine?"

Horace handed it over to Delia, "why not," she said, "After all we are on holiday," Delia quickly ran her finger down the wine list, "we will have the Vinea (2017) please."

"What are we going to do about our case?" Horace said, once the waiter had gone off to fetch the wine.

"I really don't know," Delia said, "it is a real problem, I couldn't find anything in her case, like an address or her phone number, we could google her but I don't suppose they would be giving out her personal details like her phone number on the Internet. And another thing," Delia continued, "she has what looks like some very important medication in her case that she probably needs to take regularly on a daily basis."

The waiter returned to the table with the bottle of wine and very quickly removed the cork and poured out a little into a glass for Horace to try.

Horace always felt embarrassed in these situations, never really knowing what to do, intending to move it back and forth in his mouth but the wine just shot straight down the back of his throat, making him cough.

"That's fine," he coughed, "very fruity, nice body."

The waiter half filled their glasses, gave Delia a smile and went about his business.

Chapter 8

Horace and Delia had slept all night without interruption, it may have been the very firm but comfortable mattress or the bottle of Rose wine that they had shared, or the slightly warm breeze that had blown in through the half-opened patio doors.

Delia had washed out their underwear with the hotel complementary shower gel and placed them on the small patio table, hoping that they would have dried overnight.

Horace awoke first to the sound of a cockerel and a donkey, somewhere in the distance informing everyone at the Hotel Golf and Mountain Resort Buena Vista, that morning had arrived and it was going to be another hot one.

Horace was suddenly aware of the fact that he was sleeping next to a very naked and attractive lady. He couldn't remember if they had ever slept together naked before, Delia normally wore her thick or thin night shirt depending on the season and Horace in his flannel pyjamas.

Delia was sleeping very soundly on her side, facing away from Horace, he lifted the white bedsheet and took a sneaky peak at his wife's totally naked body, he put his right hand dangerously close to her bottom, struggling with the idea of gently squeezing her bum cheeks.

Delia suddenly woke, "Is that a donkey I can hear?"

"It sounds like it," Horace chuckled, "we had a cockerel earlier as well."

Delia rolled over towards Horace and very uncharacteristically pushed all her soft body parts up against his and planted a huge smacker on the lips. Then something strange happened, the little old guy in the downstairs flat below was beginning to move around, showing signs of interest. Over the past few years, somewhere along the way, Horace had lost his purpose in life and it had affected his confidence, what with the way the firm of accountancy had changed and him not really fitting in at work anymore.

Delia pushed herself even closer, kissing Horace with a lot more passion this time. Slowly but surely the little old guy's confidence grew and within a few seconds he was ready to leave the old place behind and find something new.

Horace lay on his back, staring up at the hotel ceiling, his heart was racing and he felt very hot and sweaty, the sex had only lasted for a few seconds but it had totally worn him out.

Delia moved her hand sideways under the bed covers and found Horace's hand and gave it a little squeeze, "That was nice, darling, we really do need to do that a lot more often."

"What, you mean more than once every two years?" Horace chuckled, silently he was feeling very pleased with himself, everything seemed to have gone very well.

Delia suddenly kicked off the white bed sheet with both her feet, swinging them around sideways she stood up at the side of the bed. "Let's get ourselves showered and then a light breakfast, and then we really have to see if we can track down our suitcase."

After a light breakfast of lightly toasted long crusty rolls with marmalade from Seville and two cups of coffee from Columbia, Horace and Delia exited the ground floor breakfast bar and made their way towards the large reception desk.

Now that the picture of Spain that it mostly consisted of dusty roads and mangy dogs lying in the street had been pushed to the back of Horace's mind and filled with a new gained confidence, he approached the young man sitting behind the desk.

"Good morning," Horace began, "We have a problem."

The young man immediately jumped to his feet, with a look of concern that something was terribly wrong and it was all his fault and he was about to lose his job.

"We have lost our case."

"Somebody has taken your case sir?"

"Well yes, but no." Horace said, his confidence waning.

The young man`s facial expressions were flitting back and forth from horror to total confusion.

"We have somebody else's case."

"You have taken somebody else's case sir?"

"Yes, we have it in our room and its full of drugs and we don't know what to do with it."

The young man placed his hand over the telephone, "Shall I call the police sir?"

Horace thought to himself for just a split of a second, were the police in Spain really that helpful, would they be able to track down the rather large framed Dr Beatrice Wainwright and bring back their case.

At that point Delia stepped forward, she had decided that it was time to use all her skills of communication and talk to the young man before everything spiralled out of control.

"Hello, Buenos Dias, my name is Delia and this is my husband Horace," Delia paused momentarily for the information to sink in. "We arrived here yesterday, from England. While we were at the airport in Malaga, somebody took our case and we somehow ended up with theirs."

The young man looked at Horace and then back to Delia, did they look like con artists or drug peddlers? Then began to wish the solid mountain rock beneath him would somehow fracture and he would fall down into the fissure.

"Yes," Horace said, "correcto." Horace had no idea why he used the word correcto. "We need to trace our case."

The young man looked at Horace and then back to Delia once more, he didn't even know what the word trace meant. He had spent the last two years at evening school trying to improve his English, and even though his English teacher was from a small village in China, and after taking the final examination he had left with a diploma in the English language, there was an awful lot more of the English language that he still didn't understand.

Delia quickly realised from the expression on the young man's face even though he was very polite and was trying his very best to be helpful, there was nothing he could say or do that would bring their case back.

Delia gave the young man a reassuring smile and thanked him, dragging Horace away by the hand.

The young man watched Horace and Delia walk away, and then under his breath thanked God that they had gone, he glanced at his watch, almost ten am., then his twelve-hour shift would be over, he just had to keep his head down for a few minutes more and prayed to God that they didn't come back in the meantime.

"What now?" Horace said as he followed Delia in the direction towards the lift.

"Let's take a closer look inside Beatrice's case, maybe we can find something that may help us to track her down."

Delia pushed the key card into the slot and the door opened with a slight click, room service had already been inside while they had been out and had made the bed and tidied the room and had closed the shutters and turned on the air conditioning.

Horace opened up the shutters and then grabbed hold of the suitcase and swung it up onto the bed.

Delia very carefully lifted off the top layer that consisted mostly of Beatrice's underwear with both hands and placed it on the bed, Horace and Delia both stood at the side of the bed looking into the case.

"I didn't take anything else out yesterday," Delia said, "I didn't feel comfortable searching through other people's personal things."

Horace reached into the case and picked out a white paper bag that had blue print and a name of a chemist shop, "Levothyroxine," Horace read out the name of the tablets that was printed on the side of one of the white boxes from inside the bag.

"Those are probably for her underactive thyroid gland that she was telling me about on the plane," Delia said, taking the box from Horace and returning it back into its rightful position inside the case.

"Insulin," Horace read out aloud after he had removed another large bag of medication from the case.

"That will be for her diabetes," Delia said and then once again taking the bag full of medication and carefully placing it back into the empty space from where it had come.

Horace ran his right hand closely over the top of all the contents of the case and slightly parting everything with his thumb.

"There is a lot of medication in this case," he said, "It looks like she has a lot more wrong with her than diabetes und an underactive thyroid gland."

Horace then noticed a sticky white label on one of the bags containing medication it had information printed, in black lettering from the chemist shop.

Horace lifted the bag from the case, "Mrs Beatrice Wainwright, fifty-six long Stomps Avenue, Surrey Hills, Tadworth, KT20 7LX."

"Now we are getting somewhere," Delia said, taking her phone from her handbag, "maybe now we can find her number in the online phone directory. I have just remembered something," Delia said. "I purchased a roaming in Spain bolt on, from the phone shop in the high street and all the connection details and my mobile number are inside our suitcase. One would have thought by now that Beatrice would have looked through our case and found my number and called us, she must need her drugs and clean underwear by now."

"Maybe she doesn't need her underwear," Horace joked, "maybe she is squeezing into yours."

Delia being a headmistress at a junior school had been trained not to appreciate the use of facetious or derogatory jokes, but she hadn't ignored Horace for that reason, she was too busy typing Beatrice's name and address into the website that she had just found. Delia had found a mobile phone directory called White numbers, that claimed to find people's mobile phone numbers for the cost of five pounds.

"I think I have her number," Delia said, "I just have to save it and turn it into a new contact."

Horace watched Delia entering the information into her phone. "That's brilliant," he said, "at last, now I can get out of this darn ski suit."

"It's ringing," Delia said. "Hello Beatrice? This is Delia Dankworth, we met on the plane yesterday, we have your suitcase."

"Thank god," Beatrice replied, "I have been desperately trying to trace it since yesterday, I have been so worried. I have a whole month's supply of medication in there,"

"We just need to find some way of swapping them over," Delia said, smiling at Horace and giving him the thumbs up.

"I can come to your hotel tomorrow and pick it up," Beatrice said, "I was going to spend a few more days in Malaga and then drive to Madrid on Monday, I have enough medication for today but I will need my case tomorrow. Where about are you?" Beatrice asked.

"We are staying at the Hotel Golf and Mountain Resort Buena Vista. But I don't know exactly where we are, I know we passed Granada on the way here in the taxi, we are quite high up in the mountains."

"I am not scheduled to arrive at the Madrid university hospital of highly contagious infectious diseases and viruses until Monday, but I can leave tomorrow and get my driver to make a small diversion to your hotel on the way. I have your number in my phone now, so I can call you when I am on my way and again when I am nearby, So, we can arrange to meet."

"OK Beatrice, that will be great, we will wait to hear from you tomorrow then. Bye."

"Well Horace, my darling, just one more day of walking around in the same old clothes and then we can shower and change into something clean and fresh."

"Thank god," Horace said, "I am going to throw this ski suit into the dustbin, we are very lucky we are staying in a lovely air-conditioned hotel. I'm quite sure I will smell to high heaven if I were to attempt to step outside into the intense heat of the Spanish summer. What time did she say she would be here tomorrow?"

"I am not sure," Delia said, "she is travelling by car to Madrid tomorrow morning, so I would imagine that she will be here by mid-morning at the very latest."

Delia began to put Beatrice's clothes neatly back into her suitcase.

"So why is she travelling to Madrid?"

"Something to do with studying highly contagious diseases," Delia said, closing the lid on the case and then passing the leather strap through the chrome buckle.

"You don't think that there is anything dangerous in that case, do you?" Horace backed away, "something nasty and festering, and what with all those drugs and stuff?" Horace moved forward and grabbed the case by the handle, "maybe we should leave it outside on the balcony until tomorrow."

"I don't really think that is a good idea, Horace, especially for insulin, I'm sure it has to be kept cool," Delia said, "and besides if there was something nasty in the case, I think we would have caught it by now. Let's close the shutters and turn the air conditioning up and put the case in the cupboard and go and explore the rest of the hotel."

Horace followed Delia out from the lift, hoping that people wouldn't notice that they were still wearing the same clothes that they had arrived in the day before.

"Let's see how far it is to the golf driving range," Delia said, heading off along a brightly sunlit walkway that looked out onto a large patio with a water feature in the centre surrounded by bright pink geraniums planted in yellow pots and the odd person dotted around reading quietly.

Delia opened the door at the end of the walkway and Horace followed her out into a large square open space with shaded areas along the sides with rows of golf buggies neatly parked underneath.

"That's handy," Horace said, feeling much happier being outside and in the fresh air and away from Beatrice's contaminated suitcase.

Horace and Delia quickly read all the information signs that were printed in English, golf buggies, strictly for the use of guests only, remember to leave your key card at the reception and inform them that you are taking out a buggy.

Horace walked over to a large display case that was mounted on four legs with a slopped glass front that was situated under one of the shaded areas. Inside the case was a beautifully laid out plan of the golf course in every detail, the putting greens had small flags, marking the holes and the bunkers had been made from real sand.

"Let's take a buggy out," Delia said as soon as she had joined Horace at the display case and after running her eyes over the small scaled down buggy trail.

"It's very hot," Horace replied, "and we haven't got any sun tan lotion or sunglasses."

Delia had already made up her mind and was already heading back into the direction towards reception to hand in the key card.

"The buggies have sunshades, so we should be OK," Delia shouted to Horace as she disappeared inside the door that they had just come out from.

Delia was back in no time, smiling at Horace and waving a metal token that had a white plastic card attached with the number thirteen in black numbers.

"Let me drive," Horace said pulling rank, after all he was the experienced golfer and as far as he could remember Delia had not even set one foot on a golf course before.

Horace pushed the token into the slot of the buggy number thirteen and then very confidently drove forward out from the shaded area turned left and then left again and on to the start of the buggy trail.

Within a few minutes they had passed the first tee and they were jogging along quite smoothly.

"I am having a problem keeping my eyes open," Horace said suddenly, "I need my sunglasses; everything is much too bright."

"Don't worry," Delia said, "tomorrow we will have our suitcase and your sunglasses, even sun cream. Have you noticed there is no one playing golf," Delia said, as they passed the number two tee off position, "we appear to have the whole place to ourselves."

"That's because it's too frigging hot," Horace shouted, now sounding quite hysterical. "You would have to be mental to come out here in this heat!"

By the time they had reached the seventh tee, Horace's mood had plummeted way down into the depths of despair. "It's no good, we can't go any further, it's too hot and I can't see a thing, we will have to turn around."

"I don't think we are allowed to do that, my darling," Delia said, using her calming voice that she normally used on the school children after pandemonium had broken out, and not wanting to drive in the opposite direction to all the one-way signs that they had passed on the way. "We are almost halfway around and at the golf driving range, there should be shade there, maybe I could drive, just for a while."

Horace slid over, letting Delia take control, she slammed her foot down hard onto the accelerator pedal and they shot forward with a jolt. She had to get her husband out of the intense heat and into the safe and shaded area of the golf course driving range and quick.

Delia was pleasantly surprised by the way that Horace had quickly perked up. She had left him sitting in the buggy in a nice shaded area and he had quickly taken an interest in some elderly German golfing couples who appeared to know what they were doing.

Delia went off to investigate the wooden kiosk that appeared to sell drinks and snacks, Delia smiled at the very dark tanned guy that was almost the same colour as the wooden cladding on the kiosk.

"Buenos Dias," Delia smiled at the sun-kissed figure of the man, who was wearing a very white tee-shirt and even whiter teeth.

"What would you like, Senora?" The Spanish guy smiled.

Delia quickly ran her eyes over the menu that was fixed to the back of the kiosk. "Two cups of tea please."

While the man was making the tea, Delia glanced at Horace, he appeared to be sitting there quite happily, shielding his eyes with his hands, trying to see where the Germans balls were landing.

Delia quickly turned her attention back to the small menu; they hadn't eaten much for breakfast and it could be quite some time before they made it back to the hotel for lunch, or even dinner.

"And two toasted cheese and ham sandwiches please."

The man placed the two cups of tea onto a plastic tray. "Take your tea and I will bring your sandwiches over when they are ready," he smiled.

Delia smiled politely back, "thank you, gracias," she said.

The man checked Delia out as she walked back towards Horace, carrying the two cups of tea, she was a lot older than himself but she had very white delicate skin and a very nice firm bottom and by far the most attractive woman that had passed by his kiosk all that year.

Delia handed one of the cups of tea to Horace, he had perked up considerably, now that he was out of the sun and his blood was beginning to cool down slowly.

"Maybe we could have a go?" Horace said, gesturing and pointing the cup of tea into the direction of the Germans.

"If you think you're up to it, darling."

"Well, the Germans live in a cold country like us," Horace said, "and if they can play in this heat, so can the British."

The guy from the kiosk arrived with the cheese and ham toasties and placed them on a wooden shelf close by.

"Could we possibly hire a couple of golf clubs?" Horace asked.

"Certainly sir," the man smiled, "when you have finished your snack come over to the kiosk and I will sort you out a nice driver for you and one for the lady."

Horace put the tray with the plates and cups down onto the counter top of the kiosk, there were two golf drivers already lying on the top, waiting, Horace took hold of the longer one for men, for closer examination.

"The golf balls are in the machine and they are one Euro for twenty." The man smiled at Delia. "The clubs will be five Euros each to hire."

"I don't think that I should bother," Delia smiled, "I have never tried to hit a golf ball before."

"I will show you," the man smiled, "I will give you a lesson for free."

Delia turned to Horace for some guidance, but he had wandered off, past the Germans and was practising his swing, standing on a large rubber mat, on the edge of the golf driving range.

Delia turned back. "Are you sure? I don't want to be a nuisance."

The man looked puzzled, "Nuisance, what is nuisance."

"It doesn't matter, how much for everything?"

"Two club hire, two cups of tea, two cheese and ham toasties, twenty euros please Senora."

Delia took the fifty Euro note from her purse, up till now it had been the cheapest holiday ever, they had used their card for the food in the hotel and she still had some of the cash that was left over from the holiday they had taken the year before.

"And some change for the golf balls please."

Delia found Horace, he was checking out the golf ball machine, "I have ten Euros worth of one Euro coins and these."

Delia handed over a small plastic packet of golf tees, Horace took a plastic bucket from the pile and placed it under the shoot. Delia then pushed a one Euro coin into the slot and then with a lot more noise than one would expect, twenty golf balls rolled down the chute and into the plastic bucket.

"I am going to have a free lesson, apparently," Delia said, and then took another empty bucket from the pile and filled it with another twenty golf balls.

"That will be nice, darling," Horace smiled, "I have lost count at the number of times I have asked you to take it up."

Delia followed Horace, he had chosen a position well away from the Germans and pushed one of the plastic tees into the rubber mat.

He then balanced one of the balls on top of the tee and lined the head of his golf club up with the back of ball, then slowly moved the club back and forth, as if simulating the shot, he was about to take.

Horace didn't feel comfortable, especially because he wasn't wearing his trusty ten-year-old soft black leather golf gloves. He had never ever played without his gloves and the strange club didn't seem to sit right in his sweaty palms.

Delia had moved well away and to one side, waiting for Horace to strike the golf ball. Horace finally drew the club back behind his head, and then with all the venom he could muster he swung the club, striking the ball, causing a sort of a hollow metallic ringing sound.

"Where did that go?" Horace turned to Delia.

"Haven't got a clue," she replied. "Try another one."

Even the Germans hadn't noticed the white ball whistling off to the right side of Horace and crossing their line of fire before crashing into some pretty pink flowered hedging, over on their right side.

Jose had noticed, he knew exactly where the ball had gone, after spending the past two years cooped up inside his kiosk, just by the sound, he instinctively knew that Horace had sliced it big time and knew exactly where it was heading even before it had landed.

Horace placed another ball on the tee, after less simulation than before he struck the second golf ball, that made the same metallic sound as before.

"What about that one?" Horace turned to Delia once more.

"No, didn't see that one either," Delia said, not particularly bothered and feeling really pleased that they had come to Spain and were now spending some quality time together outside in the sunshine and the fresh air.

Jose by this time was heading towards them, holding the club that he had carefully selected for Delia, again he knew exactly where Horace's ball had landed, this time the golf club had twisted even more, now that Horace's hand was beginning to sweat even more and the ball had whizzed by, this time even closer to the Germans.

The English guy was obviously losing his grip and the club was turning in his hands every time he hit the ball. Horace searched around looking for the small plastic tee, it seemed to have disappeared also.

Keeping his distance, Jose passed by Horace and Delia and took his position on the final mat to the left side of Horace. He wasn't too bothered about the Germans, but he wasn't about to cop an extremely hard golf ball to the left temple, especially that he was only getting paid five hundred Euros a month, plus the odd forty Euros a time here and there for the extra coaching.

Delia wandered sheepishly over to Jose, like Horace, he had balanced a ball on top of the tee and was lining up the club with the back of the ball.

Then with very little effort, Jose swung the club majestically, the ball hit the four hundred metres green marker sign with a bop, Delia caught sight of it as it bounced back off, and rolled back towards them for a few metres.

Horace looked up as soon as he had heard the sound of the ball bouncing off from the wooded sign.

"That's what we do today," Jose smiled at Delia, showing at least ten of his top white teeth and ten of the bottom ones.

Horace glanced to his right, the Germans had filled up their buckets once more and seemed to be striking each ball perfectly.

Jose was explaining to Delia the basics of holding a golf club and the correct standing position using his strong Spanish accent and sparkling white teeth.

Horace pushed a new tee into the rubber mating, it was at that point that he noticed that his hands were very hot and sweaty and were also very black from holding the rubber handle of the golf club.

Horace glanced around, and then found what he was looking for, at the far end just past the wooden kiosk there was a pointed sign that read toilets.

Horace walked past the Germans, past the kiosk and followed the signs that led him under a wooden pergola type constructed walkway that had beautiful scented climate's, growing up on both side and hanging down from the roof.

Once inside the toilets, Horace washed his hand thoroughly, using plenty of liquid soap and cold water. Then after washing out the hand basin, he washed his face in fresh cold water and dried himself using the white roller towel. Then Horace set about cleaning the handle of the golf club with the liquid soap and water, it seemed to be making the handle even more slippery so he daubed it dry with the roller towel, then doing a wee in the urinal.

By the time that Horace had returned to his position at the driving range, Delia's first twenty balls were scattered about twenty metres in front and she was just about to start on her second bucket. Jose had shunted up to the rear of Delia and they were both sharing the handle of the golf club.

Jose or Delia hadn't noticed that Horace had returned, Jose was too busy praising Delia every time that she hit the ball and Delia was very uncharacteristically giggling like a schoolgirl.

Horace's head was in a bit of a twizzle, had he had too much sun? or was this guy pushing himself up against Delia, but what should he do? Maybe with the heat his imagination was running wild. Maybe that's how they did things out here in Spain?

Back home at the Belvedere golf and country club, the filthy beast would have been sent packing and his membership card unceremoniously shredded and then incinerated just for good measure. In the past, people had been banned for life for just turning up in the wrong footwear or removing their shirt.

With all these thoughts spinning around in his head Horace put down another Tee, placing a ball on the top, he took out the toilet roll from his pocket and wrapped it around the handle of the golf club. Then without any careful aligning of the ball, he wildly swung at it.

What happened next, nobody could say.

The ball whizzed very sharply to the right side of Horace and was heading towards the Germans, for the very first time Horace could see the flight of the ball and cringed, waiting for the worst to happen. Luckily for everyone, the ball struck a large square steel upright that was holding up the shaded steel structure, only a split of a second before reaching the Germans.

The ball bounced off from the steel post and then bounced off from the concrete floor and hit the roof, then somehow miraculously landed into one of the Germans' plastic bucket still full of balls.

The Germans were already on their way, shouting at Horace and gesturing with their golf clubs.

Horace took a few steps back and pointed them into the direction of Jose, muttering the words, "crazy man! crazy man."

Surprisingly, Jose could not only understand but speak German and was very quickly engaged in what seemed like a very heated argument. Horace casually walked over and took Delia by the hand, "I think it would be best if we left now."

Delia glanced back a few times, wondering what had happened to make the Germans so angry, as Horace led her by the hand and quickly hustled her onto the golf buggy.

"I enjoyed that," Delia said, once they were jogging along nicely back into the direction of the hotel, "He was a very nice man, very good at what he did."

"Yes," said Horace, smiling on the inside, "and he could speak several languages too."

Chapter 9

Sunday morning, Horace was slowly gaining consciousness to the sound of something different. It wasn't a chicken or a donkey but a strange warbling sound.

Delia suddenly leapt out from the bed and grabbed at the phone that was mounted on the wall next to the door.

"Hello."

"Miss Beatrice Wainwright at reception for you."

"My God! Horace, get up! she's here!"

Delia scurried towards her trousers and blouse stepping over her dirty underwear on the floor that had been discarded from the night before.

Horace leapt out of bed avoiding his Calvin Klein boxers with the high waistband and quickly slid into the ski suit.

"How can this be? I thought she was supposed to call first?"

"I have two missed calls," Delia said throwing her mobile onto the bed and desperately fumbling around, looking for the key card.

"Come on, Horace, grab the case!" Delia shouted from the open doorway, who hadn't had time to glance in the mirror and was suffering from serious bedhead.

Horace struggled along the corridor with the case, not even considering using the wheels for what they were designed.

As soon as Delia stepped out from the lift, she could see Beatrice standing next to the desk at reception, she appeared to be very red-faced and flustered.

Horace half Dragged the suitcase out from the lift, then at that point, Delia shoved him back inside, "You can't let her see you! She will remember you from the plane, she thinks that you are some kind of weirdo, like a pimp or sexual pervert."

Delia rushed off with the case using the handle and pulling it along on its wheels.

Horace quickly sprang out from the lift and took the long way around, using the palm trees as cover, he was able to sneak up behind the reception desk from where he could hide behind the water feature next to the pond.

Beatrice could see Delia approaching; she didn't seem to be the same very elegant English rose that she had sat next to on the plane. Her hair was all shoved over to one side and the buttons on her blouse were all crossed and one of her white breasts were quite visible through a large gap.

Beatrice grabbed the case from Delia and slung it up onto a table nearby, and then very quickly opened it, desperately tearing at bags and swallowing handfuls of pills, before plunging a syringe into her swollen pink puffy right arm.

"Your case is in the car," Beatrice said in-between gulping down mouthfuls of water.

Horace from his position behind the water feature could see everything. "The cheek of it all," Horace muttered under his breath, "it was her who ran off with our suitcase, we are not the criminals here."

Suddenly, Horace felt something very wet and cold halfway up his left leg, he instinctively looked down, making direct eye contact with a very bright green, black-eyed frog.

Whether it was the bright colours of the ski suit that had attracted the creature or merely just an easy escape route from the pond, but for Horace none of that mattered, he shook his leg violently while screaming like a girl, before slipping into the pond.

Beatrice caught sight of Horace scrambling out of the pond and immediately recognised him as the weird pervert pimp guy from the plane.

"Oh my god!" Beatrice reacted, "that's that dreadful man from the plane!"

Beatrice slammed her suitcase shut and began to drag it towards the hotel's main door, muttering. She was quickly putting two and two together and making a perfect four, these people had serious issues, big problems, maybe all those young girls on the plan were all drugged and had been transported and had been sold as prostitutes in Morocco. Whatever these people where up to, at the very least they had serious sexual hang-ups, and she needed to get away from them as fast as possible.

Delia followed Beatrice out to her car, where her driver was patiently waiting and smoking a cigarette.

Beatrice barked instructions to the driver and he quickly threw the cigarette onto the ground and took the suitcase from her. He then opened the boot and took out the almost identical brown suitcase, before putting Beatrice's case inside.

Beatrice was already seated inside the back seat of the car, the driver quickly got into the driving seat and the car sped away.

Delia, in the past, had been used to dealing with very difficult people, especially some of the unruly parents that she had come into contact with over the past years, while working at the school.

But this woman was by far the worst, just driving off like that, leaving her alone in the carpark with her suitcase, no apology, no thank you, nothing.

Horace suddenly appeared, he had watched the quick changeover of the cases in the car park, from behind the safety of the glass of the hotel entrance doors and had come out as soon as the coast was clear.

"What a horrible, nasty woman," Delia said.

Horace picked up the suitcase by the handle and began to wheel it back towards the doorway.

"I wouldn't mind," Horace said. "But all this is her fault!"

"She was the one who sat in my seat on the plane!"

"She was the one who walked off with our suitcase."

"She is the one who has ruined the start of our holiday."

The hotel receptionist watched Horace and Delia as they passed by on their way to the lift. Horace with his legs and shoes soaking wet and Delia looking like she had just had sex in the bushes outside. There was something very strangely wrong with that English couple, nothing like the English people that were illustrated in his Spanish to English exercise book that he had studied at night school.

Horace threw the brown leather case onto the bed, trembling with excitement, while fumbling his fingers, trying to open the brown leather strap.

Delia was already taking off her clothes and was heading off towards the shower.

Horace quickly popped open the two metal latches and lifted the lid.

"Noooooo!"

Horace stared into the open case, if Horace was suffering from high blood pressure, now would be the moment that his heart would have swelled and exploded, splatting blood all over the hotel walls.

This case wasn't theirs either; it was full of sex toys and party games and a white wedding gown along with all sorts of other things, like penises made from chocolate that had already started to melt in the Spanish heat and had taken on weird shapes.

Delia came bounding out from the bathroom completely naked and smelling of the very last bottle of hotel complementary shower gel. Horace was lying on the bed, facing up at the ceiling, trying to avoid a major heart attack.

"So that's why Beatrice was acting so strangely," Delia said, staring into the open suitcase. "The poor woman must have thought all this stuff belonged to us."

"What are we going to do?" Horace cried out suddenly, "I feel much worse now than what I did at poor old Trevor's funeral, and my heart is beating much too fast, I feel like I'm going to die!"

"No one is going to die, Horace my darling," Delia said, using her calming head teacher voice, "we just need to find out who's case this one is and swap them over like before."

Horace sat up suddenly, like he had just been hit with a high voltage heart starter, "It's bloody obvious! It has to belong to Trudi who is getting married to Kevin," he said.

Then at that moment the phone warbled and lit up from its position on the wall next to the door.

"Maybe that is Trudi now," Delia said optimistically and lifting the phone and putting it to her ear, "Hello."

"Mr White at reception for you."

Delia put down the phone without even answering, "Who is Mr White?" She said looking at Horace, "he's waiting for us at reception."

Sebastian White was standing in the reception area, He already had sufficient information about the Dankworths from his contact in England, and if the information sheet was correct, it shouldn't be too difficult to sell them a luxury villa, somewhere up in the mountains.

But when Horace and Delia stepped out from the lift, Sebastian was a little surprised to say the least, he had expected a very distinguished guy in his fifties and wearing a suit, and his wife a tall slim elegant lady, an English rose with a bolt upright posture.

Maybe Eric Samson from Homes in the Sun had finally taken to drink or drugs and was now sending anyone over from the UK, any old Tom, Dick or Harry, just to earn his commission. Maybe this odd-looking couple walking towards him weren't Mr and Mrs Dankworth and the guy at reception had rung the wrong room number.

This guy walking towards him, no way could he be an accountant, for a start, he had never met an accountant that went on holiday wearing some kind of coloured plastic shell suit from the eighties. And why were the bottoms of his trousers and shoes dripping wet?

And as for his wife? She appeared to be walking with a stoop, possibly a hunchback, and she looked like she had been sleeping in her clothes for at least a week?

"Mr and Mrs Dankworth?"

Sebastian held out his hand and Horace shook it very limply.

Delia sort of offered her hand from her half-stooped position, so the stranger couldn't see that she wasn't wearing a bra underneath her well-worn crumpled blouse.

Sebastian instantly pushed the play button and began to spill out the normal sales pitch that he had rehearsed in front of a mirror so many times before, and had it memorised and stored inside his head.

"Mr and Mrs Dankworth? How lovely to meet you, my name is Sebastian White, but all my friends call me Seb. I was just passing by when I thought I must pop in and see how Mr and Mrs Dankworth are finding their stay in this gorgeous setting? Well, there are two reasons actually, I had an early start this morning and this place does the best breakfast for miles. Hey, I tell you what, why don't you come and join me and then you can tell me how you are enjoying your stay in this fantastic location."

Horace and Delia just couldn't find any words to answer the stranger, and just allowed him to usher them towards the breakfast bar like bewildered sheep.

Sebastian pulled a chair out for Delia once he had selected a table with the best view looking out over the golf course and the mountains beyond.

Delia sat down and then quickly got up again as soon as she realised that the stranger was going to sit directly opposite Horace and herself, not wanting him to see that she wasn't wearing any underwear.

This caused a considerable amount of confusion, as everyone moved around and around the table; eventually, Sebastian gave up, confused and exhausted and plonked himself down into one of the leather and stainless-steel chairs.

As soon as he got back to the office, he was going to send that prat Eric Samson at Homes in the Sun the snottiest of emails that he had ever received.

Horace pulled up sharply from the game of ring a ring of roses and intended to sit in the chair to the left side of Sebastian but Delia gave him a little nudge, something that she had learnt from her hockey days, grabbing the chair from Horace and then shuffling up close to Sebastian.

Horace corrected himself with a quick shuffle of his wet feet and pulled his chair up close to Sabastian on the other side. Sebastian's sales technique was suddenly completely blown out of the water, never in his fifteen years of working for Spanish white villas in the sun, had he ever come across such a strange couple.

Normally, he would sit with his back to the window with his clients facing out, so they could take in the beautiful landscape and he would speak with a very soft-spoken voice and compliment them on their attire.

A beautiful dark tanned Spanish woman suddenly arrived at their table to take their order, and obviously knew Sebastian, starting a rapid-fire conversation with him in Spanish.

Then after what seemed to be light-hearted banter she wrote something down on her small notepad and then turned to Delia, "What would you like senora?"

Delia very politely ordered toast and marmalade and a milky coffee.

Horace on the other hand decided to go large, all in, and after a quick glance at the breakfast menu, he began to reel off a whole list of things.

"I would like fresh orange juice, then toast and butter and cereal, followed by a full English breakfast and coffee with cream."

Delia was aghast, absolutely flabbergasted, Horace must be experiencing some kind of mini breakdown, only a few moments ago he was lying on the bed and imagining that he was having a heart attack, and now he was doing his very best to eat himself into having a massive one, for real.

Opposite to Delia's way of thinking, Sebastian was absolutely delighted, over the moon, Horace had taken the bait, now he only had to reel him in and play the debt of gratitude card, maybe all wasn't lost after all. These people would never be able to afford one of the front-line villas that his company had tastefully constructed around the perimeter of the golf course, but maybe he could sell them one of the plots on the huge area of wasteland a bit further up the mountain that nobody else ever wanted.

Horace once again was feeling very good about himself; he was back in the saddle; he had made love to his wife twice inside three days and he knew exactly what this smooth-talking monkey wearing the very expensive suit was up to.

Delia on the other hand would never have the weighing of this guy, she had spent all her life surrounded by good people, teachers, doctors, parents from the school, spending all their free time fundraising to help the local charities.

But Horace had experienced really cunning and evil in the business world, pharmaceutical companies developing drugs and selling them for big profits, paying their sales reps huge salaries and very little taxes in return. Landlords who owned large apartment blocks in London, who had at least ten people living in each room but only paying the same tax as the local school tuck shop lady. Horace knew this holiday was too good to be true, this guy was obviously here to sell them something. But what?

The young waitress returned carrying a large tray containing two side plates of lightly toasted French bread and small plastic containers of butter and a selection of jams and marmalade, one each for Sebastian and Delia.

Sebastian had a cup of very black coffee and Delia had a cup of white frothy milky coffee, Horace had a glass of freshly squeezed orange juice and an empty cup along with a pot of coffee and a white jug of cream and a small bowl of sugar lumps.

Horace downed the freshly squeezed orange juice in one go, the inside of his mouth was very dry, he hadn't cleaned his teeth for two days and what with all the rushing around and everything, he was hoping the citrus juice would give his mouth a bit of a deep rinse and a good flush out.

The waitress finished unloading the tray, two half slices of toasted French bread, and some small squares of gold individually wrapped butter, a bowl of cereal for Horace and another white jug with milk and his full English breakfast, that was covered by another plate to keep it hot.

Horace flooded his cornflakes with all the milk from the jug and swiftly set about eating them before his full English breakfast turned cold.

"So, Horace," Sebastian began, "have you ever been to this part of Spain before?"

Delia glanced to her right, past Sebastian, trying to get a good look at Horace's face, looking for abnormalities or facial twitching or swollen blood vessels in and around his neck.

"No," Delia answered, "we have never ever been to Spain at all, Horace doesn't like the sun, what with his very pale skin and ginger hair."

Once again, Sebastian's sales technique was set adrift, how could he possibly sell a plot of land halfway up the mountain in the scorching midday sun, miles from anywhere to a guy with pale skin and ginger hair?

"How could you have not come to this beautiful country before?" Sebastian continued, "OK, in the summer months it is a little warmer than England I must admit but nowadays with all the new suntan creams and lotions you can use a total block for example and you can always wear a hat."

Horace finished his cereal and pushed the bowl away with his left hand and guided the full English breakfast towards him with his right, he had to give this guy credit, he had all the answers, and he was probably correct in saying they could have come to Spain before.

"So," Sebastian persisted, "what are you guys going to do with the rest of your day?"

"Well," Delia began, "we have a small problem, following our arrival at the airport in Malaga somebody walked off with our suitcase."

This is brilliant, Sebastian thought to himself, he had been presented with the perfect opportunity to be very helpful and caring and in no time at all he would be back in the driving seat.

"Oh, you poor things, how awful, don't worry, this is what I am here for, it's my job, we will have your suitcase here in no time at all, whatever it takes."

Sebastian felt a little snookered, normally he would be sitting opposite and he could have seen their response, hopefully a few tears, so then he could reach across the table and reassuringly squeeze their hand.

Horace had been pleasantly surprised by the quality of his full English cooked breakfast. The sausages were very tasty and the bacon was nice and crispy, it had been more than fifteen years since his last, especially after Dr Carolina Banks had warned him that his cholesterol level had been a little high and he was at an age where a lot of men suffered from fatal heart attacks.

"So," Sebastian continued, "have you any idea who could have taken your case?"

"It's more than likely that Trudi and her hen party has it, who were on the same flight as us," Horace said, pushing his empty breakfast plate away and reaching for the toast and butter.

"Well, it's a bit of a long story," Delia explained, "there were several brown suitcases on the conveyor similar to ours, by the time that we had collected the one that we thought was ours, everyone else had taken theirs and left. It wasn't until we opened the suitcase in our room that we soon realised that the one we had belonged to a woman called Mrs Beatrice Wainwright."

"Well, that's the answer," Sebastian said, "all we have to do is track down Mrs Wainwright."

"Well," Delia said, "we have already done that, she came here to the hotel earlier this morning but the case she had and swapped over with us wasn't ours either."

"Yes," Horace said, who by now had finished his buttered toast and was sipping his second cup of coffee, "None of this is really our fault, we just took the only remaining brown case that was left, on the conveyor assuming that it belonged to us. But now it seems that everyone else screwed up, we first assumed that Mrs Wainwright had taken our case but it turns out that she took the case that belonged to the girls from Trudi's hen party. We are now hoping that we can find the hen party and that the suitcase they have got belongs to us."

"I will make it my sole responsibility to get your suitcase back," Sebastian said, "even if I have to search the whole of Spain single-handed."

Once again Sebastian felt like he had snookered himself, but this time he was up against the cushion, surrounded by all the wrong-coloured balls. He had eaten his apricot and marmalade toast and by now he would normally be talking about a guided tour of the local area, and then slowly get onto the subject of how wonderful it would be if they owned their own villa in the sun.

Up until now all the people that he had sold villas to in the past had been reasonably wealthy people, smartly dressed and dripping in jewellery.

But these people were completely the opposite, not only did they appear not to be wealthy people, they didn't even have any clothes either, and instead of dripping with jewellery they were dripping in smelly stink water from the frog pond instead.

And besides all that, he had just taken delivery of his brand-new Mercedes CLS. That had just cost him around one hundred and twenty thousand American dollars, and there is no way he was going to let this chump set one foot inside it, looking and smelling like that, no way, never ever.

"So where do we start? How do we find this Trudi and her hen party?" Sebastian said, who by now was beginning to think he was completely wasting his time with these people, and felt that he needed a lie down and have a sleep.

"That's the problem," Delia said, "we had a lot more to go on with the other case that belonged to Mrs Wainwright but the one in our room right at this moment is full of party games and other things."

"Hotel Tropicana!" Horace suddenly said, "I remember, when we were at the airport, the girls were joking with me about driving their minibus because their goalie had a disagreement with her boyfriend."

Sebastian turned and looked at Horace in disbelief, who was this guy, whatever made that prat Eric Samson from Homes in the Sun think this guy was potential villa buying material?

"Yes," Horace continued, "they called out to me from the other side of the conveyor belt, if you change your mind, we are staying at the hotel Tropicana."

"That's it then," Sebastian said, suddenly springing up from his chair, relieved that there was possibly a way out from all this mess and a chance to get away from these couple of losers. "I will go and have a word with Jorge on the reception desk he will be able to tell me exactly where the hotel Tropicana is."

"What a lovely man," Delia said, after Sebastian had gone to talk to the guy on reception, "just like Jose at the golf driving range, those type of people would do anything for you."

"Yes," Horace replied, "they most certainly would."

Sebastian was back in no time at all. "Fantastic news we have located the hotel Tropicana it is in Marbella and furthermore I have arranged a hire car for you and a satnav."

"That's great news," Horace began, "we don't want to seem ungrateful but we don't have any sunglasses and I am having trouble seeing where I am going, what with the Spanish sun and clear blue sky, it's much too bright for my eyes."

"No problem," Sebastian said, enthusiastically, "you can leave first thing in the morning before sunrise, you will be in Marbella just in time for breakfast."

Chapter 10

It was the sound of the string section from the London Philharmonic orchestra, playing peters character, from Sergei Prokofiev's composition Peter and the Wolf that filled the bedroom very early Monday morning while Horace and Delia were still sleeping.

Just for a split of a second, Horace thought that he was back in England and it was the beginning of a normal working day and he was waking up to the sound of Delia's alarm setting on her mobile.

Delia rolled over and grabbed the phone, fumbling with the setting she managed to turn it off. "Time to get up, Darling."

"What time is it?" Horace could hear the sound of the cockerels and the donkeys in the distance, Delia had slide open the patio door and was collecting the cleanly washed underwear from the patio furniture.

Luckily for them, room service had noticed that they had used all the hotels complimentary shower gel and had replaced it with four new mini bottles.

"Five fifteen, we need to get on the road a.s.a.p."

Delia was in and out of the shower within seconds, Horace wearily went into the bathroom and put a few drops of shower gel onto his finger and rubbed his teeth vigorously and then sloshed cold water onto his face and into his mouth.

Delia was holding the suitcase, standing by the doorway primed and ready for the big adventure.

"There is no way in hell that I am going to wear this disgusting ski suit on the journey home if the girls at the hotel Tropicana have our suitcase," Horace mumbled.

"Let's hope the car is here and the key is at reception as promised," Delia said as they both stepped out from the lift.

Francisco the night receptionist opened one of the drawers and took out the key for the hire car as soon as he saw them approaching.

Sebastian had explained to Francisco the night before, what had happened to Horace and Delia, how they had arrived with the wrong suitcase and that the rather large women that they had met at reception that morning wasn't there to swap her suitcase full of money for a suitcase full of drugs.

Francisco smiled pleasantly towards Horace and Delia and held out the key, "The car is in the carpark. All ready for you sir."

Horace took the key and politely smiled back and thanked him.

"How do we know what car is ours?" Delia said once they were outside.

Horace looked at the key ring. "Well, it's a Fiat and hopefully when I push this button the hazards will light up."

"Yellow," Delia said, "that's my favourite colour."

"A Fiat Panda," Horace chuckled, as he struggled to get the brown leather suitcase into the boot. Horace and Delia opened their doors simultaneously and sat down inside.

"Phew, it's really hot in here," Horace said, "and somebody has moved the steering wheel."

"That's handy; it's my turn to drive anyway," Delia said, "You drove the golf buggy."

Delia turned the ignition key just one turn and the dashboard display lit up, Horace noticed the window control buttons and opened both front windows.

"Phew, it's just as hot outside, doesn't this country ever cool down?"

"What about air conditioning?" Delia said optimistically.

Horace run his gaze over the very sparse controls of the Fiat Panda. "No, we have a heater with hot and cold air but this morning I would imagine that it would be either hot or very, very hot."

"And a satnav, that seems to be an optional extra," Horace said, sliding the button to the on position and the machine lit up and greeting them in English, "Good morning, this morning we are off to Marbella."

"What an extremely nice man Sebastian is," Delia said, "he has programmed the satnav just like he promised."

Delia turned the key and the one point two petrol engine roared into life, and then with her left hand she instinctively felt around inside the door pocket searching for the gear stick.

"Everything is back to front," Delia said, as the confidence that she had earlier for driving the car was quickly draining away.

"Maybe we should have booked a taxi," Horace said, "We have never hired a car in a foreign country before."

At the moment the satnav butted in, giving instructions, it was a woman's voice and she sounded quite inpatient.

"After driving one kilometre turn left!"

Delia selected first gear with her right hand, pushed her foot down a little on the accelerator and gently lifted the clutch. "Well at least all the pedals are all in the right order," Delia said, feeling much happier after making a really smooth start.

Selecting second gear took a little more time, taking her foot of the gas and pushing down the clutch pedal was OK, but then finding the gear stick with her right hand was proving to be a little awkward. By the time the car was in second gear it had slowed considerably and chugged and spluttered a little before speeding up.

Very soon they were at the end of the approach road and the woman in the satnav seemed to be much calmer now, but kept repeating the instructions, "turn left, turn left."

"I am not sure what side of the road we should be driving on," Delia said, after she had successfully turned left onto what seemed like a B. Road, "there are no other cars on the road to give us something to go on."

Horace was feeling much better, now that the car was moving forward and the inside of the car felt much fresher and cooler than before, he had rolled his sleeves up and was dangling his right arm out of the window.

"Well, in England we drive on the left and the steering wheel is on the right, so in Spain everything is opposite, so the steering wheel is on the left so we should be on the right side of the road, I think."

"I think I can see something moving slowly up ahead," Delia said, "It looks like a huge bundle of twigs or straw."

"You're a bit close, Darling!" Horace shouted, and Delia swerved sharply to the left, Horace quickly pulled in his trailing hand from the outside of the window and back into the car, they were that close he could smell the donkey and its mount, a suntanned old man wearing a straw sombrero.

"That's the closest I have ever been to a donkey's arse," Horace said, quickly turning around to check if the old guy and his donkey laden with straw was still intact.

"Well, we seem to be driving on the correct side of the road," Delia said, sliding the gear stick into fifth gear, "that old guy riding the donkey should know."

"And we haven't killed anyone yet," Horace chuckled, "you are doing really well darling you just need to move away from the kerb a little and try to keep the car in the middle of the road."

By the time they had passed over at least five dry riverbeds and kilometres of open space, Delia could now see the full shape of the tangerine orange coloured sun, shining into the rear-view mirror, as it pushed upwards from behind the mountains.

Delia gently applied the brakes as they appeared to be approaching the very first whitewashed village on route. There was what looked like an animal watering trough on the right and a very old olive tree on the left.

The smell of freshly baked bread filled the car as they passed by the village baker's shop, other than a few overripe oranges dropping from the trees and rolling into the road, nothing else seemed to be moving, at that time of the morning.

After passing through the village and a lot more of open space Delia had to change down into forth gear as the road become more of a climb for the little yellow car.

Horace began to feel a little uncomfortable, they seem to be going up and up, he could feel the weird sensation in his ears that he sometimes experienced while flying. The road ahead appeared to be getting a lot narrower the more that the little car climbed, up and up. Horace would have been a lot happier if there had been steel crash barriers along the edge instead of a few withered shrubs and the occasional sign showing rocks falling down from the side of a mountain.

Delia changed down another gear into third as she steered the car around the mountain road, the white lines in the middle that she had been using as a guide to keep the car away from the edge had suddenly finished, abruptly.

Horace could see the road on the other side of the incredibly high mountain, before it disappeared around to the left-hand side and out of view.

For some strange reason, he began to think about his neighbour poor old Trever and if he had felt anything before the big blast and if they would feel anything if the car did just happen to slide over the edge, plummeting down hundreds of metres before crashing onto the rocks below.

Would they die instantaneously, or would they fill every bump as the car bounced down the side of the mountain?

Horace looked across to Delia, her face was a picture of absolute concentration, she wouldn't have had the opportunity to look out over the side of the mountain or to look down into the bottomless pit that was only a few centimetres away from Horace's side of the car.

Delia steered the little car around to the left and then to the right and then eventually back around to the left, now more or less at the point that Horace had seen from the other side a few moments earlier.

Much to Horace's and Delia's relief, the road suddenly began to widen and once again there were white lines marking the centre. Horace could see another white village about half way down the mountain and he could pick out the road at various stages as it twists and turns on its way down into the village and then much further in the distance, he could see cars moving along what looked like a motorway.

"I can see a village and probably the road to Marbella in the distance darling, and it looks like we are going down finally."

Ten minutes later, Delia was driving the small yellow car slowly through the village, it was much bigger than the first and there were lines of wires stretched across high above the road attached to the buildings on opposite side with thousands and thousands of different coloured plastic bottles hanging from them.

"How wonderful," Delia said and smiling, "it's like driving along inside a beautifully coloured tunnel."

"Maybe they were expecting us," Horace chuckled.

Unlike the first village, this one was buzzing with everyday life, there were all sorts of people, young and old, and mothers, very skilfully pushing prams along the very narrow paths on each side of the road.

"Do you think we should stop for a coffee or breakfast?" Horace said, as they passed by a small square with people sitting at tables and chairs enjoying the early morning sun and eating breakfast.

"I am not sure, darling, it might be better if we kept going before it gets too hot in here," Delia said.

"I just thought you might want a short break from driving and stretch our legs, these seats are beginning to give me a bit of a numb bottom."

Exactly three and a half hours later, Delia and Horace were driving around the outskirts of Marbella. The woman inside the satnav seemed to be having one of those days; she couldn't make her mind up, whether they should turn to the left or the right.

Horace was now suffering from a severe case of small car achy seat bum syndrome, and was doing his very best to raise his bottom off from the seat by pushing firmly down with his feet and arching his back against the back of the car seat and headrest.

Delia was beginning to feel slightly irritated; Horace was being no help, especially with the searching for the hotel Tropicana, what with his back arched and his head staring straight up at the car roof.

Delia suddenly had to stop the car at a set of traffic lights that they had already passed by at least two times before and on both occasions the stupid women inside the satnav had told her to turn left the first time and to the right the second time around.

Horace was suddenly very aware that Delia was beginning to get stressed and slowly slid back down into his seat, he scanned the crossroads through squinty eyes and miraculously notice a tall grey post with a lot of white signs with the names of hotels written in black letters, pointing into different directions.

"Hotel Tropicana!" Horace shouted, "Straight ahead!"

The traffic lights turned to green and Delia slowly passed over the crossroads, taking a long slow look at the various hotel signs that Horace had just pointed out.

The woman's voice from inside the satnav was insisting that Delia turn to the left, and then after she had driven straight ahead kept on telling her to turn around when safe to do so.

Horace leant forward slightly and slid the satnav control to the off position. "We don't want to upset her; we will need her for the journey home," he said.

Delia noticed another sign with the hotel Tropicana with a small arrow pointing directly ahead, "at last," she sighed, "finally we are making progress."

Just a few blocks later and after following the signs guiding them to the hotel Tropicana, Delia took a right turn down a wider than normal road with palm trees on either sides and also planted along each side of a wide pathway that ran along the centre.

The huge white building of the hotel Tropicana stood directly ahead, Delia, drove slowly down to the bottom of the road, looking for somewhere to park.

At the end of the road there was a mini roundabout with a huge water feature of a mermaid in the centre surrounded by pineapples squirting out jets of water. There appeared to be an underground carpark that disappeared under the building and was closed off by a large red and white striped steel barrier.

Delia slowly manoeuvred the car around the mini roundabout and back up the road. Then, very luckily, a group of black African guys were walking down the road towards them, carrying all sorts of things, trainers, watches, sunglasses, and what looked like multi-coloured Mohegan wigs.

Delia stopped the car, Horace and Delia watched as the men began squeezing themselves into a very old Ford Mondeo that was severely dented and had a different colour door and bonnet and the front bumper held on with grey gaffer tape.

The car disappeared surrounded by a cloud of black smoke.

Delia very quickly drove the car just past the empty parking space and after only three attempts backed the little yellow Fiat panda into the empty space. Horace was out from the car like a crazy horse bolting from an unsecured horse box, limping down the road towards the hotel Tropicana and frantically rubbing the backs of his legs and his bottom.

"There is no way in hell I am getting back into that car for at least another four hours!" He shouted.

As soon as Horace and Delia had stepped through the main doors of the three-star hotel Tropicana, they were paralysed with disbelief, unable to move they just stood there and stared.

They had never seen so many young people condensed into such a small area before, unlike their hotel reception there was hardly enough room to swing a cat.

There was a continuous movement of practically naked bodies, some coming in and some going out, passing through the two sets of doors, one to the right and one on the opposite side to the left.

Some of them were dripping wet and some were dressed as if they were about to go out clubbing.

"We have left the suitcase in the car," Delia said, the first one to speak, breaking the silence, "It will get too hot and all baked up in the car."

"I don't think it is much cooler in here," Horace said, taking the car key from Delia and then turning around and heading back out of the door.

By the time that Horace had returned with the case, Delia had somehow pushed her way to the sorry excuse for what supposed to be a reception desk.

"There isn't anyone here," Delia said, "Just empty wine bottles and beer cans."

Horace put the suitcase down and peered out through one of the doors, "Maybe we should have a look out here, it looks like this door goes out to the garden and pool area."

Horace grabbed hold of the leather strap and Delia followed him through the door and outside, although it was just before ten am, in the morning the bar was already open with very loud music blasting out from some very large garden shed size speakers.

Delia was very suddenly aware of the fact that they were by far the oldest people there by at least thirty years and slowed her walking, deliberately holding back, she could see that Horace was drawing a lot of attention especially from a group of young lads standing at the bar.

"Are you here on your holidays, Grandad?" one of the young lads shouted as Horace past them by.

By the time that Horace had reached the wide paved area around the poolside, he was having difficulty seeing, what with the sunlight reflecting up from the very light blue pool and the very strong smell of chemicals that were very quickly evaporating in the sun and wafting up from the pool surface.

Somebody shouted, "The mobile disco is here lads!"

And somebody else, shouted "Show us your vinyl LPs, Grandad," then there was a lot of sniggering.

Delia quickly caught up with Horace, she realised that he was having problems seeing, and was worried that he and the case were getting dangerously close to the edge of the pool.

"There is a crowd of half-naked girls waving to you," Delia said, "they are over there on the other side of the pool."

"Hey Horace! Over here!"

Horace shielded his eyes from the sun, he recognised the group of young girls from the plane and slowly began his journey around the outside of the mega-sized swimming pool, dragging the case.

By the time that Delia had followed Horace around to the other side to where the girls had set up camp, she felt like she had stumbled into a refugee camp or some sort of Romany community.

Most of the girls appeared to be unconscious or possibly dead, lying on sun loungers, some were dressed like they were about to go out to a party and others just wearing a very small bikini bottom.

"Horace!" Alice shouted, over here, excitedly, "what are you doing here! How did you get here!" She gave him a huge hug, wrapping her soaking wet almost naked body around his.

"I have got your suitcase, we were hoping that you might have ours," Horace said, very aware of the fact that he was being hugged by a very wet and naked twenty-something-year-old girl.

Eventually, Alice let Horace go and wrapped herself around Delia, "You must be Delia? This is fantastic."

Delia stood there with her arms firmly clamped by her sides by Alice's firm embrace, not knowing what to do or say and hoping that it would end very soon and she would be set free.

Alice suddenly set Delia free and spun around and turned her attention to Trudi, one of the lifeless bodies lying on one of the sunbeds.

"Trudi, wake up! Horace is here and he has brought our missing case!"

"Are you sure that she is OK?" Delia said, feeling very concerned that Trudi had made no response to Alice's vigorous shaking and shouting.

"Yeah, she's alright, she has only been asleep for about an hour we have been out all night, we don't use our rooms, we don't want to lose our sunbeds," Alice said pointing to various free-standing clothes rails scattered about. "We are out every night and then we sleep here in the daytime, we haven't used our rooms since the first night we arrived."

"That's what people do here," she smiled, "we got all these from a group of people who were going home the day after we arrived," Alice said, pointing again to the free-standing clothes rails dotted around.

"Have you by any chance got our case?" Horace asked.

"Yes," Alice said, "we have someone's, not sure if it is yours though, we were going to leave it at lost property in the airport on the way home."

Alice took the case from Horace and put it down onto one of the sunbeds and opened it up, some of the other girls began to stir and take an interest.

One of the girls pulled the specially adapted wedding dress from the case and with the help of two others they stood Trudi up and very skilfully managed to dress her with the gown, while she appeared to be still sleeping.

Trudi suddenly opened one eye and smiled at Horace, "I wish you were my dad; I really like you."

Trudi began to move forward, unaided and towards Horace, with her arms outreached in front of her, similar to a demon zombie bride.

Horace backed away, embarrassed, not wanting to be hugged by a twenty-something girl only wearing a blue thong and a very white see-through wedding dress.

Trudi lunged forward, Horace stepped back and they both fell into the pool with a huge splash, everyone around the poolside cheered, whistled and clapped and then laughed. Amazingly, Horace was totally unfazed when his very hot sweaty body fell backwards into the pool and if anything found the water quite cooling and refreshing. It had been a long time since he had swum and was amazed how easy he found it and was in no real hurry to get out.

Delia on the other hand felt terribly embarrassed and wished the ground would open and swallow her up. She was a respected member of the community, a head teacher, if the school governors could see her now standing by the poolside surrounded by almost naked women while her husband swam around fully clothed, she would be run out of town before she could say, the queen Victoria primary and junior community school.

Just when Delia thought things couldn't get any worse, the rest of Judie's hen party all fifteen of them suddenly all come to life and jumped screaming and bombing into the pool.

At that point Horace thought it was best that he got out, what with all the crazy goings on, the water had suddenly gotten very choppy and he had already taken in several large mouthfuls. Somehow Horace made his way to the steps and hauled himself out, much to the disappointment of all the girls, and they all began to chant his name, "Horace", "Horace", "Horace".

Delia quickly went over to where Horace was standing and took hold of his hand, very firmly, the man she had married all those years ago would have never contemplated leaping into the pool but now she wasn't quite so sure.

Over the past few weeks so many things had happened effecting their lives, everything had been turned upside down.

"We need to get away from this place and all these crazy young people," Delia said, tugging at Horace's hand.

Horace followed Delia's lead, slowly beginning to make their way back towards the hotel building. The cool water in the pool had very quickly revived

Trudi and as soon as she sees that Horace and Delia were leaving, she quickly got out from the pool and chased after them catching them up.

"Thank you for bringing our case, Horace, and I am sorry for pushing you in the pool."

Horace half turned and smiled, "That's OK. I needed to cool down anyway, we have had a long hot drive this morning but now we are very hungry and we need to find somewhere to eat."

"Come up to our room and collect your case," Trudi said waving her key card around, "and you can use our facilities to shower and change."

Horace and Delia were pleasantly surprised to see how tidy and clean the room was, not like the area around by the pool where all the girls appeared to be camping out.

Trudi pulled a brown leather suitcase out from the inside of the double wardrobe, "I thought this was the case that I borrowed from my parents," she said placing it on top of the bed and unbuckling the brown leather strap.

Horace and Delia stood on the other side of the bed, waiting for Trudi to lift the lid.

"Bingo," Horace shouted, at the very first glance as soon as the case was opened, they could see all their clothes and possessions and knew that it belonged to them.

Horace felt a huge sense of relief and joy, Delia uncharacteristically felt very emotional and began to cry, like she had just been reunited with her long-lost child after twenty years.

Trudi quickly moved around from the other side of the bed and gave Delia a huge hug. "Sorry for screwing up your holiday," she said.

Delia hugged Trudi, she felt very cold and wet, "you need to go and dry yourself off," she said.

Trudi broke away and went over to the window, their room was on the opposite side of the main entrance and faced out over the beach.

"When you are ready, just pull the door shut behind you, if you go out of the other door opposite, the one that leads out to the pool it will lead you out into the garden and out of a gate and onto the beach. There is a really nice fish restaurant about ten minutes' walk along the beach that has a really nice terrace that looks out onto the sea."

Once Horace and Delia had showered and changed, Delia put the clothes that they had been wearing for the last few days into one of the plastic bags that she had brought to use for the dirty laundry. Then checking that they had everything they closed the door and took the lift back down to the ground floor.

Once Horace had squeezed their suitcase into the boot of the car, they followed Trudi's instructions and passed back through the hotel and along the garden path that led them out onto the beach.

Even though Horace was wearing his leather sandals, his feet quickly sank into the deep white sand and very soon the tops of his feet began to burn.

Delia grabbed hold of Horace's hand and pulled him towards the sea, "we can paddle," she said, laughing as the sand become unbearably hot and they had to run as fast as they could.

Delia ran straight into the sea kicking of her sandals as she went; she went in far enough until the water lapped around the bottom of her patterned summer dress. Horace undid the buckles on his sandals and then gathered up Delia's and placed both pairs on the edge where the dry sand met the wet. Unlike Delia he cautiously paddled into the sea just enough for it to lap over his very white milky bottle-coloured feet.

Delia mocked Horace, laughing and trying to splash him with both of her hands. Horace turned not wanting the sea water to wet his sunglasses and fresh smelling neatly ironed summer shirt.

"I can see the restaurant!" Horace shouted. "Let's walk along the edge and check out the menu!"

Horace and Delia held hands as they walked along the water's edge, Horace on the wet compact sand and Delia paddling in the sea.

Once they were level with the restaurant Horace stopped and took off his hat and wiped his forehead with the back of his arm. "The restaurant seems to be miles away from here, we will never make it across the hot sand."

"Then we will have to die trying," Delia laughed as she ran into the sea, soaking the bottom half of her dress and then making a dash for it.

Horace stood and watched Delia while he cooled his feet in the sea, wondering if she would make it all the way across to the restaurant or suddenly turn back. Miraculously, Delia found a beach shower set into a large slab of concrete and was able to cool her feet, before waving to Horace.

Horace took a deep breath and then made a dash for it; the hot sand was incredibly soft underfoot and Horace found it very hard going. By the time he had reached the small oasis of wet concrete and wet sand surrounding the stainless-steel shower, he was making weird sounds as if he was running on hot coals.

Delia had watched him running towards her, laughing hysterically, this had been the best holiday ever, so much fun and adventure.

From the beachside the restaurant appeared to be made mostly from wood with some tables and chairs sprawling off from the wooden decking and on to the beach, with large straw umbrellas providing plenty of shade.

Horace and Delia walked up the six wooden steps and onto the terrace that projected out on either side, directly ahead through a glass door they could see the seating area inside with all the tables covered with clean white table clothes, and beyond a huge glass cabinet full of fresh fish lying on a bed of Ice.

A waiter suddenly appeared from nowhere very smartly dressed and wearing soft white cotton gloves. "Buenos Dias Senora, Buenos Dias Senor."

Delia smiled, "a table for two please?"

"Would madam care for a table on the terrace or inside."

"On the terrace if possible?" Delia smiled again, "facing the sea?"

"Certainly madam, this way please," the waiter said, heading off.

Horace and Delia followed the waiter along the terrace passing an extended Spanish family that seem to start with the great grandparents passing down through the generations with the youngest member, a baby girl sitting in a high chair holding a piece of soggy white bread.

The waiter stopped at a smaller table covered in a clean white paper tablecloth and pulled out the chair for Delia that was facing out to the sea.

A few minutes later a young woman arrived dressed in a white blouse and a black skirt, she placed a menu in front of Delia and then Horace before asking them what they would like to drink.

Delia asked for a bottle of fizzy water and for Horace a bottle of still water.

"Well, this is nice," Delia said. "It feels like we are in a completely different country and a million miles away from all those crazy young people and that ghastly hotel Tropicana."

"These prices are very reasonable too," Horace said, "and they have a good varied selection of different kinds of dishes."

By the time Horace and Delia had made their way back from the restaurant and along from the beach and back to the little yellow car, it was three o clock in the afternoon. Delia had had grilled Rosado but although they had eaten on the terrace of a really nice fish restaurant facing out towards the sea, Horace had gone for the fillet steak.

He felt that he needed something much more substantial than white fish with all the extra excitement in his life and the increase in activities like swimming, running and making love to his wonderful wife.

Delia opened the car and quickly opened both of the front windows, luckily the closely planted palm trees had provided some kind of shade to the little yellow Fiat Panda, so Delia could take hold of the steering wheel without burning her hands. Delia quickly started the car and drove directly forward and out from the parking space and turned right at the end of the road.

Horace slid the button of the satnav to the on position, luckily for them once it had illuminated instantly, the menu displayed a return to home option and Horace promptly pushed it.

In no time at all, they had left Marbella and were heading along the A7 towards Malaga and then following the road on to Granada.

Chapter 11

Tuesday morning and Horace awoke first around eight-thirty, the room was very dark and stuffy and his face felt hot and his mouth very dry. He carefully slid out from the bed, trying not to wake Delia, he opened the shutters and turned on the air conditioning on to the cool setting and silent mode.

Horace went into the bathroom to brush his teeth, looking into the mirror he could see that his face was quite red and he had white circles around his eyes and a small white line, across the top of his nose where the sunglasses had been sitting.

After taking a shower and giving his hair a thorough wash with his normal shampoo, he opened the family size bottle of after sun and squirted a generous portion into the palm of his hand, then sitting down at the bottom of the bed began to apply it all over his red legs and feet.

Delia opened her eyes, "I thought you said we were going to stay in our room all day and watch the sun go down," Horace chuckled, noticing that Delia had the same red and white pattern on her face as him.

"It was a good job that we put on plenty of factor fifty before the walk along the beach," Delia said, heading off into the shower.

Once Horace had put on a nice clean pair of Calvin Klein pants and a clean cotton short-sleeved shirt and shorts, he noticed that Delia had packed the small pair of binoculars and took them out onto the balcony to have a good nose around.

A short while later, just after Delia had put on a clean summer dress and was rubbing the Aftersun into her arms and legs, the phone rang.

"I know exactly who that is," Horace called out, from his new appointed lookout position.

"Seb wants to know if we would like to join him for breakfast?"

Horace came in from the balcony. "Well, I suppose we should, he has been more than helpful, even though I have a strong suspicion that he is going to try to sell us something."

Sebastian had planned everything out as normal the night before, he had reserved his favourite table in the centre of the breakfast area and had bought some white chrysanthemums and put them into a vase and placed them on the very clean and pressed white table cloth in the centre of the table.

He had even taken the trouble to drive into Granada to collect some colour brochures from the English mobility shop and then on to the bathroom shop that supplied and fitted baths and showers units for people with disabilities.

Even though Horace and Delia had had a bad start to their holiday, he was convinced that the pair had and were both suffering from some kind of serious disabilities, what with her stooped back, and him with his personal smelly hygiene problem.

He had set himself down in the centre of the table with his back to the window and had hidden the fourth chair, hoping that Delia would this time sit down facing the window and not pull the crazy stunt like before, playing musical chairs or let's all dance around the mulberry bush.

There was no way in hell that he was going to be shoved out from this seat and around the table playing musical chairs like last time by that half-stooped crazy bitch of a wife.

Eventually, when Horace and Delia first walked into the breakfast bar, Sebastian was completely taken by surprise, he had noticed a couple walking in his direction but didn't pay too much attention to them, except for the fact that they were blocking his line of view and he now couldn't see the crazy pair arriving that he was expecting, to be stepping out from the lift at any moment.

"Good morning," Delia said, smiling at Sebastian.

Sebastian stared up at the tall elegant English woman standing there in front of him. He vaguely recognised her face from somewhere but just couldn't think where.

"What lovely flowers," Delia smiled, "and what a beautiful morning."

Sebastian looked at Horace and then at Delia and then at Horace and then once again at Delia.

"Are you OK?" Horace asked, genuinely concerned, thinking that Sebastian was having some kind of seizure, just staring at them, like they were from planet Zongo and he didn't recognise them.

Horace slid one of the chairs out for himself so that he could sit down.

Sebastian leaped out from his chair, quickly pulling out the chair opposite for Delia, was this the same woman? She was too tall, much taller than him, and so slim and attractive, so different to the buckled and bent over old crow of a woman he had met previously.

The young waitress had been watching, she knew the drill, she had helped Seb to sell villas many times before but didn't understand why he was talking to those other people. She approached their table. "Good morning," she said, once again staring at Delia and then at Horace, "what would you like?" she said, staring at Delia, not really sure who she was.

"Just a milky coffee and toast and marmalade for me please," Delia said, smiling.

"And the same for me please," Horace smiled, "but I will have a regular coffee."

"And my usual," Sebastian said, exchanging glances with the waitress, both of them searching each other's eyes, looking for the answers—who the heck were these two people?

"Thank you for arranging the car for us," Horace was the first to speak, still not sure if Sebastian was OK, he still had a very blank expression and now seemed like he was suffering from some kind of identity crisis.

"No problem," Sebastian breathed a huge sigh of relief, his questions had been answered, these were the same people, even though the woman appeared to be much, much taller and seemed to have lost her hump. "How was your trip to Marbella, did you find your suitcase?"

"Yes," Delia smiled, "and we had the most enjoyable day, although my eyes ache a little from all the concentrating what with the bright sunlight and driving on the opposite side of the road."

The waitress returned with a tray of toast and marmalade and three coffees placing them in turn in front of each of them, still wondering who the heck they were, and who was who and what was what?

Sabastian once again felt that he was back on track, a relatively happy man, he could see that Horace and Delia were taking in the view, looking out of the window at the beautifully green landscaped golf course.

"It's fantastic, isn't it," Sebastian said, "and what a fantastic place to live or to be able to own your second home. So, what are your plans for today?"

"As long as it doesn't involve a three-and-a-half-hour drive in the blazing heat," Delia said, "we are not really sure."

"Why don't you let me show you around the local area?" Sebastian said. "I have a very quiet morning. And it's much too hot to play golf."

After breakfast, Horace and Delia went back to their room to cover themselves in suntan lotion and to collect their sunhats, while Sebastian waited for them downstairs at reception.

"I thought we could start by driving around the outside of the golf course and I could show you what our company have been doing here for the last fifteen years," Sebastian said, once they were outside, pushing the buttons on his remote control, opening up the doors and sliding back the roof of his brand-new Mercedes CLS.

Instead of turning left at the end of the road, the way that the satnav had guided Delia and Horace the day before, Sebastian turned to the right onto a wide tarmac road that had a steady climb upwards with very tall eucalyptus trees planted on either side.

"This road has been here for many years," Sebastian called out over his right shoulder, "it used to go all the way up to the top and to a very grand Spanish farmhouse, goat people."

Finally, Sebastian turned right, leaving the original partly shaded eucalyptus tree lined road and driving directly into the bright sunlight, even though the new road had been constructed almost twenty years before, it still looked very clean and well maintained.

Sebastian slowed the car down to a crawl so Horace and Delia could take everything in as they passed.

On the left were large white detached villas all surrounded by green fencing covered in the very bright pink and red colours of the Bougainvillea that interwove with the fencing.

On the right side of the road from its elevated level, Horace and Delia had a clear view out over the golf course and the hotel further over, on the other side.

The centre of the road had a raised Island running along the full length with palm trees planted every two metres, surrounded by brightly coloured orange flowers.

"So, what do you think?" Sebastian said, pulling into one of the many laybys, stopping the car and then quickly raising the roof, "we don't want the seats getting to hot and sun damaged while we are gone. This front line of villas were finished about five years ago, and up till now I have sold all of them," Sebastian said. "Now we are developing phase two and we have some fantastic off plan offers running at the moment. If you follow me, I can show you our latest project," Sebastian said, walking along the path on the other side of the road nearest to the golf course.

Sebastian stopped just in line with one of the villas, there was a much wider gape in-between this and the next, with a wide path and ramped walkway that zig zagged its way up through a mature and tastefully planted garden with shrubs and flowers.

"The villas that we are going to build will be up there," Sebastian pointed, "and will be the exactly the same as the ones on this level but because we are building on the side of the mountain you will still have a fantastic view out and beyond the golf course."

"What about the people in these villas?" Delia said, "won't they be overlooked? Won't they lose their privacy?"

"Yes, a little," Sebastian said, "but they would have seen the plans and the model of the finished development and they did buy these places at fantastically low prices, half the price of what the new ones will cost. We could walk up the path if you like," Sebastian said, gesturing with his hand across the road and up the steps, "you will get a better idea from up there, and the view is spectacular."

Horace looked up at the path, it seemed to go up and on for ever and he was already very hot and sweaty and they had only been standing out in the sun for around ten minutes.

This guy Sebastian was up to no good, Horace thought to himself, I probably wouldn't even make it to the top and even if I did, I would be delirious and suffering from sunstroke, he's probably got a contract in his pocket and probably get me to sign it before calling the ambulance.

"Maybe some other time," Delia said, "when it's not quite as hot."

"I could drive us," Sebastian said, "but it's just a dirt track up there at the moment and I don't want to get the car wheels all dusty."

"What about shopping?" Delia said, "we seem to be miles away from anywhere, don't these people feel isolated?"

"Not in the slightest," Sebastian smiled, "we are only a fifteen-minute drive from El Pueblo del Cabra Punto de Agua. Translated into English that means the village of the Goat watering point," Sebastian smiled, "it's where the shepherds used to stop, so their goats and sheep could take in water on their way up to graze in the mountains. We can go there now; I can drop you off in the village if you like and we can meet up later there for some lunch."

Once back at the car, Sebastian started the engine and turned the air conditioning on to full and shut the door.

"We just have to wait a couple of minutes for the air conditioning to work its magic and then we will be on our way." After a few minutes, Sebastian opened the car. "Twenty degrees," he said smiling, "next stop El Pueblo del Cabra Punto de Agua."

Sebastian turned the car around at a small opening in the centre of the road and soon after turning right at the end they were back on the original Eucalyptus sheltered road climbing further up the side of the mountain.

By the time Sebastian had driven them to the village of the goat watering point, almost an hour had passed. The fifteen-minute drive that he had spoken about earlier, he could only have achieved if he had been driving a jet-propelled JCB digger or possibly a gamma goat.

They had soon run out of the wide smooth tarmac road, with the surface changing to lose concrete chips and had spent around forty-five minutes on a very narrow bumpy goat track.

"It's normally much quicker if you take the main road," Sebastian said, speaking over his left shoulder.

"The roads in the village are very narrow," Sebastian said, "originally they were only built for donkeys and goat herders. There is a one-way system that runs around the outside of the village, I can drop you off in the carpark," Sebastian said, turning into a wide-open area that had the same kind of crushed concrete chips covering the surface as the goat track earlier.

Once outside the car, Sebastian took his phone from his pocket. "It's now eleven-thirty, if we can exchange numbers, you can call me if you get lost."

"I can give you mine," Delia said, "Horace doesn't have the advantage of roaming on his mobile."

Horace was happy with that arrangement, and kept his mobile safely in his pocket.

Sebastian rang Delia. "Now you have my number," He said, "If you walk in that direction, there is a gap in between the two rows of houses, just follow the street along and it will lead out into the village centre." Sebastian got back into his car. "We can catch up later," he said, driving off across the carpark and out of sight.

Delia grabbed hold of Horace's hand tugging him into the direction that Sebastian had pointed out. "This is an adventure," she said, "our first ever Spanish whitewashed village."

"Let's hope it's not our last," Horace said, "and he hasn't dropped us off here to be mugged or ambushed by bandits."

"I think you are still getting confused, Horace my darling," Delia laughed, "mixing Spain up with Mexico."

Once Horace and Delia had passed through the gap in between the two houses, that Sebastian had pointed out, they had to make a decision, turn left and walk up the road, or turn right and go down.

Just like Sebastian had said, the street was very narrow with no pedestrian pathway on either side and the cobble stone road ran right up to the edges of the fronts of the houses.

Most of the houses had small balconies on the upper floors with artistically formed iron surrounds and bright red geraniums in light blue pots.

"Let's go down," Delia said, giving Horace's hand a tug, "it is always better to start at the bottom and work your way up."

Horace and Delia followed the road down to the bottom, other than a few cats and a small white dog barking from one of the balconies, there wasn't much sign of any other life. After walking downhill for around five to ten minutes, Horace and Delia had reached the bottom of the road, they then followed it around a sharp bend to the left.

There was a continuous line of the same Spanish traditional houses on the right but to the left the houses were less frequent with narrow roads running back up the hill, in-between.

After passing three or four more narrow roads, with small houses on either side they found themselves suddenly looking up a much wider road on the left-hand side with shops and signs of life.

"This looks like the main street," Delia said, pulling Horace by the hand, starting their slow uphill climb.

The very first shop was situated on the right-hand side of the street just a few metres up from the bottom.

Horace was very disappointed to see that it was a clothes shop and knew from past experience that they would be inside for at least a half an hour, minimum.

Delia tightened her grip on Horace's hand and dragged him across the street and up three small steps and through the door. The shop was quite small inside with just enough room in the centre for a line of clothes rails running from front to back. A middle-aged woman greeted them, who was sitting at the far end behind a small glass counter.

Delia systematically moved along the left side of the shop scanning everything, occasionally pulling something from the rail for a closer inspection.

Normally, at this point, Horace would sneak out of the door and find something a little more interesting to do, and then return a good half of an hour later, but the shop was surprisingly much cooler inside than it was outside in the street.

"If we knew this village was here, we could have bought ourselves some underwear and clothes when we first arrived," Delia said, quite loudly, from the other side of the shop, assuming the Spanish lady wouldn't understand.

"Yes, and I could have had a shave and cleaned my teeth," Horace said, glancing at the Spanish lady for any signs of recognition and that she might possibly understand their conversation.

By the time Delia had scanned everything on the left and right side of the shop, she had picked out two very lightly coloured printed summer dresses and a pair of beige sandals. The Spanish shop lady pointed Delia into the direction of the small changing room that was situated at the far end of the shop, through an archway and then behind a bright red curtain.

She offered her chair to Horace and then pointed to a name badge on her blouse, "Maria," she said and smiled.

"Horace," Horace said smiling back, the women looked him up and down for a second, then she looked like she was going to repeat his name Horace but after a few facial expressions said, "que?"

"Horace," Horace repeated.

"Que?"

"Horace," he repeated once more, much louder this time. Delia poked her head from around the red curtain, wondering what the heck was going on.

The women's head disappeared down behind the glass counter, suddenly popping back up, handing Horace a small notepad and pen.

Horace lent on the glass counter and wrote down his name, and then handed the notepad back.

The women looked at Horace. "Orathee, Orathee," she repeated and smiled. "Orathee!"

Luckily, Delia suddenly appeared from out behind the red curtain, smiling, wearing one of the dresses and the beige sandals. "What do you think?"

"Very nice," Horace said. "Let's just get the hell out of here."

"Very nice," the Spanish women repeated, mimicking, and smiling at Horace.

At that point Horace couldn't give two monkeys what they looked like or the cost, he just needed to get out, he never had been very comfortable talking to foreigners, and this one seemed to be more than a little bit crazy.

Once Horace and Delia were back outside in the street and Delia was carrying both dresses and her new sandals in a white carrier bag, she took hold of Horace's hand and kissed him on the cheek, "Thank you, Orathee," she smiled.

"I wouldn't mind, I even wrote my name down on her notepad, how did she make Orathee from the name Horace?"

"I like it," Delia laughed, "it sounds very Mediterranean."

Slowly but surely Horace and Delia made their way further and further up the street, passing a butcher, greengrocers and a fresh fish shop. There was a dentist that also done implant surgery and laser teeth whitening and a lawyer's office close by. Then the street opened up with a small square on either side, on one side there was a large watering trough in the centre and a bakery with tables and chairs outside with people eating cake and drinking coffee.

On the other side there was another large watering trough, identical to the other, but with an ice-cream shop with tables and chairs and large white parasols providing shade.

"This must have been the goat watering point," Delia said, "I am going to take a picture with my phone."

Delia took some photos of the goat watering point with the shops and tables behind, a tall dark guy who was sitting at one of the tables asked Delia if she would like a photo of her with Horace.

"We need to take off our hats and sunglasses," Delia laughed, "or nobody will recognise us."

"What a lovely place this is," Delia said, as they sat on the side of the watering point once the guy had taken a couple of photos and had sat back down.

"I must admit it is very nice here," Horace said, sinking his right hand into the cool water down as far as his elbow.

After a short rest, Horace and Delia carried on with their walk, passing a hairdresser and a hardware shop that had wheelbarrows among all sorts of other things outside. At the top of the hill the road levelled off and directly ahead was a large village square with a white church at the far end.

The whole area was shaded by huge blue and white kite shaped material, all fixed together by wires and pulled tight by a series of pulleys fixed to steel posts.

Horace and Delia walked up the six steps that separated the road from the square, "How lovely," Delia said.

On both sides of the square there were small coffee shops and restaurants that had different coloured tables and chairs outside, marking out each individual area.

"Our friend Sebastian is waving to us," Horace said, "he is over there on the right, sitting at one of the tables."

"Just in time for lunch," he smiled greeting them with a firm handshake for Horace and a kiss on each cheek for Delia. "I often pop in here for lunch," he said, "everything is made from local produce and from the goats of this region. So, what do you think of our village?" Sebastian asked, once everyone was seated.

"I love it," Delia said, "the people who live here are so lucky, it is such a beautiful place."

"Have you ever considered a holiday home abroad or possibly somewhere you can retire to, Horace?"

"No not really." Horace knew exactly where Sebastian was heading, what with the free hire car, twice breakfast and now some kind of weird goatee lunch.

"Horace may have some redundancy money heading his way in the very near future," Delia said, "so anything is possible."

Horace couldn't believe what was happening, why was Delia giving this sort of personal information out to a complete stranger, or even worse a professional gold-digging salesman? She might as well have cut both of his wrists and tossed him into a pool of flesh-eating piranha.

"Really," Sebastian smiled, handing Horace a menu, "the goat stew here is really good, very meaty."

Delia in her innocence and naivety had no idea. "I will have the goat cheese salad with goat milk yogurt," she smiled and handed her menu to the waiter.

"I will have my usual, the goat stew please, Filipe, my friend," Sebastian said.

"Just a cheese salad for me please," Horace said, handing the menu back to the waiter.

"Filipe is one of the very few people in this village that can speak English fluently," Sebastian said, "he is studying economics at the university in Granada."

"So, Horace," Sebastian smiled, "what are you going to do with all that lovely redundancy money?"

"Nothing is official yet," Horace said. "There are rumours that the firm of accountants that I work for is going to be bought out and taken over by another company."

"I have just one word for you, Horace," Sebastian leaned across the table like he was about to divulge a very closely guarded secret, "property," he whispered. "Don't sit on your savings, Horace, invest in property, overseas property."

"I don't think that I will be getting enough redundancy money to buy a house," Horace said, trying to throw Sebastian off the scent, "maybe a small cheap second-hand car."

Delia laughed, "oh Horace you are so funny, you can tell that he is an accountant," she said, turning to Sebastian, "we already have money just sitting in the bank from when both our parents passed away."

Ker Ching! Sebastian thought to himself, after a bumpy start these two had come good after all, it was a pity that he had already sent the rather snotty email to Eric Samson at Homes in the Sun, calling him among other things a prat-faced son of a retarded dickhead.

Just at that point Filipe arrived carrying a tray with the drinks, two cheese salads and a weird orangey brown coloured goat stew for Sebastian.

"So," Sebastian said, "you're back to grey old England tomorrow?"

"Yes," Delia said, "I really would like to stay for another week, the time has simply flown by, what with our case going missing and everything."

"Just imagine," Sebastian said, leaning back in his chair, "if you had your own little place out here, you could come and go just as you, please."

After lunch, Horace tried to pay Filipe for the food and drinks on his way back from the toilet, but Filipe was having none of it, telling Horace very firmly that Sebastian would be very cross with him and that Sebastian had always insisted that he paid for everyone else's lunch, especially for all the clients that he had brought here in the past.

By the time that Horace had returned from the toilet, Sebastian had already very cleverly worked his magic on Delia, soon realising he wasn't going to make much headway with the tight-arsed accountant. He had taken the opportunity to work on the wife, she was much more forthcoming and more open for a little gentle persuasion.

In the few minutes that Horace had been away, Delia had spilled everything, how long that they had been married, the babies that had never happened, the performance problems that Horace had suffered from with the little old guy downstairs and that she had put all her energy and effort into teaching.

She had even outlined the tragic accident that that poor old Trevor, one of the neighbours, had recently had, and how unhappy Horace was at his work and how badly he had been treated by the bosses. But more importantly, the three hundred thousand pounds that was tucked away in the building society account, money that they had inherited after both sets of parents had sadly passed away.

"So, Horace, Delia and I have decided that we are going to have the fresh strawberries topped with strawberry flavoured goat yogurt," Sebastian said, as soon as Horace returned, "how about you?"

Horace looked at Delia. He wished that he and Delia had spent more time talking in the past, religion, politics, things that went bump in the night, about different types of characters like con men, robbers, confidence tricksters.

From a glance, he could tell that Delia had been charmed by Sebastian and it had not been such a good idea to leave her alone, maybe he shouldn't have gone to the toilet and should have tried to hold on to it for a little longer but just recently that was becoming more and more of a problem and something that he just couldn't do anymore.

"Strawberries and yogurt all sound very nice," Horace said smiling, he had to be careful, he didn't want to be the bad guy here, Delia had always been the perfect wife, loving and caring, especially when he had been ill and more recently the drunken episode with him being carried out from the toilets at the golf club by two paramedics.

Maybe they were at their time of life when they should be thinking about the future, and perhaps there should be more to Delia's life than the pressure of running a school and working tirelessly to maintain the very high standard of education.

Horace was pleasantly surprised by the fresh strawberries topped with the goat yogurt, and for one, it had taken away the horrible taste that had been left in his mouth by the goat cheese salad.

So, when Sebastian had suggested on the way back to the car, they could stop of at his estate agency to look at the model plan of phase two development of luxury villas overlooking the golf course, Horace had succumbed with a smile and said, sure, why not.

The first thing that Horace and Delia had noticed was that how much hotter it had become, as soon as they had left the shaded area of the village square.

"It's not too far from here," Sebastian said, Horace and Delia followed Sebastian down the steps from the village square, turning right and following the road along and up the hill for another four hundred metres, passing two banks a butcher shop, a hairdresser, a greengrocer shop and another bakery.

Sebastian's shop was situated at the top of the main street next to Paco's mini mart. Sebastian pushed and then turned a key into a small box that was mounted on the wall outside, and then the white aluminium shutter slowly lifted up.

Horace was very eager to get inside and out from the intense heat; as soon as Sebastian opened the glass door, he was in, like a meerkat diving into its burrow to escape the intense heat of the Botswana desert.

Of course, Sebastian had planned it that way, he knew how to sell houses on the coldest of winter months, walking the clients in the cold mountain air and then into the shop with the heating turned up, full on.

And of course, in the summer months, warming them up to a temperature just below boiling and then popping them into the wonderfully shaded, cooled air-conditioned estate agency.

The estate agency was quite small inside, nothing like the larger companies back in England, with their wide-open plan areas with men and women busily working at their computers and answering the constant ringing of the numerous telephones.

Most importantly for Horace, it was nice and cool and fairly dark inside without the neon lights switched on, that seemed to give his eyes a nice welcome rest from the glaring reflected light given off from the whitewashed buildings outside in the street.

On the left and up against the back wall, in the corner, there was a small computer desk and a chair, but on the right taking up most of the room there was a much bigger wooden table and the completed scaled model of phase one, two, three and four.

Sebastian pulled three blue leather upholstered chairs out from the table. "Have a seat for a minute while I get some cold refreshments," he said offering a chair to Delia. Sebastian disappeared behind a small partition, "We have white wine, red wine, still water or fizzy, whatever you want."

Delia looked at Horace, he was gesticulating with his hands, "no wine," he whispered, "no wine, he's trying to get us drunk."

"We will just have still water, please," Delia said.

"So, what villa would you choose if you had the choice?" Sebastian said, handing a glass of cool still water to Delia and then Horace.

Horace and Delia both looked at the model, somebody somewhere had spent a lot of time putting all the tiny parts together.

The front-line villas of phase one that Horace and Delia had seen earlier, some of them had model cars in the driveway and others had the gardener cutting the grass with a lawnmower. There were children playing in and around the pool area in some of the rear gardens, and in others there were people relaxing on sun loungers.

Horace turned his attention to phase two, his eyes running along the full length of the road and the brightly painted white villas, "Well, if I had to choose, I would choose the cheapest one and as far away as possible from all those noisy children," he said, pointing to the group of children playing in the pool in one of the rear gardens of phase one.

Sebastian laughed. "For you, Horace, they are all cheap, if you give me a deposit today you can have the choice of any one of the phase two villas at a rock bottom price of five hundred thousand euros, and for that price I can make the children disappear," he said, lifting the children from the pool and putting them into his pocket.

"That's a lot of money," Horace said, looking at Delia for her reaction.

"We don't have that sort of money," Delia said, "and that is a big decision to make, not in a split of a second over a glass of cold water."

Horace was impressed by Delia's answer, momentarily back at the restaurant he had forgotten what an intelligent and eloquent woman she was, and not the type of person to hand over all the money that their parents had worked very hard all their lives for.

To say that Sebastian was surprised and shocked by Delia's answer would have been a slight exaggeration, he was taken aback somewhat and, if anything, a little upset and for the very first time in his career lost for words.

Selling the villas of stage two hadn't exactly been a stroll in the park, but even more recently, times had changed for the worse and it was even much more difficult to find the right people. He just needed to sell the first one or two, just to get more people interested, just to get the ball rolling.

Just for a second Sebastian thought about shaving off one hundred thousand euros but that would have wiped out all his commission and that would mean clawing it back from future sales, and he was already down by two breakfasts, dinner and a hire car.

The return journey back to the Hotel Golf and Mountain Resort Buena Vista had been a quiet one, Sebastian had taken the main road and he had dropped them off outside, just inside thirty minutes. He had done his best and had used all the tricks and sales technics that he had learnt over the past years, now he just had to wait and hope that the accountant with the white skin and ginger hair would come good and take the bait.

Chapter 12

When Horace and Delia arrived back in old wet and grey England, something like how Sebastian had put it, they were both pleasantly surprised by how nice the weather was. Horace had worn a casual shirt and shorts and Delia one of the summer dresses that she had purchased from the small shop in Spain.

They had both enjoyed the taxi ride home, late Wednesday afternoon and some of the local points of interest and history that they had passed by unnoticed so many times before. And how pleasant everything looked, the different shades and colours of all the trees, and the different shades of green that surrounded them in the English countryside.

But Thursday morning, everything had suddenly changed, with a flash of lightning and a thunder clap of deafening proportion that made Horace wake up and jump out of bed all in one action, thinking that he was reliving the moment when poor old Trevor's space rocket had exploded.

In his garden shed.

Horace had reverted to wearing his flannelette pyjamas and Delia her summer bedwear of light coral-coloured silk pyjamas. Once Horace had showered and pulled on a clean pair of Calvin Klein pants, he made his way slowly down the stairs and into the living room.

Delia was busily marking exam papers and had spread herself and her work out on the sofa and both armchairs. Horace took up his position in the centre of the bay window and at the same time slid his hand into his pants, trying to stretch the elasticated crotch to make everything inside a little more comfortable.

"It's absolutely tipping down," Horace said, looking down the road to see if Richard Heed had already parked his Jaguar outside his house and in the street.

"The forecast doesn't paint a pretty picture either," Delia said, taking off her reading glasses and massaging her eyes. "Thunderstorms until Sunday and then a large band of rain moving across from the west."

"That doesn't sound like the weather we experienced in Spain then," Horace said, "factor fifty suntan cream, sunglasses and hat. I was hoping to play some golf and hit a few balls at the golf driving range."

"I have been thinking about Spain all morning," Delia said, rising from the sofa and stretching her arms up towards the ceiling and arching her back. "Yesterday coming home in the taxi was very nice, everything green and the sun shining, but this morning what with the thunderstorm and the grey sky, I am having trouble working, focusing properly. And this work is very important, the results of these exam papers will play a very big part for all these young people and how they will decide their futures."

"Why don't you take a break from work and come to the golf driving range with me and clear your head?" Horace said, resting his head on Delia's shoulder and wrapping his arms around her waist and pulling her backwards into his firm embrace.

"Yes," Delia said, "that's another problem I have this morning, I keep thinking about us sleeping naked and the sex that we had, nothing like our experiences in the past. and how different it has made me feel."

Horace quickly released his grip. "I have a terrible headache this morning," he said "it must be this stormy weather."

Yes, Spain had been very good for both of them, in many ways, but now back in England the little old guy in the flat below had slumped back into his old ways, not showing any interest or signs of life.

"I have to go into the school at some point today," Delia said, heading towards the stairs, "Ted the caretaker had left me some messages on WhatsApp, sounds like the boiler is playing up and one of the classrooms has a leaky roof."

"Well, I think I will dig out my waterproof clothing and see if I can still hit a golf ball in a straight line, and then pop into the bar and see Frank. I have to show my face there at some point, so it's better to get it over with, without giving it too much thought."

Not surprisingly, the golf driving range was completely deserted, luckily for Horace the wind and the driving rain was blowing in his favour and from behind, and it had pushed him along for most of the journey from the car to the golf driving range.

But what had worked in his favour on arrival, it was now working completely against him, in his position under the corrugated steel roofing of the golf driving range. The wind and rain were driving directly into his face and the small white golf ball had no chance of staying on the tee, gathering speed as it rolled off and then behind him and disappeared under the corrugated sheet cladding that was rattling violently on its fixing.

Horace managed to hit a few balls with the aid of a few twigs and a broken lolly stick, all the time glancing up at the corrugated roofing flapping up and down with the force from the wind.

Even when Horace managed to hit them sweetly, he had no idea where they had gone and then just after a few more balls, there was a huge flash of lightning and what sounded like a thunderbolt lighting up the sky and exploding on the other side of the corrugated sheeting just behind him.

Leaning forward into the wind and with his head down, he finally made it back to the car, he quickly threw the clubs into the boot before heading off towards the club bar.

"I thought that you had gone off to Spain with your lovely wife, Delia, not harpooning and spearing whales in the Baltic Sea," Frank called out to Horace from behind the bar.

Horace had to chuckle at Frank's witty remark and pleased that he was still a respected member of the golf club, other members nodded and laughed, sharing Frank's joke while Horace stood in the doorway wearing his waterproofs and dripping wet.

It was a huge relief to find that his name hadn't been dragged through the mud while he had been away, especially following the drunken episode and being carried out from the toilets.

Not like some of the members from the past, shunned or dragged-out kicking and screaming with their membership cards torn and shredded and thrown in their face.

After Horace had carefully removed his waterproofs and hung them up and dripping on the dark oak hat and coat stand, he made his way towards the bar where Frank and a few other members were stood waiting patiently for the story that Horace had to tell.

"So, Horace me old mate, how was Spain, was there a hotel waiting for you, or was it just a cheap con to get you there to sell you an expensive villa?"

"Surprisingly very enjoyable," Horace said, "if you make us one of your lovely cups of hot coffee, I will tell you all about it."

"So, what's the setup?" Frank said, putting a large mug of coffee on the bar in front of Horace, "the last time I see your lovely wife she was waving a couple of tickets around, saying that she had won the raffle."

Horace explained to Frank and the few other club members how horrified he had felt when Delia had arrived home slightly tipsy and that she had won the raffle and told him that they were off to Spain.

Everyone had a good laugh when Horace told them about the mix-up on the plane and how he ended up sitting at the back with sixteen young women who were drinking their way through sixteen bottles of Russian vodka. The sound of laughter in the bar had risen even louder and louder as Horace worked his way through the whole saga of the missing suitcase, first with the doctor who desperately needed her medication and then the drive to Marbella and the intense heat inside the small yellow Fiat Panda.

Then the laughter faded as Horace told them how nice the hotel was and about the pretty whitewashed Spanish village nestled up on the mountainside. And finally, about Sebastian and the villas overlooking the golf course and how much they cost.

Everyone had a story to tell, about a brother-in-law or a friend of a friend who had left the cold damp shores of England for a much more carefree life style under the blue sky and the forever shining sun of Spain. Some stories were about success, contentment and happiness, while others were about complete marital failure, bankruptcy and skin cancer.

"I have often thought about setting myself up with a small bar in Spain," Frank said, "a little place by the sea, a steady flow of customers in the daytime and family entertainment at night, like flamenco dancing or an old guy wearing a sombrero playing a Spanish guitar by candlelight."

"That company, homes in the sun that held the exhibition here have a few people booked to fly out there next month," Frank said. "Were you not tempted by this guy Sebastian's offer of the reduced price of an off-plan villa then, Horace?"

Horace took a sip from his second cup of Frank's handmade coffee, crushed and ground from the South American Columbian coffee beans.

"Well," Horace began, wiping away his dark brown frothy moustache, "it all happened so quickly, firstly we were mourning the death of my neighbour and work colleague, poor old Trevor and then a few days later we were walking around Spain in the intense heat wearing the same clothes for four days. Delia has been giving it some thought though, since we have been home, she is at home working on the exam papers that she marks every year."

"Well, she doesn't need to be in wet old England to do that," Frank said, "she could be sitting outside on the terrace of your luxury new villa while you could be out playing golf."

"I must admit, I was pleasantly surprised by Spain, nothing like I expected it to be," Horace said finishing off the rest of his coffee, "and if Delia hadn't come home with the raffle tickets we probably would have never ever gone."

"But do I want to buy a villa in a country that I know nothing about, where the sun burns my skin as soon as I step outside the house? It is a big decision and a life changing step to take and I don't think I am the type of person who could make such a big decision."

By the time Horace had pulled on his almost dry waterproofs and left the golf club the rain had eased to a light shower with just a little ray of sun peeping out from behind the dark black storm clouds.

But as soon as he steered the car right into Victoria Avenue, he was greeted with a loud drumroll of thunder and more torrential rain. Horace left the car on the driveway and bundled himself into the hallway, slipping out of the waterproofs and hanging them on the hook that allowed them to drip on the designated plastic mat.

After a long hot shower to warm his damp and cold bones, he was back downstairs, standing in the bay window in yet another pair of Calvin Klein high waistband cotton stretch pants.

Delia had settled into marking the exam papers and had turned the central heating on.

She was hoping that Horace would not have returned home until she had finished what she needed to do that day, his sudden presence, standing in the bay window was causing a major distraction and a huge cause of her annoyance.

"Why don't you pop out to the supermarket, Darling?" Delia said carefully placing the marked paper onto the completed pile that were sitting on the sofa to her right. "We need to do some shopping; I am not sure if we have anything to eat for dinner tonight."

Normally, Horace would have been at work and Delia would have been left in peace and to work at her own pace without interruption.

Horace was suddenly filled with anxiety and feelings of agoraphobia, the woman must have gone crazy, or maybe she was suffering from delayed sunstroke? She knew how much he hated shopping, he never ever went shopping, even when she had come home after catching chicken pox from the children at school, she had rolled herself out of bed and dragged herself around the supermarket while Horace had waited outside in the car.

Horace turned his thoughts back to when they were in Spain and the comment that Frank the barman had made. If Delia was sitting on the front terrace marking her papers in the shade, he would have arrived back home after an early round of golf and they could have drove into the village for a goat cheese salad and a bottle of white wine, or may be goat wine, if there was such a thing.

"Why don't we go out for dinner tonight, darling?" Horace said, desperately trying to avoid the dreaded trip to the supermarket and all those dreadful people, parking their trolleys and chatting in the aisles.

Delia stood up and joined Horace at the window. "Where would we go on a Thursday evening and in the pouring rain?"

Horace could feel the hangman noose tightening around his neck, just like in the past, when convicts were given a choice, hang by the neck or be transported to some terrible place full of hostile tribes.

"If we were in Spain, we could pop up to the village and have something from one of their little restaurants," Horace said, thinking the best way to duck out of shopping would be to divert Delia's attention.

"Oh, Horace, wouldn't that be lovely, just a little run around with a sun roof or air conditioning," Delia said, moving in close behind Horace and hugging him tightly around the waist. "I must admit it would be nice, much better than battling against the wind and rain and the ridiculous prices of the local restaurants."

"Maybe we could have a barbecue?" Horace said, realising that he was backing himself into a corner, Delia had often spoke about buying one in the school summer holidays in the past, but Horace could never bring himself to handle raw meat and the sight of blood always made him feel faint.

"Maybe we could get a little dog?" Delia said, tightening her grip around Horace's waist, "a cute little black or white one and we could call it Fluffy."

Horace's old feelings of anxiety and panic that he had briefly suffered from in his forties suddenly came rushing back, a dog? A barbeque? A barbeque was one thing, maybe he could wear dark glasses and handle the meat with tongs, but a dog. Dogs made Horace sneeze and sometimes cough and he had never met a dog that didn't want to take a huge lump out of his trousers.

"The rain appears to be easing somewhat," Horace said trying to unlock the tight grip that Delia had around his waist, "maybe I should whiz around the supermarket while I can."

By the time that Horace had arrived home from the supermarket, Delia's head was in a good place. She had put all the thoughts of Spain to the back of her mind and had reached her daily target for the amount of exam papers that she needed to mark per day.

Horace crashed through the doorway absolutely soaked with a carrier bag in each hand, his head definitely wasn't in a good place, even if they had sent an experienced rescue and recovery team down into the darkest, deepest hole, they would have never have found him.

Horace mumbled something about never ever again and there being no chance of whizzing around with all the pensioners, crawling along in the fast lane and standing around chatting and blocking the aisles.

Horace disappeared up the stairs for his third shower of the day, leaving Delia in the kitchen to sort out the soggy mess of cardboard packaging and one or two broken eggs.

Friday morning and the rain was falling down from the sky just like the day before, Delia had set her alarm clock on her mobile phone early and had managed to get two good hours of marking exam papers in before Horace took up his position in the centre of the bay window.

Only just a few minutes after the arrival of Horace, Delia was wishing that she had asked Dr Carolina Banks for a medical certificate for only one week for Horace instead of two. He would have been back to work this morning and she could have the freedom that she had enjoyed with all the school summer holidays in the past.

The days came and went but the rain stayed, sometimes easing a little, with a hint of sunshine and a colourful rainbow just before the sky darkened once again with the rain falling even heavier and joyfully bouncing off from the pavement outside in the street.

Horace was spending most of his time standing and looking out of the bay window wearing just his pants, the only thing of interest was the fact that Richard, the next door but one neighbour was still parking his car outside the front of his house in the morning and was driving it back in the evening.

There had been no chance of Horace getting out of the house to play golf, in fact the golf club had put out a notice on social media, to say that the course in some areas had been flooded and was closed temporarily until further notice.

There was also a story going around that someone pulling their golf trolley along had been struck by lightning on the ninth hole, with a picture on Facebook of a charred and half melted golf bag and clubs.

Delia, under intense pressure and determination to get Horace out from under her feet, had turned her hand to cunning and scheming; she had sent Horace off to the dry cleaners with a couple of his work suits after rubbing a little gravy powder into the knees.

On another occasion with the help of the side of the door, she managed to break off the heels from an old pair of boots that she never wore and sent him off to the shoe repairers. She managed to talk him into going to the dreaded supermarket at least three more times and to the newsagent for a different magazine each day.

But the best scheme of all was when she stripped off the bedsheets early one morning and then sabotaged the washing machine before sending him off to the launderette with a huge plastic bag full of small coins.

Finally, the week passed; Delia managed to stay on track with her school work and somehow Horace managed to get through it all without getting himself a cold, flu or even double pneumonia.

Delia awoke early Friday morning, stifled by the heat inside the bedroom, to add to the fact that the heating had been on all week, Horace had hit the override button on the timer late the evening before, after getting a good soaking while pulling all three recycle bins out from the rear garden and through the side gate and onto the grass verge by the side of the road.

Delia quickly turned off the heating override button from inside the cupboard on the landing and opened the bedroom window a little. Horace awoke about one hour later, the first thing that his brain sensed was that the constant whooshing sound that the rain and wind had been making around the outside of the house, for the last week or so had stopped, and total silence.

And then the sound of a blackbird merrily chirping away at the bottom of the garden. Slowly; with the blackbird singing and the sound of the rain absent inside Horace's head, he began to stir slowly from another really good night of deep sleep.

Some people would have had trouble sleeping the night before returning to work, especially reflecting back with what had happened over the past few weeks and with all the uncertainty of what may lay waiting for him in the day ahead.

Some people with an overactive mind could have possibly spent all night pacing up and down the bedroom with regular trips to the bathroom.

Horace hadn't been blessed with an overactive mind; in fairness, it slopped a little towards underactive. But he was incredibly good at crunching numbers, with or without a calculator, and sitting at a desk for eight hours a day without the need for a sandwich or a cup of coffee or even a good stretch.

Chapter 13

The journey to Horace's place of work normally took around twenty minutes, sometimes varying slightly, depending if he drove or went on foot. Horace would often walk, using the back alleys that ran in between the grand old detached houses and then cutting through the centre of Victoria Park.

But this morning he had taken the car, really without thinking, it had become a thing of habit over the past week, driving everywhere peering out from behind the condensation that was forever blocking his view on the inside of the windscreen. It wasn't until he turned left at the end of Victoria Avenue and onto the busy Ring Road, he suddenly realised that it was a beautiful morning and the sun was shining and he could have walked.

Horace groped around inside the glovebox, his right hand eventually finding the small electronic button, he aimed it at the large black Georgian gates and they slowly rolled backwards. He parked the car at the rear of the building and walked around to the front of what was originally a large Georgian town house.

He punched in the numbers on the key code and the door unlocked with a click, he then pushed the large Georgian door open and made his way up the wide stairway to the first floor.

The first thing that Horace noticed when he entered the large open plan work space on the first floor of the converted Georgian town house was that his old friend and work college, Trever's desk had disappeared.

He hadn't noticed that his own desk had been shunted at least three metres backward and more to the right until he found himself staring into the face of Freddie Tidmarsh, sitting at his desk where his used to be.

"Horace," Freddie said, "there have been a few changes while you have been away and your desk is over there now."

Freddie then went back to staring at his computer screen and clicking his mouse, not even with a hi Horace, how are you, are you feeling better? Nothing.

Horace went over to his desk; it had been arranged in such a way with just a few centimetres of space between the front of the desk and the face of the large Georgian style sash window.

Of course, this meant that when Horace sat in his seat, he would be facing the window with his back to everyone else.

Horace glanced around the room, some gave him a nod of acknowledgment, while others pretended that they were too engrossed in their work to have noticed him.

There had been a number of rumours going around the office while he had been away, some, that he had dropped dead in the toilet of the golf club, while others had heard that he had suffered some kind of brain seizure and was found naked in a cubicle with his tongue a bluey black colour and very swollen to the size of a giraffe's and hanging out of his mouth.

Horace sat down in his chair, he had a perfect view out of the window from his new position, in the distance he could see the beautiful green slopes of Pecton Mound and over to his left the tops of the two-hundred-year-old trees in Victoria Park.

Horace took out a small key from the inside of his jacket pocket and unlocked his cupboard and took out all the files that he had been working on, at a glance everything seemed to be in order.

Horace looked out of the window, was this promotion or was this a subtle hint that he was on his way out? Trevor had always sat by the door and it had always been a regular joke around the office that the person who worked the closest to the door would be the first one to be shoved out.

Did that apply to the window as well? Horace thought, was he about to be shoved out of the window? Horace quickly spun around in his chair, the whole office had been staring at him, then embarrassed by Horace's sudden movement and his turning around in his chair, everyone quickly looking away avoiding his gaze.

Horace swivelled back, facing the window and opened the folder marked Redmond Horse Sanctuary, he had already worked his way through a huge plastic carrier bag containing all the receipts, the day before Trevor's funeral.

Mostly for hay, for feeding and bedding, processed grain, barely, oats, carrots, apples, vets bills for tooth filing and injections for coughs and sneezes.

Horace's mind began to drift away from voluntary donations and the unbelievable cost of the stable roof repairs, thinking about the events that led up to when he had overheard his two bosses discussing his future.

Was what he overheard that day for real? While he sat on the toilet paralysed with the alcohol from Dave's spritzers? Did he really hear them light-heartedly talk about poor old Trevor's death as being a major bonus to the firm and now he was gone, they could offer the redundancy package to him?

Had they moved his desk next to the window, the first of many cunning schemes that they had contrived, slowly one by one inflicting the psychological pain and humiliation until he cracked and resigned or even worse driving him into a complete nervous breakdown and then being dragged from his chair, hissing and spitting?

Horace looked out of the window, whatever happened he had to remain calm and stay focused, gazing out of the window he could see a figure in the distance slowly descending Pecton mound and a dog playfully running around and the owner throwing something for the dog to fetch.

He thought about Delia at home, systematically working her way through the heap of exam papers.

And then the time that they had spent in Spain, the cool tranquillity of the hotel and sleeping naked and cleaning his teeth with shower gel, just using his finger as a toothbrush, Horace turned on the desk top computer and opened the current files and then double clicked on the file marked Redmond horse sanctuary, he was going to knuckle down and focus and complete the file before lunch.

There were two types of people that worked in the open plan office space at Squirrel and Squirrel, there were those who went out to lunch and those who would stay and sit at their desk with a small snack in one hand and the computer mouse in the other.

Horace never ever went out to lunch, but today, at one o clock precisely when the regular band of people were starting to show signs of life, putting on their jackets and mumbling, Horace had the overwhelming desire to get out of the office and walk to the top of Pecton mound.

Without any thought or planning, Horace stood up from his chair slid into his jacket skipped down the stairs and out into his car.

Horace drove to the local super market and bought himself a meal deal, a chicken and bacon salad sandwich, a packet of plain crisps and a high energy sports drink, then he drove the car directly to Pecton way.

Horace, parked the car as close as he could to the opening between the black steel railings, passing through the gap he started the steady climb up to the top of Pecton mound.

As far as Horace could remember he had never been up to the top of Pecton mound, the whole of the slope was covered in different types of wild grasses and different coloured wild flowers, with just a natural pathway, that had been worn away from the people who had gone up and down before.

Horace hadn't gone too far when he realised that his nice black leather shoes had gained a lot of weight and girth from the wet sticky mud caused by all the recent rain fall.

Undeterred, he pressed on, stepping sideways off from the muddy path and onto the long-wet grass, over to one side.

This seemed to help Horace gain a little more traction and the wet grass helped to clean most of the mud from his black highly polished shiny shoes.

Horace was making good ground and was at least two thirds of the way up from the bottom when he felt a sharp pain just behind his left knee, stopping quickly in his tracks he glanced down, he could see the cause of the problem instantaneously, from both of his knees all the way down to the bottom of his trousers were completely covered in hundreds of round silver very prickly balls.

Instinctively, Horace grabbed at the area behind his left knee with his thumb and forefinger pulling at the nasty little invader. "Shit!" Horace shouted out. "Shit, shit, shit!" waving his hand around trying to dislodge the nasty grey prickly ball from his finger and thumb.

Finally, after a lot of frantic hand movements, the silver ball flew off from his hand but leaving behind the small prickly pins firmly embedded into his finger and thumb. Horace looked around, the whole area seemed to be deserted, what should he do? He was much closer to the top than the bottom, he would press on and finish off what he had set out to do.

At the top of the mound, the path carried on and disappeared down on the opposite side to what Horace had just climbed, the grass was much shorter up there and there were three seat type benches equally spaced where people could sit and rest and take in the view.

Horace chose the middle seat and carefully sat down with his legs outstretched in front of him, that seemed to be more comfortable and kept the pesky prickly balls from sticking into the backs of his legs.

Horace opened his high energy drink and took a long swig, then he quickly ate his chicken and bacon salad sandwich, he had come up here to clear his head and think about his future, but now he had more important things to do.

After a couple more swigs of his drink, he finished off his sandwich and then swiftly moved on to the bag of crisps. Horace finished off the remainder of his drink, washing down the sandwich and the crisps and then put the packaging and the empty plastic bottle into the bin.

Just the short journey to the bin and back to the bench, Horace could feel the prickles pushing through his trouser legs and prickling his skin, he would never make it down to the bottom, he thought, somehow, he had to remove all the small alien balls from his trousers.

Horace glanced around, still no one about, he quickly undid his shoelaces and stepped out of his shoes and trousers, holding on to the back of the bench for support. Then grabbing them at the waistband he began to shake his trousers around violently, some of the balls came off but the majority were stuck, as if they had been applied with the aid of a hot glue gun.

Horace then tried running the trousers back and forth over the top part of the bench, this method was much more effective and he was relieved to see all the silver balls dropping from his trousers one by one and on to the grass.

Phillis Headblugger always took her English bulldog, Barny, for a walk just after lunchtime and if weather permitting, they would climb to the top of Pecton Mound, hoping that she would burn off some calories from her huge solid frame, that was very similar to her pet bulldog's, Barny.

She was a very big and a very strong women and only at the young age of sixteen, her school careers advisor had suggested that she would make an excellent lady rugby player or a prison officer.

She had never married or even dated and now after serving her time as a prison warden and then later in life as the governor of a lady's correction centre, she now spent most of her time walking Barny or running the local self-defence classes for women.

That afternoon although the ground was still very wet underfoot, Phillis woke poor old Barny up from his afternoon snooze and dragged him up to the top of Pecton Mound.

As soon as she spotted Horace waving his trousers around, above his head, she knew instantly and without any doubt that he was the Pecton Mound flasher, he was a man and he wasn't wearing any trousers, he fitted the police description perfectly.

Fortunately for Horace, Barny was dribbling and snorting through his nose violently by the time that he had reached the top, Horace had just managed to put his trousers back on when he heard Phillis and Barny slowly stalking up from his rear.

Horace quickly spun around.

"You worthless piece of shit!" Phillis shouted at Horace, full of rage and furious with herself that she hadn't gotten quite close enough to Horace to make that final killer charge.

Horace picked up his shoes and ran down the muddy pathway as fast as his legs would allow, he had almost reached the bottom before he glanced around to check that the massive crazy red-faced women wasn't behind him.

It was at that point his tired legs, unused to running, buckled and crumpled beneath him and he fell backwards, sliding five metres or so on his bottom before coming to a halt.

Everyone had settled down at their desks just after lunch, when the sirens from the police cars broke the silence inside the office at Squirrel and Squirrel and then just a few minutes later everyone's mobile phones were buzzing, announcing on Facebook that the Pecton mound flasher had just been sighted, once again.

Horace arrived back at the office about a half of an hour later, he took a deep breath and passed through the glass doorway as quickly as he could and then scurried directly to his desk and sat down.

Everyone in the office had noticed that his chair was unusually empty when they had returned from lunch and wondered what had happened to him, Horace never ever went out to lunch, someone said.

As soon as Horace returned, the whole office had followed him with their eyes, all the way from the door and right up to the point where he had sat down at his desk. The bottom of his jacket was all creased and covered in silver balls, the type that you would find up at Pecton Mound.

The back of his trousers was all wet and muddy and he was walking funny like he had just spent the last hour and a half being treated with the Chinese therapy of acupuncture.

"It's the Pecton Mound flasher!" Freddie Tidmarsh shouted out, at the top of his voice, sarcastically. Some people in the office laughed out quite loudly while others sniggered, but some looked at Horace with suspicion, horrified, was Horace, the quiet introvert guy of the office, really the Pecton Mound flasher?

By the time the big hand had reached the number twelve and the little hand was now pointing to the number three on the large wall clock mounted on the office wall, everyone had settled down and were busily working away, staring at their monitors and clicking away with their mouse's.

Horace had opened and worked his way through all the accounts of the independent cat's home in Prendick and had just pushed go and sent everything off to the tax man for approval.

Jean the company secretary had come up from her office on the ground floor and was standing close by, waiting patiently for Horace to finish off what he was doing.

"Hello Horace, how are you feeling now?" Jean by far was the nicest person that worked there and never ever said anything bad about anyone, and always enquired about people's health and their family. "Are you still suffering from the dizzy spells?" Jean continued, Jean never seemed to go anywhere without holding a huge file of something or other or some papers always with both arms clamped tight up against her chest.

Jean had been sent up by the two bosses to check on Horace's mental health status, after Freddie Tidmarsh had slithered down the stairs and boasted to the bosses that he had just sold a huge pension plan for all the workers at the enormous canning factory at Seawick.

And furthermore, that Horace had returned from lunch a half an hour late and covered in mud and prickly silver balls.

"Hello Jean," Horace smiled, "I am fine thanks, thank you for asking, how are you?"

"Oh, you know," Jean smiled pleasantly back, "overworked and underpaid and the usual ongoing women's troubles."

Jean could see the mud, now drying on Horace's trousers and some dust and a few pieces of dried mud and silver prickly balls, lying underneath his desk where they had dropped off from his trousers.

"Your face looks quite red, Horace, like you have been running or something, or you have spent too much time in sun?"

Horace had a little think to himself, he had to be careful what he said, Jean was absolutely correct on both accounts, yes, he had been running and yes, he had been out in the sun, the Spanish sun.

"Yes," Horace replied, "I am quite hot, it is very hot here, working so close to the window, with the sun shining through, directly into my face."

"Well, it's good to see you back, Horace," Jean said, sounding very sincere, "I will leave you to it."

Jean went back down the stairs and politely tapped on the door of Cedrick's office, Cedrick and Cyril had both been waiting for her to report back on the general wellbeing of Horace.

"Well, he seems OK," Jean started, thinking that the two bosses were genuinely concerned for Horace's health and were not hoping that he was on the verge of a heart attack or about to crack up, saving them thousands of pounds in redundancy money, just like they had done with poor old Trever.

"His face appears to be quite red," Jean continued, "and his trousers are rather muddy, I am worried that he may still be suffering from bouts of dizziness and may have fallen over."

"Well, that sounds promising," Cyril said, once Jean had left the office and closed the door behind her, "hopefully he is suffering from high blood pressure and he is about to pop, we still have a week left before the takeover is finalised, hopefully we can get Horace to crack before the weeks out."

"I will get on to the contractor," Cedrick said, "and get him to pop over tonight and take the blind down from Horace's window, Jean said that he looked red-faced and hot, maybe we can warm him up a teeny-weeny little bit more."

Delia was still sitting in the rear garden when Horace arrived home around five thirty, Horace opened the front door and went straight up the stairs, taking everything off and kicking all the muddy clothes under the bed before taking a shower. After showering and changing into his casual trousers and tee shirt and making sure his clothes were kicked under the bed far enough so Delia wouldn't see them, he then went down the stairs to find her.

Delia had taken advantage of the sudden change in the weather and had taken the garden table and chairs out from the shed and after a quick clean, set herself up with all her school work, putting it into the relevant piles on the table top.

"Hello darling," Delia smiled as Horace came towards her, "how was work today, did the bosses talk to you?"

Horace sat down in one of the chairs. "They have moved my desk over by the window and poor old Trever's desk has already been taken away, but other than Jean asking me how I was feeling, it seemed to be business as usual."

"No mention of redundancy then?" Delia said, sounding rather disappointed that Horace hadn't arrived home with a massive redundancy pay-out package. "Guess who called me today?" Delia said.

Horace's heart fluttered before going all out, pumping his blood like it had never been pumped before, sending him into a hot sweat, that women from Pecton mound, Horace thought, or the police or possibly both?

"Seb," Delia smiled, "Seb from Spain."

Horace could feel the sweat on his body rapidly cooling and his heart slowing down to a near normal speed, he actually felt relieved and quite pleased to hear the name Seb and not the police or the crazy woman from earlier.

"How is he, how many houses has he sold today, or more to the point how many has he sold to you?" Horace said, giving a little chuckle, mostly brought on by the relief from all the nervous exhaustion that he had suffered from that day.

"He asked how we were and that he has a plane full of potential customers flying out there very soon. And he was wondering if we had thought anymore about his offer, and was worried that we might miss out on our first choice of property, once all the other people fly out there. What do you think, Horace?" Delia said, "I have been thinking about it all day, we could retire of semi retire, maybe spend the winters in Spain and the summers here in England."

"What about your job?" Horace said. "You love your work; you have put your whole life into that school."

"I used to love it," Delia sighed, "but so many things have changed over the past few years, the parents seem to be getting younger and younger every year and our staffroom is full of teachers most of them younger than the parents."

"The young women teachers now days, only talk about hair and makeup and spend all their spare time out running or at the gym, and then once they have achieved their perfect figure, they get themselves pregnant and spend most of the day in the school toilets throwing up."

Horace was quite shocked, why hadn't she mentioned none of this before? He had always thought that he was the only one in the family who had the shit job, and Delia's life was full of sweet young children singing and clapping and happily skipping around the school playground.

Horace suddenly realised that he was sitting facing the bomb site were poor old Trever's shed had once stood, maybe like Trevor, Delia could possibly be suffering from some kind of middle life crises, just like the programme they had recently watched on television about when people get to a certain age, the phycologist had called it a bump in the road, maybe Delia was at that time of life where she had hit that bump?

"I have been looking on the Internet," Delia continued, "I could get a job at the English college, it's only a forty-minute drive from the goat water point village and you could work in the local Asesoria, that's an office where they deal with people's accounts and taxes among other things."

Horace sat back in his chair, blimey, he thought to himself this isn't just a bump in the road, this is a bloody great mound, Delia had driven into Pecton Mound.

This is bombshell, similar to all those years ago when Delia had asked him to marry her after he had completely bungled their very first night of sex and sleeping together.

"Well," Horace said, "if the rumours are correct and they really are going to make me redundant then maybe we could keep this house and still afford to buy one in Spain, using our savings and the redundancy money."

Delia leapt out of her chair and did her very best to give Horace a huge cuddle but found herself hugging mostly the back of the plastic chair. "Oh darling, that will be wonderful, we could be sitting outside like this every evening and watching the sun go down."

Chapter 14

The fine warm dry weather continued throughout the whole weekend, Horace and Delia spent most of their time in the garden, Delia methodically working through her school work and Horace pottering around, weeding and picking up small pieces of poor old Trevor's space rocket, whenever he found them.

Saturday evening, they went out for a meal at a Spanish restaurant that Delia had found, on a where to eat web site on the Internet, Horace was surprised to find that goat wasn't on the menu and they shared a chicken paella for two and a bottle of Rioja.

Delia had bought a new Spanish phrase book that the waiter had found quite amusing, him being a cockney, born and bred in London after his grandparents had moved to England, arriving from Madrid many years ago.

Horace woke up Monday morning forgetting how unpredictable the English weather was and was halfway to work, walking through the park when he heard the first rumble of thunder and felt the first few spots of rain.

He had arrived at work just before the first real clap of thunder and the heavy downpour but his spirits were still dampened by the huge carrier bag of receipts, mostly handwritten that had been dumped on his desk, from a market trader who sold wet fish and was under investigation from the tax man.

Later that morning around ten o'clock, Jean had handed out white sealed envelopes to everyone in the office.

Inside was a letter that read, following our meeting last Monday, informing everyone about the possible takeover, we are pleased to inform you that our negotiations with the new owners have now been completed and the company will commence a transitional period starting from next Monday.

Horace sat back in his chair, taking time to read the letter, they obviously had some kind of meeting while he had been away in Spain, maybe that was what Freddie Tidmarsh had meant by the changes that had taken place around the office.

Horace had a quick glance around; some people had opened the letter while other just left it sitting on their desk as if they knew what it contained and all the relevant information in advance.

Horace wondered if there had been any mention of redundancy, normally he would have asked Trevor to bring him up to speed while he had been away, but now there was no one working in the office that spoke openly about anything.

Horace turned his attention back to the new file he was creating for the wet fish market trader before submitting it to the tax man.

His hands smelt of fish as if the carrier bag containing all the receipts had been used for carrying fresh fish home from the market beforehand.

For someone who seem to spend most of his time driving back and forth to the Billingsgate fish market, other than the hundreds of receipts for thousands and thousands of pounds' worth of diesel and a new cold store room that the guy seemed to have had replaced every year for the last ten years, everything seemed to be in order.

First thing Wednesday morning Horace had an appointment at the dentist that Delia had made for him on Monday.

Telling him that he should have a check-up while he still had the benefits of the company medical cover, just in case he was going to be made redundant in the near future.

Horace arrived at work around eleven with a very numb mouth, after a mouth full of injections and four small fillings, two at the top and two at the bottom, for some strange reason he couldn't stop himself from dribbling profusely.

To make thing worse there was another bag of receipts from the wet fish market trader and the bag was moving around with two fresh fish thrashing around inside, flapping their tails around and gasping for air.

Horace picked up the plastic bag, there was a yellow sticky label attached reading, sorry I missed you, enjoy the fish, Horace quickly made his way back down the stairs and filled up one of the wash basins with water inside the gent's toilet and carefully slid the fish into the almost overflowing basin.

"You're not allowed to accept bribes from the client," Freddie Tidmarsh smirked, as Horace made his way back to his desk, "or pets."

The two senior partners had spent a lot of their time talking to the new owners that morning and Cyril had informed them that the gross yearly salary bill for the entire company had been reduced to the agreed amount before the pending takeover.

And that the new bosses were bringing five of their own staff on Monday as planned and the relevant spaces would be ready for the arrival of their desks and equipment.

Cedrick had become very stressed with all the negotiating and especially up tight and agitated mostly brought on due to the fact that Spankworth was still working steadily away at his desk, and they hadn't managed to get rid of him.

Horace was also feeling the pressure, trying to make head or tail of all the latest pile of receipts that the wet fishmonger had left, it had been a beautiful warm sunny morning and now the sun and moved around and lined itself up perfectly with Horace and was shining directly through the window and onto the top of his head.

The smell of fish seemed to be getting stronger and stronger as the late morning seem to be getting hotter and hotter, Horace had already opened his cupboard underneath his desk twice beforehand to check that there wasn't a fish or two, hiding in between his cardboard folders.

The effects from the dentist's numbing needles had shown no signs of wearing off and with the sun shining directly into his face, he found it very difficult to concentrate and couldn't stop himself from dribbling over everything.

Jean suddenly appeared alongside Horace, clutching a huge pile of papers tightly against her chest. "Good afternoon, Horace, how are you?" Jean had caught Horace at a bad time, before he had the chance to wipe the dribble from around his chin.

"I am fine, Jean, how are you?" Well, that was what Horace had intended to say, but he wasn't sure if Jean had understood him, he hadn't spoken to anyone since the dentist, and his tongue was also feeling very numb and had slid out between his teeth when he had tried to talk.

Jean had heard some of the rumours about Horace and the toilets at the golf club and his oversized black tongue, hanging out from his mouth, and she had instantly dismissed them as poppycock. But know, seeing Horace this way, for herself, his tongue hanging out and sweating, she felt genuinely concerned, he also seemed to smell weird, like, wet fish.

"The bosses would like to talk to you this morning, before lunch, Horace, mostly because you missed the meeting that had taken place last week while you were off sick. They are both waiting for you in Cedrick's office when it's convenient and you are at a point where you can leave what you are doing."

Horace done his very best to smile without dribbling. "Thank you, Jean, I will be down in a couple of minutes," Horace slobbered.

Horace's heart somehow had missed first and second gear, skipped third and fourth, and was instantly pounding away, moving directly into fifth, this was the moment he had been anticipating.

This is it, he thought to himself, he was nervous but excited, he could imagine Delia sitting in the garden when he arrived home later that evening, unable to control himself and blurting everything out, that he had been made redundant with a huge package and then Delia throwing her pencil into the air and then throwing herself into his arms.

Horace skipped down the stairs two at a time and into the gent's toilet's, he had to calm himself down, as far as everyone else was concerned, nobody knew about his pending redundancy and it was only by chance that he knew the reason for what and why he had been summoned by the Bosses for.

The two fish that Horace had put there earlier seemed to be doing remarkably well and much happier in the hand basin than inside the carrier bag along with all the fraudulent receipts, left by the dodgy wet fishmonger.

Using one of the other washbasins, Horace splashed some cold water over his face and then looked into the mirror, he had a little play around with his cheeks, squeezing them here and there trying to restore some life back into his face.

Horace took in a deep breath and knocked on the door of Cedrick's office and looked through the top glass panel and waited to be beckoned in.

Horace opened the door, Cedrick's office was very cool inside, much cooler than the large office space upstairs and especially cooler than where Horace's desk was now situated, next to the window and directly in the sunlight.

Cyril had wheeled his large black leather executive chair into Cedrick's office and the two brothers were sitting side by side staring at Horace with their usual fixed expressions, somewhere in-between crying and frowning or if they were both suffering from heart burn or trapped wind.

As far as Horace could remember he had never seen the two bosses sitting together in the same office before and they had placed an extra chair the other side of the desk so Horace could sit opposite.

The walk from the door to the chair seemed to take forever and Horace could feel the start of a panic attack, and his legs beginning to turn numb, almost the same sensation he was experiencing with his mouth.

Horace sat down in the chair, wiping the slobber away from his mouth with the back of his hand.

"We are very concerned about you, Horace," Cedrick started, "you don't seem to be coping with your work and some of the other people in the office have noticed that your level of hygiene has slipped."

This was a bombshell; a megger bomb, Horace hadn't seen this one coming, even though he had overheard their conversation from inside the toilet, talking about getting rid of him; he had never thought that the pair of shitheads would be going ahead with it, especially now that poor old Trever had gone.

Horace could feel himself dribbling again and quickly wiped his mouth with the back of his hand.

Cyril picked up what must have been the certificate that the doctor had written out for Horace. "These dizzy spells that you're suffering from, we are worried that it could be leading up to some kind of brain seizure or a stroke," Cyril said, watching the line of dribble running down from the corner of Horace's mouth.

Horace quickly wiped his mouth with the back of his hand. He didn't know what to say, he had come here expecting an offer of redundancy, but this pair of scheming backstabbing bastards were trying to stick the knife in right between the shoulder blades, or at the very best, they were trying to convince him that he was suffering from ill health and he was on his way out, literally.

Horace made sure that his tongue was wedged firmly behind his front bottom teeth before speaking.

"No, I am fine now, thank you for your concern, I suffered from a little dizziness a couple of weeks ago but I am fine now."

Cyril fumbled around with the certificate that Dr Carolina Banks had written out. "Maybe we should send you to one of our doctors, for a general health check," he said, "we wouldn't want anything nasty to happen to you."

Horace instantly thought about poor old Trevor, did he have a meeting similar to this? Something very nasty definitely happened to him, maybe this twisted pair sneaked into his shed and planted a detonator?

"Oh, that would be fantastic," Horace slobbered, forgetting about sorting his tongue out before answering, "my wife and I have been a little concerned and a full health check would put everyone's minds at rest. I love this job," Horace continued, with his tongue rolling around inside his mouth, "and my wife Delia and I are thinking about trying for a baby," Horace said, lying through his teeth, "so as far as I'm concerned, this is my job for life."

All things considered, Horace thought that he had coped with the impromptu meeting very well. Especially after the initial shock and quickly realising he wasn't being offered the redundancy package that he had been expecting.

And that they had summoned him down to their office, thinking that they could just ambush him and wheel him out the door, totally humiliated and a broken man.

Well, Horace thought to himself, as he climbed the stairs and then back to his desk, now the gloves were off, and he would have to fight for everything, his redundancy pay-out, his very loyal wife Delia, his now departed friend, poor old Trevor, and all that he had worked for over the past twenty-five years.

"Getting rid of Spankworth is going to be more difficult than we thought," Cedrick said, as soon as Horace had left and closed the door, "maybe we should offer him the redundancy package after all?"

"We still have a few days left," Cyril said. "We will be saving ourselves a lot of money, we just need to put him under a little more pressure, he definitely has a problem; did you notice all that dribbling?"

"He is definitely cracking up," Cedrick agreed, "and what was all that about him having a baby? And at his age?"

When Horace arrived home that evening, he opened the front door with his key and then passing through the hallway and through the kitchen and out into the rear garden to find Delia. All the thoughts that he had earlier about coming home excited with a huge pay-out and Delia falling into his arms had been totally smashed and then crushed by the two bastard conniving bosses.

Delia could see that Horace looked more dejected than his normal weary self as he came towards her and then slumped into one of the garden chairs.

"Hello my darling, how was the trip to the dentist?"

"The dentist was nothing compared to the meeting that I had with the two bastard, backstabbing bosses today," Horace said. "If I hadn't overheard their conversation at the golf club, I wouldn't have had a clue to what I was walking into this afternoon and what the hell is going on at that crazy place at the moment."

"Apparently, they had a brief meeting while we were away, and everyone was handed a letter, outlining about the company being taken over, and that everyone's jobs were safe and they would remain working there with the same contract and the same salary as before. I asked Jean if I had a letter and she told me that the bosses wanted to talk to me in person as my circumstances were slightly different."

"I managed to retrieve one of the letters from the wastepaper bin that someone else had put there," Horace said, pulling out a piece of crumpled paper from his trousers pocket and handing it to Delia.

Delia felt a little uncomfortable reading a letter that had been pulled out from the rubbish bin, especially a private letter that had been addressed and intended for someone else.

"This is exactly what Hilary was telling me at Trevor's funeral," Delia said, putting the letter down onto the table, "the bosses are selling the firm and retiring, and that two people were going to be made redundant, one being Trever." Trever was being offered redundancy and for some strange reason they had singled you out for the chop as well.

"They have never liked me," Horace said solemnly, sinking further down into his chair, "ever since I refused to take the job of selling those doggy shares and the really expensive life insurance policies."

"You're better off out of it, my darling," Delia said, reaching across the table and squeezing Horace's hand, "we just want what they owe you after all those years of loyal service; maybe we should seek advice from a lawyer."

Thursday morning, Horace left Delia in the garden, sitting in the sunshine with a cup of coffee and one slice of toast and marmalade. They had spent a lot of time Wednesday evening talking about poor old Trevor and the possibilities of what could have happened to him. Had the bosses somehow forced him into taking early redundancy, or even worse, forced him into a corner where he had thought the only way out was to blow himself up?

Horace and Delia also spent a considerable amount of time searching the internet for solicitors who specialised in the mistreatment of people in the workplace and their rights, regarding redundancy.

Delia said that she would ring and make an appointment for Horace around ten o clock that morning as soon as they were open.

In spite of everything, Horace had slept very well and felt much happier about his future, knowing like always that he had the support of a good women and that Delia was now on the case.

Horace had left the car on the driveway, deciding to walked to work, the gardeners were already busy cutting the grass and tending to the rosses in

Victoria Park as he passed through, following the pathway, that led from one gate and out through the one on the other side.

He had to be careful, stopping and then timing his run to dodge the water spraying from the water sprinklers.

Horace arrived at the office just before nine, unusually, the whole place seemed to be in turmoil, everyone was standing around, scratching their heads, all the desks had been moved around and there were a couple of guys from an I.T. company rerouting all the internet cables.

Remarkably, Horace's desk was exactly in the same place, like a remote island, over by the window, exactly where he had left it the night before. Horace took off his jacket and placed it over the back of the chair and then turned on his computer. Then, swivelled around one hundred and eighty degrees in his chair to have a good look to see what the heck was going on.

Everyone's desks had been moved and they now formed two straight banks from left to right and another two rows of desks had been turned and were now facing the others with a light grey vanity board in-between, so one wouldn't be staring into the face of the person sitting opposite.

Horace could see that there were five very new different types of desks that had somehow been squeezed into the new formed rows of two, making everything even more crowded in the already very tight office space.

"It's just like a call centre," somebody said quite loudly, nobody seemed knew what to do, some people were trying to identify their chairs over in one of the corners of the room while other were looking for their desk, opening the cupboards underneath, looking for their personal belongings.

Horace swivelled back around, facing his computer, instead of his home page being displayed as normal with all the icons of the client's accounts, in perfect order, his computer appeared to be logged into some kind of an online bingo game.

Horace pushed his chair backwards, looking at the computer tower sitting on the shelf underneath, checking to see if this was his unit and had not been switched from another desk in all the confusion.

It was very difficult to know, all the computers in the office were supplied from the very same company and he really hadn't paid that much attention to its appearance in the past.

Then Horace tried to find a way to exit the game, he had never played online bingo before or any other computer game, he could never understand how grown men could possibly spend hours locked away up in their bedroom, night after night playing on their computers after spending all day at work staring into them.

Suddenly, Jean was there, looking over his shoulder, expecting to see the normal spread sheets and rows of detailed accounts, instead Horace was frantically clicking his mouse at large black numbers that looked very much like an online bingo game.

Horace, very aware of the fact that Jean was probably thinking that she had caught him red-handed playing online bingo, clicked even more frantically, trying to exit the site. Then to make things look even worse, a pop up appeared on his screen advertising south American red-hot totties', and a very attractive beautifully bronzed woman with enormous breasts.

Horace turned off his screen, quickly clicking the small off button on the front. Horace swivelled his chair to the left, almost facing Jean, Horace looked at Jean, and Jean looked at Horace. For a split of a second it looked like Jean was going to say something but just stood there looking at Horace, red-faced and embarrassed.

"Good morning, Jean, how are you?" Horace said turning in his chair a little more and smiling.

Jean looked very red-faced and very different from her normal self and even more surprisingly, wasn't clutching her normal load of papers, just holding a single white envelope. Horace was expecting her normal answer, the very same that she had said for the past twenty years or more, something like being over worked and about her forever suffering from women's problems.

"My whole life is changing and filled with uncertainty," Jean suddenly blurted. "I am not even sure if I will still have a job here in the very near future. All these changes and new bosses and there are two men in my office moving everything around to make space for their young twenty-two-year-old secretary called Tracey."

Horace looked at Jean and then quickly glancing around the office at all the pandemonium. He had been so wrapped up inside his own small world with his own problems and thinking everyone else in the office were all sunny day sailing with a light breeze.

Of course, everyone's life had been thrown into turmoil with the company takeover exactly the same as his, and he was probably better off out of it, as long as he got a good redundancy pay-out.

Nobody was sweetly sailing along on a sunny day spring tide; everyone had been flung into the cold murky waters of uncertainty or possibly unemployment.

Horace had never been one for hugging, he wasn't the type of person who could throw their arms around any old Tom, Dick or Harry, but without thinking, he was already on his feet with his arms wrapped around Jean's soft spongy fifty-something portly frame. This hugging experience was also very new to Jean and made her feel very uncomfortable.

She could feel Horace's breath on the side of her cheek and on the back of her neck and began to worry that he may be dribbling, or even worse, his tongue may be black and slip out from his mouth, staining the neckline of her freshly washed and ironed dress.

Jean wriggled and wiggled, moving backwards at the same time, "I have a letter for you, Horace, it's an appointment at the Mountfitchet Medical Centre, you have to be there at one-thirty this afternoon."

Jean handed Horace the letter from a good distance of arm's length and from a much safer place. "The bosses said you can take the day off, so you have plenty of time to get yourself over there."

Horace reached out and took the letter, Jean smiled at Horace, "good luck, I hope everything is OK."

Horace sat back down and opened the envelope, inside was something that Jean had typed out, the name and address of the medical centre and the time of the appointment.

Horace pushed the small button on the front of his monitor, luckily, the bingo game had finished and was giving him two options, start new game or quit game.

Horace quickly clicked on the quit game option before the computer had a chance to change its mind and then had a glance around the office, nobody seemed to had noticed and were all still trying to sort out who's desk was whose and who was now sitting where.

Horace grabbed his jacket from the back of the chair, luckily someone had thrown him a lifeline, a means of escape from the crazy place, and he went out through the door and down the stairs.

Once outside, he wished that he had driven the car into work and not decided to walk, his mind was in a muddle and he needed Delia to talk to or maybe the solicitor that she was supposed to ring at ten. Horace was halfway through Victoria Park when he received a message from Delia: *have made you an appointment for four pm this afternoon, you have to be home by three-thirty.*

Delia was standing in the kitchen holding a fresh cup of coffee when the front door suddenly opened.

"You have made good time, I only sent you the message just five minutes ago."

"I have been sent home just like a naughty schoolboy," Horace said, not really sure if he should laugh or cry.

Chapter 15

Horace or Delia had never seen or heard of the Mountfitchet Medical Centre before, even though Mountfitchet was only a half hour drive or so in the car, so they left the house early, at around twelve-thirty, giving them a little extra time to find the place and park the car.

Horace and Delia travelled the full length of Mountfitchet Avenue until they reached the roundabout at the bottom, Horace had entered the address into the satnav and they were expecting to see a new suave sophisticated building with a lot of glass and light-coloured bricks.

Horace drove as slow as the traffic behind allowed him on the way back, unfortunately there was a white builders van directly behind and Horace could see the guy in his rear-view mirror flapping his arms around.

The satnav had told them to turn right into Rectory Lane as they passed on the way down, but it didn't seem to make any sense as the medical centre was supposed to be situated on Mountfitchet Avenue.

The satnav was now instructing Horace to turn left into Rectory Lane once again, Horace indicated and rapidly swung a left, mainly because the women's voice in the satnav kept on at him and secondly to get away from the inpatient guy behind in the white van.

Just a few metres down Rectory Lane on the left there was a black sign with gold letters that read, Mountfitchet Medical Centre with a white arrow pointing into a car park.

Horace parked the car on the end of a row of three cars, the only ones in the car park, as soon as he switched of the engine, they could hear the sound of crows cawing as they circled overhead.

"That's a bad omen, isn't it? If a crow suddenly appears, doesn't that mean that somebody is about to die?" Horace said, looking up at the sky and wondering if the car will be covered in bird poo when they return.

"I thought it had to be a black cat crossing your path," Delia said, looking up at the sky, "besides there are a lot more than one, and have probably nested in this area for years."

Horace and Delia made their way across the car park towards the large old house, quite similar to the converted Georgian house where Horace worked, Horace turned the handle and opened the solid oak door.

A doorbell rang somewhere in the building and a few seconds later a woman appeared dressed in a very white uniform similar to a nurse, she looked at Horace and then at Delia, waiting for them to introduce themselves.

"Good afternoon, my name is Horace Dankworth and I have an appointment for this afternoon?"

"Ah yes, Mr Dankworth, please take a seat and if you would be so kind and fill in this form, we will call you when we are ready."

Delia followed Horace over to what appeared to be the most comfortable chairs in the room and they both sat down.

Horace quickly worked his way down the health questioner after filling in his name, address and age. The rest was very simple with, a lot of questions, that just needed a yes or no to be ticked off inside the small boxes alongside, starting with did he smoke? Did he drink? Was he currently taking pills for depression?

"Doesn't seem much like a medical centre," Delia whispered, looking around the room at all the different types of chairs, "and there is no one else here, just us two."

Horace leant forward and sifted through the selection of magazines that were lying on the top of a glass coffee table. "There is nothing here less than a year old," he said sitting back.

"Maybe they picked up the magazines along with all the second-hand chairs from the local boot sale," Delia whispered into Horace's ear.

Horace looked around the waiting room, there was a large poster opposite, asking if you were travelling overseas to a diseased infected country, and to make sure you had the relevant protection, with a list of injections available and a price list. There were also posters advertising the services of a therapist that helped people who suffered with self-confidence problems like stammering and bed-wetting.

"I am getting a very bad feeling about this place," Horace said, shifting around in his bright red upholstered cottage chair.

"Well, it's been a long time since you had any kind of a health check or medical," Delia said, "and besides, it's free and you have been given the day off and it leaves us plenty of time to see the solicitor after."

"Nothing makes sense anymore," Horace said, "and why have they sent me here? this must be costing a fortune, why would they send me for a health check if they are about to make me redundant?"

The women suddenly reappeared. "My name is Vivian and I am a nurse technician and we will be running a few tests for you today." She reached out and took the medical questionnaire from Horace. "This will take about two hours," she said turning to Delia, "if you prefer to come back?"

Delia waited for Horace to disappear behind the closed door with Vivian and then went out to the car, two hours was a long time to spend in a room with a handful of out-of-date magazines and nothing else to do.

One hour and forty-five minutes later Delia turned the car left into Rectory Lane and left again into the carpark, Horace was standing there, waiting, feeling abandoned like a small child waiting in the School playground for his mother to come and pick him up.

"I didn't know what to do or where you had gone," Horace said, practically falling into the car, "they took so much blood for all the different tests, I can barely stand, and I had to wee into about six bottles."

"Just sit back and relax, my darling," Delia said, doing her very best, sounding sympathetic, knowing the fuss Horace normally makes at the first sight of blood, "well, it sounds like they were very thorough, we have to get a move on, we just have enough time to drive to the solicitor's office."

The solicitor's office from the outside looked nothing like the old building that they had just left, unlike the medical centre it looked modern and airy and there were no crows circling overhead.

The building sat back from the main road heading towards Bingham and it had been tastefully constructed from bright red bricks and had white Georgian style windows.

Delia had entered the coordinates into the satnav and the journey had been straight forward, she lightly touched the brakes and turned into the gravel forecourt.

"This is a nice building," Delia said as they both walked towards the main entrance door, passing by all the brass plates that were mounted on both sides of the front entrance that displayed all the information about the solicitors that worked there.

"If they are charging two hundred pounds an hour, I am surprised it's not a gold-plated palace," Horace said begrudgingly.

"Well, at least now you have had a full medical and health check for free," Delia smiled, "now we can move to Spain without any worries."

Horace pulled open the glass tinted door, using the stainless-steel tubular handle that ran from top to bottom, he could feel a little stiffness on the inside of his elbow where the sticky plaster was covering the drain hole where the nurse had sucked out all of his blood.

It was very cool inside and very white and a lot off light coming in from the tinted glass frontage. Just inside the door stood a large reception desk made mostly from opaque glass with led lighting Shining out from the inside.

A young woman was sitting behind the desk talking on the phone wearing a very lightweight headset and looking at her computer, she glanced up at Delia and Horace and directed them to the black leather chairs opposite with her left hand.

Horace sat down next to Delia, checking the time. "We have made good time," he said pushing the mode setting button on his watch, turning it to stop watch mode, "if we are paying two hundred pounds an hour, I am going to make sure we are getting our money's worth."

At four o'clock precisely, the young women came around from the other side of her desk, "Would you follow me please, Mr Pendleton will see you now."

Horace pushed the start button on his stop watch, it was four o clock to the second, the women opened one of the glass doors, situated halfway down the passageway and invited Delia and Horace into Mr Pendleton's office.

Mr Pendleton could have been anywhere between fifty and sixty-five years of age, he had the type of face that oozed wisdom and authority, he had stylish brownie grey hair that suited a well-established solicitor perfectly but probably wouldn't sit right on the head of a front man of a heavy metal rock band.

He was wearing a very expensive looking suit that Horace recognised instantly as a Brioni Vanquish II, similar to the suit that James bond wore and strangely enough, Freddie Tidmarsh back at the office.

He was sitting behind an enormous hardwood desk that had a light green leather inlay sunken into the top surface.

There was a notepad with a dark wood surround, sitting on the desk in front of him and a piece of polished marble with quill pens fitted into a row of holes on the top.

"Mr and Mrs Dankworth, please take a seat."

Horace and Delia sank down into the soft brown leather chairs, opposite.

"So, Mr Dankworth, how can I help you?" He glanced down at a few notes that he had made on a writing pad, "you feel that you are being singled out at work by your bosses and you feel that they are trying to get rid of you?"

Horace had wished that he had worn his best suit, this man obviously had very expensive tastes and he might have made a better impression, but that would have been a bit stupid having the medical earlier that morning and now he was sure that what little blood they had left inside his body, was now seeping out from underneath the sticky plaster on his arm.

"Well, it all started when we were attending our neighbour Trevor's funeral," Horace began. "When I overheard my two bosses talking, while I was in the toilet. One of them was saying that our neighbour and my work college Trever had done them a huge favour by blowing himself up, saving them a small fortune on a redundancy package that they had been negotiating."

"Then they said, now that Trevor had departed, instead of having to find a way of getting rid of me, maybe they would offer me a redundancy package, similar to the one that they had offered to Trevor."

Mr Pendleton put his pencil down and sat back in his chair, he was expecting some hard evidence of mistreatment in the workplace, so he could make notes that would help him to put together some sort of strong case. Usually starting with a strong-worded letter to Horace's employers, outlining his demands or what action he was about to take, but in this case, he had absolutely nothing to go on.

Just some kind of story that sounded very similar to a TV soap drama, involving the men's toilets and someone called Trevor who had recently accidentally blown themselves up.

"Trevor's wife, Hilary, told me exactly the same story," Delia interjected, "that Horace overheard from inside the men's toilet at the golf club. That they were going to find a way of getting rid of Horace," Delia, continued, feeling Horace hadn't explained himself properly and his story didn't sound quite right and needed substantiating.

"And they have just given me a new account to work on," Horace added, "some bogus fishmonger from Billingsgate fish market. And someone left two live fish on my desk, in a plastic carrier bag and they have moved my desk over to the window, directly in the sunlight and they have taken the sunblind down."

Mr Pendleton had taken on many, many redundancy cases over the years, none of them had been so bizarre as anyone blowing themselves up and that somehow involved a bogus fishmonger from Billingsgate.

"When you were in the toilet and overheard your bosses talking, did they actually mention your name or you in person?" Mr Pendleton asked.

Horace felt a little embarrassed, he felt that he hadn't explained himself very well, probably because they had just arrived, immediately after him having the medical and them taking all that blood. They never even offered him a cup of tea and a biscuit, just like they do at the mobile blood donor van, they had just sent him on his way, more or less shoving him out the door.

"They referred to me by another name," Horace said sheepishly, "Spankworth."

Horace watched Mr Pendleton as he wrote in his notepad adding the name Spankworth to his notes.

"Have you had any kind of meeting with your bosses where they mentioned that you may be made redundant?"

"Yes," Horace replied, "last Wednesday, but they didn't say anything about redundancy, I got the impression that they were trying to make me feel uncomfortable and inadequate. They told me that they were concerned about my health and I was falling behind with my work and I had a personal hygiene problem."

Horace watched Mr Pendleton while he added, a hygiene problem and the word inadequate and falling behind with the workload, to his notes.

"Did they give you a verbal warning?" Mr Pendleton asked.

Horace had to think back about the meeting that he had with both bosses, they never had been very good at talking with their employees, there was a definite lack of communication and they had a cunning way of telling you things that were normally clouded by smoke.

"I don't think so," Horace said, "they said that they were going to arrange for me to have a medical. I find them very difficult people to talk to."

Horace watched Mr Pendleton as he wrote the words unsure, finds it difficult to focus and finds it very difficult to talk to people.

Horace sat back in his chair. He could feel very strong feelings of misrepresentation building up inside his body, as if it seemed like this very expensive lawyer was actually building a case against him. It was a good job he wasn't being accused of murder; this guy would have him hanged outside the courtroom just inside the hour at the rounded cost of two hundred pounds.

"Well, Mr Dankworth," Mr Pendleton started, "I can see that recent events have caused you and your wife a lot of stress and worry and concern. You have worked for the company for a considerable number of years and from what you are telling me it sounds like your bosses are treating you like an office junior, and they are obviously trying to belittle you and that obviously will make you feel very uncomfortable and inadequate."

"These people cannot get rid of you, just because your face doesn't fit any more, or you just happen to have drifted out of your bosses' favour. By law, they can only get rid of you if the job is redundant and not the person, and as you work at a firm of accountants and I assume that you all more or less do the same job, they cannot single you out and make you redundant."

"But what they can do," Mr Pendleton continued, "they can offer you a voluntary redundancy package, probably similar to what they offered your friend Trevor where you can accept and agree to their terms and the amount of pay-out, they are offering you. My advice would be for you, Mr Dankworth, if you feel they are trying to get rid of you, would be to carry on at work as if nothing has happened, work hard and don't give them any reason that they could possibly use to try and get rid of you."

"Try to be extra nice to everyone in the office and try to be as helpful as possible, if they are set on getting rid of you, at some point they will approach you and offer you some kind of redundancy package."

Horace handed his visa debit card over to the receptionist on the way out and in an instant, with just a click of a button, two hundred pounds had gone from his and Delia's joint bank account.

Chapter 16

Monday morning, the two new bosses had almost taken control of the company, they had spent the whole weekend alone at the office, going over all the accounts and now felt confident to make the final payment, that would make them both the new owners and concluding the takeover.

There were just a few loose ends to tie up, that they felt needed some clarification or an explanation, number one being, who was the guy who seemed to smell of fish, working away on his computer, sitting all alone over by the window?

Unable to answer, some of their awkward questions, Cedrick had somehow managed to bundle Cecil out from the office for an impromptu meeting in the café of the local supermarket.

"I said we should have offered Spankworth a redundancy package," Cedrick said glaring at Cecil across the wobbly table, spilling the froth from the top of both cappuccinos. "Now we are stuck! What the hell are we going to do? We have even taken his name off from the payroll!"

"This could jeopardise the final transaction," Cedrick spat out the words at Cecil, his face bright red with anger and the veins in his neck swollen and bulging.

"Oh no, you can't blame me entirely," Cecil said calmly, him always being the calmer brother of the two. "I don't remember you offering to stick your hand into your pocket to pay Spankworth out! We will have to offer him a deal," Cecil said, "We will have to either ask him to come into the office early tomorrow morning or stay late tonight, when the other two are not around."

"Maybe we should wait until we get his medical report back from the medical centre," Cedrick said callously, "maybe he has something wrong with him and it could be terminal, he might only have a few more weeks to live."

"Or preferably just a few more days," Cecil said, showing no emotion, "that will save us any further embarrassment and a lot of money."

Tuesday morning, Jean came into Cedrick's office, Cecil had moved out from his office, and the two new bosses had established themselves in Cecil's office and were now both working away inside.

Cecil was working in the corner of Cedrick's office using a very small table, just big enough for his computer.

Jean, as usual was carrying the morning post, it was her job to open everything and only bring in anything that needed the immediate attention from the two bosses.

"I have wonderful news," she said, waving an A4 sized folder around, "we have the medical report back from the medical centre, Horace is one hundred per cent fit; if anything, he has the constitution of a twenty-eight-year-old and could quite easily live to be one hundred."

Jean placed the open three-page report onto the top of Cedrick's desk before leaving and closing the door behind her, on her way back to her own office who she now shared with the beautiful very slim twenty-two-year-old Tracey.

"I can't believe it," Cedrick said, after quickly thumbing through the three-page report, before throwing It into one of his drawers, slamming it shut. "Tidmarsh said he was lying lifeless on the floor, inside the toilet with his tongue hanging out, all blue and swollen, his information is normally very accurate, how could he have made such a huge mistake?"

"A blooming expensive one too, I have a good mind to take the money out from his bonuses this month," Cecil snapped from his new work space cramped up against the wall, over in the corner.

"Well, we are wasting our time trying to stress him out," Cedrick said, "If anything, all the extra workload and the smell of fish seems to agree with him, if anything it has brought him out from his shell. Tidmarsh said that he turned up after lunch yesterday with boxes of fresh cream cakes and handed them out to everyone, saying that he and his wife are trying for a baby."

"We will have to get him in here, and quick," Cecil said, his voice sounding panicky, "before he starts to breed, there is no way we will be able to make him redundant when he has half a dozen ginger-haired runts running around the place."

Wednesday morning, after beginning the week with some hot humid weather, it had ended abruptly with a huge flash of lighting and a loud bang and then a rumble of thunder.

Horace ran from the car, quickly fumbling with the door, desperately trying to escape the enormous drops of rain. Horace was startled by the ghostly figure of Cedrick, lurking in the shadows just inside the doorway.

"Horace, I am glad I caught you, would you mind stepping into the office for a second?"

Horace followed Cedrick into his office, Cecil was already sitting there, but this time not in a grand black leather executive chair but perched on a small very cheap-looking swivel chair like a vulture waiting for something to pass him by, gasping its last breath.

Horace looked around the office, there was nowhere for him to sit, so he guessed whatever he had been called in there for, it wasn't something that was going to take a very long time.

"Well Horace, we won't beat about the bush," Cedrick began, "we have to lose bodies before the final takeover. The two new company directors are not accountants; in fact, you have much more qualifications than the pair of them put together."

"The new company will be mostly interested in selling stocks and shares and insurance policies, they will still be providing accountancy for the big company's but they are not interested in the small fish."

Horace guessed where this conversation was heading, most recently he was the guy in the office who dealt with all the small fish. Horace thought about the two live fish that had been left on his desk the week before, and what had happened to them? They had simply disappeared from the men's washroom, as quickly as they had arrived.

"So, you see, Horace, we have to shed bodies," Cecil said, taking the reins from his brother, "we have to lighten the wage bill."

Horace thought again, are these pair of conniving bastards playing with him like cats with a captured mouse? Small fish? Sheds and bodies, after all that had happened to Trevor and all the recent events that had happened to him in his own life recently?

"So, Horace, how would you feel about voluntary redundancy? We can offer you a lump sum of a year's salary in advance, and then pay you monthly for the second year, that will free you up for whatever you want to do for the next two years. Giving you more time to have babies and start a family," Cedrick said, then sort of wincing at the thought.

Horace was instantly filled with happiness, totally overjoyed, so much so that he wanted to punch the air and shout out, yes, yes, yes!

Of course, if this had happened to him only just a year ago, he would have been devastated, after working there for so long, it would have been a massive blow, like being hit by a juggernaut, travelling at seventy miles an hour.

That would have corresponded with his midlife crises, when Dr Carolina Banks said that he was suffering from at the time, on the very rare occasion that he had sought her medical advice.

But now after what had happened most recently, Trevor, the funeral, overhearing the way that the two bosses had spoken about him, the holiday in Spain, sleeping naked and making love to his wife, this was perfect timing, this was going to be the first day of their new life.

Horace skipped out through the doorway and around the side of the building towards the car.

The rain had gotten even harder and the drops were huge, even the sky had turned blacker, Horace didn't feel the huge drops of rain soaking through his jacket and then through his shirt, he just felt overwhelmingly happy as he splashed his way to the car, skipping through all the puddles.

Delia had finished all the school work and had decided to take on the huge task of cleaning out all the kitchen cupboards. She had taken all the tin cans out, placing them on the kitchen tops and was just running some warm water into the washing up bowl, so she could wipe clean all the shelves, when Horace came crashing through the front door.

Horace stood on the piece of plastic matting especially reserved for the wet days when he returned home from golf, he pulled of his soaking wet jacket and then peeled of his shirt, then slid out of his shoes, trousers and pants all in one move.

Delia was standing by the kitchen sink when Horace burst in, only wearing his damp socks, lifting her up into his arms and began to make his way to the foot of stairs.

"Let's go upstairs and make love!" he shouted.

Horace had never carried Delia up the stairs before and on hindsight this had not been the right time to start, the first stair he kind of managed, the second step seemed to be much higher than usual and he just about managed the third after a prolonged teeter on the edge.

All the extra energy Horace's body had generated from the excitement had suddenly drained; Delia sensed this and with a little wiggle slid out from Horace's shaky hands and put her feet down firmly onto the stairs.

"Let's have a nice cup of strong coffee," she said heading back towards the kitchen.

Horace crawled up the stairs like an undernourished stray dog, then across the landing and into the bedroom and pulled on a nice warm track suit, that he had recently purchased after returning from Spain.

The sky outside had gotten even darker and Delia could see the leaves blowing around in the back garden, she turned on the kitchen lights after she had poured out two cups of coffee.

Horace suddenly appeared, wearing his royal blue tracksuit, he looked so different in casual wear, normally during a working day he would be wearing one of his suits.

"So, Horace why are you home? It must be good news otherwise you wouldn't be so happy."

"Finally, they have come clean, just like the solicitor said, they have offered me voluntary redundancy. They took me by surprise this morning, they were both waiting for me, when I arrived first thing."

"Yes," Delia said, "how much?"

"Not enough to buy the villa in Spain, but it's a start."

"How much?" Delia said, the suspense killing her.

"Not as much as I expected, I bet Trevor was offered more."

"How much!" Delia shouted, her patience running out.

Horace had been home now for at least half an hour and she still didn't know any of the details.

"A year's salary in the form of a lump sum and then the following year, my monthly salary paid every month for one more year."

"That's a very good offer considering that we heard rumours that they were trying to get rid of you," Delia said, "what did you say to them, did you accept it?"

"To be honest, I was completely bowled over, they caught me by surprise, I told them that I would discuss it with my wife, then Cedrick more or less shoved me out the door as if they didn't want me there anymore. Now that the dust has settled and in view of what has happened, I suppose it is a reasonable offer," Horace smiled.

"The only thing that worries me is the monthly salary part for the following year, will we get it? And if not, where will the pair of rats be in a year's time?" Horace said, then finishing the rest of his coffee.

"Yes, I agree," Delia said, putting the two empty coffee mugs into the washing up bowl and rinsing them out, wiping the insides with a small sponge.

"This time next year, they could be anywhere in the world, we would have no chance in tracking them down and getting the rest of our money."

"And this time next year we could be moving into our new villa in Spain, Delia said, smiling."

"Maybe I should go back and ask them for the two years' redundancy upfront as a lump sum," Horace said. "A hundred thousand, that would be peanuts to them."

"You mustn't seem too eager though, Horace, remember all this has come out of the blue as far as they know, we didn't know anything about this, we have to box very clever."

"Maybe I should go in earlier tomorrow and get myself working at my desk, before they arrive, try to appear shaken and upset."

"Well, they seem like they want to get rid of you in a hurry, I am surprised at the amount of money that they are offering you," Delia said, carrying the washing up bowl over to the largest kitchen cupboard, and then beginning to wipe the shelving.

Horace looked out of the kitchen window, "what are you supposed to do on a day like this? The golf course must be like a bog; this is supposed to be our summer."

Chapter 17

Thursday morning, Horace was the first one to arrive at the office, after handing out the cream cakes a few days previously and the talk about trying for a baby, all his other work colleagues were surprised to find Horace working away on his computer as they all slowly filtered in.

"The baby making can't be going too well," Freddy Tidmarsh shouted out, so everyone could here, "what's he doing here and not at home, making love to his wife, and putting all his effort into trying to make a baby?"

Most people nodded or said good morning, waiting for Horace to give some sort of explanation, or maybe that he had already done the deed and his wife was already banged up. But Horace said nothing, he just clicked away at his mouse, just giving them a wave of acknowledgment with his left hand.

He had completed all the accounts for the dodgy fishmonger but was still in two minds whether the guy was fictitious or not, and decided not to forward all the relevant paperwork off to the taxman for the time being.

Freddy Tidmarsh had been summoned downstairs to speak with the bosses and gave Horace one of his sideways sneering looks on his return as normal.

He obviously hadn't been told anything about the pending redundancy offer, otherwise he would have made some kind of wise crack, loud enough for everyone else to hear.

Horace needed to keep busy, He closed the file on the uncertain fishmonger and clicked his mouse on to his diary, the file on the small chain of family run sweet shops, sweetly named the gob stopper, was the next on the agenda.

The young Mrs Molly Smith who had taken over the running of the shops from the Mrs Molly Smith Senior, had always sent the accounts in well before time and in good order and presented everything perfectly, leaving Horace very little to do.

Mrs Smith senior had come to Horace, carrying a shopping bag of purchase orders and a big pile of cash, more than twenty years ago when she first started the business, selling sweets, like sherbet lemons and gobstoppers from a market stall in Bingham.

Suddenly, Jean was there, standing next to Horace clutching her normal bundle of papers.

"The bosses would like a quick word with you, Horace, I think it might be urgent."

Horace followed Jean out from the office space and down the stairs, he felt quite nervous, he was guessing that they wanted an answer.

Jean tapped politely on the boss's door and then opened it for Horace to enter.

The door was barely shut when Cecil began, "Well Horace, have you got an answer for us?"

"My wife and I spent the whole evening discussing it and we have a lot of reservations," Horace began, after taking a deep breath, "our main concerns are, will I be able to find myself another job at my age. If you maybe paid me two years' salary as a lump sum, that would give me more breathing space and confidence to search for the right job in the current market place."

Cecil stared at Horace and then looked across to his brother, this guy Spankworth wasn't going to be that easy to get rid of after all, he was as healthy as a workhorse and apparently was going to live for ever.

Cecil opened the top drawer and took out the company cheque book and quickly wrote the words, 'pay Horace Dankworth the sum of one hundred thousand pounds', and then after tearing the cheque from the book, passed it over for his brother to countersign.

Cedrick held out the cheque for Horace. "Take the cheque and walk away," Cedrick said using a cold dull tone, "you don't go back upstairs, you don't talk to anybody, you walk straight out of that door."

Horace took the cheque from Cedrick, turned around and went out of the door, there wouldn't be any card signed by his fellow workers or a small farewell party, no small talk about how it had been a pleasure working with him. Nothing.

Horace turned the car into the driveway and parked it just in front of the garage, after driving the car home on auto pilot with the cheque for one hundred thousand pounds sitting on the passenger seat in the front of the car beside him.

He felt nothing, unlike the morning previously where he was full of excitement and his hormones raging, if anything he felt a little weary and sad.

Delia was upstairs cleaning the bathroom; she had just finished brushing on a tile cleaner inside the shower cubicle when she heard the sound of Horace's car pull up outside.

Horace wearily climbed the stairs with the one-thousand-pound cheque hanging limply from his hand.

"That's it, I'm on the scrap heap with all the other middle-aged losers," Horace said solemnly.

Delia put her arms up, resting them onto Horace's shoulders and gently squeezing both sides of his neck with her forearms, not wanting to contaminate him with her stinky yellow rubber gloves.

"You're not a loser, darling," she said, "they are, they are the losers, and they have just lost their best accountant, the best accountant in the whole wide world."

Horace went into the bedroom and took off his suit. "I won't be needing these anymore, unless there are more funerals to attend," he said, hanging his suit into the wardrobe, along with all the rest.

Delia went back into the bathroom and unscrewed the shower head from the hose and quickly washed off all the tile cleaner from the tiles inside the shower cubicle and then unrolled the plastic gloves from her hands and dropped them into the shower tray and then washing her hands in the hand basin.

Delia then went quickly into the bedroom, seeing the cheque on the bed she quickly picked it up, "Wow, one hundred thousand pounds," she said, "what happened, what did they say?"

"Not much," Horace said solemnly, "they handed me the cheque for one hundred thousand pounds and then shoved me out of the door into the pouring rain."

"Let's get out of here," Delia said, quickly changing into a long-knitted woollen dress, "the rain has eased, we can drive into town and put the cheque into the building society and then have lunch somewhere, maybe have a wander around the shopping centre."

Friday morning, Delia was out from the bed at seven thirty, sharp, "Come on," she said, giving Horace's side of the bed a good bounce up and down with both hands. "Let's strike while the iron is still hot, let's get you back in the marketplace and find you a new job."

Delia was already inside the shower, giving the tiles their final rinse, when Horace's feet first touched the bedroom carpet, he shuffled over to the wardrobe and slid all the hangers to one side that were holding his work suits and pulled out yet another new track suit that he had just purchased before, at the weekend in shopping centre.

The house had suddenly turned very cold inside, what with all the wind and rain, and now that he was unemployed, he didn't want the extra expense of turning the heating on.

Horace then slid his laptop out from one of the shelves from inside the wardrobe along with the power adapter and then went down the stairs, putting the laptop onto the dining room table and then plugging it into the socket close by.

He looked out of the dining room window, the weather wasn't helping his mood, instead of the morning sky getting lighter, it was becoming much darker by the minute, with thick black clouds that seemed to be closing in on him and all around the house.

Delia suddenly appeared wearing the same tracksuit as Horace, her one being the women's version, in bright pink. "Now we are a proper team," she said smiling, putting her laptop down opposite Horace and sitting down.

"Thirty-six degrees and sunny in Marbella today." Delia smiled from across the table at Horace, as she quickly glanced at the daily weather reports, along the coastal resorts of southern Spain, on the website that now came up on her laptop every time, she switched it on.

Horace looked out of the window; the rain somehow was holding off but the sky seemed to be getting even darker by the minute. "If the clouds get any lower, they will be coming into the house through the upstairs windows," he said, wearily.

"This weather is only supposed to last for a few more days," Delia said, as she started to sift through the different employment agencies.

"Let's move to Spain!" Horace shouted suddenly, leaping out of his chair. "Let's buy one of Sebastian's white villas in the sun, while I am still young enough to breathe and walk unaided! Let's get away from all this depressing gloomy weather," Horace said, "this is supposed to be our English summer, everything will be sliding downhill from here."

"Oh Horace, my darling, that would be wonderful," Delia said leaping out of her chair, wrapping her arms around his body so that their brand-new tracksuits made maximum contact.

Delia quickly rang Sebastian, before Horace had the chance to change his mind, forgetting that England was an hour in front and it would only be six forty-five, early morning there in southern Spain.

Sebastian leapt out of bed, telling Delia that he would e-mail her all the details within the hour, despite him being up all night, trying to sell one of the luxury villas to a couple of Germans who just happen to stop in the street to admire his new car.

Delia was searching through the employment agencies at around eight forty-five British time when her laptop pinged, giving her notification of the e-mails that had just arrived and were now in her in box.

Sebastian had sent a plan of the proposed phase two site, asking them what plot number they preferred.

And more importantly, asking for the initial payment for the sum of three hundred thousand euros for the deposit, that being the first of two down payments for an off-plan villa to be built just inside the year by the company, Spanish white villas in the sun.

Sebastian had also sent them details of a company who specialised in changing pounds sterling into foreign currencies, informing them that they were offering the best exchange rate from pounds Sterling to euros at the moment. Advising them to change their pounds into euros as quickly as possible as the exchange rate could plummet within the hour, with all the uncertainty surrounding the negotiations around Brexit.

Despite the dark black clouds surrounding the house outside and the wind whistling an eerie sound around the patio door at the rear of the dining room, Horace's mood had risen from a lacklustre life with no purpose or meaning, to a very bright future.

Now potentially purchasing a brand-new villa in Spain and a job interview lined up for the very first thing, the following Monday morning.

With Horace's natural skills in number crunching, he had achieved the very best deal, changing his pounds sterling into euros and sent them off using the services of internet banking. Directly depositing the money into the business account of Spanish white villas in the sun.

In the meantime, Delia had found Horace a reasonably small manufacturing company, whose in-house accountant was about to take a year out for maternity leave, and the company was looking for someone to take up the position for just one year only.

The very first thing, the following Monday morning, Horace had steered the car to the industrial area at Bingham, doing his very best to avoid the huge puddles of rain water that seem to be lying around on every corner.

Mr Mumford, the boss and co-owner of Bakelite Electronics, had been impressed right from the very first minute after meeting Horace, not expecting anyone with Horace's years of experience to apply for the job.

Horace began at Bakelite Electronics on the first Monday of September that coincided with Delia returning to her school for the start of the autumn term.

Horace settled down into his new role remarkably very quickly and very soon was doing much more than his old job where he had just been crunching numbers. He was very quickly put in charge of the payroll system on the computer and given more control over the company's accounts.

Delia had submitted her resignation to the school governors, giving them plenty of warning and a year's notice and that she intended to leave the following year.

By the time that the cold grey days of November had arrived, Horace and Delia's lives had settled down into some kind of normality and a steady rhythm of work and long dark evenings, watching and criticising British television.

Trevor's wife, Hilary, had decided not to return to Victoria Avenue and had put the house, next door on the market and had been advised by the local estate agent to put the house up for sale for the sum of five hundred and fifty thousand pounds.

In no time at all the Christmas holidays had arrived, with Delia's school closing for the two weeks' holiday period and Bakelite Electronics shutting down for seven days over the Christmas holiday.

The very first day of the Christmas holidays, Delia spoke to Sebastian on the phone, telling them that they were thinking of spending the Christmas holiday over there in Spain, and if possible, they would like view the new villa and see how things were moving along.

Sebastian's tone had suddenly changed from a racy upbeat tempo to a more unusually sullen one, telling Delia that, the building of the villa had gotten off to a very slow start, and at the moment there wasn't very much there to see.

He then went on to explain to Delia in great detail that before any kind of building project of this kind were undertaken, all the services had to be sunk down into the ground with a lot of time-consuming excavating work.

Especially for the huge network of drainage pipes that have to be buried into the ground a long way down.

Sebastian then went on to explain, telling Delia that the groundwork contractors had hit a very hard seam of dense rock, almost impossible to excavate and it had slowed the work down to a snail's pace.

Delia was horrified at all the bad news and felt quite sick and shaken and quickly poured herself a large glass of lemonade from the fridge, hoping that it would settle her stomach.

Luckily, Horace was out of the house, playing a round of golf with his new found friends and golf buddies, taking advantage of the clear bright days that had just arrived with the start of the Christmas holidays.

Horace had mentioned to Delia the week previously that he was interested in entering the golf tournament at the club and also asked if she wanted to attend this year's annual Christmas meal. Delia had said that it would be nice to do something different this Christmas and had mentioned to Horace about going to Spain, and keeping their options open.

By the time that Horace had arrived home from his eighteen holes, it was late afternoon and almost dark, the smell of freshly backed mince pies, greeted him as soon as he opened the front door.

Delia didn't want to worry Horace too much, by sounding the alarm bells, telling him that all was not well with the construction on their new villa in Spain, and she was hoping maybe things could improve and speed up in the new year.

Delia had tried to put the bad news about the villa in Spain to the back of her head and busied herself making some homemade mince pies from a recipe from the new television program, lets bake with Daphne Cranebrook, who just happened to be one of the latest TV. personality pastry cooks.

Horace arrived home in a good mood. He didn't have to stand on his plastic protective carpet to take off his shoes, and he had played one of the best games of golf for at least a year.

"Golf is a much easier game to play without all that wind and rain," he said chirpily, "the ball goes exactly where you expect it to, my game should improve by at least twenty per cent when we move to Spain. The golf course is very dry at the moment and the ball is bouncing and rolling much further," Horace continued, "the game is much more enjoyable when you don't have to prise the ball out from the mud."

"Would you like a hot mince pie and custard, darling?" Delia smiled at Horace, lifting back the tea towel revealing her freshly baked home-made pies, done to perfection.

Horace sat down at the small round kitchen table, "my hands are frozen," he said, "even wearing my golf gloves, a hot mince pie is just what I need."

"I was thinking," Delia said, "as the weather is fine and we can get out more, maybe we should stay at home this year as this could be our last Christmas here in England for some time. Is there enough time for you to enter the golf tournament, darling? Maybe I could take a few lessons at the driving range and we could attend the Christmas dance."

"That will be great," Horace smiled, helping himself to another mince pie. "I was talking to Arthur, who works at the golf club, and he told me that we are going to have this very fine dry weather all week. This would be a good opportunity for you to have a few lessons," Horace said, "and hopefully, you won't need too many when we go to Spain."

And that will keep you away from that filthy leacher Jose, over there in Spain, Horace thought to himself. *Or maybe they could try another golf course in Spain, where the coach didn't have a mouthful of brilliant white teeth and isn't quite so tanned and he keeps his hand on his clubs and not on Delia's arse.*

The Christmas period passed by relatively quickly, Horace and Delia attended the Christmas dinner and dance at the golf club. On Christmas day after a quiet lunch at home, they went for a brisk walk before it got too dark, as the fine dry weather had continued, just like the groundsman, Arthur had informed him up at the golf course.

Horace and Delia like most years also attended the New Year's Eve dance at the golf club, normally, over the past years they would have booked a taxi cab there and back, sharing the fare with the neighbours, Trevor and Hilary.

The evening didn't seem the same without Trevor and Hilary attending, and Horace and Delia weren't in the mood for revelling and the evening dragged and it seemed to take for ever for the clock to tick away the last few hours of twenty nineteen.

2019 eventually slipped away with 2020 starting with a lot of uncertainty.

Delia couldn't stop herself thinking about her conversation with Sebastian about the villa in Spain. It was the first thing on her mind in the cold January mornings when she first awoke and she was thinking about it more and more in the daytime, with every day that had passed.

Horace had gone back to work and Delia was left at home on her own for another week before the school term started.

Delia and Horace had both agreed not to discuss the villa in Spain with anyone, especially at the school where Delia, still worked, the following July was a long way off, and she didn't want the young teachers talking about her in the staff room.

But now Delia felt that she needed to share her concerns with somebody, but who? Maybe a professional like the solicitor that they went to see, Mr Pendleton, he was very expensive but he seemed to know what he was talking about.

The day before Delia was due to return to work, she decided that she would call Sebastian in Spain, one more time.

She had prepared in advance what she would say to him, she would be polite but firm, and tell him that she needed answers or they would like their three hundred thousand euros returned very promptly and in full.

Delia waited until eleven o clock, thinking that it would be ten o clock in the morning over there in Spain and she would catch him at the start of his day.

She scrolled down her list of contacts on her mobile and pushed Sebastian's number, the same as the last time it took a few seconds to make the contact before dialling. Delia went into the kitchen and leaned against the kitchen units waiting for Sebastian to answer, the phone rang for a few seconds and then was switched off. Delia felt a little anxious, Sebastian had her number entered into his list of contacts on his phone, so he would know that it was Delia trying to contact him.

Delia made herself a cup of hot strong coffee and wrapped her fingers around the hot mug, maybe he is busy with another client, she thought, maybe she should wait for him to call her back?

By the time that Horace was due home from work that evening, the anxiety had built up inside Delia's head, Sebastian had not returned her call and she had tried to reach him on more than four or five occasions, ringing him throughout the day. She had busied herself that day in the kitchen preparing vegetables and some lamb and had put everything into the slow cooker and left it simmering in the kitchen.

Chopping the vegetables and peeling the potatoes had helped her think more clearly, and it was while she was scraping the carrots, she decided that she would have to talk to Horace about the problem with the villa. She would break the news to Horace slowly and calmly over dinner, later that evening.

But just like Delia, she would have to be very tactful, like always, very careful to protect Horace, so that he wouldn't get himself worked up and into a right old state.

Horace in the past had always sent himself into a panic, especially where money was concerned.

As soon as he arrived home that evening and was just inside the front door, he blurted out the big problem that was developing at work, and much worse all around the world.

Horace explained to Delia, telling her that the company had been waiting for a huge shipment of electronic parts to arrive from China, in December, but they had never arrived.

Mr Mumford the boss of Bakelite Electronics had been assured by his contact in China that the very important parts would arrive by early January. After Mr Mumford had spent most of his time on the phone that day, he eventually learned that the very important parts hadn't even been shipped out from China. The contact in China had told Mr Mumford that the parts wouldn't be arriving after all and the factory in China that made the components had been temporally closed, but nobody could tell him why.

Horace went up the stairs for a shower and to change into his warm casualwear, Delia went into the kitchen and switched off the slow cooker, preparing the table for their evening meal.

The problems at the company that Horace now worked for sounded very serious, and Horace was genuinely concerned, about the whole affair. What should she do, about the villa in Spain? she was walking around with all this worry building up inside her head, but now wasn't the right time to tell Horace, but she will be back to work at the school first thing in the morning.

Chapter 18

January rolled into February with more and more uncertainty building every day.

Mr Mumford had called a meeting with all the workers at Bakelite Electronics, telling them that things were getting very difficult. He explained to them that their customers were getting very cross and were demanding their electronic assemblies, but without the very important supplies of electronic parts from China, there was nothing much that they could do.

Delia had made some kind of headway with the villa in Spain, she had called a number on some of the paper work that Sebastian had originally emailed over, it was a solicitor, Angel Benítez whose name was printed on some of the documents. Angel had answered the phone immediately, unlike Sebastian, after just one dialling tone, he was very polite and spoke excellent English.

He thanked Delia for contacting him and then very politely explained to her that although he was the solicitor who drew up the sales agreements and that his name was on the top of all the documents, all the agreements had been made with Horace and Delia and Spanish white villas in the sun.

Delia explained to Angel that she had been trying to contact Sebastian for over a month but he wasn't answering her calls. Angel said that he hadn't seen Sebastian for some time but he would ring him and tell him that Delia was still waiting for him to return her call. Delia felt much better after talking with Angel, although things hadn't improved, at least now she had Angel as a contact over there in Spain, and he did say that he would contact Sebastian.

Horace arrived home that evening, telling Delia that the reason that the electronic parts were not arriving from China were because of the mysterious flu type virus that was going around over there, and everything had been closed down, and it was now being reported all over the world news.

Monday morning, on the sixteenth of march, at around eleven thirty, Delia received a call from Sebastian in Spain.

Delia was sitting in her office with the school secretary sifting through all the paperwork concerning the COVID-19 virus and the latest recommendations by the government on how to protect the school children.

Delia answered her phone in a hurry, not looking at the name displayed and not checking who it was calling. She was very surprised to hear Sebastian's voice and she recognised it instantly.

Sebastian spent the first two minutes apologising profusely, telling Delia that things had been extremely difficult and he had spent a lot of time at meetings trying to resolve the problems and didn't want to call her until he had some positive news.

But then Sebastian's tone changed to an even sullener one, much more than before. He explained to Delia that even though work had progressed at the site but very slowly, the whole of Spain had been hit by the COVID-19 virus.

And the whole of country had been shut down as from that weekend and nobody were allowed out of their houses and the country had almost stopped functioning completely.

Delia put her mobile phone down onto the desk top.

"That was someone in Spain," she said, looking across the desk at the school secretary, "the whole country has been locked down and apparently no one is allowed out from their houses."

That evening when Horace arrived home from work, Delia greeted him in the hallway, breaking the news to him about the delay with the building of the villa in Spain, before she had the chance to change her mind.

Horace took the news extremely well, shrugging his shoulders and saying that this new virus was spreading all over the world and soon they may have to close the factory. Only just a few days later all the schools in the United Kingdom were instructed by the government to close their doors, and Delia spent the whole of the next two weeks, working with computer experts, setting up online tuition for all the pupils at her school.

Horace carried on working in the offices above the factory of Bakelite Electronics even though all the staff working in the factory below had been sent home.

Mr Mumford, the boss of Bakelite Electronics, had found a small company of general contractors and they set about moving all the work benches around and installing plastic screens to protect the workers in the factory from the now deadly virus. By the end of May most of the workers had been allowed to return to the factory but now having to wear face masks and protective rubber gloves, while working at their benches behind a plastic screen.

Remarkably, the very important shipment of electrical components arrived from China and Mr Mumford organised the people in the factory into shifts, paying the workers extra money, hoping to clear the backlog of orders.

Delia continued to work from home, and by the time that June had arrived, it had been agreed by everyone, that the school would remain closed until the start of the new term in September. The decision to keep the school closed until the following term filled Delia with mixed emotions, after working at the school for so many years, this would mean that she would be leaving the school in July. Not having the chance to say goodbye to the staff or pupils in person.

Wednesday morning, the fifteenth of July, the last day of school term, there wasn't really very much for Delia to do. Normally, over the past years, once all the pupils and staff had left, Delia would have a short meeting with the school caretaker and then everything would then be locked up for the duration of the school summer holidays.

This year had been a disaster with all the children losing out on a huge chunk of their education as the school had already been closed since March.

Delia turned on her laptop around nine o'clock and was instantly bombarded with a whole new line of emails and e-cards saying how much that she will be missed and wishing her the very best in the future.

By the time eleven o'clock had arrived, Delia had taken delivery of a huge bunch of flowers and a lot more cards, wishing her well and that she will be missed, all dropping through the letter box and onto the mat in the hallway.

By the time Horace arrived home around five o'clock, Delia had placed the flowers on the dining room table, surrounded by all her cards.

"We need to go to Spain," Delia said, greeting Horace in the hallway, "as soon as possible, there is a lot of talk about a second wave of the dreadful virus, and now is probably a good time as any to fly, before things get any worse. We need to see for ourselves what is happening with the villa and talk to Sebastian face to face," Delia said, brimming over with nervous energy.

"Yes," Horace agreed, "on hindsight it wasn't a very good idea to have a brand-new villa built in Spain, especially when we were heading towards a world-wide pandemic."

The very next morning Horace spoke with Mr Mumford, telling him about his and Delia's concerns and that he would like to take some time off work so that he and Delia could travel to Spain.

Mr Mumford was very accommodating, he told Horace that Melisa the young lady that had gone off to have her baby was now chomping at the bit and was very eager to get out of the house and back to work, and was more than happy to leave the baby at home with her mother.

Mr Mumford thanked Horace for all his hard work and said that he had been a great help to the company, working through the most difficult times the business had ever experienced. He told Horace that he would be able leave at that weekend and that he would pay him up in full, up to the full term on his one-year contract.

The flight over from London Gatwick to Malaga in Spain the following Tuesday, was nothing like the flight that Horace and Delia had experienced the year before. There were no hen parties, no lively young women at the back of the plane, systematically working their way through unlimited numbers of bottles of gin. There was no sound of laughing and joking and no one flinging sex toys around.

There were no larger-than-life women doctors or scientists occupying Horace's seat, in fact the plane was less than half full and had plenty of spare seats, with just a spattering of people dotted around. All the passengers were wearing face masks, and constantly rubbing alcohol-based gel into their hands, nobody was talking and everyone had spread themselves out, keeping as far as away from each other as possible.

For Horace, the flight seemed to take forever, Delia had sunken herself into a very thick book that she had chosen from the bookshop at the airport.

Horace never had been much of a reader, nothing much held his attention for very long, he was never interested in big boy's books, like war or gang warfare with blood and guts being splattered all over the place.

He had run his eye along the shelves at the airport, but nothing there had caught his eye, so he had wandered out of the bookshop settling for a large cardboard cup of coffee in the very quiet coffee shop.

Horace had prepared himself much better this time for the journey to Spain, especially for the bright sunlight and the intense heat of the sun scorched country; he had worn a light cotton shirt and lightweight trousers, and had purchased a good quality pair of sunglasses and had them polished and ready for action, sitting in the top pocket of his lightweight shirt.

On arrival, they didn't even have to cram themselves into a bus, waiting for them on the baking hot tarmac like before, along with at least another hundred sweaty bodies.

Malaga airport had been very quiet on arrival and the plane had taxied straight into the main arrival's bay, and after a short wait, Horace and Delia were able to disembark through a long tunnel and found themselves in the luggage reclaim hall in no time at all. For clarity and not wanting a repeated episode of case identity crises, like the year before, Delia had stuck a large round bright yellow sticky label to both sides of their brown leather suitcase.

The luggage reclaim area had been incredible quiet with just a few ghostly figures standing in the shadows of the half lit area around conveyer number seven. After waiting for five minutes, conveyer number seven suddenly broke the silence and began to trundle around, all the luggage on the conveyer had been spread out and Horace had no problem pulling their case off from the conveyer and was more than happy he had chosen the correct case this time.

Delia had reserved a hire car for seven days when she had booked the plane tickets and amazingly, it was sitting there waiting for them in the carpark, that was just a short walk and down a ramp after leaving the baggage reclaim hall.

Horace had decided that he was going to drive the metallic gold-coloured Seat Ibiza, setting the air con at a cool twenty degrees and wearing his new sun glasses, he felt cool and in total control and the journey to the Hotel Golf and Mountain Resort Buena Vista had gone very smoothly, following the instructions of the satnav the whole journey passed without incident.

After two and a half hours, Horace was driving along the approach road towards the Hotel Buena Vista, by now he was feeling a little weary after concentrating for the whole journey and didn't even notice that the carpark was uncharacteristically completely empty. Even Delia hadn't noticed that there was only one vehicle standing solely in one corner of the carpark.

She was desperate to get out of the car and into the lady's room, having not wanting to use the confined space of the toilets on the plane. As soon as Horace stopped the car, Delia was out, not even taking the time to close the car door and was making great strides towards the hotel entrance.

"Don't you think that we should have booked?" Horace shouted, as he got out of the car and walking around to the other side and closing the door.

It was at that moment Horace noticed that the whole carpark was completely empty, with the exception of a small white van, parked in the corner with security written on the sides in large red letters.

Delia, by now, was pushing and pulling at the large door handle, trying to get in. After the short walk from the car, Horace was already feeling the hot sun of July burning the top of his head, he had thought of almost everything beforehand, except a straw hat, "The place looks deserted," Horace said, taking off his sunglasses and shielding his eyes with his hands and peering through the glass.

Delia gave the door one more shake, mostly out of frustration, she should have booked in advance. but the last time they were here there were plenty of spare rooms and she wasn't sure how long they were going to stay.

Suddenly, a man appeared on the other side of the glass, he was obviously the driver of the van outside. He was wearing a dark brown jacket and trousers, with the word security stitched with yellow cotton onto the flap of the breast pocket on his jacket.

"Closed!" he shouted through the glass, and then said something else in Spanish.

"May I use the toilet?" Delia shouted anxiously back through the glass.

"Closed!" the man repeated, "closed!"

"Must be the virus," Delia said, "I wouldn't have thought a place like this, miles from anywhere would not have been effected by COVID-19 and still be closed."

"I thought the whole country closed down for eight weeks, to stop the virus from spreading," Horace said, turning away, feeling the top of his head. "Let's get out of the sun and back into the car, we can drive to the goat village or whatever it's called along the main road, maybe stop at a service station or something for a toilet."

Delia reluctantly let go of the door handle and followed Horace back to the car.

"Let's drive up the lane towards the villas," Delia said, overtaking Horace and quickly getting into the car and shutting the door. "You will have to stop the car at a quiet spot," Delia said, "I will have to go in the bushes, it must be a lot safer than some dirty motorway service station and besides, I can't hold out much longer."

Horace turned right at the end of the approach road and then right again and steered the car at a steady speed up the steady rise of the Eucalyptus lined road.

"I don't know why you didn't use the toilet on the plane," Horace said, "I was in and out every twenty minutes after drinking all that coffee."

"It's alright for men," Delia said, "you don't have to make any kind of contact with the dirty filthy things, women are different, and besides, I didn't see it get cleaned once during the flight and the virus can live on surfaces for about two hours. Stop the car here!"

Horace hit the brakes and the car slid a little before stopping, on the fallen eucalyptus leaves that carpeted the lane. Delia leaped out of the car and disappeared behind the tall trees and into the sun parched undergrowth beyond. Delia kicked off her sandals and then her knickers, quickly hanging them on a small branch that was conveniently growing out from some kind of wild shrub with small yellow flowers.

Delia had never ever had to do a wee in a public place before, and certainly not in the undergrowth, squatting down like a nomadic woman. Only just a year ago it would have been unthinkable, her being the headmistress of the local junior school and a respected member of the local community.

But now so much had changed in such a short space of time, she wasn't the headmistress anymore and people were being advised to stay away from confined spaces and doing a wee in the bushes would now be good advice to offer to any protective parent.

As far as anyone knew the local wild life population and the pig community in Spain had not been affected by the COVID-19 virus outbreak, at least not directly. But with the very strict lockdown measures that lasted for eight weeks and a lot of people not being able to work, who were already living very close to the breadline, the local people in the area who owned guns, caused by hunger and desperation, had taken to hunting.

There was a healthy population of wild black pigs in the area that were quite friendly and were easy victims even to the poorest of shots, before the covid lockdown they would quite often forage around on the golf course and some regular golfers would often feed them with apples.

The little one-year old black male found himself staring at Delia's very white but nicely shaped bottom. This was the first human contact the young black male had, had for over two weeks after being chased across the fairways by two very hungry Spanish gypsies and had been split from the rest of the herd.

Delia hadn't even thought about what wildlife that may be living and lurking around in the undergrowth in the countryside of southern Spain.

Luckily for Delia, she had just finished her extremely long wee when she felt the cold wet snout of the young one-year-old black male checking out her bottom.

Horace had spent his time while Delia was in the bushes by checking out all the controls in the hire car and fiddling with the radio and had found a station that was playing classic music from his teenage years and beyond.

With the car engine running and the air con on, accompanied by Cindy Lauper singing, girls just want to have fun, Horace would have never heard Delia's screams, as she ran towards the car barefoot, holding her sandals, abandoning her knickers snagged on the wild shrub.

"Drive!" Delia shouted. "Drive!"

Horace instinctively glanced to his right, a small black pig came trotting out of the undergrowth sniffing the air with its snout and looking very lonely and abandoned. Horace laughed. "You should have used the toilet on the plane," he said, putting the car into first gear and driving slowly away.

Delia looked at the little black male pig standing there all alone by the roadside, watching them slowly drive away. "It gave me quite a fright," she said, "all my feet are dusty and I have left my knickers behind."

Horace laughed even more, turning the radio down a little and then putting the car into second gear. Horace instinctively drove up the lane, turning right and then driving along the road that looked out over the golf course to the right, passing the line of villas on the left and parking in one of the empty laybys, more or less the same spot where Sebastian had parked his very expensive car the year before.

Delia leapt out from the car as soon as it had stopped, crossing the road and standing on the first few steps in the gap between the villas.

Shielding her eyes from the sun with her hands, she peered up the rest of the wide steps that ran up in between the landscaped garden area and then beyond to where the phase two development should by now, be already partly built.

Her heart sank, there was nothing to see, not even the odd brick, or a pile of sand, not even a bag of cement, nothing.

Delia began to cry. "Oh Horace, what have I done? This is all my fault; I have lost all our money, we are miles from home and we are both unemployed, what was I thinking?"

"Let's get back into the car and out of this heat," Horace said, putting his arm around her shoulders and guiding her back across the road and quickly into the car. Horace started the car, this was only the second time he had ever seen Delia cry, ever since they were first married.

"Let's drive back to the main road and up to the goat village," Horace said, "we will go to Sebastian's shop and see what is happening."

Horace put the car into first gear and drove to the end of the road, steering the car around the roundabout and driving back the way that they had come.

Chapter 19

Horace drove the car down the ramp leading back onto the motorway and then after only a few minutes more, he took the next exit and drove up the ramp and along the road towards the goat watering point, village.

Once they had reached the outskirts of the village, Horace drove the hire car around the one-way system and then turning into the wide-open space of the make do carpark, parking the car as close to the exit as possible between the whitewashed terraced houses.

Horace glanced at Delia over the car roof as he pushed the black button on the key, locking the doors, she had dried her eyes but still had a sad expression, the very same after her mother had died five years ago unexpectedly.

Horace reached out and grabbed hold of Delia's right hand as they headed towards the gap between the roughly rendered whitewashed houses, even though it was late afternoon it was still unbearably hot.

It may have been a mistake to have the air conditioning in the car set so low, Horace thought to himself, it felt like he had jumped out from the freezer and into the baker's oven.

A Spanish lady suddenly appeared through the gap and was heading towards them, she was struggling with two with very full carrier bags of shopping, she appeared to be very hot and struggling to breathe behind the black face mask covering her mouth and nose.

"We are not wearing our face masks," Delia said, turning around and heading straight back towards the car. "It's the law here, we have to wear them at all times, even in the street."

Horace reached into the car and retrieved the two face masks from the glove box, even though the car had only been parked there for just a few minutes, it was already incredibly hot inside and the masks were quite warm as if they had been left in the oven on a low gas.

Horace had thought it unnecessary to wear a mask to protect himself against the COVID-19 virus outside in the fresh air in England, but now they were in Spain and the laws were completely different and here it was compulsory, or face the cost of a huge fine.

They had just passed through the gap in-between the whitewashed houses and turned left to begin the long steady walk uphill to the top of the high street, when Horace's eyes began to sting.

Horace soon realised that his sunglasses had steamed up with his breath, causing them to condensate on the inside and that he couldn't see a thing.

He stumbled into a shop doorway and into the shade. "I can't see!" He shouted out to Delia. "My eyes are really stinging."

Delia stopped and then turned around, her spirit and confidence were in tatters, and at an all-time low, and now her husband for some mysterious reason had been struck down blind, in the street.

Horace pulled off his sunglasses, the lenses on the inside were dripping with water. "It must be my hot breath from behind the mask," he said, "it is causing my sunglasses to mist up. What do we do now?" Horace said, drying the sunglasses the best he could with his shirt. "We have to wear a mask but I can't see in this bright sunlight without my sunglasses?"

Delia glanced around and then up and down the street, there weren't many people around, the village was much quieter now than their previous visit. Just a few people scurrying back and forth all wearing face masks, all going about their business as quickly as possible so they could get out and away from the intense heat and into the shade away from the heat of the late afternoon sun.

Delia then noticed a shop, just a few metres up on the other side of the road, they had various things on display on the path outside, one being a hat stand full of straw hats.

"Wait here," Delia called out to Horace, walking quickly up the street. "I am going to buy us some straw hats."

Although it wasn't the perfect solution, once Horace had pulled the extra wide-brimmed straw hat down shading his eyes, it enabled him to carry on up the hill and towards the top of the street and hopefully a meeting with the recently very elusive Sebastian.

Wearing her new sun hat with the pretty material tied around the brim, finishing at the back with a large bow and the two ends trailing down behind, Delia had picked up the pace and even in the heat of the day seemed to be walking faster and faster, attacking the incline of the high street like a professional speed walker.

Horace was a walker, he loved walking, he had spent a lot of his spare time walking around the golf courses back home and to and from work, weather permitting. But here in all the heat of the late afternoon, he was struggling to keep up with Delia, as if she had used her sadness and had turned it into aggression and she seemed to be getting faster and faster as the gap widened between her and Horace.

It had been a long day, other than the coffee at the airport, Horace had drunk nothing else and he suddenly felt very hungry and very, very thirsty. Maybe a couple of energy bars and a bottle of water, from one of the small supermarkets that they kept passing by, just to tide him over until they had the time to eat a proper meal. Horace wanted to call out to Delia, but with the extremely fast pace and his throat so dry, he barely let out a warbled squeak.

Delia disappeared out of view as she followed the natural bend in the road that slightly veered off to the left, Horace put his head down, doing his very best to up his pace. His wife was heading uphill all alone in the intense heat of the day, in a foreign country, anything could happen to her.

Horace pulled his face mask down, just a little so he could breathe out through his nostrils, he could now see Delia up ahead and in the distance beyond was the colourful signage of Paco's mini mart that he remembered from their previous visit, the year before.

Paco's mini mart appeared to be two of the regular small shops joined together that was situated adjacent on the left-hand side of Sebastian's estate agency.

By the time that Horace had caught up with Delia, and he had reached the top of the hill, Delia's energy and aggression had fizzled out and she was standing outside the estate agency staring at the closed white aluminium shutter.

Horace turned immediately to the left and in through the open doorway of Paco's mini mart. He opened the tall door of the chiller cabinet and took out a large bottle of water and then following the one-way system marked with the bright blue arrows that had been painted on the floor, he eventually arrived at the cereals aisle and chewy bars.

Once back outside, Horace opened the bottle of water and handed it to Delia.

Delia took a few sips from the bottle before handing it back to Horace, Horace drank as much as he possibly could, without drawing a breath, then took out his clean hanky from his pocket and soaked it with the bottled water and then wiped his forehead and face.

Delia had already taken out her phone from her small bag and was standing there with the phone next to her ear listening to the sound of the phone calling Sebastian's number.

Horace poured some more of the water onto his hanky, this time spending more time cooling down his forehead before moving the hanky to the back of his neck. Then he turned all his attention to the fruit and fibre of the muesli chewy bars, tearing the lid off from the thin cardboard box and eating three of the cereal bars and then almost finishing the rest of the water.

Delia put her mobile back into her small bag. "He's not answering," she said, her voice sounding sad and dejected once again.

"Maybe he is at a meeting or with a client," Horace said, "he could be anywhere." Horace held out the box of cereal bars offering them to Delia. "Would you like one of these, darling? You haven't eaten a single thing all day."

Delia looked at Horace, his gesture that she should eat something was hopelessly futile, she felt sick with worry, right down to the bottom of her stomach, she couldn't eat anything even if she wanted.

They were standing at the side of the road in the late afternoon sun, in a foreign country, they had nowhere to stay not even a bed for the night.

And most probably, lost all their inheritance from both sets of parents and all of their hard-earned life savings.

Delia took her small Spanish phrase book out from her handbag, quickly flicking through the pages as she walked into Paco's mini mart. Paco was sitting behind the small counter next to the exit.

Delia quickly glanced at her phrase book one last time before speaking, "Donde esta Sebastian?" she asked. Paco looked at Delia and then at Horace, who had followed Delia around the one-way system of the mini mart and was now standing a few paces behind. Horace didn't have a clue what Delia had just said except that he recognised the name Sebastian, so he imagined Delia was asking Paco where he was.

Paco answered Delia's question with a quick return of rapid-fire Spanish, as if he was mimicking a machine gun, occasionally looking at Horace as if he was including him in the conversation as well.

"What did he say?" Horace said, he had already retreated a few more steps, and was feeling very uncomfortable being talked at in a strange language.

Delia didn't know what to say or do, all the past events of the day had suddenly caught up with her, the sleepless night, the early morning start, the stress of wearing a face mask with the thought of the risk of catching the Corona virus never far from her thoughts. She thumbed through her small Spanish phrase book, keeping her head down, avoiding any sort of eye contact with Paco.

Paco stood up from his chair and then walked to the back of the shop, disappearing through a small doorway, then Horace and Delia could hear footsteps and muffled voices coming through the ceiling from up above.

Horace took a few steps forward. "He must be upstairs," he said, "what the heck did you say to him?"

Then there was the sound of more movement and footsteps, coming from overhead and then suddenly a young boy appeared, followed by Paco a few seconds later.

He could have been anywhere between eight to twelve years old; he was very slim and his hair had been cut very short around the back and sides with the remainder greased down onto the top of his head. He smiled, first at Delia and then at Horace. "How can I help you?" he asked in perfect English.

Horace retreated a few more stepped backwards, for one, the young lad wasn't wearing a face mask and secondly, Horace wasn't very comfortable talking to children, especially ones who appeared to be much more intelligent for their years.

Delia smiled back and completely opposite to Horace she took a few steps forward, she was more than happy to talk with the young lad, much more comfortable talking with children and in most cases much more so than their parents, that had been her job for so many years.

"We are looking for the man who works in the estate agency next door, Sebastian?"

The boy turned slightly and spoke with his father.

His father replied and seemed to be rattling off everything that he had said before but this time even faster and seemed to be getting a little more excited.

Paco eventually stopped talking after waving his arms around and pointing out into the street several times and then panting and sweating, he then slumped down onto his chair behind the counter.

The young lad took in a deep breath and then began.

"My father said that Sebastian has gone, vamoosed, taken off, many people appear to be looking for him, and only yesterday some very big ugly men came into the shop and asked my father if he knew where he was. They were very rude and one of the men took cans of beer from the cooler and they drank them in the shop without paying for them, and one of the other men shook his can violently before opening it and aimed the squirting froth towards my father."

"They said that they would be back in a few days and then left, my father is worried that Sebastian has gotten himself involved with the wrong type of people and is worried they will soon come back."

Delia didn't know what to say or do, she turned to Horace, he was standing there, just a few steps behind, motionless, as if he had been frozen or turned to stone.

"It's like all my worst fears and nightmares about buying a villa in Spain have actually happened, for real," Horace suddenly blurted out, before his mouth turned very dry inside and his throat felt like it was slowly closing up, he then wished that he had saved some of the bottled water.

Delia turned around once again, facing the young lad and Paco who was still sitting down, opening her small bag she took out a sales document from Spanish white villas in the sun. "Do you know where this man's office is?" Delia pointed to the name and address of the solicitor that was printed in bold letters at the top of the paper.

The young lad took the piece of paper from Delia and handed it to his father.

Paco's face looked much relieved, he didn't understand what was written in the letter but he immediately recognised the solicitor's name on the heading. Paco stood up and then handed the letter back to Delia, he appeared to be much happier now, knowing that Horace and Delia seemed to be law-abiding citizens and were not there to smash the place up. He now spoke with a much slower calmer voice.

"My father said that Senor Benitez is a good honest man," the young lad translated, "he is the best lawyer in town, but he won't be at his office now, it is too late in the day."

Delia turned once again to Horace, this time even more desperate than the last, hoping for some kind of input or guidance or advice on what they should do next. Horace was now feeling very hot and faint and was also having problems with his breathing.

Delia's and Paco's eyes followed him as he slowly made his way towards the chiller cabinet, opening the door and taking out a bottle of water. Everyone watched Horace as he gulped down the cold water, eventually taking the bottle from his lips and holding on to the chiller cabinet, he looked at Delia and said, "I feel like I am going to faint."

The young lad was the first one to respond; shuffling past his father, he dragged the chair from behind the counter, placing it in front of Horace, the young lad's father quickly cleaned the chair with an alcohol solution before gesticulating to Horace to sit down. Horace sat down on the wooden chair.

"What is your name?" Delia asked turning to the young lad, feeling so grateful that Paco had such an intelligent helpful young son, she would have felt very proud of him if he had attended her school, the perfect student.

"Paco," the young lad answered, "me llamo Paco."

Delia smiled affectionately, she had understood exactly what the young lad had just said.

"Me llamo Delia," she replied, "me llamo Delia."

Sitting much closer to the floor on the wooden chair didn't seem to be helping Horace to feel any better or to cool down, the marble flooring of Paco's mini mart had slowly warmed up over the summer months and if anything, Horace was now feeling even hotter.

He probably would have been much better off standing inside the drinks chiller cabinet or clinging on to the outside of the cold frosted door. His head and thoughts were now in a complete mess, he had arrived in Spain full of confidence and feeling really good about himself. The short period of time that he had spent working for Mr Mumford at Bakelite Electronics, the self-confidence and self-esteem that he had built up from the feelings of being wanted and being a valuable asset to the small company had now all totally gone.

All the thoughts of owning a new villa in Spain and playing golf when he felt the urge had all been flushed down the crapper along with his three hundred thousand euros.

Delia was also feeling bad, all her dreams and enthusiasm that she had built for moving into a brand-new white Spanish villa and building a new life in Spain had suddenly rocked and then crumpled into the dust.

She looked at Horace sitting there in the chair, sweating and panting like a tired old dog, she had made a huge mistake bringing a man with milky white freckled skin and ginger hair to Spain.

She turned once again to young Paco. "Does your father know where we can find a bed for the night?"

Young Paco once again turned to his father, "She wants to know where they can buy a bed tonight?"

Paco senior scratched his head, why would these people want to buy a bed?

There is nowhere around here, he thought, they would have to travel back along the motorway to one of the big towns.

As far as he could remember, no one had ever bought a bed in the village, everyone's beds had been made from solid wood and had been handed down through the generations. Occasionally, some people would buy a new mattress, but most people would just get the old one refilled.

Paco looked at Delia and then towards Horace, sitting in the chair, his face and neck all red and sweaty.

He turned to young Paco, "Ask them if they want to rent our flat for a few days, tell them they can have it for fifty euros a night."

Young Paco looked at Delia, "my father said you can rent our flat for a few days if you want for fifty euros a night."

Delia turned and looked at Horace, "what do you think?"

"Anything," Horace said, "anywhere where we can get out of this heat and have a nice cool shower."

"Yes, that would be fine," Delia said, "thank you very much, you have been more than helpful."

Delia then paid Paco senior for the bottle of water and they both followed young Paco out of the shop and back down the hill, the way they had come earlier.

The path was old and narrow and was never built with the idea of social distancing in mind, Delia followed Paco and Horace followed Delia, occasionally passing by the odd person on their way up, walking in the opposite direction.

Horace was now feeling a lot better, the sun was now behind them and walking back down the high street was much easier than the journey that they had made earlier, coming up.

Delia and then Horace, followed young Paco all the way down to the bottom of the road, passing the gap between the two rows of town houses and the carpark, where they had left the hire car. There were passing more houses than shops now, Horace and Delia could now see that they were heading down towards the quieter end of the village.

The road then began to curve around to the left and by now there were only a few houses on either side, some of the houses had their front doors open.

Delia and Horace both looked into some of the open doorways and into the darkness and the stillness as if everything and everyone were still taking an afternoon siesta, sleeping.

Then what seemed like the end of the village and sitting a lot further back from the road, unlike the painted white town houses that sat on the side with the narrow pathway somehow squeezed in front, there stood a large white apartment block. There was a wide grass area that sat well back from the road and in front were orange and lemon trees planted, and well-maintained gardens with colourful flowers.

There was a wide pathway that had been laid with orange bricks that led directly to the black steel fencing that surrounded the building and a large steel gate.

Horace caught up with Delia for the first time since leaving the shop they were able to walk side by side. Horace grabbed hold of Delia's hand. "This is a lot better than what I expected," he said. "I imagined a pokey little room above a shop with no air conditioning and a load of washing hanging out in the backyard."

Young Paco took a small white card out from his pocket and ran it past a small scanner mounted on the wall and the black steel gate opened with a click.

He then held on to the gate handle, holding it open for Horace and Delia to pass through and then let it go and the gate closed with a bang.

They then followed Paco through an archway that went under the building that led them through to a private garden with palm trees rising up from a square grassed area with a swimming pool in the centre and a pathway running around the outside. They followed Paco along the pathway and around the pool to the other side, he then pushed a door bell on one of the doors.

Horace and Delia stood on the wide pathway that seemed to run along the front of the apartments with a stairway at each end, rising up to the three floors of apartments above.

A minute or so passed, there didn't seem to be any sign of life coming from the other side of the door.

The whole journey from the shop with Paco junior had been done in silence and now Horace and Delia felt awkward standing there, they didn't know who or what was on the other side of the door or why they were there.

Young Paco reached out and pushed the doorbell once again, but this time holding it in for an embarrassing amount of time before letting it go, he smiled at Horace and Delia and raised his eyebrows as if all three were sharing some kind of a joke.

Horace, not knowing what to do or say, turned away and glanced around the pool area, it was very quiet, quiet enough that he could hear the sound of the water pumping out from the nozzles around the edge of the pool. Then suddenly, breaking the silence, there was the sound of locks and catches being undone and slid back. The door slowly opened just wide enough for a very old looking, sun-dried wrinkled face to peer out.

Young Paco began to talk very quickly in Spanish, the old woman muttered a few words, looking past Paco and towards Horace and Delia. Young Paco then turned and spoke to Horace and Delia. "This is Maisie," he said, "she is an English lady and she will show you the flat."

Then Paco was gone, walking back around the pool, before disappearing through the archway.

Maisie muttered something and then closed the door.

Horace turned to Delia, "What did she say?"

"I am not sure, I think she said mask," Delia replied.

After a few minutes more, the door opened again and Maisie stepped out into the bright late afternoon sunshine, she was wearing a dark blue track suit and a larger than normal black face mask. Maisie pulled the door shut while giving Horace and Delia the once over, looking at them both up and down.

"Didn't expect to see anyone from England this year," she mumbled from behind her mask, "don't blame me if the place is all dirty, and it will be red hot inside, the air con hasn't been on for almost a year."

For someone who looked so old and leathery, Maisie seemed to be very sprightly on her feet and moved very quickly along the path and up the stairs to the first floor.

Maisie suddenly turned, "Where is all your luggage?" she said, from behind her mask and looking at them through her squinty eyes.

Horace had maintained a safe distance behind Delia, he wasn't expecting to meet anyone else along the way, especially Maisie.

She seemed a little bit scary, even more so than before, especially now with the black face mask, he thought it would be best leaving Delia to do all the talking, while he maintained a safe distance off around two metres.

"We don't have much," Delia answered, "just a couple of small cabin bags and one suitcase that are in the hire car."

Maisie turned, unlocking the door, "You stay here," she said, "I will have a quick flit around and turn on the aircon."

Maisie came back out after around ten minutes, sweating profusely, her head was all hot and sweaty and her strawberry blond sun-kissed hair was all stuck to the top of her head. She had droplets of sweat on her forehead and they were running down her face and onto her face mask, making it all wet.

"You can't go in there for at least an hour," she panted. "I have left the aircon on high boost, normally in the summer months, I would normally turn the aircon on at least a day or so before anyone arrives. If you go for a slow walk and collect your car, there is a carpark around the back, the entrance is just past the apartments, you will easily find it."

"Where can we find somewhere to eat?" Delia asked.

"If you go back out of the main gate and turn right, then if you cross the road, about fifty metres up on the left there is a pathway that runs in between two houses, you should find something through there."

Maisie held out her hand, offering the door keys to Delia, then a white key card for the entrance gate.

"If you have any problems, you know where to find me," she said, then moving forward with both her arms out to the sides as if she was shooing sheep, she ushered them back down the stairs.

Horace was now feeling much better than he had felt earlier, even though it was still very hot, the sun had gone down much lower in the sky and he didn't need to wear his sunglasses. He had pulled his face mask away from around his nose a little, that allowed him to breathe a lot better.

Once back at the hire car, Horace opened the door and was immediately hit by the rush of hot air escaping from the inside.

Horace leaned inside and quickly started the car, then he turned on the aircon, before quickly retreating and shutting the door, a trick that he had learned from Sebastian the year earlier.

Once the car had cooled sufficiently enough to enter, Horace drove the car out of the carpark, finding the journey around the one-way system and then to the carpark behind the apartment block amazingly, straight forward and simple.

They had both decided not to bother with unloading the suitcase, they both by now were feeling desperately hungry, holding hands they followed Maisie's directions through the gap in-between the houses and into a small square.

Horace or Delia didn't feel the need to stop and take in the surrounding architecture, or admire the four-tear water feature, with the water cascading down from the top tier. They both had immediately spotted a small restaurant directly ahead and a friendly waiter standing outside, he seemed equally pleased to see them as they were to see him.

They both sat down at the nearest table in front of the restaurant, normally Horace would check the prices on the menu and Delia would look around to see what other people were eating but there was no one else there, and Horace needed to eat something and quick, whatever the cost.

Carlos, the waiter, with all his years of experience could tell that Horace and Delia were both English and handed them both an English menu, as soon as they had settled.

"Good evening, sir, good evening, madam," he smiled, "would you like a drink?"

Delia had already run her finger down the menu, "water for me please and the sirloin steak with vegetables, por favor."

Horace felt so hungry he would have eaten anything, "Yes that's fine," he said, "and the same for me please."

Carlos was back within a few minutes, carrying a tray containing two glasses, two bottles of water and a small boat-shaped basket with warm crispy bread rolls cut into halves, with garlic butter slowly melting on the top.

Within a few minutes, the warm bread had all disappeared and Horace and Delia had finished off their small bottles of water.

As if Carlos had been watching them, waiting for his cue, he reappeared carrying a bottle of red wine, "our house red," he said, "compliments with the meal."

Carlos turned over the upturned wine glasses on the table and then pulled the cork out from the bottle, after placing the bottle on the table, he went back inside the restaurant.

Horace was relieved that he wasn't asked to sample the wine first, and swiftly poured Delia and then himself a full glass. Horace had never been much of a wine connoisseur, but this tasted good, quite sweet and fruity and it had been a real long pig of a day. Delia also felt the strong need to drink, and by the time their steak dinner had arrived, between them they had polished of the whole bottle.

"Another bottle of your excellent house red," Delia said, her voice sounding uncharacteristically slurry.

Later that evening somehow, they both made it back to the apartment.

The credit card-sized key card had been a blessing, and once through the gate, they only missed falling into the pool by a few inches. Delia somehow managed to push the key into the front door of the apartment and they both bundled in together. Horace tugged at his clothes at the same time as he fell face down onto the bed.

Delia, while sitting on the bed, managed to get undressed and then sliding under the duvet, she mumbled, "We have no work, we have lost all our money and now we are both a couple of winos."

Chapter 20

When Horace awoke the next morning, he didn't have a clue to where he was or how he had managed to get there. He was lying on the top of a strange bed, fully dressed and his head was hanging over the side. Even though he had slept fully clothed, the whole of his body was freezing cold, with the air conditioning set on high boost, pumping out very cold air directly onto him.

Desperately, he grabbed at the bedclothes, doing his best to defy gravity, trying to pull himself back onto the bed. Slowly, he slid downwards, his head hit the hard white marble flooring first, followed by the rest of his body and then the lightweight printed patterned summer duvet, dropping down, covering his head.

Somehow, he managed to roll over onto his front and crawl out backwards, along the gap between the bed and the wall.

Slowly he stood up, the room was very dark with no natural light coming in from anywhere, rubbing his head he looked around the room, Delia was still sleeping, her white body easily visible, lying there on the bed naked.

Horace very carefully covered her over with the duvet and then began the search around, looking for the air con controller. He soon realised that he would never find it, not without switching a light on, and not wanting to wake Delia, he abandoned the search for a more urgent need, like a desperate trip to the bathroom. He groped his way out of the bedroom and into the small hallway, looking for the toilet.

Once inside the toilet, Horace felt much warmer, He slid his trousers and pants down and sat down on the seat, then resting his elbows on the top of his knees and holding his head in his hands, he drifted back to sleep.

Sometime later, Horace was awoken by Delia, frantically calling his name, then the toilet door burst open, Delia was standing in the doorway, completely naked, except her black face mask, hanging from one ear.

"Oh god, Horace," she said, "Thank god, when I awoke and you weren't there, I was so worried, I thought I might have left you somewhere. I need to use the toilet, darling, and then have a warm shower, I am freezing cold, I feel like I have been sleeping in the fridge all night."

Horace closed the bathroom door behind him and then turned on the light switch, while standing in the doorway of the lounge area.

It felt just as cold inside as it did in the bedroom, he then spotted the controller, sitting on a bracket mounted on the wall, he quickly pushed the red button at the top. He then set about opening the shutters that were all closed down on every window, pulling down on a woven material band, he slowly raised the shutters, one by one.

Then he set about searching through the kitchen cupboards in the kitchenette, opening all the doors, hoping to find some coffee.

Delia appeared in the doorway with a white towel wrapped around her body. "Well, it's nothing like the Hotel Golf and Mountain Resort, Buena Vista," she said, looking around, "and this towel could be a lot softer."

"There's no coffee," Horace said, "nothing, maybe I should take the car and go and buy a few things."

"I don't think you should be driving just yet," Delia said, "we don't want any more problems, but you can fetch the case from the car, and then we can go out for something, and then maybe call the solicitor."

Horace's need for a cup of hot coffee was much greater than his need to have a warm shower. His throat felt so dry, He desperately needed to drink something, anything would do, even water, there was nothing in the apartment, the fridge was completely empty and he didn't want to risk drinking the water from the tap.

By the time he had fetched the case from the car, Delia had slipped into a summer dress, she had managed to find the controller for the air conditioning unit in the bedroom and had turned the darn thing off.

Delia had just enough time to grab her small bag and her face mask, before Horace hustled her out of the apartment and down the stairs.

As soon as the steel gate had slammed shut behind them, Horace soon quickly realised that he had been much too hasty, and he had forgotten his straw hat and sunglasses and he hadn't covered his face and neck in factor fifty sunscreen. The sun was already up high above in the sky, and now that they were outside, it felt so much hotter than the day before, Horace grabbed hold of Delia's hand. "Let's see if we can find something in the small square, where we were last night," he said, putting his head down and pulling her along.

The small restaurant, where they had eaten the night before was all closed up, all the tables and chairs had been taken away and the shutters were down.

To the left-hand side, there was what looked like a bakery, with tables and chairs outside with large white parasols shading the people, who were drinking coffee and eating churros. Horace and Delia sat down at an empty table, a young woman, wearing a black blouse and skirt, came over, smiling, "Buenos Dias."

"Dos café con leche por favor," Delia said, she had been practicing her Spanish phrases from her pocket book on the journey over on the plane and what to say, when asking for two coffees, along the way.

"Grande," Horace croaked, gesticulating with both his hands the size of cup that he would like, more like the size of a bucket than a cup.

The young woman beamed a huge smile towards Delia and then chuckled.

Horace had picked up the word, grande, from Paco the shop owner, he had used the word repeatedly when describing the big men that had come to the shop and had squirted him with the can of beer.

Delia looked at Horace, he had surprised her, he had already learnt a Spanish word, but he did look a complete mess, like a wino living in a shop doorway.

What was left of Horace's hair was all sticking up and the smart summer shirt that he had worn the day before was now all creased and stained from the red wine that they had drunk the night before.

The young lady swiftly returned with two large cups of milky frothy coffee and placed them in front of Horace and Delia.

"Churros?" she smiled.

Horace and Delia looked at each other, Delia had exhausted her knowledge of Spanish, asking for two coffees with milk and Horace had already stepped out from within his comfort zone, surprising her with the word, grande.

"Si," Horace replied, "grande."

The young women returned, within two minutes carrying a tray with a huge plate of long round pastry shapes, two medium sized cups of liquid chocolate and a pile of paper serviettes. Horace and Delia both looked at each other and then at the huge pile of round light brown objects piled up on the plate in front of them.

"Well, at least we won't be hungry today," Horace said.

Delia had a quick glance around, most of the people sitting at the other tables were eating the same thing, some of them were dipping them into their coffee, but most of them into their chocolate before biting off the end.

Delia broke off a small piece and put it into the chocolate, just enough to coat the end.

"They really are very good," Delia smiled, "some kind of a fried batter mix I would imagine, must be very high in calories."

Horace picked up one of the pieces and plunged it into the cup of chocolate until it hit the bottom, somehow, he managed to get the whole of the end into his mouth before the brown liquid dripped off, onto his already wine-stained shirt.

"Yes, they are," Horace smiled, quickly finishing the rest and then reaching for another.

Delia lifted her small bag from the table and took out her mobile.

"I am going to call the solicitor, Angel Benitez," she said, "I'm hoping that he can help us get our money back."

Angel Benitez didn't occupy a grand building with a large frontage with its own carpark and grass and shrubs, like the solicitor back in England, Mr Pendleton. His office was a small commercial building that could easily be converted back into small restaurant or a shop or a bar.

When he answered his phone, he wasn't surprised to hear the sound of Delia's voice, but he was surprised to hear that she was here in Spain, and from what she had described, she was sitting in the square, just outside his office window.

Looking out of his office window from the first floor, he could see the English lady sitting there at one of the tables, with the phone to her ear.

Delia took the phone down from her ear, and then put it back into her bag, "He is coming to meet us here," she said, "in about five minutes."

Delia then took out a small packet of cleansing wipes and a small make up mirror from her bag. Then looking into her mirror, she wiped around her mouth, before applying some light pink lipstick.

What with the intense heat, and Horace waking that morning with a very dry sore throat, he had momentarily forgotten about the reason for what they were doing and why they were there in Spain. As soon as Delia had picked up her phone, his feelings of panic and anxiety had all come flooding back.

The thought of losing three hundred euros with both of them now unemployed felt like a recurring nightmare, and his throat began to tighten up again, like it was slowly closing up. Dunking the churros into chocolate seemed to be helping lubricate his throat and keep the airway open.

The sweet tasting chocolate seemed to be keeping him calm, as if it was acting like some kind of happy drug, making him feel slightly better and a little less anxious. One by one he worked his way through the whole plateful of churros, finishing off his cup of chocolate before sliding the second cup towards him, and swiftly downing it in one go.

Angel Benitez arrived at their table only a few minutes after Delia had put all the things back into her bag and Horace had just polished off the very last of the churros and the two cups of chocolate.

He was a slim man, in his early fifties, he was wearing a short-sleeved white shirt, black trousers and a light blue medically approved face mask. In normal times, he would have shaken Horace by the hand and given Delia a kiss on either cheek, but nowadays, in Spain, everyone was following the very strict rules of social distancing.

He introduced himself from the other side of the table, pulling out the chair opposite and sat down, siting back in his chair and raising his right hand, catching the young women's attention, he said, "Hola."

The same young woman who had served them earlier came over; Angel ordered a black coffee and then asked Delia and then Horace if they wanted anything. Delia said that she would like a glass of water and Horace said that he would have another coffee.

"It is a pleasure to meet you both," Angel started, "I only wish it was under better circumstances."

Angel looked across the table towards Delia, he hadn't been disappointed, she was exactly how he had imagined her, tall, slim with good posture and beautiful white skin. Mostly all Spanish women were beautiful, with their very dark hair and olive coloured skin, but Angel had always preferred very white English women, ever since he fell in love with his English teacher, when he was studying at the university in Madrid many years ago.

"Do you think you could help us?" Delia asked. "We drove past the site on our way here yesterday, there doesn't appear to be anything there, nothing at all."

"Yes," Horace interjected, "it looks like this Sebastian guy has taken all our money and buggered off."

Angel looked across the table at Horace, how did this chump manage to snare and catch such a beautiful woman like Delia? This guy looked like a complete slob, for one, he looked like he was still wearing the same clothes from the day before, and it looked like his shirt was all stained from red wine, he hadn't even bothered to shave or comb his hair.

"My fee is fifty euros an hour," Angel said, "I can do a lot of work in an hour; if you want, I can go back to the office and start straight away."

"That is so kind of you," Delia said, at last having some feelings of hope and all was not lost, then suddenly feeling very emotional, her eyes filling with water.

Angel wanted to take Delia into his arms and wipe away her tears with a white silk hanky. He looked across the table at Horace, the sun had just crept around slightly and was now just catching the side of Horace's neck and left shoulder.

Amazingly, Horace hadn't noticed that his head was slowly getting hotter and the chocolate around his mouth was beginning to trickle down onto his chin. Hopefully, this guy will catch sunstroke before the day is out, Angel thought to himself, just enough for him to be rushed off in an ambulance to the hospital in Granada. Just for a few days, then he could spend more time talking and getting to know the beautiful, elegant white-skinned English woman, Delia, who was sitting opposite.

Angel finished his coffee. "I must get back to the office," he said, "we can meet here again tomorrow morning at around ten thirty. It's much better that we meet outside in the fresh air than sitting in a stuffy office with all of us having to wear face masks."

As soon as Horace had left the table and the refuge of the shade under the large white parasol, he could feel the full strength of the July sun burning down directly on to the top of his head.

"I am going to make a dash for it," he said to Delia who was still sitting under the parasol finishing her glass of water.

"I won't be able to get back through the security gate," she said, quickly finishing her drink and following Horace, who by now was speed walking with his head down towards the gap that led out of from the square.

Walking with his head bent forward, like a hunchback, soon created a new problem, he could feel the sun burning the back of his neck. "I must remember to wear my straw hat at all times," Horace shouted to Delia, then doing his very best to up the pace.

Delia quickly spotted the dangers of walking along on such a narrow path, with one's head down. Fearing Horace could quite easily crash into someone, she quickly overtook Horace, clearing the way and forcing anyone walking towards them, off from the path and into the road.

Once they were back safely inside the apartment, Horace leapt into the shower, leaving Delia in the kitchenette, trying to remove the stains from his shirt with their holiday-size bottle of shower gel. Delia passed the shower gel through the sliding door of the shower to Horace and then went back into the kitchenette to check out the washing machine. Then she set about gathering up the rest of Horace's clothes and put them into the machine, then collecting her own dirty laundry from the bedroom, she pushed it into the washing machine and closed the door.

The apartment was beginning feel very hot and stuffy inside so Delia opened all the windows, hoping to catch some of the fresh mountain breezes that seemed to blow towards the rear of the building. Quickly checking through the cupboards, it was obvious there was no washing powder for the machine, and there was nothing inside the fridge either.

Delia went into the bedroom and rubbed a generous portion of suntan lotion onto her face and neck and then her arms and legs.

"I am popping out for some washing powder, darling," she shouted through the bathroom door, then putting on her sun hat and gathering up the keys, she exited the apartment, checking that she still had her Spanish phrase book safely tucked inside her bag.

Not wanting to walk back up to the top of the hill to Paco's mini mart, Delia walked up as far as a smaller shop that she had noticed, on the way down, the day before.

Delia purchased some freshly sliced ham from the fresh meat counter and then a bag of fresh mixed salad, a tub of spreadable butter, a carton of long-life milk and two long, freshly baked French sticks, a one litre bottle of liquid soap for the washing machine and a large bottle of drinking water.

Delia walked slowly back down the hill, carrying the carrier bag with the groceries in one hand and the five litres of bottled water in the other.

She was feeling pleased with herself, in spite of having the money worries concerning the villa always at the back of her mind, she had successfully completed her first shop in a Spanish village, and with the help of her phrase book everyone seemed to have understood her. She rather liked the idea of staying in the apartment in the village, mixing with the local people and having to speak Spanish.

Staying at the Hotel Golf and Mountain Resort Buena Vista, had been a wonderful experience and she would have never ever dreamed of renting an apartment in a Spanish village before.

Horace would have never agreed on such a crazy notion, but now that they were here, she was enjoying the new experience of Spanish village life. As soon as Delia opened the front door of the apartment, to the sound of Horace, shouting, shoo, shoo, she dropped the shopping at the door and rushed inside.

A very large ginger fluffy cat was guarding the bathroom door and continuously meowing at Horace, who was trapped inside. As soon as the cat spotted Delia, it abandoned Horace and began to affectionately rub itself around Delia's legs and purr.

"Get rid of it!" Horace shouted. "Before I have one of my allergic reactions, I have been trapped in here for at least an hour."

Delia tried to lure the cat towards the open doorway, but the large ginger puss, was having none of it. Instead, it boldly walked into the sitting room and jumped up onto the sofa. Delia fetched the bag of groceries from just inside the door and carried them inside to the small kitchen area, then unwrapping the freshly sliced ham, she tore off a small piece and waved it around in front of the ginger furred fluff ball.

The cat quickly jumped off from the sofa and followed Delia to the front door, she flung the ham into the passageway and slammed the front door shut.

"I don't understand how the darn thing got in here in the first place," Horace said, walking into the bedroom, checking his sinuses for mucus.

"That is probably my fault," Delia said, smiling to herself, "I opened all the windows before I went out."

Delia went back into the kitchen and poured some of the detergent into the washing machine and then selected a forty-degrees coloured wash.

Horace was then suddenly screaming and sneezing in the bedroom. "It's back in here again! It's on the bed!"

Delia quickly moved around the apartment closing all the windows, then tearing off another piece of ham, she went into the bedroom. Horace had opened the wardrobe door and was standing behind, with his head peering around the side, while the cat was playfully rolling around on top of the bed. As soon as the cat spotted Delia and the ham, it was off from the bed like a rocket and was already standing, purring, waiting for Delia to open the door.

The cat darted into the passageway outside, waiting for Delia to throw the ham, meowing excitedly in anticipation.

Delia tossed the piece of ham out into the passageway, quickly closing the door, Horace was back inside the shower, rubbing shower gel all over his body, as if he had been contaminated by a sudden nuclear fallout.

Delia put the shopping away and then decided to check out the cupboard in the hallway; much to her delight there were two comfortable relaxer chairs sitting just inside the door.

Horace came out of the shower, mumbling to himself about cat hair and the effect that it had on him. Delia went into the bedroom. "Maybe we could sit around the pool today," she said, "it is much too hot to do anything else.

Delia put the suitcase onto the bed and began to unpack, putting their clothes into the dark wooden double wardrobe. Then she flung Horace's swimming shorts across the bed towards him, then quickly getting undressed, she pulled on her swimsuit.

"There's no point in us getting dressed," Delia said, "it is much too hot in here and we can't have the windows open, because of the cat."

"I think I may have some cat hair stuck in my throat," Horace said, "and my arms feel all itchy."

"You can relax now, darling, it won't be able to get back in here now and I will make us a nice cup of coffee."

"Did you get any biscuits?" Horace said, making sure all his lumpy bits were tucked away inside his new black elasticated swim shorts.

"No," Delia replied, "but we can have some nice fresh ham and salad rolls for lunch and we can eat them around the pool later."

Chapter 21

The next morning, the Spanish solicitor, Angel Benitez, arrived at his office around nine thirty as normal. The office being situated on the first floor had its advantages and disadvantages.

The main advantage being the view from the window into the pretty square down below and the mountains of Granada in the distance always surrounded by the pale blue sky. Then, of course, the very big disadvantage, was being on the first floor, much closer to the sun, with no shade, and the excessive heat, with the aircon switched on all day and night. His wife, Catalina, hadn't been to the office for over six months, she had just taken off suddenly one morning, saying she was going to visit her mother.

Then, with the COVID-19 pandemic and her mother being of the age of the most vulnerable, Catalina had decided to stay for a while.

Angel had met Catalina at University, at that time she was very close to her father, who spoilt her rotten, he handed over a huge wad of money to Angel on their wedding day, telling Angel to look after his baby girl and set up their own business.

For the first ten years of their marriage, life was very good for Angel and Catalina, him being a solicitor and her being an accountant, both working together in the same office, situated on the first floor and the view of the pretty square down below.

Behind their main office, was a much smaller room, just big enough for a double bed, where Angel and Catalina would take their afternoon siesta, making love every afternoon before falling asleep in each other's arms.

But then suddenly, Catalina began to take on too much work, instead of jumping into bed with Angel and giggling, she would go downstairs to the bakery and then return with a huge take away coffee and a large bag of fresh cream cakes.

Then sitting at her desk and working through the whole lunch period, systematically clicking away on her computer and filling her mouth with huge mouthfuls of cake.

Angel at first was devastated, desperate and longing for the feel of her naked passionate body against his, he would try to lure her into the backroom with packets of cakes or large bars of chocolate. Instead of filling her afternoons with wild passionate sex, every lunch time, Catalina would be munching on cakes and biscuits.

She began to call her mother, by this time her father had moved on to his fourth wife, always opting for a much younger woman, the new one only being two years older than Catalina.

Catalina quickly got very fat and began to look very much like her mother, she began to wear glasses and would be forever sliding them up and down her nose, which annoyed the hell out of Angel, who was always sitting opposite.

Over the years, Angel had remained loyal to Catalina, occasionally, they would still have sex, normally at home very late at night, after Catalina had bombed herself out on her favourite Spanish red wine.

Angel checked the office phone for massages, then gathering up the A4-sized file he had prepared for Horace and Delia, he locked up the office and quickly made his way down the stairs and into the square.

He chose a good table with a large white parasol that provided a lot of shade and he ordered a strong black coffee without sugar.

Around ten-twenty, Angel ordered himself a second cup of coffee and a croissant, while he watched the opening between the houses that led into the square. He was very pleased to see Delia walking towards him, she was wearing a large lemon coloured sunhat and a long flowery patterned summer dress.

His heart sank when Horace appeared a few seconds later, he had been hoping that the knob of an English guy had been incapacitated with severe sunstroke or at the very least, a severe case of Spanish tum.

To make things even worse, it looked like the white-faced English guy had upped his game a little and had spent the whole morning in the shower; he had brushed his hair and smelt of scented soap or shower gel. Hiding his disappointment, Angel stood up and greeted them both with a Buenos dias and a smile.

Angel called the young waitress over, Delia said that she just wanted a cappuccino and Horace said he would have the same. Angel then started by opening the folder and taking a deep breath. "I have spent some time looking into your problem and have compiled this report. Some time ago, a large body of investors purchased a huge area of land from the regional government. They built the Hotel Golf and Mountain Resort Buena Vista and the surrounding golf course. After the golf course had been completed, over to the north side, they had a wide strip of land reserved for a road and a row of front-line villas. They offered the contract for the construction of the villas to a company called Spanish white villas in the sun."

"When the first of the villas were almost completed, the construction company gave the job to the local estate agent, Sebastian Blanca, to market and to sell all the villas. Sebastian Blanca originally arrived here in Spain from south America, at that time he had set up a small estate agency in the village, but was struggling to survive."

"When Sebastian was approached by the company, Spanish white villas in the sun, he very conveniently changed his name to Sebastian White, giving people the impression that he had a strong connection to the company whom he was marketing the villas for."

"Sebastian did extremely well, selling all the villas at the top asking prices and made an awful lot of money for the large company that built the golf course and Spanish white villas in the sun, and for himself with the large commissions."

"One of the big selling points that Sebastian used was that the potential buyers would have fantastic views, out over the golf course from the front of the villas. And uninterrupted views, looking out over the unspoilt open space of the Spanish countryside, and in the distance the mountains of Granada, from the rear of all the villas. At that time Sebastian genuinely believed that he was telling the truth and all the land that had been originally purchased for building, had been built on, with the line of the rear gardens running along the edge of the boundary."

"Then after the success and the completion of all the sales of the villas and making a good healthy profit, Spanish white villas in the sun then decided to apply to the regional government to buy some more land, big enough to build another road behind and another row of villas."

"Spanish white villas in the sun didn't want to risk all their profits purchasing the extra land, so they then approached Sebastian, asking him to sell the idea of off-plan properties, hoping to accumulate enough money to buy the extra land, then they would use their own money for the construction."

"When the lorries and diggers arrived and began to clear a space for the new road, all the people in the original villas got very angry and complained to the major and the local council. The mayor and the local council didn't have the power to do anything, the land had been sold by the regional government for construction and they had to grant the planning permission for the road and one more row of villas."

"But you drew up all the sales agreements for us," Delia, interjected, "why didn't you warn us if you thought the building of the extra houses were if not illegal, morally wrong?"

"Sebastian and Spanish villas in the sun, at that time, were my clients and up to that point they had acted very professionally. My hands were tied," Angel said solemnly, "there was nothing I could do, they weren't breaking any laws and I was still their legal representative. If I hadn't drawn up the agreement, they would have found someone else, and I was their solicitor."

"So, how do we get our money back?" Horace said, wishing that he had been born with a much stronger physique, enough to be able to punch Angel one in the eye, maybe give him a bit of a kicking while he rolled around on the floor.

Angel turned the first page of his report over and continued, "last November, while the construction workers were laying the pipe work for the drainage for the new houses and the road, they discovered some Roman artefacts. As soon as the mayor got to hear about it, he could then use his power and declare the site an archaeological dig and closed the whole place down."

"A team of experts arrived from Madrid and they spent the whole of November, December and January, sifting through all the site, using small hand trowels, and gently cleaning everything with small brushes. February, the site was officially recognised by the Spanish government as a site of historical interest and gave the go ahead for a full-size archaeological dig. Then in March, Spain went into a full national lock down in an effort to stop the COVID-19 virus from spreading any further."

"Somehow at that point, Sebastian disappeared," Angel continued, "his apartment appears to have been abandoned, his mobile phone has been turned off and his car has gone."

Horace suddenly felt very sick, and his arms were itching like crazy, not knowing if it was an allergic reaction from the ginger cat or the dreadful news, that Angel had just presented him with.

Delia was also suffering, her lips felt very dry and all the feelings of guilt and anxiety had all come flooding back. "Could I have a glass of water please?" she asked.

Angel looked around for the waitress, then springing to his feet, "I will fetch us some water," he said, before disappearing inside.

"The bastard has probably done a runner, like the other crooks," Horace said, angrily, scratching his arms, "the bastard is probably climbing out through the toilet window right now as we speak."

Angel returned just a few minutes later with the young waitress, she was carrying a tray with various sized bottles of water and three glasses. Delia poured herself a glass of cool still water, while Horace opened a bottle of sparkling spring water.

"I have contacted Spanish white villas in the sun," Angel said, "I have sent them an email, informing them that they have broken their contract, failing to build your villa as agreed, asking them to return your money in full."

Angel pushed the cardboard folder across the table towards Horace and Delia, "I am still waiting for them to respond," he said. "I do feel very bad about all this, I won't charge you for any of my time," Angel said, "not until we get all your money returned in full. I must now get back to the office," Angel said, quickly standing up, "I have paid for the coffees and the water, hopefully, I will have some good news for you very soon. I will leave my report with you, it has my office number and email and my personal mobile number, as soon as I hear back from Spanish white villas in the sun, I will call you."

Delia lent back in her chair and poured herself some more water, all the feelings of guilt and anxiety that she had suffered from in January, were all now flooding back in a huge way, once again she felt really bad about everything, all this was all her fault. If she hadn't been so naïve, being lured here to Spain on a whim and what now seemed to have been a bogus raffle ticket and the thought of a free holiday.

Since she had been sold that winning ticket, it had changed their lives completely, most probably forever. This time last year, she was the headmistress of the local junior school, taking on the extra work, marking exam papers for schools and colleges during her holidays. But now, one year later, she was a nobody, a nobody who had nothing, stranded helplessly in a foreign country.

Horace appeared to be suffering much more than herself, as well as scratching his arms he was now rubbing the top of his head, just sitting there, rocking slightly back and forth, just staring, not saying anything.

She was so thankful that Angel had dealt with the legal side of things and not turned Sebastian away. Like Angel had said, Sebastian would have easily found another solicitor, maybe someone from South America, just like him, disappearing, as soon as things got a little bit too sticky.

At least while they had Angel, there was hope, he seemed to be a good honest decent man, and hopefully he will be able to get their money back, hopefully very soon.

"Let's get out of here," Delia said, suddenly. "Let's take the car to Marbella, it's not going to do us any good hanging around here and moping."

Delia took hold of Horace's hand and led him out of the square and back towards the apartment and the car, like before, when things had gotten a little rocky in the past, she somehow had to be the strong one. Somehow, she had pull Horace out from the very dark black hole that they had both fallen into and out of this huge mess that she had caused.

Surprisingly, Horace still insisted on driving the hire car, and as soon as they were back on the main road, heading towards Marbella, Delia tuned the radio in to the English-speaking radio station that played music from the seventies and eighties.

The journey passed without incident and on arrival they navigated the one-way system without any help from the satnav and found the Hotel Tropicana the first time around. Unlike the year before, the approach road had more than enough parking places and the whole area seemed mysteriously silent and empty.

Horace slowly drove the car down to the bottom of the road, turning at the end and around the roundabout, as they slowly passed the hotel Tropicana, they both stared in amazement, the whole place was closed.

The huge entrance had been closed off with a large set of steel gates locked shut, and a heavy-duty lock and chain wrapped around the centre.

Horace parked the car by the side of the road and they both got out, after being in the car with the air con set at twenty-two degrees, it felt incredibly hot outside.

So different from the year before, there was no sound of hundreds of young voices all talking excitedly at once and the sound of the young people, jumping into the pool and splashing.

Delia was the first to speak. "All those young people," she said, "they had no idea that their lives would be so different this year."

"All those young women," Horace said, "drinking gin and sleeping around the pool, so they wouldn't lose their sunbeds. And young Trudi, she was so lucky to have gotten married before all this happened, and the women's football team, all having to stay at home and no football."

"Let's get out of here," Delia said. "It's much too hot to walk along the beach, we can find a restaurant and have some lunch, we only had coffee for our breakfast."

Horace and Delia arrived back at the village and the apartment, around eleven thirty that Thursday evening. They had left the aircon running, set at twenty-three degrees, and as soon as they arrived back, Delia switched it off and opened the bedroom window, just enough to let a little air into the room.

Horace didn't like the idea and it took him much longer to drift off to sleep, watching the window, expecting the large ginger cat to squeeze itself through the two-inch gap at any moment.

Friday morning, Delia popped out to the local shops and bought some fresh bread and a jar of apricot jam for their breakfast. After breakfast, they pulled out the sun chairs from the cupboard in the hallway and carried them down the stairs and set them up in the shade under a large palm tree.

Delia opened her book, the one that she had purchased at London Gatwick and had started to read on the plane, saying to Horace that she would like to finish it before she forgot all the different characters that were involved in the very complicated plot.

Horace soon got bored, just sitting there, under the shade staring at the water that was being pumped out of the nozzles around the sides of the pool.

Occasionally, someone would come down the steps from one of the other apartments, they all had the appearance of local people with their dark coloured skin and dark hair.

They all seemed to be very surprised to see the two very white-skinned holidaymakers just sitting there, by the pool, all alone.

Some people nodded, others smiled and said hola, others quickly checked, making sure that their face mask was covering their nose and mouth correctly, before quickly scurrying past on their way out through the main gate.

After fidgeting around in his chair for almost an hour, Horace went back up the stairs to the apartment and switched on the TV, flicking through the channels with the controller. Everything was in Spanish, just like daytime TV in England, a pile of rubbish but even more annoying, not being able to understand any of it.

Horace then thumbed through the small selection of books that were sitting on the dark wooden wall unit, just under the television. Some of the books were very old and the pages had all turned a yellowy colour. Most of them were directed towards the female reader, about love and romance, and the rest were all written in Spanish.

Horace then searched through the four remaining drawers, lower down in the unit, there was a chess set and various board games in one, and boxes of jigsaw puzzles in another. There were batteries and lightbulbs, hover bags, and various other bits and pieces that made up the contents of the junk drawer. A pair of binoculars, some candles and a torch and a box or matches and a cigarette lighter in the remainder.

Horace went back out of the apartment and back downstairs and sat back down in his chair next to Delia, giving her the full report about the rubbish on Spanish TV. And what he had found inside the drawers of the wall unit.

"Why don't you piece together one of the jigsaws?" Delia said, putting her book down onto her lap, reaching across and holding Horace's hand.

"I wonder how long it will take for Angel the solicitor to come back to us, talking of jigsaws," Horace said, "and how long should we stay here?"

"It is only Friday today, we have only been here for four days," Delia said, "I will call him on Monday, if we haven't heard from him by then."

Monday morning, around nine thirty, Horace and Delia made their way to the bakery in the small square for coffee and a ration of churros each. Once they had finished their breakfast, Delia took the packet of cleansing wipes and a small mirror from her bag and wiped around her mouth and then her hands, then taking out her mobile she called the solicitor. Angel answered his phone straight away, telling Delia he would be down in a few minutes.

After the normal greetings, Angel ordered himself a cup of strong coffee, he said that he had been very busy, chasing people all over the place, doing his very best to get all of their money returned.

"I managed to get through to the head office of Spanish white villas in the sun," Angel said, "after getting no response from the numerous emails that I had already sent to them. Surprisingly, their office is in northern France, I spoke to one of the senior partners, He told me that they are waiting for compensation from the Spanish government and they would get back to me as soon as they hear."

"I then spoke with our local mayor, asking him for a favour, if his office could find out from the regional Government anything about Spanish white villas in the sun and their pending claim. Friday afternoon, a young woman from the mayor's office called me, she told me that she had contacted someone that she knew in the regional government office."

"She informed me that there is no pending claim, because Spanish white villas in the sun had never purchased the land in the first place, they hadn't raised sufficient funds. The area of land had been marked out and the purchase price agreed but the regional government had never received any payment what so ever. I then called the contractors who had started the work, clearing the site, on behalf of Spanish white villas in the sun, Miguel and sons, excavators."

"I had a very long and interesting conversation with Miguel junior, he informed me that Spanish white villas in the sun had paid them the initial payment to start the work, clearing the site and had promised to make more payments as the work progressed."

"Miguel Junior then told me that they still had a large sum of money sitting in their bank account, because they hadn't gotten very far with the work when the digger driver uncovered some very valuable Roman artefacts and coins. Only a few minutes ago, just before you called me, I sent off a letter with a special recorded delivery, informing Spanish white villas in the sun that they must return your money in full within seven working days, after taking delivery and signing for the letter, or we will have to begin legal action."

"How much will that cost?" Horace said. "And how long will that take?"

"Here in Spain and our very slow legal system, it will probably take forever," Angel said. "I am hoping that it will never come to that, you are both the victims of very unfortunate circumstances. I have never dealt with a case were Roman coins and archaeological digs were involved before."

"What about these digger people, Miguel and sons," Delia interjected, "if they still have the money from Spanish white villas, why can't they just pass it on to us? after all it's probably our money anyway."

"That would be very nice," Angel smiled at Delia, "But highly illegal, but it would suit everyone, it would certainly make my job a lot easier. Fingers crossed, Spanish white villas in the sun will ask for the rest of their money to be returned and pass some of it directly on to you."

"We could be stuck here for months," Horace said, "and if we have to take legal action it could go on for another year, maybe two, possibly forever!"

"What about this Sebastian guy?" Horace said, "and his brand new one hundred- and fifty-thousand Pounds Mercedes car, did you find out what happened to him?"

"Sebastian was only an employee," Angel said, "contracted to sell the houses for Spanish white villas in the sun. Besides, some of the people that live in the front-row villas, saw him digging in the ground, out at the back, several times during the lockdown period, at the peak of the pandemic."

"When legally, no one was allowed out from our houses, not without a special license or permission from the local police. Some of the times, the local residence were woken up in the middle of the night, by Sebastian and the sound of digging, dressed all in black and wearing a head torch. There are rumours that he uncovered and stole some of the gold coins from the site, the police are trying to track him down, right now as we speak. He could be anywhere in the world," Angel said solemnly, "South America, most likely."

Horace suddenly stood up, banging his head on the corner of the large white parasol, falling back into his chair. "This can't be happening," he said, "this can't be for real?"

Delia reached to her right and under the table, taking hold of Horace's hand, up till now he had been taking everything remarkably well.

He had a very hot sweaty hand, and he had a nasty red mark in the centre of his forehead, but thankfully, he hadn't reverted to the rocking and the staring.

"We might as well go back home to England," Delia said, "there isn't much we can do here, it's much too hot for us, and we are paying fifty euros a night for the apartment just to be here."

"Under the circumstances, that will be the best thing to do," Angel said, "we must remain positive, Spanish White villas in the sun up till now have done nothing illegal, except gloss over the truth, hopefully the cheque will arrive in the post sometime next week."

Once Angel had left, promising them that he would keep the pressure on, doing his very best to get their money back, Delia checked out the flights back to London Gatwick, using her mobile phone.

"There is a flight tomorrow morning," Delia said," it leaves Malaga airport at eleven forty-five?"

"Book it!" Horace said. "Book it!" then starting to rock slightly back and forth in his chair, "book it, book it!"

Chapter 22

The flight back to the UK and London Gatwick left Malaga airport bang on time, similar to the flight coming out, the plane was only around fifty per cent full, giving all the passengers plenty of room to spread out, maintaining a good level of social distancing.

Delia and Horace had seated themselves more towards the front of the plane, Delia taking the window seat and Horace, next to the aisle.

Shortly after take-off, Delia settled down with the intention of finishing her book, Horace had decided to waste as much time of the flight eating and drinking, this allowing him to keep his face mask permanently down, sitting half under his chin, allowing him to be able to breath more freely.

Taking as much time as possible, he worked his way through two toasted cheese and ham sandwiches, a tube of Pringles and a box of Maltesers, while slowly sipping his way through five cups of coffee. He then slowly sipped his way through two large glasses of red wine, then finally purchasing a bottle of very expensive fizzy mountain spring water, taking the very last few sips, during the plane's final descent, into London Gatwick.

The last few miles, just before they arrived back home at Victoria Avenue, the taxi passed through a light shower, just heavy enough for the taxi driver to have to turn the windscreen wipers on, just for a few minutes.

Nothing seemed to have changed in the last eight days while Horace and Delia had been away.

The highly polished Jaguar, belonging to their next door but one neighbour, Richard Heed, was parked in the road as normal, directly outside the front of his house.

The familiar sound of the local Black birds singing, and the cooing of wood pigeons, much happier now that the rain had stopped.

Horace dumped the case down in the hallway and after spending some time in the downstairs toilet, promptly turned his attention to the gas boiler.

Turning the heating on to full and then turning the thermostat up in the hallway to maximum, saying that the house felt very cold inside.

Delia was pleased, she also wanted the heating to be turned on, not wanting to say anything to Horace, now that they were both unemployed, but inside the house felt very dark and cold and unwelcoming. Delia quickly ran up the stairs to change out of her lightweight summer dress and into something much warmer.

Horace went directly out to the back garden, after sliding back the patio door, drawn towards the huge weed type plants, that seemed to have sprung up everywhere while they had been away. Horace opened the door of the garden shed and reached inside, grabbing his garden gloves, then going to the bottom of the garden, towards the very sad looking fire damaged conifers.

Most of the weeds were growing in the areas where Horace had worked in the soil, especially under and around the conifers and along the border of the chain link fencing, Horace, then looked around, singling out the fattest and tallest green stem that was growing along the border, where poor old Trevor's shed had once stood.

Bending down to one side and wrapping both of his hands around the base, he pulled at the mysterious green plant, attempting to pull it out from the damp soil.

Delia, for no particular reason, just happen to glance out of the bedroom window as Horace was falling backwards into the long wet grass. "Horace!" Delia shouted, running out into the garden through the half open patio doorway.

"Looks like some kind of root vegetable," Horace said, holding the plant up and wiggling it, for Delia to see.

"Thank god you're alright," Delia said, "for a moment, I thought you had had some kind of heart failure or something."

"The ground feels quite wet," Horace said, slowly getting to his feet, "we must have had a few showers while we were away."

"Let's go back inside and have a nice cup of tea," Delia said, "I think we have some fruit cake left in the bread bin."

Delia took hold of Horace's arm, leading him back towards the house and through the open patio doorway, "it doesn't feel much like summer this evening," she said, looking up at the sky and the black thunderclouds overhead.

In spite of all the worries and the thoughts of losing, three hundred thousand euros, and the huge difference in temperature, travelling from one country to another, Horace and Delia slept the whole night without interruption.

Delia was already sitting on the sofa with a cup of coffee resting, on the top of a small side table, when Horace came down the stairs, resuming his old position, standing inside the bay window. Unlike before, he was wearing a lot more than his Calvin Klein high waistband, cotton stretch pants.

"The house feels so cold," he said looking down the street, to see if the highly polished Jaguar was parked in the road outside Richard's house. "I don't remember the house ever feeling so cold after our summer holidays in the past," Horace said.

"It's most probably that our bodies had gotten accustomed to the heat in Spain," Delia said, "I have read that the blood gets thinner and the body quickly adapts to the heat and the change of temperature. And besides, in the past, we have always gone somewhere much cooler, like skiing, or walking in Scotland."

"I am going to put the heating on," Horace said, "just for this morning, just to take the chill off, it might have been cheaper to stay in Spain after all."

"I am just writing an email to Angel," Delia said, "thanking him for all his help and that we will wait to hear from him with any further developments, and to make sure he doesn't forget about us, now that we are back home, here in England."

"I think that I will go for a round of golf after breakfast," Horace said, "I feel like I need to walk, tire myself out, hit a few balls, I feel so frustrated and helpless, maybe take up boxing, learn to punch people."

After eating breakfast of poached eggs and a mug of coffee, Horace set about preparing for a day out at the golf club.

"Would you like to come, darling?" Horace asked, as he rinsed off the breakfast plates under the tap in the kitchen.

"No thank you, I would only slow you down," Delia said, "and I really don't feel like talking to anyone today, especially at the golf club, I feel embarrassed after what has happened, what with the raffle tickets and everything."

After Horace had left the house, Delia washed up the breakfast things and opened the kitchen window to get rid of the smell of eggs.

Then she carried the suitcase from the hallway and lifted it onto the small kitchen table, then put all the dirty laundry into the washing machine, setting the machine at a forty-degree wash. After carrying the suitcase up the stairs and emptying the rest of its contents and hanging the clean clothes back into the wardrobe, she was suddenly hit with the realisation that she was all alone in the house with nothing else to do.

Maybe she should have gone for a round of golf with Horace? For the very first time she missed him not being around, getting under her feet, keeping her busy with his juvenile comments about the neighbours and looking ridiculous just wearing his pants.

Delia walked from one bedroom to the next, opening the small top window in each room as she went, letting in the fresh morning air and the sound of the blackbirds singing, breaking the silence inside the large four-bedroom house. Delia sat on the single bed in the smallest of the four bedrooms, as far as she could remember, nobody had ever slept in the bed, and the room had never been redecorated.

Horace, in the past, had always summoned Peter the painter who he had been recommended by other members at the golf club. Over the years, Peter had repainted the whole of the downstairs at different stages, while Horace and Delia had been out of the house, busy at work. Somehow Peter had never worked his magic upstairs, although he had suggested it in the past, Horace and Delia had never felt the need, they had never smoked and the rooms were very rarely used.

Maybe now was the right time to move? Delia thought to herself, there didn't seem any point in living in such a big house, having no children or grandchildren to visit, for an occasional sleep over. She now felt she had stopped at the crossroads, with no signs, pointing in any direction in which direction her life should take. Up till now, she had been in the driving seat, forever moving forward with the responsibility of running the school and the education of the local young children.

She needed a project, something with a purpose, she would do some decorating, she thought to herself, starting with the painting of the walls in the small room, then if things don't turn out so well, they could always call in Peter the painter to patch things over.

It had taken Horace around four and a half hours to complete the eighteen-hole circuit of the golf course.

Wednesdays, especially in the mornings, were always very quiet, he had no one on the fairways behind him, so he had decided to play two balls at the same time.

It had been a good morning, with a lot of white cloud overhead, protecting him from the sun, and the ground had been perfect, the grass had been a little damp at the start but had soon been dried out, by the light breeze.

Frank, the barman, was sitting alone in the member's bar when Horace walked in, He was wearing his normal white golf shirt and slacks but in addition wearing a black silk face mask with the name Belvedere Golf Club, embroidered with gold stitching, under the chin.

There was a large dispenser of bacterial hand cleaner next to the doorway, accompanied by a sign written in bold black letters stating that face masks must be worn at all times.

Horace quickly pulled his mask out from his pocket and slipped the elastic over his head, then applied a liberal amount of hand gel to both palms.

"Horace, my old mate," Frank boomed out from his position behind the bar, "How are you? I thought you and your beautiful wife had jetted off to Spain, to view the new villa?"

"Frank," Horace bleated out from behind his white face mask, "there's nothing there to view, no villa, nothing, we have lost all our money, I don't know what we are going to do?"

"Looks like you could do with a large brandy," Frank said, genuinely concerned for Horace's wellbeing, but at the same time desperate to make an improvement on the bar's very poor takings off late.

"I will just have a fresh orange juice and a Slim line Tonic in a big glass please, Frank," Horace said, not wanting to complicate things even more so, with the pickling of his brain with any more alcohol.

Normally Horace would shuffle up, and onto one of the barstools, but even after a round of golf, He still felt very agitated and didn't feel much like sitting.

"What's happened," Frank asked, sliding Horace's drink across the bar top towards him.

"Well," Horace began, "this time last year, we were promised a brand-new villa, on the hillside overlooking the golf course. Delia had been worrying since as far back as January, we were supposed to get regular reports and updates, on how the building work was going, we were even promised photographs.

"Delia kept sending emails and ringing the agent's number, she was getting more and more worried and very anxious even back then, we hadn't received no progress reports, as promised, nothing. Then we had this terrible pandemic, While Delia was working from home, she kept trying to ring the agent, over there in Spain, by then he wasn't even answering his phone.

"I was always very busy, working at Bakelite Electronics, I had no idea how bad things were, Delia was at home, working and worrying and still trying to ring the agent."

"Blimey," Frank said, "I thought I had money worries, what with this dreadful pandemic, having to close the bar, and then people staying away frightened of catching the virus."

Normally, Frank would offer good solid advice for anyone whom may need it, nobody at the golf club ever thought of him as just Frank the barman, he was the guy who seemed to know something about everything.

He was always there, ready to listen with a sympathetic ear, ready to help, as much as he possible could, depending on the size of the problem, much better than any guidance councillor or therapist.

"Did you visit the site?" Frank asked, "have they started any building work, this dam pandemic has slowed everything down."

"We didn't actually physically walk right up to the position where the villa was supposed to be," Horace said, "you wouldn't believe how hot it is in the south of Spain in early August, we looked from the side of the road, we could easily see that there was nothing there. We have hired a local solicitor," Horace continued, "he has already informed us that there is no villa and there will probably never ever be one. Directly underneath where our villa was supposed to be built, they have uncovered some Roman ruins and some very valuable gold coins, now it's been declared an official archaeological dig, and a historical site of interest."

Frank just stood and stared at Horace, he couldn't think of anything positive to say, in most cases he would normally offer good solid advice.

"Like, go home to the wife, tell her that you're deeply sorry."

"Take her away for the weekend, apologise to her for shouting at her after she had smashed up the brand new family car."

Horace suddenly reached into his golf trousers and pulled out the plant that he had pulled up from the back garden the night before.

"What do you think these are?" Horace said, dangling the plant in front of Franks face, "they seem to be springing up everywhere all over the back garden."

Frank reached out and took the plant from Horace, "looks like a very young seedling, a root vegetable, most probably a radish."

Although Frank felt very sorry for Horace, with all his money worries, what with the Spanish villa and everything, he couldn't think of anything positive to say, no words of encouragement, nothing. Horace had bought himself into a financial minefield, and it seemed like there was no way out.

Frank was very relieved to see the root vegetable, something that he knew a lot about and could give Horace some good sound advice, getting away from the subject of tossing all your money into a huge hole, somewhere on a mountainside in southern Spain.

"They were the first thing I noticed, when I looked out into the back garden, when we arrived home from Spain yesterday evening," Horace said.

"They must have come from poor old Trevor's shed," Frank said, "he was always talking to me about starting a vegetable patch in the back garden, he must have bought some packets of seeds and had them stored away in the shed."

"If you intend to keep them, you will need a good vegetable granulised fertiliser," Frank said, "and work it in around the base of the plants, there might be other things growing there as well, if Trevor had bought everything, I told him to get."

"It's very strange," Horace said, "he never ever mentioned any of this to me, all the time we had spent together on the golf course, he never ever said anything about starting a vegetable garden, and he certainly never ever said anything about building a space rocket."

Horace suddenly felt very sad, let down, betrayed, all the nervous energy, generated from all his frustrations and anxiety that had him pumping earlier, just flopped out from his body, leaving him a little shaky and unsteady on his feet.

"I will have that double brandy after all, and have one yourself, Frank," Horace said, pulling his wallet from his pocket and climbing onto the barstool, "surely things can't get any worse than they are now, can they?"

Horace left the car at the golf club with the golf clubs securely locked away in the boot, he wasn't really in the mood for the forty-minute walk home, after pulling the golf trolley around the eighteen holes earlier that morning.

He had never ever mixed alcohol with driving, with the exception of Trevor's funeral, he never ever drunk in the afternoon. The two large glasses of double brandy had relaxed him, probably too much, by the time he arrived back at the front door, he felt more than a little drunk and very light-headed and barely had enough energy to turn the key.

Normally, at this time of the year when Horace arrived home in the afternoon, Delia would be sitting on the sofa or at the dining table, rechecking disputed exam papers or deeply engrossed in some kind of school work, for the coming year.

"Darling, are you home?" Horace called out; the house seemed strangely empty with no sign of Delia anywhere.

Horace very wearily went up the stairs, he was quickly greeted at the top by all of the furniture from the small bedroom sitting on the landing, leaving no space for him to pass by.

They were being burgled, Horace thought to himself, opportunists who always seemed to know when people were away on holiday and then somehow get themselves inside and clear the place out. There was a weird rubbing and scraping sound coming from inside the small bedroom, the robbers were obviously still inside, he had caught them red-handed.

What should he do? If he called the police, they would surely hear him, and these people were normally huge violent guys with tattoos of snakes and devils inked onto the side of their necks and all over their heads.

Horace grabbed the aluminium lamp stand that was lying on the top of the bed, it had a very heavy round steel base, and a long round aluminium shaft, maybe he could keep them in the room, using it as a weapon until the police arrived.

Horace grabbed hold of the plug and pushed it into the wall socket and switched on the power, he could use it as a stunner, maybe, pocking them with the bulb end, possibly breaking the bulb on their heads and exposing the live filament.

Suddenly, there were footsteps, somebody was on their way out, Horace raised the lamp up high above his head.

Delia stepped out from the doorway, completely naked, except for wearing the white lightweight paper boiler suit that she had purchased along with the sandpaper and the coloured paint test pots.

At the very same time, the electric wire pulled out from the lamp base, the exposed live wires first making contact with the back of Horace's neck, then the back of his left leg.

Delia screamed, Horace screamed even louder, throwing the lamp down onto the landing floor, before spinning around and then collapsing onto the bed.

Delia reacted very quickly, sitting astride Horace, she ripped open his short-sleeved golf shirt and began to treat Horace like she had been trained, when someone had just suffered from an electric shock. Delia had just placed both her palms onto Horace's chest and administrated only the very first pump when Horace's eyes suddenly flicked wide open.

Horace rolled Delia over on top of the single bed, tearing at her white paper boiler suit, shredding it like a wild animal, kissing her passionately on the lips. Horace then quickly rolled up all the paper into a large ball and flung it down the stairs, closely followed by his Adidas golf slacks.

During their thirty-five years of marriage, Horace had never ever once acted this way, all sorts of thoughts were rushing through Delia's head. Especially the words that were regularly echoed by Dr Carolina Banks, a highly sexually active man is a very well-balanced healthy man.

Delia was surprised by Horace's wild animal like actions, and why he was acting in this way, she couldn't possibly think. It could have been an inner rage, unharnessed, fuelled by the sense of anger and frustration, fermenting, building up inside Horace's body, deep within. The two double brandies, consumed at lunchtime, possibly the electric shock to the back of the neck or the appearance of Delia, standing there suddenly, practically naked, just wearing the paper suit.

Whatever the reason, Delia was pleased that Horace had acted in this way.

After arriving back home from Spain, Delia was expecting Horace to go under, sink down to the bottom very quickly, with her doing her very best to keep his head above the water.

Never, even in her wildest of dreams had she expected Horace to make love to her on the single bed in the middle of the afternoon, just above the stairs on the landing.

Chapter 23

Delia had been very pleased with all her recent achievements, decorating the small bedroom had given her a new set of skills. She was feeling much better within herself, just like Horace she was driven on with an excessive amount of nervous energy, once again pushing the Villa worries to the back of her mind.

The guy in the local family run DIY shop had been more than helpful, he had walked her through every step, firstly starting with dust covers and masking tape, then the preparation of the different surfaces and then the different types of paints and the best way to apply them.

By the time Delia had finished the room and put all the furniture back, August had slipped away and they were now in the first week of September.

They hadn't received any word from the solicitor, Angel Benitez, over there in Spain, so the very next morning after Julia had finished decorating the small bedroom, she sent him an e-mail.

Angel returned Delia's e-mail straight away, apologising for the lack of correspondence, explaining that he was still chasing Spanish White Villas in the sun, he said that they seemed to have buried their heads in the sand and were ignoring all his calls and e-mails.

Even though he had sent them the letter, using special delivery, informing them that they would be facing legal proceedings if they didn't return the three hundred thousand euros in full, he had never had anything back from them.

Angel then went on to say that he hadn't e-mailed Delia before and that he had been waiting for some better news to send to her.

Angel's return e-mail had not offered any comfort to Delia what so ever, as soon as she closed down her lap top, the feeling of anxiety and the deep sense of helplessness and remorse quickly filled her body once again.

Just like before, she quickly decided to throw herself into the decorating, running up the stairs, using any method she could, pushing, dragging and rolling, clearing all the furniture out from the third bedroom and shoving it out onto the landing.

Horace had also kept himself very busy, amazingly, he had suffered no ill effects following the electric shock, or the crazy ten minutes of love making, that had taken place, on the small bed at the top of the stairs, on the landing.

The weather had been very kind, and he had spent a lot of his time outside in the garden, over a period of two weeks he had dug out and prepared a vegetable patch right at the very bottom.

One by one, he had carefully dug out the young vegetable plants from in and around the garden and replanted them in the new designated area. Following each round of golf, Frank the barman, had identified the different vegetables and salads, that Horace had presented him with. He had then planted them in their correct individual rows in the garden, and worked in a good granulised fertiliser that Frank had recommended. Horace had also turned his hand to DIY, and on Delia's recommendation, had visited the friendly, helpful guy at the local DIY shop.

Horace had returned home with a car full of planks of pinewood, shelf brackets and an electric drill with boxes of screws and various wall fixings.

After spending more than ample time, measuring and marking, for the very first hole to be drilled in the garage wall, Delia suddenly appeared, all flustered and panting wildly, temporarily, unable to catch her breath.

"I have just received the strangest call, from Angel Benitez," Delia, panted excitedly after running around the garden searching for Horace, then eventually, finding him in the garage.

Horace put down the electric drill onto the garage floor and switched off the power, waiting for Delia to tell him the news.

Delia then walked from the back of the garage and out through the open doorway and began to pace up and down outside.

Horace followed her outside, "Well, what is it?"

"A new house," Delia said, "A different house, a big house, set in its own grounds, private, not overlooked by anyone."

Horace looked at Delia, she was bubbling with excitement, she was still pacing back and forth, "What house?" he said, "where?"

"At the very top of the lane," Delia said, "the one that takes you up and past the golf course, but at the very top, on the grounds of the old derelict farmhouse."

Delia wasn't making any sense, Horace grabbed both her hands, stopping her in her tracks.

Delia stared into Horace's eyes, "oh, Horace, this is our chance, a new life, Like, phoenixes, rising out from the ashes of the gloom and doom and into the bright light of the Spanish sunshine. Please say yes."

"How can I say yes, if I don't have a clue what you are talking about and what I am saying yes to?" Horace said.

"Angel, the solicitor, has had many meetings with the mayor of the village and between them they have devised a rescue plan, one that will work for everyone. The money that Spanish white villas in the sun paid to the excavators, Miguel and sons, with the money that they still have, they have agreed to clear the site and connect all the services from the new villas, up to the land of the old farmhouse."

"Angel can do the legal documentation, changing the plot from the one that we originally purchased to the plot where the old farmhouse once stood."

"How is that supposed to help us?" Horace said, grumpily, "then we would have paid out three hundred thousand euros just for an empty plot of land, in the middle of nowhere."

"Yes," Delia said, "but it is a very big plot, much bigger than the original one and Angel said that we could build a much better house, for less money, much less than the five hundred thousand euros that we were going to pay out originally, for the other villa."

Horace felt very disappointed. From Delia's first reactions, when she first burst into the garage, he had expected something much better, possibly all their money had been returned in full, or that they had won the jackpot on the lottery.

"Why can't we just get our money back?" Horace said, not sharing Delia's enthusiasm, thinking that everything she was telling him all sounded a bit dodgy.

"Angel has tried," Delia said, very disappointed with Horace's reaction, "he says it could take us years, if we act fast, Angel can put everything in motion straight away."

"So why can't we just have the money that the excavators have?" Horace said, "why can't they pay it back into our bank account?"

"I have already discussed this with Angel," Delia said, "that would be illegal, besides the contractors are very keen to hang onto the money that they already have. Angel has had a meeting with the boss, Miguel and he is more than happy to connect all the pipework and clear the site with the money that they have already been paid. This way no laws have been broken, they were contracted by Spanish White Villas in the sun to clear the ground and put in the pipework and that is exactly what they will be doing."

"Well, if that is our only option," Horace said, unenthusiastically, "we have nothing more to lose."

Delia, kissed Horace on the lips. "Thank you darling, I am going to ring Angel back right away," she said, rushing off as quickly as she had appeared.

Horace went back into the garage, he had suddenly lost all his enthusiasm for drilling holes, once again his head was filled with the goings-on in Spain, he closed the garage door and went back inside the house.

Delia had just put the phone down, "That's settled then," she smiled, "isn't that wonderful news," she said, greeting Horace in the kitchen with another huge smacker on the lips.

"How long is this all going to take?" Horace said, "What if Spanish White Villas in the sun ask Miguel and sons for their money back?"

"Angel, says that Spanish White Villas in the sun have cut and run, they have pulled out of Spain completely, Miguel and sons, need the money and are desperate to keep their men working, they are going to start the work right away."

"What about the house?" Horace said, "who is going to build that?"

"Angel, is going to arrange everything," Delia said, excitedly, "he has a lot of connection from previous clients and similar work, he knows a good architect and a good local builder."

"Well, we are not going to pay out any more money until we get everything written down on paper," Horace said, "and another thing, how much is this solicitor, Angel, going to charge us for all this?"

Horace still couldn't feel the same enthusiasm that seemed to have taken over Delia. He suddenly felt the urge to start the drilling of the holes into the garage wall once again.

"I am going back out into the garage," he said, "I need to put the shelves up, so we can get all your painting materials of from the garage floor, before somebody trips over them and kills themselves."

September slipped away into the first week of October, it had taken Horace a long time to put all the shelving up in the garage. Delia had glided through the redecorating of the third bedroom and had presented Horace with a lot more half empty paint tins and roller trays.

At first, Horace had struggled, drilling the holes, after marking out the holes in the wall, the electric drill seemed to have a mind of its own and either wandered off from the mark, spinning out of control or snapped the drill bit into two pieces.

Early one morning, Horace and Delia had spent a considerable amount of time at the local hospital in casualty, having a load of brick dust washed out from his left eye.

Angel had sent Delia endless amounts of e-mails, some of them, the plans of the house that had been forwarded on from the architect, and an artist's impression of what the house will look like, once completed.

As the weeks had past, Horace had gained more and more interest and his enthusiasm for living in Spain had increased as the time passed by.

Delia had to pop out one morning for a new black ink cartridge, so she could print of all the plans that the architect had sent on to them.

Horace had laid them all out onto the dining room table and had spent a whole day studying them.

At first not understanding any of them, but then, finally, page by page, slowly piecing everything together.

Following the guidelines of the local village council, the architect had been instructed to design a farmhouse type building, with outbuildings, that reflected its agricultural heritage and the surroundings and the original buildings history.

towards the end of October, Horace had been instructed to transfer, two hundred thousand euros into the bank account of Angel the solicitor, so he could pay the Architect and the Spanish builders.

By the end of October, unfortunately for everyone living in England, the amount of people being affected by the covid 19 had risen rapidly.

The government had to announce new measures to try to combat what was now being called the second wave.

Angel, the solicitor Called Delia, early one morning, informing her that they had to come over to Spain to sign the legal documentation for what was now being called, the farmhouse.

By that time Delia had, had enough of painting and decorating and had decided not to move on and repaint the master bedroom.

Horace had successfully stored all the paints and rollers along with the trays and brushes, onto the new erected garage shelving.

Angel had sounded quite anxious on the phone, and said that they should come over as soon as possible, just in case any new travel restrictions were announced.

As soon as Delia had put the phone down, Horace was gripped by panic, telling Delia to get on her laptop and book up the next available flight out of London Gatwick right away. By this time, Horace was more than ready to get away from the house and the garden once again.

His life, once again, had lost all purpose and without meaning or direction, spending more and more time, wearing just his pants, standing in the area, looking out from inside the bay window.

He had given up on the vegetable patch, Frank the barman, had given him a lot of advice on how to grow vegetables but he hadn't said anything about insect infestation or how quickly the slugs and snails chomp their way through everything that was fresh and green.

That very next morning, Horace and Delia were on the morning flight, flying out from London Gatwick, on their way back to Malaga.

The plane touched down onto the tarmac at Malaga airport twenty minutes ahead of schedule, Horace and Delia whizzed through the airport, pulling their small cases behind them like experienced travellers.

There had been no que at the desk for the hire car and within a half an hour, Horace was in the driving seat and Delia was familiarising herself with the controls inside a shiny new white Citroen.

Although, now they were in Spain at the end of October and the intense heat of the summer had come slowly down by ten degrees, the car was still very hot and stuffy inside and Delia set the aircon at a comfortable twenty-three degrees.

As soon as Horace had steered the car out from the darkness of the underground carpark, he was suddenly hit by the brightness of the Spanish sunlight and had to pull the car over while Delia grabbed his case from the back seat, searching for his sunglasses.

The rest of the journey passed without incident and later that evening, Horace and Delia had arrived back at Paco's apartment.

Parking the car behind the apartment block, they had let themselves into the apartment, finding the key inside the huge ceramic pot just outside the front door, as Paco had promised via WhatsApp.

Maisie from the apartment downstairs had been in and had cleaned everything and had left the aircon on, set at comfortable twenty-four degrees.

By the time that they had put their clothes into the wardrobe and then showered, Delia had slipped into a light summer dress, and Horace, into his shorts and tee-shirt, they both were more than just a little hungry.

They both quickly made their way to the small square and the friendly restaurant that they had eaten in, on their previous visit's before.

It was a beautiful warm evening, the whole of the square was illuminated by colourful festoon lights and there was a couple of musicians playing their Spanish guitars, both sitting on wooden chairs in the middle of the square.

Even though the restaurant appeared to be full with a lot more tourists than their last visit, the friendly restaurant owner, recognised Horace and Delia instantly, after shouting a few words in Spanish, into the open doorway, a table and some chairs were quickly carried out from inside the restaurant.

After their meal of steak and vegetables and they had swiftly moved onto the second bottle of red wine, the musicians, suddenly upped the tempo and a few couples got up to dance, while others clapped or stamped their feet.

A more than friendly Spanish couple, danced their way over to Horace and Delia, insisting they joined in, pulling Delia from her chair, Horace resisted by firmly holding onto the bottom of his seat.

Fearing that he may not be able to stand up, or even worse, catch the deadly Covid virus.

Horace, watched Delia as she danced, trying her best to copy everyone else, Horace drunk more and more of the red wine Sinking further and further down into his chair, occasionally clapping, and stamping his left foot, not wanting to appear to be a complete party pooper.

By the time Horace had finished off the second bottle of red wine, he was feeling unusually very happy.

Delia had done the right thing, initially, dragging him off here to Spain, the last twelve months had been a nightmare, what with the Covid virus and the building of the villa completely going tits up.

Somehow, the nightmare had turned into a dream, now they were living the dream, with all these wonderful friendly people, here, in this wonderful country.

Without any warning, Horace, suddenly slid from his chair and onto the ground, rolling around under the table, franticly doing his best to stand up.

Everyone cheered, as Horace, moved towards them, doing his very best to blend in with the crowd, he raised his hands above his head and began to clap and stamp his feet.

Someone shouted, "Ole!" from the inside, Horace felt like he was a very dark tanned Spanish flamenco dancer, but from the outside, he looked completely all wrong, like cross between a very sick leper with no coordination and an incredibly anaemic space alien.

Chapter 24

Wednesday, 28th of October, the start of Horace and Delia's first day back in Spain.

Unusually, Horace awoke first, for the past hour or so, he had been aware of something pushing down on his lower legs, but he had been much to tired and still under the influence of the red wine, unable to do anything about it.

He opened his eyes and starred up at the ceiling, unlike the night before, it seemed to have stopped spinning around but legs still felt extremely heavy, he managed to raise his head from the pillow very slightly, looking down, towards the bottom of the bed.

Horace screamed out in horror!

Delia leaped out from the bed, "what is it?" she said, looking around the room, expecting to see something horrid or evil.

"That ginger cat!" Horace shrilled, "it was sitting on my legs, at the bottom of the bed!"

Delia went out from the bedroom, searching around the rest of the apartment for the overfed ginger fur ball.

"Nothing here," she said, poking her head around the bedroom door, "you must have had a bad dream."

Horace slowly got out of the bed, "that ginger cat was here, on the bed," he insisted, "I felt it, it was lying on my legs, I saw it with my own eyes."

"Well, I am going to take a shower," Delia said, feeling a little grumpy after being broken from her blissful deep sleep.

"What if it comes back?" Horace said, watching Delia as she disappeared into the bathroom.

"We need to get a move on, if we are going to meet Angel in the square at ten thirty!" she called back.

Horace slowly made his way into the small kitchen area, opening one of the cupboards, where he had left the large jar of Nescafe.

"Nothing," he mumbled to himself, the fridge had also been emptied, there was nothing to drink, only tap water.

Delia suddenly reappeared. "Well, have you found the cat yet?"

"No," Horace, replied, now feeling very grumpy and hungover, "it seemed to have disappeared, along with our jar of coffee."

"If you quickly take a shower and change out of those cloths, that you are still wearing from last night, we can have some coffee in the square," Delia called out, as she disappeared into the bedroom.

The walk to the small square was now a lot more comfortable than their previous visit, Horace still needed to wear a hat, to protect his head from the sun but it had lost its intensity and was now shielded by the white occasional cloud.

There were already a few people sitting at some of the tables outside the coffee shop, by the time that Horace and Delia arrived.

They sat at the middle table furthest from the small frontage, the young lady, that had served them before, on their previous visits gave them a welcoming smile.

Delia told her, that they didn't want churros and that they just wanted coffee.

After drinking three cups of coffee, Horace was beginning to feel slightly better although he still needed to wear his sunglasses, and still couldn't open his eyes fully.

Angel, the solicitor, arrived, just before ten thirty, although Horace was very pleased to see him, much to his disgust, he still looked very tall and slim, his face still very tanned and unlike Horace, he didn't seem to need to wear dark sunglasses.

"Buenos Dias," he beamed at them both, genuinely relieved and very happy to see them both. "So, what do you think of Spain in October?" he smiled again, "much cooler, better for your skin."

"This morning I am going to drive you to the farmhouse," Angel smiled, again, "I have arranged for us to meet the architect there, if that is OK with you both?"

"That's fantastic," Delia said excitedly, "thank you ever so much for everything that you have done for the both of us."

Angel led the way through a small gap between the buildings in the corner of the square, through a narrow walkway and into a car park.

"We have to keep wearing our face masks in the car," Angel said, "it's the law here and it makes good sense, considering that the whole world still seems to be gripped by this dreadful pandemic."

"Your English is very good," Delia said, "much better than some English people that we know."

Angel smiled, "Thank you, a lot of my work involves talking with English speaking people. How was the flight over here?" Angel said, as he opened the back doors for Delia and then Horace to get inside.

"Very good," Delia replied, "very quiet, not many people traveling from the airport in England."

"We can use the back road," Angel, said, speaking over his left shoulder, "the local council have done a lot of work to it, people are now using it a lot more, now that the surface is a lot easier to drive on."

The journey along the back road was much more comfortable than their last trip with Sebastian.

It appeared to be much wider, all the large pot holes had been filled in and it has been covered with some kind of white concrete chipping.

Just before the ninety-degree bend in the road that took you off to the left and down the lane, lined with eucalyptus trees on either side, then passing the villas and then down towards the golf course, Angel turned the car, sharply to the right, onto the new run in, that lead up to the farmhouse and stopped the car.

"Well, what do you think?" he said, as Delia and then Horace got out from the car.

"It's very big," Delia said, facing towards the new farmhouse building that was already half built, above the ground floor windows.

"There is a lot of land," Horace said, looking around at the different colours of the yellows and browns of the surrounding dry parched landscape.

"It does look a mess at the moment," Angel said. "But it is a construction site and we haven't had any rain since last April. Follow me," Angel said, "I can introduce you to the architect, Juan Jose Carlos. I know that he has already arrived, I can see his car."

Horace and Delia followed Angel around the side of the building and to the back, where a group of men were standing chatting, drinking coffee.

Jose the architect came towards them as they approached, "this is Mr and Mrs Dankworth," Angel said, carrying out the introductions, "and this is Jose, the architect."

Jose was holding a leather case, he raised it slightly in recognition and smiled, "welcome to Spain," he said. "If you would like to follow me, please."

Jose led them over to a makeshift table that the builders had put together with wooden trestles and some of the internal doors.

"In normal times, we would have met at my office," Jose began, "this is how we do things out here now; all our meetings are now carried out here, in the fresh air."

Jose put his case down onto the table, taking out some drawings of the completed farmhouse building, laying them all out, showing how it will look, once completed.

"As Angel has already explained," Jose began, "we are standing on agricultural ground, the building has to resemble a traditional Spanish farmhouse and I was given very strict instructions by the local council on how the house must look. Everything that I am showing you now has been approved by the local council, and we must work to the strict guidelines that has already been agreed."

"The house is more or less standing on the same position as the original house that was built more than one hundred and fifty years ago, but we have been allowed to turn its standing position, so the large roof area faces south, and the all-day sun. Electricity here in Spain is very expensive," Jose said, then handed Horace a booklet containing pictures and information about solar panels that produced electricity.

"We are going to fix solar panels to the roof for all your electricity needs, and a different kind of solar panels for your hot water. We are also going to fix solar panels onto the barn roof, they will provide the hot water for the swimming pool and the pump and filters we can install inside."

"When the house is nearer completion, you will be asked to pick out the wall and floor tiles and the fixtures for the bathrooms," Jose smiled towards Delia, "that will probably be your job."

"When do you think it will be ready?" Horace asked, "And how much is all this going to cost?"

"The house should be ready in around two- or three-months' time," Jose said, "You will have to talk to Angel about the cost. I have already been paid my fee," Jose smiled.

"This is going to be a much better house than one of the villas that have been built on the edge of the golf course," Angel said, "everything will be perfect, a dream house in a dream location."

"So why hadn't somebody come along and built on this land before?" Horace said, thinking that everything here was much too good to be true.

"A lot of builders have tried in the past to develop the land and squeeze as many houses as they possibly could onto the site, especially after the golf course was completed, but all their plans have always been rejected. The land was handed back to the government many years ago and is strictly for agricultural use only and can only be used for farming," Jose said.

"If this land has been vacant for so many years, why hasn't a local farmer bought it?"

"The local farmers in this area are very superstitious," Angel said, "there are a lot of old stories about what happened here years many ago, they think the land is cursed."

Delia, at the start, had been annoyed with Horace, with all his questions, appearing to be ungrateful not appreciating everything that Angel had done for them both. But now, even she was more than interested to hear the history of what had happened here at the original farmhouse, all those years ago.

"What happened here years ago?" Delia asked.

Jose suddenly cut in, "I am very sorry, I have another appointment very soon and I have to say goodbye now."

Delia thanked Jose for all his efforts and said it had been a pleasure to meet him. Jose said that he had enjoyed working on the house and that he was very pleased with what they had all achieved. Angel walked with Jose towards his car, speaking in Spanish, then they both touched fists and then elbows. Then Jose got into his car and drove away.

Angel came back over to the table, where Horace and Delia were still standing, "I suppose we should leave now and get out of the way of the builders, so they can push on with what they are doing," he said.

Angel then picked up all the drawings and various information sheets that Jose had left for them and handed them over to Horace. "You can study all this more closely, later, if you have any questions, you can give me a call."

Angel led the way back to the car, Delia was still very keen to learn what had happened to the people who had lived in the original farmhouse, all those years ago.

Delia opened the front passenger door and got in next to Angel, "So what happened to the farmer and his wife?" she asked.

Angel was surprised by Delia's actions, it wasn't what respectable people normally did in Spain, sitting in the front seat with another man while the husband sat in the back seat, all alone.

Angel started the engine and pushed the gear stick forward into first gear, he could see Delia's very white English knees, just a few centimetres away from his right hand. Angel looked into the rear-view mirror, immediately making eye contact with Horace. "So?" Horace said, "what happened?"

"The village was built many years ago around a very strong farming community," Angel began, "there are many stories from the past that have been passed down through the generations over the years. I am still considered to be an outsider here, by the local farming community, even though I have lived here for many years now," Angel said. "And that I am the only solicitor who lives in the village and over the past years have helped or represented almost everyone at some point. I spent a considerable amount of time searching through the old documents and records for the names of the couple that lived at the farmhouse."

"I found a record of them getting married at the old local church in the village. But then, nothing, I couldn't find their names on any of the old land registry records. No records of them ever owning the land, my search was very thorough, searching through all the old documents, just in case somebody turned up at your door in years to come, claiming that the property is theirs. Some of the stories that the local people have told me, during my search sound like complete nonsense, they couldn't possibly be true."

"But what about the farmhouse?" Delia said. "What is the story behind that?"

"The people that originally lived there were pig and sheep farmers," Angel began, "senor Mateo Morales and his wife Mencia. They only had a small herd of pigs but they had a huge heard of goats and sheep, the biggest in the region. The husband, Mateo, spent most of his time away from the house, grazing the goats and sheep up in the surrounding mountains, while the wife, Mencia, stayed at home, looking after the pigs."

"Mateo would sometimes be away from the house for weeks and weeks on end, leaving his wife all alone in the farmhouse. Like all the farmers and shepherds back in those days, he drank very heavily and gambled, he would often leave the dogs to look after the heard in the hills behind the village and walk down to the local bar to drink and play poker."

"All the men that he met at the bar, like him, were farmers and shepherds, none of them carried money for the fear of being robbed up in the mountain's, so they would use dried beans for currency and the barman kept a book in a safe, behind the bar of who owed who and what."

"No money ever changed hands, they used to pay off their debts with goats and sheep, there was a lot of disagreements and often the game would end in a huge drunken fight. Mateo very rarely lost at poker, and all the other farmers were always accusing him of cheating, over the years he had won a lot of goats from all the other farmers."

"Mencia, his wife, desperately wanted a child, but Mateo wasn't interested and would rather spend his evenings gambling and sleeping on the slopes of the mountains with his sheep. Sick of his drinking and gambling, Mencia took in a lover, a huge man, called Don Carlos. While Mateo was in the bar, drinking and playing poker, Don Carlos would go to the farmhouse and make wild passionate love to Mencia."

"One night, there was a huge fight at the bar, Mateo had just won one of the farmers' prized goat, the farmer said that Mateo was a cheating son of a bitch and his wife was a cheating bitch too, making rude gestures of what was happening to his wife, while he was away from the farmhouse, drinking."

"Gripped by a blind rage fuelled by alcohol, Mateo stumbled his way back to the farmhouse and took the shotgun from the barn and shot his wife Mencia and Don Carlos dead in the bed while they lay sleeping in each other's arms."

"So, we are buying a farmhouse from a drunken gambler and a murderer?" Horace said. "What if he comes back, while we are sleeping in our bed."

Delia chuckled, she hadn't taken Angel's story very seriously. "He should be quite harmless, he will be around one hundred and fifty years old by now," she chuckled. "What happened to Mateo?" Delia asked.

"He disappeared into the mountains," Angel said, "along with all his goats and sheep, he was never ever seen again from that day on."

"So, Mateo still owns the land?" Horace said, worried now, that his initial loss of three hundred thousand euros, had almost doubled to five hundred.

"No," Angel said, "the house stood empty for many years, after a set period of time, unclaimed land is taken back by the government, I think you will find, that the same laws are very similar in England."

"I have the deeds to the land and all the required building certificates in my office, everything is now registered in both your names, the house and land is now legally yours. We do have one small problem," Angel said, "you will have to buy some farm animals, there is no way around it, I have tried my best, the land is registered as farm land and all the buildings are for housing animals."

From the moment Horace had seen the new farmhouse and all the land that went with it, he had been overwhelmed by it all, Delia, originally, had persuaded him to buy a nice new clean white villa, looking out over the golf course, not some place miles from anywhere, full of pigs and chickens.

"Stop the car!" Horace shouted suddenly, "I think I am going to be sick!"

The disappointment from seeing the house, the large meal from the night before and the best part of two bottles of red wine, all being shaken around on the backseat of Angel's car, had all been too much for Horace's delicate English stomach.

Horace opened the back door and stepped out onto the white dusty track, hoping to take in some clean country fresh air, the air was warm and thick, not giving Horace any comfort, and his head started to bang even more.

He stumbled his way around to the back of the car, over to a very old looking olive tree, putting his arm forward onto a strong branch, he then rested his head onto his arm, facing down, looking at the ground.

Delia half turned in her seat, her white knees moving even closer towards Angel's hand, "I hope he is going to be OK," she said.

Angel turned, looking over his right shoulder, Horace was still in the same position, holding onto the olive tree, making weird gestures with his mouth, like a huge goldfish gasping for air.

"Yes, I am sure he is going to be fine," Angel said, turning back, glancing down at Delia's beautiful white knees, her dress had now risen up slightly, showing more of her beautiful firm white thighs.

Angel had a very strong impulse to drive off, slamming the gearstick forward into first gear, leaving Horace stranded there, in the middle of nowhere. It was a huge shame it wasn't August, he wouldn't last very long out here, exposed to the intense heat of the Spanish August sun, maybe, getting bitten by a poisonous snake or a scorpion.

After a short period of wearing black and mourning, Delia, maybe, would ask him to move in with her at the farmhouse. Then everyone in the village, especially the farmers would watch him with envy as he drove past in his new white Mercedes and his very white rose of an English wife. Every evening, he would fill the bathroom with scented candles and sit and watch Delia while she bathed her beautiful white naked body in goat's milk.

The back door suddenly opened and Horace got back into the car.

"Sorry about that," he said, "I think that I must have drunk too much red wine last night," wiping some red-tinted slobber away from his mouth with the back of his hand.

Angel started the car. "That OK," he said, suddenly being broken away from his beautiful, wishful daydream. "That happens a lot out here in Spain," he said.

Chapter 25

Horace awoke early the next morning feeling much better, after Angel had dropped them both back at the small square, they had spent the rest of the day discussing their future and what they should do, now that they were officially the owners of a new farmhouse and the surrounding land.

Angel had said to them both, in the first instance everything had gone completely wrong for them, mostly due to circumstances way out and beyond their control, but with his help, they had landed on their feet and now they were the owners of a new farmhouse, probably worth at the very least four times more than what it had cost them to build.

These few words from Angel had changed Horace's opinion on the farmhouse completely, he had cheered up considerably. Thinking to himself that they could sell the place, once it was finished and buy themselves something else, much more suitable for their needs.

The bathroom door suddenly burst open and Delia came into the bedroom, a towel wrapped around her body, the room was filled with the smell of strawberry, peach and apple shower gel.

"Good morning, farmer Horace," she smiled, "will you be going out drinking and gambling tonight? Or will you be staying home and making love to your adorable wife?"

Horace smiled, he would never be a drinker, or a gambler, he had never played poker, he would be hopeless at it, he would never have a poker face, or be a good bluffer, his face always got too red and flushed.

"I think I will just settle for a shower," he said, quickly getting out of the bed, not really feeling in the mood for lovemaking and not wanting to disappoint Delia with another lacklustre performance.

Once Horace had taken his shower, they both walked into the village high street, the sun was much gentler now and Delia didn't feel the need to wear her hat or her sunglasses. Horace still felt more comfortable wearing a straw hat and his sunglasses, even though he was still having problems with condensation caused by the wearing of the protective face mask.

They managed to walk the full length of the high street, all the way to the top, stopping at Paco's mini mart. Paco seemed genuinely pleased to see them both, and asked Delia if everything was good at the apartment, this time speaking very slowly in basic Spanish so Delia would understand. Paco wanted to ask Delia about Sebastian, and about the villa, and about the huge dig that was now taking place up at the site, but knowing Delia's Spanish was still at the very early stages, more like, good morning or good night, he thought it would be best to wait until another time, when he's son would be there, so he could translate, so in the meantime, settled just for nod and a smile.

Horace and Delia slowly worked their way around the shelves of the mini mart, Delia reading the labels on the jars and packaging, using Google translate on her phone and consulting her small Spanish dictionary.

Delia enjoyed the whole new shopping experience, after a good half an hour, they left the shop, both carrying a plastic reusable shopping bag, containing, two cartons of fully skimmed long-life milk, a jar of decaffeinated coffee, four long freshly baked bread sticks, butter, without salt, and two types of marmalade, and a large bottle of water.

After breakfast, Horace and Delia explored the rest of the village a little more, now that the temperature was more favourable, there was no need to rush from one place to another, seeking the shade. There seemed to be a lot of walking trails that led out and away from the outside of the village, up into the surrounding countryside.

Horace and Delia both enjoyed walking, and decided to walk out from the village following one of the trails, marked out by wooden posts and small blue arrows, pointing the way.

Right from the very beginning, the trail took them up the side of the mountainside, the pathway had been cut in such a way that it didn't take the most direct route up to the top.

It had been cut in the shape of a zig zag, firstly, veering off to the right, and then bending ninety degrees to the left, making the climb more possible, with much less of a slope.

There didn't seem to be anyone else around, Horace pulled off his face mask and put it into his pocket. "Phew, that's better," he said, "can't see the point, struggling to breathe when there is no one else around."

After two or three kilometres or so, the open barren landscape changed and they found themselves following the trail through a shady pine forest. The hard rock path was now much easier to walk on, covered by hundreds of years' worth of falling pine needles, forming a thick golden-brown carpet. After two hours of steady walking, Horace and Delia reached what looked like the end of the trail.

The woodlands, opening up into a large flat area with a viewing point that looked out over the village, then the golf course far beyond in the distance.

"It's a shame we didn't bring a picnic," Delia said, looking at her watch, "it will take us another two hours before we get back down to the village."

Horace held onto the sturdy ranch style wooden fencing that formed a safe barrier on the edge of the mountainside. "I can see how what's his name, Mateo, disappeared off into the mountains after murdering his wife, it is such a big country, with so much open space, we haven't seen a living soul since we left the village. All this space up here, you could very easily murder and bury someone, no one would ever know."

"They must have sent the police out looking for him," Delia said, "if the story is to be believed, surely a man with all those goats and sheep can't be that hard to track down and find, especially with sniffer dogs."

"I wonder if the police have caught up with Sebastian yet?" Horace said, "the police would soon find him if they used sniffer dogs, the rat. This seems to be a very easy place to go missing from, especially if you have just murdered someone, or just screwed them out of all of their life's savings and everything that they have worked for," Horace said, kicking the wooden safety rail.

"Maybe we should start heading back down to the village," Delia said, "I wouldn't like to be stuck up here after nightfall."

Horace looked around, the whole place suddenly felt very eerie and creepy, he had a strong sense that someone was watching him, lurking in the shadows of the dense pine forest.

Delia was already fifty metres away on the start of her descent.

Horace quickly caught Delia up, holding on to her hand, then turning around, nervously, just to make sure that there was no one behind them.

"Imagine sleeping up here on the mountainside with all those sheep and goats, with all those eerie shapes moving around in the darkness, with blood on your hands," Horace said, looking around over his shoulder, once again just to make sure that no one was there, stalking them.

By the time that Horace and Delia, arrived back at the small square in the village, it was somewhere between mid to late afternoon.

The restaurant was already open, with just one lonely figure, sitting outside, drinking a glass of larger.

The lonely figure watched them as the they drew closer and then gave them a wave. "It's Maisie, from downstairs," Delia said, waving back enthusiastically.

Horace was now close enough to see the very dark-skin of Maisie's wrinkled face, her face mask sitting under her chin.

"Let's go somewhere else," Horace said, pulling at Delia's hand, just wanting to have a quiet meal with his wife and not wanting to be trapped by something so sun-baked and intimidating.

Delia slipped her hand free from the sweaty grip of Horace's sweaty left palm, walking directly to where Maisie was sitting.

Horace hung back, hoping that Delia would just say a quick hello and then move away. Delia half turned. "Horace," she said, "Look it's Maisie, from the flat below, it's Maisie."

Suddenly, the restaurant owner was there, laying out two extra napkins and two sets of knives and forks. He pulled out a chair for Delia to sit down, Maisie looked towards Horace, offering him a combination of a pitiful pathetic stare and a wry smile, like an abandoned moggie on the side of a motorway or at an overcrowded cat's home.

Slowly, Horace moved forward and sat down, doing his very best not to make eye contact with Maisie, mumbling good afternoon and then quickly ordering a bottle of red wine.

Both Horace and Delia felt very hungry, the vigorous walk and taking in the fresh mountain air, had worked wonders for their appetite. Delia ordered, the charcoal grilled fillet of chicken with new potatoes and vegetables, Horace said he would like the same.

"Maisie looked across the table towards Horace, you should have ordered white wine with the chicken," she said, "White meat, white wine, red meat, red wine. There is nothing that I don't know about fine wines and alcoholic beverages," Maisie said, putting the glass of larger to her lips and downing what was left in one go.

Horace, couldn't think of anything to say in return, His thoughts returning to Mateo, wandering alone, high above the village up in the mountains.

Preferring the company of the goats, rather than sleep in a comfortable bed with his wife, especially if she looked anything like the women who was sitting directly opposite him.

The restaurant owner returned with a bottle of Horace's and Delia's favourite red wine, he turned Delia's glass over and poured in the wine, half filling her glass, then stood there holding the bottle, waiting for the inevitable.

"Would you like some red wine, Maisie?" Delia asked, Maisie turned over her wine glass, "oh go on then," she said, "I am having goat meat balls in tomato sauce, a perfect combination with red wine," she said, narrowing her eyes while looking across the table at Horace, disapprovingly.

"Shall we hold on to your meatballs for a while, Senora? so you can all eat together, the waiter asked, pouring the red wine into Maisie's glass, knowing that he was onto a winner, a perfect opportunity to shift a few more bottles of red wine."

"That's an excellent idea," Delia smiled, it can't be much fun eating on your own."

Horace's mind slipped back to the thought of Mateo, bursting into the bedroom, blasting his wife, from point blank rang with a shotgun.

Looking across the table at Maisie, he could see why Mateo had killed his wife and why he had been driven into such a dreadful act, solely out of never-ending mental torture and desperation.

"We used to own a restaurant like this," Maisie said, then taking more than a huge sip of wine, "My husband, Frank and I, down on the cost, we were there for thirty years or more. We fell into the trap of drinking too much, it killed my husband in the end, we were both alcoholics, the doctor warned him, if he didn't stop it would kill him."

"So how long have you been living here?" Delia asked, not able to think of anything positive to say about alcoholism or her dear departed husband, Frank.

"I sold the bar, ten years ago, after my husband Frank died, the doctors said that I needed to get away from working in and around alcohol, or I would be following my husband's footsteps and would be dead just inside the following year. I went to live with my brother at first, in a little mountain village called sweet water, he owns a small farm there and lives with his Spanish wife, Maria."

"When I arrived there, my brother, Ron, was in a bad way, I thought it was a bit strange when he didn't show up to pick me up from the bus station as arranged. He was too drunk to drive the truck and was lying in one of the barns with the goats, by the time that I had arrived. I stayed there for almost a year, helping Ron and Maria to get the place back onto its feet, Ron and I, joined alcoholics anonymous, we both helped each other to kick the booze."

Maisie put the wine glass to her lips and finished off what was left in the glass.

"Then I found this place, I couldn't live there at Sweet Water, it was much too quiet for me, nothing happening there, I was so bored, I was very tempted to start drinking again. Don't fall through the dark hole of the drinking trap to hell," Maisie said, looking, directly across the table at Horace, "it's much too easy especially if you are thinking of living out here permanently."

"So, what is happening with the new villa, that you are supposed to be buying?" Maisie asked. "I see that the estate agent in the high street has closed down, and that they have found some Roman ruins up at the site."

The waiter arrived at the table with the food, "Would you like another bottle of wine to go with your meal, senora?"

Delia picked up the bottle and poured what was left into Maisie's glass and handed him the empty bottle, "yes please," she said smiling, "this food looks delicious."

Luckily for Horace, now that the food had arrived, Maisie had stopped talking, and was now putting all her effort into eating her meatballs.

This gave Horace the opportunity to get on, allowing him to eat his meal in peace and have a few mouthfuls of the red wine before Maisie finished off the second bottle.

Maisie couldn't eat nowhere near the speed that she could drink, just about finishing her plate of meatballs by the time that Horace and Delia had eaten a complete chicken dinner.

The waiter returned to clear the table, asking if they wanted anything else to eat, quite disappointed to see that the second bottle of red wine was still not quite yet empty.

Horace answered very quickly, "No thank you, and could we have the bill please," not wanting to spend the afternoon on a bender, drinking red wine with Maisie.

"So, what happened with the villa?" Maisie asked.

"As soon as they uncovered the Roman ruins, all the work stopped, luckily for us we found a good solicitor and we have now bought a new farmhouse on a different site," Delia said, pouring what was left of the red wine into her own glass and refilling Maisie's.

"I never realised that you were looking at properties as big as farmhouses," Maisie said, "you could have bought my brother Ron's place. They are both desperate to sell their farm, and move into a village like this, Maria says, that she is sick of farming and she now wants to enjoy life while she still can. They still have a small goat herd that they are desperate to sell, but because of the recession caused by the Covid virus, nobody wants them."

"Maybe we could buy them," Delia said, "apparently, we have to keep animals on the farm, part of the agreement, so that we can live there."

Horace almost choked on what was left of his red wine, looking across the table at Delia. She couldn't be drunk, she had only had one or two glassfuls, if that, she would never joke about something like that, especially with someone like Maisie, who by now was looking at least two parts pissed.

"Goats!" Horace said, "I thought once we had settled in, we could possible get a rabbit or maybe a tortoise."

Delia leant back in her chair, laughing uncharacteristically. "Oh Horace, you're so funny sometimes. I have read through the small print of the translated agreement that we have both signed, I don't think a rabbit or a tortoise really qualify as farm animals."

"Well, we can't buy goats," Horace said, sounding quite hysterical, "that's a ridiculous idea, we don't know anything about them, who would look after them when we are not here? I am an accountant, not a goat herder, I crunch numbers for a living, that's what I spent all those years studying for."

"You wouldn't even notice that they were there," Maisie said, grasping at the opportunity to sell her brother's goats and possibly get back the ten thousand euros that he still owed her. "You would save them all from the slaughterhouse," Maisie said, adding a bit more girth to her sales pitch. "Horrible place," Maisie said, looking across the table at Horace, "nothing humane there, they just come out and shot them through the head with a nail gun, right where they stand, blood everywhere. We are probably too late," Maisie said, "It's a shame, they are probably being slaughtered right now as we speak."

"Can't we at least go and look at them?" Delia said, "I am sure they don't cost too much to feed, and they would keep the garden under control."

"There would be goat's crap everywhere," Horace said, not understanding why Delia was suddenly so interested in keeping goats, "smelly things, you wouldn't be able to step outside the front door."

"We used to take the school children to an urban farm," Delia said, "they had goats there, they were always nice and clean and smelt of shower gel, the children loved them."

The waiter came back with the bill and placed it in the middle of the table.

Horace quickly picked up the paper bill and slid the money under the clip of the small silver tray provided.

Maisie sort of fumbled around with her small bag, her fingers fumbling around with the clasp, asking Horace how much she owed him.

Horace by now was already on his feet and was slowly backing away, and could have quite easily turned and broken into a gallop.

"Don't worry about that," Delia said, "our treat, talk to your brother about the goats, tell him that we may be interested," Delia said, before turning, then breaking into a little jog to catch Horace up.

"Goats," Horace mumbled, he was still going on about it, by the time that Delia had caught him up.

Delia grabbed hold of Horace's hand, "we will have to talk to Angel," she smiled, "he said something about, we need to apply for a farming licence, maybe it's just a technicality, and somehow we can work around it."

Horace couldn't think of anything else to say, Delia must have drunk much more of the red wine than he had thought. It had been quite a long day, what with the long walk up the side of the mountain and the fresh mountain air, now they both felt a little light-headed and tired.

They both would have an early night, Horace thought to himself, and in the morning all this talk of goats would have been forgotten.

Chapter 26

Around eight thirty Friday morning, there was a light tapping on the door of Horace's and Delia's apartment.

"Horace," Delia said, "did you hear that?"

Horace had awoken a half hour earlier and was now drifting in and out of sleep, "hear what?" he asked.

There was another tapping on the door, this time much louder, more like a knocking.

"There is somebody at the door," Delia said, quickly getting out from the bed, pulling on her lightweight dressing gown.

"Don't let that cat in!" Horace shouted, as Delia disappeared out of the bedroom and into the small hallway.

Horace could hear voices, talking at the doorway, then the door closed and he could hear whoever it was passing through into the small sitting room.

Horace quickly got out from the bed and pulled on his clothes from the night before.

"This is Maisie's nephew, Alberto," Delia said as Horace entered the room.

Maisie was sitting in one of the small armchairs, wearing a black facemask that was covering her nose and mouth. Alberto moved forward towards Horace, smiling from behind his facemask, offering his elbow for Horace to touch with his, "My friends call me Bert."

Horace wiggled his elbow, returning the gesture from a safe distance, mostly from embarrassment than the fear of catching Covid.

"Alberto stayed over last night, he is staying for a couple of days at Maisie's," Delia said, "and they were wondering if we would like to go with Alberto this morning to see the goats?"

Horace didn't know what to say, he had been taken completely by surprise, ambushed, trapped, in the corner, there was no escape.

And what a stupid question, of course he didn't want to go and see a field full of smelly goats. In the small space of time that he had been allowed, Horace couldn't think of any plausible excuse why they shouldn't go, Maisie was sitting there, squinting, starring at him, waiting for him to reply.

Horace looked at Alberto, he looked nothing like his aunty, he was a young man in his early twenties with dark hair and lightly tanned golden-brown skin.

"I can drive you both there now," Alberto said, smiling at Horace, "after breakfast, we would be there in no time at all."

Horace looked at Delia, He could see that she was bubbling over with excitement, he had to say yes, there was nothing else he could do or say.

"Give us a knock when you are ready," Alberto smiled, "and wear some warmer clothes, it's a lot cooler up in the mountains this time of year."

After Delia had seen them both out, she came rushing back into the sitting room. "Thank you, darling," she said, wrapping her arms around Horace, thinking about the school trips in the past and the beautiful well-behaved goats that smelt of shower gel.

After eating their breakfast of toasted bread rolls and marmalade and a large mug of coffee, Delia took her shower, followed by Horace, then following Alberto's advice they both togged up with the warmer clothes that Delia had packed for the return journey back to England.

After pulling the front door shut, Horace followed Delia down the single flight of stairs, hanging back while she knocked on Maisie's front door.

Alberto was out just a few seconds later, "that's good," he said, "you remembered to wear some warm clothing."

"So, how many goats are there?" Delia asked.

"Not really sure on the exact numbers," Alberto said, "it is only a small herd, they are always out grazing on the slops around the farmhouse, I grew up with them, to me they have always been part of the landscape."

By now, all three were in the small carpark, directly behind the apartment block. Horace and Delia's eyes suddenly focused on the very old white Peugeot 207, that was sitting all alone over in the far corner, like it was waiting for the scrap dealer to arrive and tow it away. Up till that point, Horace and Delia hadn't even thought about what mode of transport young Alberto might be using.

Delia had been too excited, looking forward to the trip ahead as a new adventure, traveling more into the interior of Spain, passing through remote villages, maybe having lunch, sampling the local produce in the village of Sweat Water.

"Maybe we should take the hire car," Horace said, now close enough to look inside at the very small space between the front and rear seats.

"It's much better if I drive," Alberto said, unlocking the doors, which seemed to be a pointless exercise as the tattered vinyl roof had been left down all night. "It might look a wreck but it goes like a bomb," he smiled, "the roof is stuck down so we will be getting plenty of fresh air into the car, no need to wear our masks."

Reluctantly, Horace and Delia squeezed themselves into the back seats, they had very little padding offering very little support or comfort. Horace and Delia both had to turn their legs to one side, so their knees didn't push into the seats at the front.

Alberto turned the key in the ignition, the engine didn't sound like it was going to start, Horace was desperately hoping, praying that it wouldn't, so they could use the hire car, or better still abandon the whole trip all together.

Suddenly, the engine roared into life and with one quick action, Alberto selected first gear, dropped the clutch and Horace and Delia were flung back in their seats. Horace had remembered to wear his sunglasses but had forgotten his straw hat, not that it mattered. He would have soon lost it, once they had left the village and Alberto had an open road ahead and was able to put his foot down.

Surprisingly, it wasn't as windy as Horace and Delia had anticipated, with the moulded windscreen giving them a lot of protection.

Once Alberto had taken the second turning off from the roundabout and down the ramp and merging into the traffic on the main road, any sort of conversation would have been out of the question.

The noise from the passing traffic, the sound of the wind being displaced around the car and the noise and vibration now coming from the gearbox, was nothing like the trip that Delia had imagined.

Horace began to fill his head with worry, did this crazy young man have any form of motor insurance, or even worse, did he even have a driving licence?

Were Delia and himself covered by their holiday insurance? would it cover the cost of all the emergency services, cutting them out from the tangled mess and flying them to an adequately equipped hospital by helicopter?

By the time that Alberto had taken the exit from the main road that was signposted Bengaluru and Sweet Water village, only one hour and thirty-three minutes had passed. Although to Horace, it had seemed like a lifetime, with him checking his watch every few minutes along the way.

The sun had been shining directly into Horace's face, and with the combination of the wind, he could feel his face burning, feeling hotter and hotter with every kilometre that had passed, and to make things much worse he had also lost all the feelings in both of his legs.

Thankfully, Alberto had slowed the car down considerably, and the vibration and the noise from the gear box had suddenly stopped.

Delia now felt more comfortable, she had managed to shift her knees from one side to the other and was now taking in the view and the sudden change in the landscape. Most of the journey up till now that they had passed by had been mostly agricultural land with huge greenhouses set-in wide-open spaces and fields full of different types of fruit and vegetables.

But now, once they had left the main road, they seemed to be heading up into the mountains, the road following the outside edge of one mountain side that veered to the right and then at the next bend the road took them around the next mountain edge off to the left, all the time climbing steadily upwards.

Thankfully, the road was still of a good quality with always the mountain to one side and a crash barrier on the outside edge of the other.

At some point, just before the car turned off to the left, as it approached a ninety-degree bend, Horace and Delia found themselves looking straight ahead, over the side of the mountain and into the distance they could both see a whitewashed village, brightly illuminated by the October sun.

"The village of Sweet water!" Alberto shouted over his left shoulder.

By now, Horace had had enough, the pain in his legs had become unbearable and his thoughts had turned to deep vein thrombosis and blood clots. Also, with all the vibration coming up through his legs from the gearbox, there was something going on downstairs, he wasn't sure if he needed to do a wee or not, or if it was already seeping out into his pants.

"How much further?" Horace called out.

"A half an hour at the most," Alberto shouted, "almost there."

Horace glanced sideways at Delia, considering everything, she seemed quite relaxed and comfortable with no sign of pain visible showing in her face.

Delia was aware of Horace, studying her face, she shifted her knees to the other side once again and then reached across, holding Horace's hand, "we will soon be there, darling," she said.

Horace glanced down at his crotch area, he couldn't see any visible evidence of wee or blood, but he now was experiencing a strange tingling sensation, he was now desperate to get out of the car, whatever the cost. If only he had worn his straw hat, he could have allowed the wind take it off from the top of his head and then call out to Alberto to stop the car.

He tried to shift his knees from one side to the other, like Delia had done, many times over the course of the journey, but his legs were much longer than hers and they felt like they had been cast in concrete, stuck in the same position that he had adopted right from the start.

"Look!" Delia suddenly shouted. "The village of Sweet Water."

Horace glanced past Delia, out over the huge chasm of open space, the village of sweet water was just on the other side of the mountains, now, much, much closer than it had been before.

Horace was filled with hope, maybe there would be a restaurant or something on the approach to the village of Sweet Water and they would be able to stop for a toilet break.

After another agonising ten minutes had passed, there was still no sign of the village of sweet water, but the road had now levelled off and Alberto had turned the car off from the mountain road and down a side track.

Alberto put his foot hard down on the accelerator, causing a huge cloud of dust that was now floating along behind the car, "almost there!" he shouted.

After eating up a few more dusty kilometres, Alberto took the left fork at the end of the track, not bothering to take his foot of the accelerator, for any need to slow down.

Since they had left the mountain road, there had not been any sign of life, they seemed to be in the middle of nowhere surrounded by miles and miles of open scrubland.

"Just as well we didn't use the hire car," Delia said, "they would have never found us if we had broken down out here."

"It's nothing like this from Christmas time to late spring here," Alberto called out, sensing the disappointment in Delia's voice, "everywhere is covered with different types of wildflowers, the whole place is alive with colour. We have had a very long hot summer in this area, not much can survive out here, that's why we keep goats and not sheep, we still haven't had any rain here in this area since last March."

Then, suddenly, without any prior warning, Alberto swung the car to the right, turning onto yet another dusty track and now in the far distance, Horace and Delia could see the outline of some kind of building.

"That's our place, up there, straight ahead," Alberto shouted.

Alberto skidded the car to a halt about fifty metres from the house, beeping the horn and then leaping out from the car all in one continuous action. Delia was also out of the car, pushing Alberto's vacated seat forward and then springing out like a greyhound at the starting line, racing out from its trap.

After all the time that Horace had spent secretly praying to himself that the car would break down or the engine would explode, so that he could escape from this pile of shit, he now found himself paralysed, unable to move. The dense trail of dust that had been following them, all along the way, had now caught them up and had engulfed Horace in and around the car, before slowly drifting on towards the house.

Horace leant forward and pushed the empty passenger seat in front of him as far as it would go, but he still was unable to move his legs, as if all the lines of communication from his brain to the whole region below his waist had been severed.

Then, in front of him, out from the dust, appeared a very dark Spanish lady, as if she had risen up out of nowhere or from a hole in the ground.

Alberto swiftly moved towards her, they both embraced, kissing each other on both sides of the cheeks, as if he had been away for at least two years and not just one single night.

Delia was suddenly aware of Horace's absence, not wanting to be formally introduced to Alberto's mother without Horace by her side.

She turned and walked quickly back to the car, "Horace, are you alright?"

"I can't get out of this damn car," Horace replied, "I can't move my legs!"

Delia turned around, she could see Alberto and his mother, moving towards them, talking in Spanish and both looking curiously in their direction.

Delia opened the driver's door, grabbing hold of both of Horace's ankles, lifting his feet slightly and gently swinging his legs around, towards the open doorway.

"See if you can slide yourself out now," Delia said, now that Horace had swivelled his body around on the seat and his legs were hanging out over the side of the car.

Horace slowly slid off from the seat until his feet touched the ground, and then with one hand on the metal and Delia pulling the other, Horace slowly stood up.

By this time, Alberto and his mother had reached the car and were both standing there, looking at Horace and then Delia, talking in Spanish.

"Why have you brought these people here to buy our goats?" Alberto's mother was saying, "this guy is obviously a cripple, how will he take care of them?"

"He didn't seem like a cripple earlier," Alberto said, "I saw him walk down the stairs and to the car."

"Aunt Maisie said nothing about him be a cripple, she told me that he is a big wig accountant from England with pots of money, and he is having a huge farmhouse built on acres of land."

Alberto stepped a little forward, "This is my mother," he said, "she doesn't speak any English, she says, welcome to our house."

Delia gave a little wave, "Buenos dias," she said. Politely smiling.

Horace mumbled, "hola," still not happy with being dragged all the way out here to the middle of nowhere, to this dusty shit hole of a place, and in a shit heap of a car.

"My mother has prepared lunch for us on the back terrace," Alberto smiled, still wondering about Horace and if he needed to be carried into the house.

Slowly, step by step, Horace had found his walking legs once again, and was able to glance around, on his way to the house, looking for any signs of the demon goats.

Delia also looked around, on her way into the house, she was bitterly disappointed, this place was nothing like she had imagined.

She thought they were going into the village of Sweet Water and to a farm possibly sitting on the outskirts, with a long driveway up to the entrance, lined with orange and lemon trees, and a stream of crystal-clear water passing through a green meadow. A grandly well-organised place, where all the goats were soft and cute, little black and white fellows all neatly kept in pens and bleating affectionately.

Alberto's parents' farmhouse was built from solid stone with a pattern of good thick veins of mortar, bonding everything together. Alberto's mother had left the front door wide open, she half turned in the doorway as she went inside beckoning them to follow her in.

They followed Alberto's mother along a short hallway and into the main living area, there was a large patio door in front of them that had already been slid back, wide open.

Horace and Delia were more than pleasantly surprised by the rear garden and the patio area, as if they had stepped through a portal from hell and into an oasis of sanctitude. The whole area had been closed off, with attractive green fencing with shrubs and climates planted all around the edges and neat tidy borders full of different types of plants and flowers. There was a huge swimming pool that had blue tiles and patterns of dolphins, set into the tiles on the inside edge, just below the water line.

There was a very attractive barbeque area over in the far corner, all finished with very colourful mosque tiles.

Alberto's mum had been busy, she had put a white tablecloth, covering the patio table and had laid out the cutlery and placed upturned wine glasses sitting on top of red serviettes. She beckoned with her hand for Horace and Delia to sit down at the table and then disappeared into the house, quickly returning with a jug of water with slices of lemon and ice floating around.

After the very long drive in the back seat of Alberto's car, Horace was very reluctant to sit down, but the chairs seemed extra comfy with a very thick, brightly coloured padding.

Horace sat down, stretching his legs out under the very large solid looking oak table, his knees had now stopped hurting, but now he seemed to have developed a pain in the left side of his back that seemed to go away if he cocked his head over to one side.

Alberto's mother was now sitting at the far end of the table, staring at Horace curiously, Alberto was standing by her side, pouring some water into her glass.

"There is definitely something wrong with this guy," she was saying loud enough for everyone to hear, assuming that Horace and Delia didn't understand a word of Spanish. "He doesn't appear to be the type of person who could look after a herd of goats. Especially with his ginger hair and his very white freckled skin, he wouldn't last five minutes out there in the open countryside."

"My mother has prepared us a salad for lunch and wants to know if you would like to eat now or wait for my father to come home with the goats?"

"It would be better if we waited for your father," Delia said, "we don't want to inconvenience anyone."

Alberto put the water jug down on the table next to Horace and Delia and told them to help themselves.

Then after a short conversation with his mother, she took out her mobile phone and held it up to her ear.

"She is ringing my father," Alberto said, "to see how far away he is and what time he will arrive home."

Sitting out there in the middle of nowhere with no background noise was incredibly quiet, and everyone sitting around the table could easily hear the sound of Alberto's mother mobile calling her husband.

After what seemed like a very long and embarrassing period of time for everyone sitting there in absolute silence, listening to the sound of Alberto's mother's dialling tone from her mobile phone calling her husband, she took the phone from her ear and put it down on the table in front of her.

She then got up from the table, mumbling away to herself, Alberto quickly got up from his seat also and followed his mother back into the house.

They both quickly returned, carrying plates and glass containers, containing cheese, ham and tuna, also bowls of salad, arranging everything on the table before going back into the house.

"My mother thinks it will be better to eat now," Alberto said, placing more bowls of food on the table, "before everything gets spoilt."

Horace had cheered up considerably, the pain in his back had slowly ebbed away and the food that Alberto's mother had prepared was excellent.

Delia talked to Alberto across the table, "please thank your mother for this marvellous food," she said, "and this bread is the best that I have ever tasted."

Alberto's mother smiled at Delia, while talking in Spanish for her son to translate.

"My mother says you must call her Maria, and she says thank you for the compliments, she makes the bread herself and the cheese is made from our own goat's milk."

After lunch, Maria came out from the house carrying two large jugs of homemade Tinto Verano, and Alberto handed out the tall wine glasses, "take it easy with this stuff," he smiled, "it's quite strong, an old family recipe, handed down from my grandmother."

After a glass of Maria's Tinto Verano, Maria asked Horace and Delia if they would like to swim in the pool.

Delia said that would be lovely but they didn't have any bathing costumes with them, "I suppose I could swim in my dress." She giggled.

Horace turned his head, so he could look at Delia's face, as he had suspected, she had drunk the Tinto Verano much to quickly and her face now looked flushed, a crimson red. Everything was now feeling a little strange, they had been driven out here in the middle of nowhere to look at some goats, but now Delia was acting a little tipsy and was contemplating swimming in the pool fully dressed.

Maria took Delia by the hand and led her into the house, talking to her directly, using very basic Spanish and gesticulating.

Horace was more than happy to lay down on one of the sun loungers, under the shade created by a wooden pergola with a white material roof covering, situated at the far end of the pool.

Delia reappeared with Maria, both giggling like school girls, Maria diving into the pool and going the full length of the pool under the water. Delia choose to use the stainless-steel steps, expecting the water to be cold, now that the intense heat of the summer had passed.

Alberto suddenly appeared, sporting a very small tight pair of light blue speedos, running from the house at full pelt and making a huge splash.

Luckily for Delia, she had seen him coming and had quickly let go of the steps and belly-flopped into the water, making sure to get her shoulders under before the impact.

Horace finished off what was left of the Tinto Verano inside his glass and slid it under the sun lounger, then laid back and closed his eyes, it had been a very eventful four days, suddenly Horace felt very tired.

Sometime later Horace was abruptly woken by what sounded like raised voices, shouting at one and another over the loud noise of what sounded like the revving of a motorcycle.

Horace opened his eyes, he had been left in the garden all alone, he got up out of the sun lounger and went into the house through the open patio doorway, along the hallway and out through the wide-open front door.

Most of the shouting was being done by Maria, who was doing her very best to hold on to a man on a quad bike who Horace could only assume to be Ron, her husband. Alberto was doing his best to stop the guy from driving off, holding on to the chrome steel bar behind the rear seat, still wearing his blue speedos.

Delia spotted Horace coming out from the house and began to walk towards him, "It's Maria's husband," she said, "he has been drinking in a bar all day and left the goats up in the mountains with a friend."

After Horace's sleep, and being awoken abruptly, he had woken up feeling a little grumpy, his first impulse was to grab Delia by the hand and get the hell out of there.

Spain was beginning to seem unreal, a little bit crazy, this sort of thing would never have happened back home in England, in Victoria Avenue. Maria then somehow managed to pull the keys from the ignition, turning the engine off, then fleeing into the house being chased by her husband, Frank.

Alberto pushed the trike around to the side of the house, parking it under the shade of a car port, next to his mother's car.

"I am very sorry about all this," Alberto said, "my father has taken to drinking, he had only come back to the house just to get some more money."

Horace looked at Delia, he didn't know what to do or say, normally in this kind of embarrassing situation, one would leave, politely say your goodbyes and call a taxi. They were stuck there, calling a taxi was out of the question and there was no way that Horace could endure another two hours in Alberto's car.

And besides, how much of the very potent Tinto Verano had he drunk? Would they all end up plummeting over the side of a mountain in the shit heap of a car?

"Let's go back into the house and have a nice cup of coffee," Alberto said, talking as if everyone had had too much to drink, confirming Horace's suspicions that Alberto may have over indulged himself.

Horace and Delia stood in the kitchen, watching Alberto making coffee, using a very grand coffee machine that ground its own beans. After all the noise and commotion that had occurred outside only a few moments earlier, the house now seemed to be very quiet inside, with no noise coming from the upstairs, and no sound or sign of Alberto's parents.

Alberto turned away from the coffee machine, "what kind of coffee would you like? Strong, no milk, cappuccino, whatever you want."

Alberto's mother suddenly appeared in the kitchen doorway, she put both of the flats of her palms together. "Sleeping," she said, speaking the one word in English.

Alberto handed his mother a mug of coffee and she then sat down at the large kitchen table, gesturing to Horace and Delia to sit also.

Once everyone was settled at the table, Maria began to talk very quickly with a lot of emotion, Alberto done his very best to keep up with the translation.

"My mother wishes to apologise," Alberto, began, "My father is in a bad way, what seemed like a good idea many years ago, moving out here in the middle of nowhere, recently has become a huge strain for everyone. My parents have sold the house to a German couple, who plan to use it as a holiday home and rent it out for the rest of the time when they are not here."

"We have a meeting booked for next Friday in what we call here, a Notaria, once everyone signs the documentation and the money is handed over the house will no longer be ours. I am going back to university at the end of the month and my parents are going to rent somewhere by the coast."

"We have been doing our best to sell the goats, but because of the Covid pandemic and what with everyone being locked inside their houses for three months and a huge slump in the economy, we cannot find a buyer. Our only option now is to sell them to the slaughterhouse, for their meat, just having one week left before we move out."

Delia suddenly felt very sick in her stomach, picturing the scene that Maisie had described back at the restaurant, of men chasing the poor defenceless goats, firing nails from a nail gun, the whole area being turned into a bloodbath.

"Who would want to eat goat's meat," Delia said, sounds horrible, her mind flipping back to the school trips with the children at the petting zoo.

"Goat meat is eaten all around the world," Alberto said, "more than beef, it is considered to be very healthy, much less cholesterol than other meats but very high in protein."

Delia reached across the kitchen table and took hold of Horace's hand, "we could buy them, darling, couldn't we?" her thoughts once again returning to the cute little black and white fellows from the petting zoo and the small baby one being hand reared, being fed with a baby's bottle.

"It's not that straightforward," Alberto said, "you would need to get a licence to keep goats and you are supposed to have a license to transport them."

Delia took her mobile out from her dress pocket, calling Angel the solicitor.

Angel responded immediately, seeing Delia's number coming up on the caller display screen, hoping that she was stuck out in the countryside somewhere all alone, broken down in her car. He was very disappointed to learn that she just wanted some info about goats and what paperwork she might need.

"As I explained before," Angel said, "the land you now own is agricultural land and it is a vital requirement that you have to keep animals, goats are a perfect solution."

"That's settled then," Delia said smiling, putting her phone back into her pocket, "we don't have to get a license, apparently, we already have one."

Alberto broke the good news to his mother.

Maria leapt out of her seat, tears of joy rolling down her cheeks, flinging her arms around Delia and hugging her. "Gracias," she said, "muchos gracias."

Horace put the mug to his lips and drunk the very last drop of his coffee, he felt very unsettled, considerably worried, not really sure where all this was going. Delia had just agreed to buy these people's goats, goats that they hadn't even seen, not even knowing the cost.

"How many goats are there?" Horace asked, "and what is the total cost?"

Alberto had a brief conversation with his mother.

"Normally, here in Spain you would expect to pay around five hundred euros per goat," Alberto said, "but at the moment, what with everything as it is, the best price we have been offered was one hundred euros per head from the people at the slaughterhouse."

"What about if we give you two hundred euros per goat?" Delia said, thinking that under the circumstances that was a very good fair offer.

"Three hundred," Maria said, looking directly across the table at Horace, remembering the story from her sister-in-law Maisie, about Horace being a bigwig with pots of money.

"Two fifty," Horace said in return, thinking that if there were roughly ten goats that would shave the total price down from three thousand to two thousand five hundred euros, still a lot of money to pay for a load of goats that he didn't even really want.

Maria once again got out from her seat this time shaking Horace's hand, sealing the deal, and then turning to Delia kissing her on each side of her cheeks.

Suddenly, Ron, Maria's husband, appeared in the doorway, looking very sheepish, not making any eye contact with anyone, his head bowed slightly, with his hands in his pockets. He appeared to be a much smaller man to what he had appeared to be earlier, when he was sitting astride the huge powerful quad bike.

His appearance was very much similar to his sister Maisie, a small wiry man, wearing a short-sleeved cotton dark green T shirt and casual grey trousers which had lots of pockets, running down the outside of each leg.

Maria got up from her seat at the table, not saying anything, she flicked the switch, reheating the coffee that was left over in the machine from earlier.

"More coffee?" she said, turning to Delia and Horace, tapping the side of her empty coffee cup.

"Si, por favor," Delia answered, getting from her seat and placing hers and Horace's mug on top of the kitchen worktop.

Maria poured the coffee into the mugs, then taking a jug of milk from the fridge, placing it next to the coffee mugs, so Delia could help herself. Then she handed a mug full of very strong black coffee to her husband, talking to him in Spanish. Ron looked towards Horace and Delia, not really believing what Maria was telling him. "These people look nothing like goat herders," he said.

Ron pulled one of the empty chairs out from under the kitchen table and placed it in front of the cupboards opposite and sat down.

"So, you have bought the goats," he said, "I hope you both know what you are taking on, you can't just put them in a field and forget about them."

"We haven't got a clue," Horace replied, hoping that Ron would see how crazy all this was and stop the sale. "I don't even like cats or dogs, I have no idea why we have to buy a load of goats."

"It's a long story," Delia answered, while giving Horace a long hard disapproving stare, "we have recently purchased a farmhouse, on agricultural land and we have to keep animals, to live there apparently, and if it would save your goats from being butchered, this arrangement seems to suit everyone."

Ron took a long drink of coffee, this woman was much to posh to keep goats, he could imagine her as a public speaker at a seminar, at Oxford University, or maybe doing the voice over for the talking clock from all those years ago. But walking around the Spanish countryside, searching for goats in the dead of the night, meeting up and drinking and playing dominos with the other herdsman in the local bar?

Maria, not understanding what Ron had said but recognising his tone and the way he was looking at Delia, snapped at him, talking very quickly with the sound of menace in her voice.

"We could round them up early tomorrow morning," Alberto said, recognising the tension building between his parents, "we can get Salva to transport them in his wagon."

Alberto then had a short conversation with his mother in Spanish, before turning to Horace and Delia.

"My mother thinks it would be better for everyone if you have dinner here with us and stay the night, there doesn't seem any point in me driving you all the way back at this time in the evening."

Delia looked across the table, smiling at Maria, "thank you so much," she said, "we hope it's not too much bother."

Horace was also more than happy with these arrangements, the thought of traveling back along that mountain winding road in a car with no roof, in the dark, had been a constant worry, niggling away at the back of his mind as the afternoon had pushed on.

Chapter 27

Saturday, the last day of October, the sun in the morning was rising up from behind the mountains much later now.

On Maria's advice, Horace and Delia had closed the shutters in the guest bedroom before they had slid under the covers of the very comfortable king-sized bed. Horace was the first one to wake up, not really sure where he was, he had slept in the same bed on the opposite side to the window for the past thirty years or so. Within the last five days, he had already slept in two different beds, both facing in two different directions.

Even though the bedroom was situated at the rear of the farmhouse and with all the shutters closed, he still could hear the sound of the revving coming from Ron's quad bike.

There seemed to be a lot of Spanish voices shouting to each other and the hissing of air brakes and the sound of a heavy vehicle moving slowly backwards.

"What time is it?" Delia said, sensing that Horace was already awake, "I feel so sleepy still, like I have been drugged, it must have been Maria's Tinto Verano yesterday."

"It sounds like our goats are being loaded up onto a lorry," Horace said, unenthusiastically.

"I do hope we have done the right thing," Delia said, getting out from the bed and opening one of the shutters, immediately being blinded by the bright sunlight and then quickly closing it down again.

"I hope we have enough money to pay for them," Horace said, sounding a little anxious, "our bank account is almost empty, there is plenty of money going out, but nothing going back in. We have bought a herd of goats for some reason I don't know why, and we don't have any furniture to put inside the new house when eventually it is all finished."

Delia was suddenly gripped by anxiety and panic also, she sat back down on the bed. "Everything has happened so quickly," she said, "with no real time to think things properly through. What with all the disappointment and worry, firstly with the villa and then covid, everything that has happened recently, has happened so quickly, most of it happening way far out beyond our control."

Up till this point, Horace had never ever suffered from any kind of worry with money problems, over the years he had helped a lot of his clients with a lot of good sound advice, when starting out, setting up their new small business adventure. Some businesses had taken off right from the very start, especially the ones that had been planned properly, with sufficient funding and organised cash flow.

People who had researched the market and had sorted out their finances, with the help of Horace and his cash flow forecasts. Others had crashed and burned, within a few months, not taking the solid advice offered from Horace, not starting out with sufficient funding, no business planning or projections, nothing.

Horace and Delia were now one of those small businesses that had just dived into the murky waters of unplanned business ventures, with no planning and insufficient funding. They had spent all their inheritance, his redundancy pay-out had all gone and now they were eating into their life savings.

It was too late to cancel anything now, Horace wasn't about to wander outside amongst all the chaos, and shout out above all the noise, "the deal's off!"

What would the consequences of such actions be? Would Ron get straight onto the slaughter men? What other option would he have, now that Ron and Maria's moving date was only a few more days away. How would they get back to the apartment? Would Alberto still drive them? Would the slaughter men turn up within a few minutes?

Before they had the chance to leave, chasing the goats around all over the place, firing the nails from their guns, willy-nilly, just like Maisie had described in great gory detail, back at the restaurant.

After spending a considerable amount of time in the shower, adjusting the shower head, concentrating the main jet flow of water onto her face, head and shoulders, Delia then washed out her underwear placing it on the electric heated towel rail in the bathroom.

Horace had quickly got himself dressed, settling for cleaning his teeth with his finger and splashing some warm water onto his face.

They both found Maria in the kitchen preparing breakfast, she smiled at them warmly, greeting them both and then led them outside, sitting them both down at the large oak table on the patio.

Horace had been placed at one end, with Delia to his left, Maria, returned holding a tray with seven large empty mugs placing, them around the table, putting hers down next to Delia.

Horace and Delia were both unaware of the fact that all the noise coming from the front of the house had now stopped and all the goats were now loaded into Salva's truck.

Slowly, one by one the men filtered around to the back of the house, through a side gate. They all assembled around the barbeque area, taking it in turns, washing their hands in the stainless-steel sink, looking towards Horace and Delia, laughing and joking.

Maria quickly filled the table top with two large pots of coffee, bowls of scrambled eggs, cooked tomatoes, grilled bacon and avocados.

Alberto introduced the two new arrivals to the table, "this is Salva," he said "he is very kindly going to drive your goats to your new farmhouse in his truck."

Salva gave Horace and Delia a very slight movement from his right hand, offering his acknowledgment. He was a very thin sun-tanned wiry man; he gave the appearance that he was still drunk from the night before and that his legs didn't have the strength to hold up the top half of his body.

"And this is Thiago, but everyone calls him Go, Go."

Go, Go, was a much younger looking man, he had very dark skin, much darker than everyone else who were now sitting around the table. He was wearing a straw hat and clothes that looked like he had stolen them from the nearest scarecrow.

Nobody spoke during breakfast, the coffee and food was passed from person to person around the table, starting with Delia, finally ending up with Maria.

Horace was already thinking and becoming increasingly concerned about the journey back in Alberto's car, to the village and how they were going to pay for all the goats.

Nothing had been discussed, would they want cash? Or would he be able to transfer the money directly into their bank account.

Delia was thinking about Maria, and what a remarkable woman she was, living out here in the middle of nowhere, organising her home and garden and everything. The way that she had easily prepared the evening meal the night before and the breakfast this morning for seven people at the drop of a hat.

Everyone had finished their breakfast, except Salva, who seemed to be having a lot of difficulty keeping any of his food to stay attached to the end of his fork.

Maria began to clear the empty plates away, Delia swiftly got to her feet, wanting to help, asking Alberto to thank his mother for all the wonderful food that she had presented them with, the evening meal the night before and breakfast.

After another ten minutes had passed and all the men had finished the rest of the food and drank all the coffee, they got up from the table and slowly made their way out through the side gate.

Horace had been sitting there in silence, slightly embarrassed and feeling awkward, Delia hadn't returned from the kitchen, and all the Spanish men were laughing and joking, occasionally glancing in his direction.

Horace waited for the last man to disappear through the side gate, before getting to his feet, slowly following in their footsteps. All the men were standing next to Salva's huge truck, smoking and drawing patterns in the dust with some sticks.

Alberto came over towards Horace, "We are just planning our route," he said, "Salva's truck is a little sluggish, just in case we get split up, it might be better if you ride with Salva and Delia comes with me."

Horace looked at the very old dusty truck and then towards Salva, it was a very difficult decision to make, being squeezed into the back of Alberto's car, or ride in the truck with the very strange looking Salva.

Delia, followed by Maria, came out of the front door, "See you there," she said, obviously briefed about the travelling arrangements and not too concerned about traveling all the way back in Alberto's car.

Maria and her husband, Ron, stood and watched as Horace tried his very best to get into the truck. The little step that should be in position just below the door had rusted through five years previously and had dropped off somewhere in the Spanish countryside.

Suddenly, Thiago was there, bending down next to Horace, cupping his hands together making a stirrup for Horace's foot.

"Foot here," he said, speaking the two words in English.

Horace put both hands on the side of the seat and then put his foot into Thiago's cradled hands, within seconds, Horace was launched up and inside the cab, face down, with his head only stopping when it slid up against the side of Salva.

Horace managed to sit himself into the passenger seat, then smiled at Salva. "Buenos dias," he said.

Salva looked at Horace for a brief second, then turned and pulled out a large bottle of something from behind his seat, and took a long drink and then burped.

Horace's suspicions had been confirmed, he was traveling in a huge lorry that was being driven by an alcoholic or at the very best, a drunk. He then noticed that the handbrake was missing and there was a piece of stout wood wedged between the footbrake pedal and the underside of the steering wheel. Horace could see Delia sitting in the front seat of Alberto's car, she had half turned in her seat and gave Horace a wave.

Alberto's car slowly moved forward, Salva unwedged the piece of wood from under the steering wheel and put it on the seat next to Horace. The huge truck jerked forward, Horace unhooked the seat belt from its clip, but there was nowhere to put it. Alberto had already gained around one hundred kilometres, kicking up a huge dust trail in his wake.

Horace tried to shut the passenger side window but the handle just turned around and around with nothing happening.

Salva took another huge slug of drink from his bottle, this time offering it across to Horace. Horace took the bottle, maybe it wasn't alcohol, perhaps it was something medicinal, or herbal, or possibly green tea? Horace took a small sip, raising the bottle up and down in one quick motion.

Whatever it was, it definitely wasn't herbal, or green tea, as soon as it hit his tonsils, Horace began to cough uncontrollably.

Salva grabbed the bottle from Horace giving him a sideways sneering glance, before finishing what was left in the bottle himself, and then tossing the empty out of the open window.

Slowly, Salva's truck gathered speed, Horace looked around for something to hold on to, double checking, to see if there was somewhere to engage the strap of the seat belt into, but there was nothing.

Salva produced another bottle from behind the seat and pulled the cork out with his teeth, then popping it out onto his lap, he took a long swig and then offered it across to Horace.

Horace felt obliged to take the bottle, taking a small sip like before, this time he managed to swallow it down without coughing. Salva smiled approvingly and spoke for the very first time, saying, "eeehh?" Salva took back the bottle, taking another long swig before searching for the cork between his legs.

Up till that point the truck had been slowly building more and more sped and they were now travelling at a speed around fifty kilometres an hour. Salva was having trouble finding the cork and was now searching around on the floor and under the seat of the truck. Horace wasn't sure if he was supposed to take hold of the wheel, like if there was some kind of an unwritten code between truckers and farmers.

It was at that point the lorry crashed through the very old flimsy wooden fencing that surrounded the two-hundred-year-old dry-stone building, hitting the two feet thick wall, right at the point of the corner and then stopping instantly.

Salva had been in a better placed position before the impact, already being so close to the floor, Horace flew out from his seat, landing in the footwell, crashing against the bulkhead with the side of his body.

Salva picked up the cork that suddenly appeared and was rolling around on the floor and popped it back into the bottle. He then climbed back into his seat and restarted the engine, looking down at Horace accusingly, as if everything that had just happened was all his fault.

Somehow, Horace managed to pull himself up and back onto his seat, allowing Salva to move the long shaft of the gear stick, forward and over to the left, crunching the gears into reverse.

Horace could feel the back wheels of the truck trying to pull the front half of the truck backwards away from the old house, but it wasn't budging, like it had reached its final resting place and was refusing to go.

Salva revved the engine a lot more, this time rocking back and forth in his seat, as if he was trying to encourage the old truck to move.

Ron suddenly appeared on the trike with Maria on the back and Thiago standing up on the small tow bar mounted on the back, pulling up alongside the high revving smoking lorry.

Alberto had turned the car around and had parked on the road, next to the huge hole in the fence that had been made by Salva's truck. Ron was shouting in Spanish at Salva and making gestures with his arms, that even Horace could understand, to cut the engine.

Salva revved the engine even more, rocking back and forth, with his body, much more than before, by this time, everyone was standing outside the front of the cab, shouting at Salva to quit. Eventually, Salva turned off the engine, opened the door and slid down from the cab, walking around to the front of the lorry, looking underneath to see what all the fuss was about.

Something had come adrift from the steering and was hanging down underneath and one of the front wheels was facing in the wrong direction.

Ron and Salva had engaged in what looked like a heated discussion, then Salva turned and pointed an accusing finger at Horace. "Stupid ginger-haired pale-faced goat man," he said in Spanish, "he wouldn't take hold of the steering wheel."

Horace opened the door and slid down from the truck, everyone was looking at him, as if he had committed some kind of evil wicked crime.

"Why didn't you take hold of the wheel?" Delia said, caught up in all the drama, after Alberto had explained to her in English Salva's misconstrued story.

Horace couldn't believe what he was hearing, Delia had never ever spoken to him in that way before, not even in the past when he had deserved it.

Horace walked around the front of the truck to inspect the damage. "The guy is a pisshead and a drunk," he said, "he shouldn't be driving a huge lorry like this, they should have taken his licence away years ago!"

By this time, everyone had moved around to the back of the truck, Ron lifted the retaining pins out from their locations, then with Maria helping, all the men slowly lowered down the tailgate.

Horace and Delia were stood by the side, watching in anticipation, waiting for the goats to appear from the inside.

Thiago gave a whistle, and a few weird noises calling the goats, that sounded like words of encouragement.

Suddenly there was a lot of bleating and the sound of hoofs on the wooden floor of the truck as they flooded down the tailgate and onto the safe firm ground.

Horace did his best to count them as they came out, thinking about the total cost, still not knowing exactly how many goats he had agreed to buy.

It was an impossible task, the goats were piling out from the truck four, five or six at a time, Horace done his best to guesstimate, it seemed like there were hundreds, they just kept coming and coming. Delia hadn't even thought about the number, she just stood there agog, they were nothing like she had imagined or expected.

There were no small black and white cute little fellows, like the ones she had seen on her previous trips out, or the ones illustrated in the colourful children's books back home at the school. These were big brown smelly things, some of them bigger than the size of a miniature Shetland pony.

They all very quickly spread out, frantically searching around for something to eat, as if they had just arrived from a long coach journey, like a lot of tourists at a motorway service station.

Some of the goats had already passed through the whole in the fence and had surrounded Alberto's car, putting their heads down inside through the open roof, eating whatever it was that was stuck to the carpet before quickly moving on.

Horace looked at Delia, he could see the disappointment on her face, now was the time to get her away from her crazy romantic notion that she had built up inside her head about keeping goats.

"It looks like the deal is off," Horace said, sounding very disappointed, hiding his immense relief.

"There seems to be so many of them," Delia said, "not really sure if we would have had enough room for them all at the farm anyway."

"We would have had to sell the house in England to pay for them all," Horace said, hoping to convince Delia even more, that it had been a crazy notion, a bad idea right from the start.

Maria came over to Delia, looking very sad, speaking in Spanish, Delia, opened up her arms and pulled Maria towards her, hugging her, rubbing her hand up and down her back, similar to what she had done to their neighbour Hilary at Trever's funeral.

In less than the twenty-four hours that they had known each other, they had formed a very strong friendship, they had bonded instantly. In spite of their language difference, they had formed a connection that would normally take most people months' possibly years to achieve.

Ron, had spent the last five minutes talking on the phone to the local mechanic, telling him what had just happened and asking him how soon he could come out and fix the steering on the truck.

"Thursday," Ron said, loud enough for everyone to here, "the very earliest he can get out here, and he said that it will probably take him all day."

Ron then spoke to Maria and Salva, Salva shrugged his shoulders, not appearing to be too concerned, he climbed back into the cab and shut the door.

Horace and Delia both watched him through the windscreen as he made himself comfortable, spreading his body across both of the front seats and then raised a new bottle to his lips and took a long drink.

"There is no way I am going to wait around here until Thursday," Horace said, looking at Delia, expecting her to agree, "and there is no way I am getting back into that lorry, with that crazy drunk. How far would we get after he has been drinking for six more days, and how much drink has he got stashed away inside that old truck? He most probably won't even be capable of steering it back through that massive hole in the fence that he has already made, let alone all the way back to the village with a truckload of goats. So, what happens now?" Horace asked, as Alberto came over, putting his arms out slightly to one side and shrugging his shoulders.

"We will have to get on to the slaughterhouse, I suppose, there is no guarantee that the mechanic will be able to get out here on Thursday and even then, he may not be able to fix it."

"Maybe we could buy just a few of the goats," Delia said. "Maybe ten? Then perhaps we could arrange alternative transport, like a small van or something."

Horace thought that was a bad idea, under the circumstances, it would be better for everyone if they just walked away, somehow call a taxi, leaving these people to sort everything out for themselves. Maybe they could get a couple of donkeys and a few chickens, keep them out at the back as far away from the house as possible.

Delia had walked out through the gap in the fence and was talking to Thiago, he was feeding the goats with something from a shoulder bag and offered a handful to Delia.

A one-year-old female goat took the food from the palm of her hand and then rubbed its body back and forth against Delia, similar to what a cat might do. Suddenly, Delia was surrounded by most of the herd, Thiago handed her the shoulder bag of food to Delia.

She did her very best to share the food out fairly and equally, in spite of all the shoving and pushing and the constant bleating. Now that she was much closer to the animals, they didn't appear to be quite so ugly or smelly, Thiago began to explain in a few words in English, who was who and what was what.

"Emily," he said, pointing to the goat Delia was now feeding, "mother of four, this year."

Ron and Maria came over and began to speak to Thiago, talking in Spanish. Thiago quickly became very irritated, waving his stick around, obviously not very happy with what he was being told.

Delia carefully picked her way back through the herd, passing back through the hole in the fence. Horace slowly backed away, as Delia approached.

Most of the goats had stayed with Thiago but a few had followed Delia, and were now heading his way.

Alberto met Delia halfway. "Thiago has been caring for the goats for the last two years," he said, "he has grown very attached to them. He is saying that he is not going to stand here and watch them all being murdered."

Maria and Ron were talking to Thiago, it looked like they were trying to calm him down. Thiago then shouted across in the direction of Delia and Horace, who had backed away even more and was now standing behind the front of the broken-down truck.

"We walk," he shouted, "vamos, we walk!"

"What's he saying?" Horace said, calling across to Delia from behind the truck, where he was still standing, more or less out of view, while hiding from all the smelly goats.

"We walk," Thiago repeated, "venga, vamos, we walk!"

Ron and Maria came over to Delia, "He wants to walk," Ron said.

"Walk where?" Horace shouted, from his safe position from behind the truck and away from the goats.

"To the village," Ron shouted back, "back to your house!"

"Why does he want to walk to our house?" Horace shouted back.

"With the goats!" Ron replied.

"Is that a possibility?" Delia said, "it must be at least a hundred kilometres?"

"It's possible," Ron said, "but it is a crazy idea, it will take days."

Maria began to talk very quickly to Ron in Spanish, occasionally looking at Delia and then across to Horace.

"Maria thinks it's a good idea," Ron said, "To be honest I haven't had much to do with the herd for more than three years now. Not since Thiago arrived, he knows every single one of them, he has even given them all names."

"How long will it take?" Delia asked?

"Goats aren't like dogs," Ron said, "they won't just walk along, they are grazing animals, they walk and eat, they will probably cover about twenty kilometres a day."

"We are going to walk," Delia shouted across to Horace. "I will see you back at the apartment next Thursday or Friday."

"That's ridiculous!" Horace shouted. "You can't just walk halfway across Spain with a load of goats, let alone with a complete stranger, anything could happen!"

"One hundred and fifty euros a head," Ron said, "you can send me the money when they arrive."

Delia turned. "Vamos!" she shouted, across to Thiago, "We are going to walk."

Thiago's face lit up, smiling and waving his stick around like he had just won the lottery. "Vamos," he shouted, "venga, vamos!"

Thiago began to walk along the lane in the direction that they had been heading earlier, before the truck had ploughed through the wooden fence.

Delia followed, walking out into the lane through the large gape in the fence.

Alberto came over to Horace. "I will give you a lift back to the village now if you like," he said, not really knowing what else to say.

Horace glanced across to Alberto's car, remembering the dreadful journey out here, and then down the lane to Delia. She was walking alone, surrounded by goats, she was still wearing the same dress and sandals from the day before.

Even if he did accept Alberto's offer, they would have to drive past Delia and Thiago, very slowly, picking their way through all the goats.

It would be an impossible thing to do, like total abandonment, like not turning up at his own wedding, just leaving her there and driving off into the distance, not knowing if he would ever see her again.

Horace turned to Alberto, "No thank you, I better go after her."

Horace followed in Delia's footsteps, out through the gap in the fence then turning left, she was about one hundred kilometres up in front.

Thiago was about another hundred kilometres in front of Delia, with the goats now spread out in between them both.

Horace looked at his watch, it was still only ten o clock in the morning, he would follow Delia until she got tired and bored with the idea of walking with a load of goats, then they could call a taxi.

Delia knew instinctively that Horace wouldn't be too far behind, hanging back, not wanting to get to close to the goats. Frightened that they might affect his hay fever or cat allergy, or all the other thing that made him cough and sneeze.

The goats had now spread out, there was no fence along that particular stretch of road, they were moving along fairly quickly, searching for things to eat. They were all competing with each other, to be the first one to reach the small wild flower or weed, quickly munching their way through anything that lay ahead in their pathway.

Delia was now walking alone, only around fifty metres up in front of Horace, she could hear his footsteps on the loose white concrete chipping that covered the surface.

"I hope you know what you're doing," Horace said, catching Delia up, now that the goats had moved away and that Horace now considered it to be a safe distance.

Delia reached out her hand, grabbing hold of Horace's. "this is such a beautiful country," she said, "even though it hasn't rained here since last spring, look at all the different types of wild shrubs that are still growing."

"What about all the other stuff?" Horace said, "like scorpions, snakes, biting spiders and poisonous toads and possibly wolves."

Delia laughed, "We should have done this years ago," she said, "what would you be doing if you were still back in England right now? Playing golf in the wind and rain, or standing inside the bay widow, spying on the neighbours, wearing only your pants?"

"We're not really dressed for the occasion," Horace said, "I haven't got a hat, we don't have any sun cream and these small stones are really annoying, they keep getting in between the holes in my sandals."

"I must agree," Delia smiled. "We could have planned things a little better if we had known, maybe we will pass a small village along the way and we can buy some more suitable clothing. And some new clean underwear," Delia said, "in all the confusion, I have left mine behind in Maria's bathroom, sitting on the radiator."

Horace had a good look around, "I didn't notice any villages on the way up here, only the village of Sweet Water and that is on the other side of those mountains."

Delia paused for a while and opened her small holiday shoulder bag, taking out a small tube of factor fifty sun cream and offering it to Horace.

"We don't even have anything to drink," Horace said, covering his face with the thick white cream before moving down to his arms and then his legs. "We could easily die of dehydration, how far are we going to last out here without water?"

"Thiago must know what he is doing," Delia said, "if he has spent the last three years looking after the goats out here in the open countryside."

"And another thing," Horace said, "if we ever get there, where are we going to put them all? Are we just going to turn up at the house, which is still only half built and just turn them loose amongst all the chaos and the builders?"

"We have been a little premature," Delia said, "but we do have an awful lot of land out at the back, there is no fencing, we don't even know where our boundary ends."

"And what about this Thiago guy, what is he going to do? Is he just going to turn around and walk back again? This is a crazy situation we have gotten ourselves into," Horace whined, "we have only been here for five days and our whole life has been turned upside down."

Chapter 28

After around an hour had passed of steady walking, they had reached the point where the roughly covered track joined onto the hard surface of the road, the road that had brought them here in Alberto's car the day before.

Horace was just beginning to wonder how the heck they were going to get all the goats safely back down on the very dangerous narrow mountain road, when Thiago suddenly took a left turn.

Thiago had turned off from the road and was now walking with all the goats down a gentle slope that seem to go on for ever down into the open mountainside, re-joining the mountain road far below in the distance.

All the goats suddenly became more vocal, much happier with the new terrain, spreading out and then slowing their pace down, taking more time, eating what looked like dried wild grass and weeds.

Later on, after yet another hour had passed of steady walking downwards, they had reached a more level area where olive trees were growing.

These trees were nothing like the ones that Horace and Delia had seen previously, planted in rows and cultivated in huge areas, these trees were growing haphazardly, all different shapes and sizes.

Thiago stopped under the shade of a huge olive tree and took off his straw hat, then bashing the branches with his stick, catching some olives in his hat.

The goats were already busy, mopping up all the fruit that had already ripened and had fallen down some time before, along with any small twigs and leaves that were also lying around.

Horace and Delia stopped under the tree also, Thiago held out his hat, offering the olives to Delia and then Horace.

"I would rather have a bottle of water," Horace said, now feeling very thirsty.

"Agua, comida," Thiago smiled, "Water and food."

Horace took a handful of olives from the hat, in the past he could never ever see any reason for eating olives, they took an awful lot of work for what you got in return. Thiago began to eat the olives very quickly, spitting the small seed from the inside as far as he could and then laughing. Then, turning and looking at Horace, smiling, nodding his head, laying down the challenge.

Delia quickly took a tissue from her bag and handed it to Horace. Spitting had always been strictly forbidden at the school at all times for any reason in any type or form and especially now what with the highly infectious spread of the Covid nineteen virus.

Thiago could see Delia's displeasure and moved off, over to another tree, sitting down, resting his back against the tree, facing the other way. Horace sat down also, resting his back against the tree, Delia looked around for somewhere more comfortable, then sitting down next to Horace.

"Where do you think we will be by nightfall?" she said, her mood had changed. "I wouldn't like to be stuck out here in the dark."

"Maybe now is the right time to call a taxi," Horace said. "We have showed a little willing, now let's get the hell out of here, we can leave the goat man alone to do his job."

Delia took out her phone from her handbag, "We don't have any internet," she said, "I can't use Google to find a taxi or to find out where we are. Maybe Thiago could help," Delia said, "he has a phone, he must have a taxi number?"

"I can't imagine the goat man in the back of a taxi," Horace chuckled, "sitting in the back smelling of goats and spitting olive seeds everywhere. Besides, how are we going to get a taxi out here? The Uber drivers are very keen on picking up every fare, but I can't imagine anyone driving down the side of a mountain for fifty euros."

"Hopefully we will reach the road we saw earlier, before it gets too dark and call one from there."

Although the walk had been relatively easy, forever walking downwards with very little effort, by the time the sun was disappearing down behind the mountains in the far distance, Horace and Delia were practically dead on their feet.

They had booked themselves on walking holidays in the past and were quite used to walking all day. But that had always been with an organised group and they were always greeted at the end of the day by the bright lights of a comfy hotel and the smell of a good evening meal.

The light was now fading, Delia, grabbed hold of Horace's hand, suddenly everything began to feel very eerie, even the goats looked spooky, moving around in the fading light. Thiago hadn't spoken a word to them all day, not since they had left the safe shaded area of the olive trees. He had spent the last twenty minutes looking at his phone, the light from the screen now lighting up his face.

Horace's head was now only filled with dark negative thoughts, as if they were slowly walking down into the pits of hell. He knew that there was nothing behind them, nowhere where they could have taken refuge for the night, a small hotel, or even the very smallest of family run places that only done bed and breakfast.

Now looking ahead into the darkness, there was no sign of life, not even a flicker of a light in a window that maybe coming from a small dwelling in the distance, nothing.

They hadn't met anyone all day along the way, not a soul in any form of human shape or size, not even in the distance, during their journey down the side of the mountain. They had now reached an area much lower; they had been walking all day, down into what looked now like a valley with the shapes of two huge mountains on either side.

Horace kept turning around, he was experiencing strange feelings as if they were being followed, like someone had been tracking them all day waiting for the right opportunity to pounce.

Who else would be out there, miles from anywhere, stumbling around in the dark, and for what reason?

Maybe the ghost of Mateo's wife, Mencia Morales, or that huge crazy psychotic women from Pecton mound, her overweight dog, slowly but surely sniffing the ground and tracking him down.

Thiago suddenly stopped, "We stop here," he said.

Delia's mood had also darkened, for the last hour or so, she had kept herself going with happy thoughts by thinking about all the good times that she had experienced in the past with all the children back at the school. She wanted to ask Thiago what the heck he thought he was doing, leading them down the mountain to the middle of nowhere with nothing to eat or drink and nowhere to sleep.

If only they had come to Spain better prepared, spending a least a couple of years beforehand, attending evening classes, at a night school, learning level one Spanish. Thankfully, it was a warm evening with a full moon, giving them some kind of light, now the sun had completely disappeared.

The half-moon then suddenly slipped behind a small black cloud, Horace was filled with panic, he couldn't see no more than a few centimetres in front of him and he felt like he was suffocating, like there wasn't any air.

Thiago was using the light from his phone, pulling up dried grass and weeds, building what looked like the start of a fire.

Delia took out her phone also, beginning to wander around, looking for stuff to burn, Horace quickly followed, not wanting to be left standing there in the dark all alone. Miraculously, they stumbled across a piece of a dead tree, Horace dragged it back and dropped it down next to Thiago.

Everyone was now working together for the common good, Thiago had successfully started the fire. Horace and Delia, with the aid of the torchlight from her phone, carried on their search for more fuel. The fire was now burning brightly, Thiago was using the light from the fire to build himself a seat from any loose rocks that he could find that were lying around, piling them up in the shape of a makeshift stool.

Copying Thiago's rough design, Horace and Delia worked together, deciding only to make just the one seat for now. It was much harder than what it had looked, and by the time the pile of stones and rocks were high enough for Delia to try out, another hour had passed.

Already the pile of wood that they had collected for the fire had been burnt, Horace looked around from the safe haven of the light of the fire to see if there was anything else lying around that they could burn.

Peering out into the darkness, he could just make out the shape of another dead bow from a tree, similar to what they had found earlier, only a few metres away.

Horace picked up the dead wood, and then peering out into the darkness, suddenly as if they had been waiting for the right moment, he could see lights appearing and the sound of engines.

Something was heading towards them, possibly three of them, their headlights shining towards them out from the black backdrop.

Horace's mind was instantly racing, unusually much more active than what it was normally.

Maybe, brought on by the fact that they had eaten very little that day practically nothing except for some olives and a few figs, or he had taken in too much of the fresh thin mountain air.

He broke off a branch from the dead tree, he would have to stand and fight.

Him being the first line of defence, against the mindless zombies or the ageing hells angels that they had passed on the motorway on their way from the airport, in the hire car.

Thiago for some reason was now waving the light from his phone around and shouting in Spanish, as if he was trying to draw them towards him.

Horace raised the dead branch high above his head, the heavy weighted end then dropped off onto the ground behind him.

Leaving him standing there with just a small piece of light dry tinder wood, just as Ron and Maria sped past, riding on the quadbike, only a few metres away.

Ron parked the bike at a safe distance away from the fire, Horace threw what little fuel he had left in his hands into the flames. Ron and Maria quickly undone the rope that was securing everything that they had brought that was piled up on top of the toolbox at the rear of the quadbike.

Maria carried over two folding chairs, holding one out, offering it to Delia, "Buenos noches," she said, smiling, her face lit up by the firelight.

"We have bought everything you need for a night out, sleeping out under the stars," Ron said, putting another folding chair down in front of the fire, quickly sitting down and rubbing his hands together.

Maria then handed out plastic containers of still hot paella and warm homemade brown bread rolls.

Delia was so happy and relieved that she felt like crying.

She would have never ever imagined that Ron and Maria would come riding through the darkness in the middle of the countryside, bringing them all the home comforts and food. Horace was equally impressed, now the quadbike made sense, his opinion of Ron in the first instance of him being a mindless drunk, riding around on his big macho machine had been a little harsh and a little premature.

How else would you travel around in this type of terrain? He probably connected with Thiago every evening, bringing him food before disappearing into the night, and into the bright lights of the local bars.

After they had finished eating, Ron and Maria produced two sleeping bags and a small two-man tent that they fixed down onto the ground in no time at all.

Then Maria handed Delia a pair of jeans and a warm casual top and her clean underwear that she had found in the bathroom that Delia had left behind that morning.

Ron lifted a box of red wine out from the large toolbox. "This will help you sleep," he laughed, emptying the first bottle into plastic beakers, pouring it out into equal measures for five people.

Delia disappeared into the darkness to change into the clothes that Maria had brought for her.

Ron, now holding Thiago's mobile phone, showed Horace the trails that they were supposedly following.

A route that would hopefully and would eventually lead them down the side of the mountain and then along the valley and then eventually into the village, then on to the land at the rear of their new farmhouse.

Delia had never ever slept outside before; it was something that she had never ever contemplated. In the past, some of the younger teachers from the school had returned after their camping holiday, telling stories of high winds and persistent rain and a possible trial separation.

Horace, on the other hand, was more than pleased with the sleeping arrangements, only a couple of hours ago they had nowhere to go, and nothing to eat or drink. Now, looking at the tent being illuminated by the firelight, it looked so inviting and he couldn't wait to get inside and rest his head on a pillow and close his eyes. He had taken Ron's advice and had matched him beaker for beaker, drinking the red wine like it was water.

Occasionally looking around, checking where the tent had been erected, just in case he lost his bearings and got too drunk and stumbled off into the night and the darkness.

As more and more time passed, Delia began to worry about the sleeping arrangements. From the outside, the tent appeared to be very small, and she wouldn't want to share such a small space with Thiago.

He was obviously very good at what he did, but he had some filthy habits, and on the few occasions that Delia had been a bit closer than the recommended two meters, to maintain social distancing, he had smelt like a goat.

Ron stood up. "That's it, I am off to my bed," he said. "From tomorrow you are on your own, we have booked you in at a small family-run hotel, about thirty kilometres from here for tomorrow night. Hopefully, you will be there before nightfall, don't worry about all this stuff, we will be back in the morning to collect everything."

Maria gave Delia a big hug, kissing her on both cheeks, saying a few words in Spanish, Ron started the quad bike, and Thiago wandered off into the darkness to sleep with the goats.

It was Delia who awoke first the next morning to the sound of the goats and Thiago's voice shouting commands and whistling. She had slept through the whole night, not waking once, the wine that Ron had brought on the quad bike the night before, certainly did the trick, as promised, she had slept like a baby.

She now desperately needed a wee, she unzipped her sleeping bag, Horace must have struggled with his the night before, as he was curled up in the corner, the sleeping bag still rolled up and he was using it like a pillow.

Delia crawled out through the doorway on her hands and knees, it was a cool cloudy morning, Thiago was already on the move, he and the goats were already a few hundred metres away.

She quickly pulled down the jeans that Maria had given her, sitting on one of the stools that they had made from the loose stones and rocks the night before, she used it as if she was sitting on the toilet.

Delia looked around, checking that no one was watching, some of the very white powdery ash from the fire was blowing around with the light morning breeze. There were empty wine bottles and the plastic containers that Maria had brought the food in the night before, still lying around.

Delia suddenly felt very hungover and depressed.

"What the heck are we doing here?" She muttered.

This was nothing like the life that she imagined when they had agreed to buy one of the front-line villas, overlooking the golf course. They had been much too hasty, they should have spent a lot more time looking into things, getting professional advice. But then the whole world had been hit by this dreadful pandemic, no one saw that coming and all the problems that it would bring.

Delia stood up, because the landscape was still falling away, deeper down into the valley, from her viewpoint, she could see Thiago and the goats slowly moving down the slope of the mountainside.

Delia crawled back into the tent, leaning over Horace, just by looking at him, she could see that it was going to be very difficult, very close to impossible to wake him up.

Maybe it would be best to leave him there to sleep it off, what on earth were they thinking, drinking the night away like a pair of teenagers.

What should she do?

Thiago obviously had his own agenda, he wasn't interested in Horace or herself, only the goats, and the promise of a new home for them all, far away as possible from the risk of being slaughtered and then butchered.

She could catch Thiago up, leaving Horace to sleep it off, maybe Ron could catch them up and bring Horace on the quad bike later, when he came back to pick up the tent and everything else that was still scattered around.

Or she could wait, ask Ron to book them a taxi for later, but then they would have to walk back up the mountainside the way that they had come.

That would be such a waste, after spending all the day before walking here in the first place and then spending the whole night sleeping rough and then spending the whole day walking back.

She could be hanging around for hours, waiting for Horace to sleep off all of the red wine, and Ron might not come back until later that evening.

Delia grabbed her handbag from inside the tent, taking out her pen she quickly wrote Horace a message, on a small piece of paper.

Gone with the goats and Thiago, follow the signs.

Delia then quickly, made the shape of an arrow with some small loose rocks, pointing in the direction in which Thiago was now heading, remembering some of the skills she had learnt from her younger days as a girl guide.

Then with her bag on her shoulder, she grabbed her dress and the bottle of water that Maria had left for her the night before, and headed off down the slope to catch Thiago.

After about one hundred metres, Delia turned around, looking back up the slope, she couldn't see the small tent, she could just about make out the position where they had camped the night before. She then tied her woollen knitted dress around a shrub with small bright yellow flowers, leaving it blowing in the light morning breeze.

Hopefully, with the note and the arrow made from stones, pointing in the right direction, and her dress that must be easily visible from above, it should be enough pointers for Horace to set him on his way and hopefully help him follow their trail.

After around five hundred metres, Delia stopped walking and turned around, maybe she was being a little hasty, she thought, it would be very difficult for Horace to find her.

Looking around at the landscape, everywhere looked the same, with areas of dry brown wild grass and loose rocks, that were roughly the size of small pineapples.

And the same shrubs growing everywhere with the small yellow flowers, all roughly similar in size. It would be pointless writing Horace another note, even if you were searching for one you would never find it in this kind of landscape.

Thiago was only about fifty metres up ahead, she had caught him and the goats up very easily, they were moving much slower than the day before, finding more things to nibble at and eat.

Thiago had turned initially, and had given her a wave of acknowledgment, raising his stick, not even bothering to ask where Horace was or what had happened to him.

Delia, stood behind one of the larger bushy shrubs and quickly took off her bra, then hung it on the highest tip, of the long twig covered in bright yellow flowers, bending down, allowing the bra to hang unsnagged, clear of all the others.

Horace would never recognise one bra from another, but she was the only women out there, he should be able to spot it, he must be able to put two and two together, even in his condition.

Delia took a small sip of water from her bottle, the walk down the slope hadn't done anything to shake off the morning after feeling from drinking all the wine the night before.

Maybe it would be best for her to go back, she thought to herself, to check on Horace, it would only take around a half hour or so to walk back up the slope to the tent.

Especially now, and the way she was feeling, she would be better off crawling back into her own sleeping bag and going back to sleep.

And Horace could possibly be violently sick, Delia thought, chocking on his own vomit, especially after his last drinking episode at the golf club, where he was in urgent need of medical attention.

But this time he had only drunk red wine, unlike before, with all the vodka and all different coloured syrup and sugar of the vodka based spritzers, Delia thought to herself, it would be much better for him to wake up when he was ready.

She had made the right decision, she would follow the heard, slowly moving down the mountain, her head was still very fuzzy and the walk in the fresh air should do her good.

Even if she had stayed with Horace, how would they know where to go and what direction to head off in? They would never find the small hotel that Ron had already made reservations for them both.

Even if and when Ron returned on the quadbike, both of them couldn't fit on the seat behind, and either of them were not young or foolish enough to stand on the toe bar, especially across this terrain.

Chapter 29

From the moment that Delia left, more than four hours had passed, before the brain inside Horace's head, slowly, little by little became more active. He raised his right arm, trying to brush away the fly that was buzzing around his head and continuously landing on his nose.

Slowly, his senses were beginning to function more and more, picking up on the fly, buzzing around and then landing, taking a few steps up inside his nostrils. The tickling on the inside of his nose as the fly's feet moved amongst the ginger hair, jumping from one strand to another, was becoming more and more irritating.

Horace rolled over onto his face, pushing his face down into the soft fabric of the quilted sleeping bag, burying his nose deep down into the soft muzzling. The fly was now much happier than before, Horace's ears were a much better landing strip, with many more places to explore.

He swiped at his right ear; the fly, unrelenting, landed inside his left. Buzzing around the opening. Then, as if his body had suddenly been taken over by the devil, Horace suddenly stood up, his head bulging up into the roof lining of the two-man tent. Now it felt like the fly was trapped inside his brain, buzzing frantically, much, much louder, sounding really pissed off and disorientated.

Horace pushed himself forward, miraculously, finding the door, the small steel tent pegs, pulled out from their securing points and the whole of the tent raised up to the level of Horace's head.

Just like the fly before, the tent fabric had now become a huge sense of annoyance, Horace pulled at the fabric, blindly, frantically, his brain not yet signalling correctly, not sending the correct signal for him to open up his eyes.

Somehow Horace pushed himself out through the unzipped doorway and into the open space of the Spanish countryside. Leaving the tent crumpled behind him, in a pile on the floor. Still moving forward with his eyes still closed, he walked directly into Thiago's purpose-built stool and fell head first onto the ground.

Rolling over into the white ash and debris from the outside edge of the fire from the night before. Horace rolled over onto his back, then opening his eyes, blinking up at the colours of the blue and the wispy white cloudy sky.

Even though, now they were in the month of November, the light was still much too bright for Horace's light-sensitive blue eyes. Instinctively, now on all fours, he crawled back towards the tent, pushing his head under the fabric, searching around frantically, trying to find his sunglasses.

Then, suddenly, the realisation of something much worse, his wife and long-life partner for the past thirty-five years had also gone missing, vanished or kidnapped from right under his nose, where she had been sleeping.

Horace backed out from the tent and half stood up, part of the tent, still covering his head and shoulders, his back covered in white ash and dead leaves. He stumbled towards the edge of the level ground where they had spent the night and shouted out his wife's name, "Delia!"

His voice, ringing out down into the valley, a similar tone not much different from the cry from the top of the cathedral in Paris, all those years ago, from the hunch back of Notre Dame.

Delia would never ever have heard Horace's cry, echoing out her name, not even if Horace had linked arms with Quasimodo in person and they had both bellowed out her name together, from the top of the highest mountain.

She was now feeling much better within herself, after around four hours of slowly walking downwards, the mountain eventually bottomed out into the valley.

Almost linking with the bottom of the mountain on the opposite side, only separated by a wide dusty track.

Thiago had shouted a few commands to the goats and they all stopped moving forward and spent a few minutes of their time cropping the much healthier looking grass that was growing along both sides of the track.

Thiago had cautiously approached Delia offering her a cereal chewy bar from his man bag, speaking a few words of English.

Only then had he inquired about Horace and his whereabouts.

Delia had put both her palms of her hands together then against her left ear and had answered, "sleeping."

Thiago had laughed approvingly. He had then raised his right hand, gesturing to Delia that he was holding a bottle, laughing and rubbing his belly, before setting off once again along the dusty track.

Delia slowly raised the water bottle up, pressing the neck gently against her lips, then with her head leaning back, she finished off what was left inside, before squashing it flat and replacing the top.

She took out her mobile phone from the inside of her bag, checking the time, almost five hours had now passed since she had left Horace behind, sleeping like a baby, inside the two-man tent.

If only Horace had sorted out his mobile before coming to Spain, she thought to herself, or even connected to a Spanish site using roaming while he was here, she could have stayed in touch and rung him after a few hours had passed.

The rapid advancement of mobile technology had arrived very quickly and at the same speed, passed Horace by. He hadn't embraced the idea of WhatsApp, he had no friends on face book, he didn't take selfies and then forward them on with outrageous captions, like the majority of the world's current population. He had always commented on the amount of time, one could waste every day, playing with a mobile phone, he had no interest what so ever, nothing.

They could have kept in contact by mobile phone so easily, Delia thought, that was the point of modern technology. He could have even tracked her whereabouts, once he had woken up, using his phone, instead, it was just sitting in the drawer, switched off, back at Paco's apartment.

Suddenly, Delia's thoughts were broken by the heavy drone of a large engine, approaching from behind. She turned around, coming towards them on the dusty track was a green Land Rover with an open back, similar to a small truck with a group of people standing in the back.

The land rover pulled up alongside Delia and all the people jumped out and began to take photos of her, some with cameras others with their mobile phones.

Delia's level of French was good enough to understand most of what they were saying, "How cute," one lady said, "a Spanish goat herder and his wife."

Thiago turned and quickly made his way back towards Delia, the herd separating in the middle, letting him pass through. He picked up the smallest and cutest goat from the herd, a one-year-old female called Sonja, handing Delia his long stick, he stood by her side, holding the young goat and smiling.

Everyone clicked away approvingly, Delia didn't feel very much like smiling.

She felt like she had fallen out from the tallest tree, from the dizzy heights of her profession, as a well-respected school teacher and headmistress, to the bottom of the food chain as a goat herder's woman, just within the period of a few days.

A smartly dressed middle-aged man stepped forward and pushed a ten-euro note into Delia's hand. "What a great life these simple people have out here," he said, "no stress of the modern world, no threat from these darn Covid viruses."

Then, as quickly as they had all arrived, everyone jumped back into the back of the Land Rover and the driver moved forward slowly through the herd before disappearing into the distance in a cloud of sandy coloured dust.

Delia instinctively handed the ten euro note sideways, like a prostitute would hand over her hard-earned cash to her pimp. Thiago took the note without any hesitation, kissing it before tucking it away inside his man bag. "Muchas gracias," he said, "buen trabajo, good work."

Thiago then took his mobile phone out from his bag, after a few seconds, handed it over to Delia, pointing out the small family run finca, the place where her and Horace were hopefully going to spend that coming night together.

"Three horas' mas," he said, "we walk for three hours more."

By the time that Thiago, then the herd of goats, followed by Delia, arrived at the finca, a traditional styled farmhouse, surrounded by orange and lemon trees, it was six o'clock in the evening.

All the other ten guests were already seated in the dining room, that had a good view out through the large glass windows, from the front of the building, along the track and the surrounding countryside.

They all quickly abandoned their starter of a prawn cocktail or alternatively grapefruit and water melon, and had all come charging out of the front entrance, as soon as they had spotted the lonely figure of Thiago, followed by the goats.

Just like the French people in the Land Rover they all clicked away with their cameras and mobile phones, enthusiastically. This was the type of thing they had hoped to see when they had found the farmhouse advertised on the Internet.

Offering it as a real-life slice of Spain, when they were looking to book up their yearly summer vacation away from the overcrowded resorts and away from the dreaded covid nineteen viruses.

Delia hung back as soon as she could see what was happening up ahead, taking refuge amongst the orange and lemon trees. Nobody had noticed her, lurking amongst the shadows of the fruit trees, what was she going to do? She felt like a dirty filthy criminal, she hadn't washed for two whole days and had slept rough in a tent the night before.

When Maria's husband Ron had made the booking, for a Mr and Mrs Horace Dankworth, they must have been expecting a middle-class accountant dressed in a suit and a school mistress turning up at the front door.

She hadn't even looked in a mirror, what must she look like? and she hadn't even brushed her teeth or her hair for two whole days.

Thiago suddenly spun around, turning very quickly one hundred and eighty degrees, calling out her name, with perfect pronunciation, "Delia!" he shouted.

All the other guests stretched their necks from side to side, shielding their eyes from the now very low sun in the sky, with their hands, trying to see who the goat man was talking to.

Delia stepped out from the shadows of the orange and lemon trees, everyone gasped with horror, Delia looked straight ahead, focusing on the open doorway of the Spanish finca.

"O my god, that must be his wife," one lady gasped.

"Judging by the state of her, he probably beats her with that huge stick," said another middle-aged woman who preferred to travel alone.

Thiago walked over towards the few steps that led up to the main entrance and spoke a few words of Spanish to the lady standing at the top, she had bleached blonde hair and was dressed like a waitress.

After a very brief conversation with Thiago, Julia, the retired nurse from Basingstoke and co-owner of the family run Spanish finca, came rushing down the stairs to meet Delia, like someone who had just witnessed a horrific car or train crash, and now was helping to pull the injured survivors from the wreck.

Putting her arm around Delia's shoulder and walking very slowly and talking very quietly to her, guiding her forward towards the open doorway. The crowd parted, letting Delia pass by, being gently ushered by Julia, talking words of comfort. At that point if Delia could have melted and drained away into the hard baked soil, she would have done so, this must be the worst day of her life by a long shot.

Thiago shouted out a few commands in Spanish and all the goats bleated in reply and began to hurry forward along the dusty track.

A tall slim woman with a tattoo of a swallow on her neck, shouted out to Thiago, "you big ugly brute of a man!" By that time, he and the goats were all out of earshot, disappearing around the bend in the lane.

Once inside, Delia, quickly took off all her clothes and dumped them down onto the floor and stepped into the free-standing Queen Victorian styled bath that was situated in the corner of the tastefully modernised studio styled room.

Never before in her whole life had she realised what comfort and relaxation a bath had to offer, her whole body ached after the walking and sleeping on the hard ground.

In the past she had taken just the simplest of things like hot water and scented soap for granted. Reaching forward she picked up a bar of lavender scented soap from the chrome plated soap dish that was slotted in between the chrome plated free standing bath taps, that were rising up, fixed independently onto the white and black marble flooring.

Unfortunately, the warm scented water hadn't completely relaxed her like she was hoping, in fact, the combination of the worry that she may never ever see Horace again and the fairly hot water, was making her heart beat faster and then began to thump, rapidly.

So many thoughts were now rushing around inside her head.

Where was Horace? Had he successfully vacated the tent, or was he lying lifelessly in a pool of his own vomit? What was she thinking, just walking off like she did, with Thiago and the herd of goats? Did he find the note? Did he see the arrow that she had made from the stones, pointing out the direction that she had taken?

And what about her dress, had Horace spotted it hanging from the tallest shrub, blowing gently in the light breeze? On hindsight, it had been a really stupid thing to do, especially leaving her bra behind dangling there in the wind.

What would he be thinking? Had she been attacked and then raped? Hopefully not, and Horace had managed to calmly untie the bra and her dress, unsnagged and not to dirty, and was now heading towards her at that very moment.

But Horace was hugely lacking in the most basic of life skills, especially the ones that involved outdoor pursuits. The natural survival skills one learns from the boy scouts or the girl guides, skills that one learns as a child, but his childhood had passed him by without any kind of adventures or obtaining any of these basic skills.

His parents hadn't enrolled him in any local clubs or organisations like the army cadets, or sea cadets, or even the boy scouts, so he did lack the life skills one needed to go successfully forward in life.

Delia, like Horace, was the only child but her parents had sent her out into the big wide world as soon as she could walk. Starting with a nursery school, her mother passing her over as soon as she were able to return to full time employment and her career. Delia had attended brownies as soon as she was old enough, then graduating on to the girl guides.

She had successfully completed all the tasks that had been set for her and somewhere in the loft, she still had her uniform and all the badges of her achievement neatly sewn on. She should never have left Horace alone, still sleeping in the tent, it was a really stupid thing to do.

She may as well have left a six-month-old baby, sleeping alone, wrapped up in a blanket. What was she going to wear? Maybe she should have hung on to her dress, on hindsight, it would have been the most sensible thing to do.

Now she was trapped inside the hotel room with nothing to wear, there was no way out, she was like a prisoner. She was starving hungry, and she had smelt the freshly cooked food, wafting out from the kitchen doorway on the way in. But she couldn't face all those gawping people, once again, all staring and wondering who she was and what the heck she was doing there?

She couldn't go downstairs still wearing the same dirty clothes that she had arrived in, all dusty and covered in wild grass seeds, she was trapped, she was a prisoner of her own making.

She had a quick wash, then getting out from the bath she dabbed herself dry with the fresh soft white towel. Then moving over to the double bed, she unfolded the freshly pressed white bathrobe and slipped it on.

Then there was a light knock on the door, Delia opened the door, Julia, the lady who had helped her earlier was standing there smiling.

"Good evening," she said, "my name is Julia and my husband, Eric and I run this little place together. Would you like me to take your clothes away and get them laundered for your departure first thing in the morning," she said.

"That would be marvellous," Delia, replied, "that is so thoughtful of you, I really didn't know what I was going to do."

"Will your husband be joining us for dinner?" Julia said, gathering up all the clothes from the floor.

"I really don't know," Delia replied, "at this moment in time I really don't know where he is," not knowing what else to say.

"The goat herder told me what you and your husband were doing, giving all those goats a new home and saving them from the slaughterhouse, I think that is a marvellous thing to do."

Delia suddenly felt very proud, the last few days had been a huge challenge and the lack of a good night sleep plus the alcohol had made her feel down.

Now her spirits were lifted, yes her and Horace were doing something good, and it had been recognised by other people, now all she had to do was somehow find Horace, and then they would be back on track.

Chapter 30

After spending at least five minutes searching through the material of the collapsed tent and around the surrounding area on the ground, desperately looking for his sunglasses, Horace began his descent, stumbling down the side of the mountain.

He hadn't found any trace of blood while looking around for his sunglasses and had come to the conclusion that Delia must have left by her own accord and had not been dragged of by some kind of wild animal. He also had failed to see the note that Delia had left and the arrow made from the small loose rocks and stones, pointing the way that he should have taken.

Even now in early November, the sun was beginning to irritate Horace's eyes, and he was even more irritated by the fact that his sunglasses seemed to have disappeared along with his wife. He had found the bottle of water that Ron had handed to him the night before, even though the outside of the plastic bottle was all wet with condensation and covered in yellow dust.

There was no visible sign of a pathway or track running down the mountainside for him to follow. Thiago, much earlier and with the aid of Google Earth, knew roughly what direction to head off in, and after that had just followed his nose.

Without giving it any thought, Horace, more or less, carried on roughly in the direction that they had been heading, the day before. It was what Freddie Tidmarsh back at the office would have called, a no-brainer.

Horace wouldn't turn around and go back up the slope the way that they had come, or turn to the left or the right, walking down the mountain at a weird angle would be a waste of time, pointless.

Thiago had taken the direction of a very slight angle, slowly descending down to the left, his own instinct telling him where the village of the goat watering point was in the far distance and then having his instincts confirmed once again by Google Maps.

Horace, on the other hand, didn't have a clue to where he was or where he was heading. The journey by car on the road up here originally had so many twists and turns, so right now he could be facing in any direction and heading anywhere.

Horace had chosen a route that veered off very slightly to the right, an almost perfect opposite angle to that of Thiago's but on the opposite side of the compass.

Even without his sunglasses and still hungover from the night before, he was able to make good progress, much quicker than Thiago and Delia who would have been slowed down by the goats grazing and nibbling their way down the gradual slope of the mountainside.

By the time Horace had reached the bottom of the mountains and down onto the wide-open flat area of the valley, the sun was slowly disappearing and the daylight was now fading fast.

The mountain had eventually bottomed out, separated by the same track that Thiago and Delia had connected with much earlier. The route that he had taken had eventually brought him down onto the very same track but much further back by around eight kilometres.

He turned roughly ninety degrees to the left, unknowingly following the track, heading off in the right direction, towards the small family run country retreat and Delia.

Horace also drew comfort from the fact that there were small dwellings scattered around, mostly hidden behind tall trees, with the flickering of lights shining out through the foliage.

The small hotel or guest house that Ron had booked for them the night before, looked very likely to be along the route that he was now traveling on.

This had been the first sign of civilisation that he had come across since he had left Ron and Maria's Spanish finca, practically two days before.

Luckily for Horace, there was a clear sky and a bright full moon that lit everything up in and around the surrounding area, making everything the colour of a pale warm yellow.

For an evening in November, it was still very mild and the track in that particular area was very soft and spongy underfoot, covered with thousands of fallen eucalyptus leaves.

Horace had always enjoyed walking, something that he had discovered at the still very young age of fourteen, when his parents had absent-mindedly driven off, leaving him stranded at a book fare thirty miles from his home.

He would have enjoyed the walk that evening had it been under different circumstances, it was a beautiful evening with the smell of eucalyptus oil filling the air.

His headache had now subsided and his eyes felt much better, now rested away from the bright sunlight of the day.

His thoughts returned to Delia, and why had she taken off like that?

Abandoning him, leaving him sleeping alone in the tent, choosing to go wandering off at the break of dawn with a herd of goats and the goat man.

Occasionally, a dog would bark, its bark breaking his thoughts and the silence, echoing out from behind the trees and inside one of the small dwellings, sensing Horace's presents as he passed by.

A small cat suddenly appeared, out from behind the foliage, meowing, getting under Horace's feet, craving for human company, rubbing its thin body against Horace's legs.

Horace, stopped in his tracks, not knowing what to do, fearing that at any moment his cat allergy would send him reeling, coughing and scratching wildly at his arms.

Horace stood perfectly still, as the cat snaked itself around Horace's legs, he could feel the warmth from its body as it squeezed itself through the gap, purring while rubbing it head against the inside of Horace's legs.

Then as quickly as it had appeared, it squeezed itself through a small gap in the hedging and disappeared.

Horace began to walk again, much faster than before, now with a more sense of urgency, the cat suddenly came running out onto the track in front of Horace, darting around playfully.

Horace moved up through the gears, now doing his best to jog, if only he had his mobile phone, he thought. All the times that he had carried it around in the past with no real reason or need, never fitting into any of his pockets, always causing a nuisance.

He could have called Delia, as soon as he had woken up, they could be chatting away right now, with him describing the landscape and Delia confirming his whereabouts with the aid of google maps.

Horace had suddenly broken out into a sweat, jogging along on the spongy surface of the eucalyptus leaves was hard going, and it seemed like he had been making much better progress earlier, with the speed walking.

He decided that it would be better to slow himself down, giving up on the jogging and walk at a much steadier pace, taking in deeper breaths.

Suddenly, from behind he could hear the sound from other footsteps, rustling, walking on the eucalyptus leaves other than his.

Horace stopped walking and turned, expecting to see the cat, there was no cat, but a huge dog, the biggest dog that Horace had ever seen, it had also stopped, cocking its head to one side, checking Horace out.

Horace's heart rate instantly shot up, now beating much harder and faster than previously, than when he was jogging, Surprisingly, he didn't lose total control of his nervous system completely, running away, becoming hysterical and screaming like a girl.

The words of wisdom from the park ranger from a very expensive holiday on safari in Africa that he had shared with him and Delia, echoed around inside his head. When being threatened by a wild cat or a savage animal and you think that your life may be in danger, never run, don't make eye contact, make yourself big, like a goalkeeper before a penalty kick, walk away slowly and boldly. Horace turned, and then slowly walking on tip toe he stretched his arms out to the side, stretching them out as far as he could.

The huge dog also moved forward very slowly, following in Horace's footsteps, maintaining a safe distance, not sure what to make of his new found friend who smelt like a heard of goats.

After a few seconds, Horace stopped and turned his head slowly, following the rules of the wild perfectly, the dog also stopped, cocking its head to one side yet again, totally bewildered by Horace's actions.

Horace turned back, slowly moving forward, his plan of action seemed to be working, the animal hadn't charged, dragging him to the ground, biting into the back of his neck, cutting of the blood flow to his brain.

The huge dog also was quite happy with its progress, this human seemed to be friendly, unlike some others in the past who had chased him away, throwing stones and shouting.

After a few more minutes had passed, Horace was finding it very difficult to walk on the tips off his toes, he was beginning to experience severe pain from his calf muscles and the back of his ankles.

Slowly, while still moving forward he adapted a more comfortable walking position, placing his feet firmly down onto the ground, but now limping slightly, caused by the pain shooting up the back of his legs from the both of his ankles.

The pain from his shoulders was also becoming unbearable, holding one's arms out to the sides wasn't that easy either. Slowly, Horace lowered them down, hoping the wild animal behind wouldn't notice.

Slowly, stride by stride, the dog's confidence grew and little by little he closed the gap between Horace and himself. Horace, suddenly was aware of the huge lumbering beast breathing very close to his backside, he stopped and turned, unwittingly breaking the most important rule of the wild.

He made eye contact, the dog stared back, deeply into Horace's eyes, searching for any sign of human kindness, longing to be beckoned forward for a comforting stroke. Horace turned and set off once again with the thoughts of finding Delia, this animal at the moment didn't seem to be posing any kind of immediate threat. Maybe it had just recently made a kill and was still digesting its last victim.

By the time that Horace had reached the small family run country retreat that was run very efficiently by Eric and Julia Simson, he had had enough of walking and felt completely all out and done in. By its appearance from the outside, it did look like some kind of guest house or a very small family run hotel where maybe he could take a room for the night. Just somewhere to sleep, then he could resume his search for Delia in the morning.

Horace turned ninety degrees off from the track and walked up the wide-open approach, towards the brightly lit building.

The huge dog by now was walking alongside Horace quite happily, but was also feeling tired and very hungry.

Horace first pushed and then pulled at the front door, it moved very slightly as the triple locking system prevented it from opening. Horace searched around for a bell or some kind of door knocker, he could see a very small reception desk through the glass and a sign that read, for late arrivals ring a telephone number that was written in bold black numbers.

Horace cursed himself for not carrying a mobile phone once again before giving the door a good rattle, hoping someone might come.

Horace walked back down the few steps and turned to his left, passing the glass frontage of the dining room that had been cleaned and everything had been tidied away for the night.

Then reaching the corner of the building he turned left again, passing what looked like individual rooms that all had the same curtains drawn shut and appeared to be in total darkness.

Turning left again, Horace found himself at the rear of the building and a well-stocked organic garden, illuminated by a selection of solar powered lights of all shapes and colours.

The dog went off to investigate, sniffing around the garden amongst the vegetables before cocking its leg up next to a row of bamboo canes, supporting the rows of runner beans and then did a very long wee.

Then suddenly, Horace noticed a shadow in the shape of a human form as it passed by a low-level light of some description. The huge mutt came bounding back playfully to Horace's side, seemingly to have gained a lot of pleasure from one of the basic functions in life like doing a wee.

Horace moved forward along the paved area that separated the back of the building and the organic garden, towards the light shining out through the glass and hopefully what was the rear entrance.

Horace stepped into the light that was shining out through the large floor to ceiling window.

Immediately, coming face to face with a very tall and a very slim naked woman. She had very white milky skin and small round firm breasts and the hair around her vagina, cut and styled to the shape of a Brazilian. She was standing only millimetres away on the other side of the glass at full stretch, her arms both stretched out to the sides at the point where she was just about to pull the heavy duty crushed velvet curtains shut.

She stared directly into Horace's eyes and then at the huge dog, and then at the white slimy drawl hanging from its lips. Letting out a scream so loud and piercing that it could have easily been heard as far away as the checking desk, in the departure lounge at Malaga airport.

The whole building was instantly illuminated and the sound of voices and people moving around. Horace just stood there, rooted to the spot, as the woman turned, opened her bedroom door and disappeared into the hallway.

Even Delia had heard the scream, even though she had fallen asleep only moments before and was sleeping very deeply, lying on top of the bed, still wearing the hotel dressing gown.

All the guests quickly gathered in the small reception area, some arriving more quickly than others, only wearing their dressing gowns, while others had taken the time to get fully dressed and were carrying all their personal belongings and valuables.

"There was a man!" the tall slim woman was shouting hysterically, "staring at my naked body, and a huge ugly slobbering dog."

Julia, the owner, looked genuinely concerned, in all the years that Eric and herself had been running the place they had never had a night prowler before, or anything that had woken everyone up in the middle of the night.

Eric, on the other hand, wasn't so sure, most evenings the corridors smelt of something like dried leaves burning, obviously some of the guests liked to relax in the evening with a smoke of the wacky-backy. A lot of the people who booked the type of holiday that they provided, seemed to be the type who liked to relax in the evening with a joint of pot or a bottle of wine.

Suddenly, Horace appeared at the front door, the motion sensors picking up the movement of his body and lighting him up with the beams from the very bright spotlights.

"That's him!" the woman shouted, pointing at Horace through the glass. "The sex pervert!"

Everyone stared at Horace, he didn't seem much like a sex pervert, more like someone who had fallen on harder times, losing his home and sleeping rough. Or one of those people who had stored themselves away in the underbelly of a passenger jet and had fallen out just after take-off.

Delia was positioned quite a long way back down the hallway, behind most of the other guests and the reflection from the glass was working against her, making it very difficult to see out.

"I think that might be my husband," she said.

Everyone turned and stared at Delia, as if she was cursed and had somehow invited the dark spirits of black evil into the building.

Delia moved slowly forward, trying to focus her tired eyes on the lonely desperate figure, illuminated on the other side of the glass.

"Horace?" she said.

Julia took the keys from her pocket and unlocked the door, Horace slowly walked into the small reception area followed by the huge dog and then the cat.

Everyone gasped and quickly shuffled back.

"Horace," Delia said, "what on earth are you doing with that huge dog and a stray cat?"

Horace hadn't uttered one single word of English to himself for around five hours and the bottled water had run out way before that. His throat suddenly felt very dry and sore, he wanted to speak to Delia, telling her what a dreadful day he had had. Walking around the mountains all alone, he opened and closed his mouth like a goldfish when gasping for air, but nothing came out.

"Let's get him into the kitchen and get some hot warm drink inside him," Julia said, reaching out and taking Horace by the arm, very similar to the way that she had assisted Delia all those hours before.

Eric explained everything to the tall slim woman, telling her Horace and Delia's story and what they were doing and how they had come to be separated. Everyone slowly filtered away, happy with Eric's explanation and returned to their rooms.

Julia handed Horace a warm thick hot chocolate drink, laced with half of a small bottle of brandy. Horace sat at the huge solid wooden kitchen table, taking small sips of his bedtime drink and blinking at Delia and Julia, like a small child who, for no reason at all, had been dragged from its bed in the middle of the night.

Suddenly, everyone was aware of the horrible smell wafting up from the dog, who had made himself at home underneath the kitchen table.

Julia opened the fridge door and filled a large cereal bowl with some of the leftovers from earlier. The huge hungry mutt got to her feet and followed Julia out through the side door, Julia placed the food outside on the ground, then coming back inside, shut the door and turned the key.

Horace finished off his drink and followed Delia up the stairs to their room on the first floor. Horace immediately collapsed onto the bed, and fell into a deep sleep, just within a few seconds. Horace awoke around midday the following morning, he opened his eyes and looked around the room. For the second time in two days, Delia was already up and out, leaving him all alone while still sleeping.

He rolled over and closed his eyes, wherever she was or whatever she was doing, he didn't care, there was no way he was getting up from such a comfortable bed and go wandering off in search for her.

Delia returned to the room around two o clock in the afternoon, "You have missed breakfast and lunch," she smiled, relieved and happy that somehow Horace had found her and they were now back together again.

"I am starving," Horace said, "I haven't eaten for almost two days."

"Eric has loaned you some clothes," Delia smiled, "you can take a shower and then, Julia said to go down stairs into the kitchen for something to eat. They are marvellous people," Delia said, putting the shirt socks and casual trousers onto the bed, "everyone here in Spain seems to be so helpful and friendly. We will have had to pay for an extra night," Delia said, "we were supposed to vacate the room by ten am this morning, maybe we can even stay for one more extra day or possibly two. And Julia and I have bathed your dog," Delia beamed a smile once again, "she smells much better now, much better than what she did when she arrived at the front door with you last night."

"It's not my dog," Horace mumbled, as he opened the door to the bathroom, "I don't even like dogs."

By the time Horace had showered and followed Delia down the stairs and into the kitchen, there was a steak dinner waiting for him. Julia had selected one of the finest steaks from their meat freezer and had fried it in a light garlic oil and it was presented with small new potatoes and a mixture of fresh vegetables from the organic garden.

Horace, as far as he could remember, had never gone two whole days without eating any source of food before. He found it very difficult to maintain his dignity and table manners, resisting the temptation to gulp everything down like a wild animal. The dog stared at him wistfully, licking her lips and pushing her head up against the glass on the other side of the door.

Horace finally looked up from his plate to take a drink of water, only then did he notice the huge mutt peering through the glass at him.

"Who's dog do you think it is?" he said, before putting his head down once again and finishing off what was left on his plate.

"Nobody's, probably," Julia answered, "turned out by a farmer or abandoned by a shepherd because she couldn't keep up, it's quite common here in this part of Spain."

"I thought we could take her home with us," Delia said. "She could help us look after the goats."

Horace looked out through the glass, making eye contact with the dog, her huge brown eyes staring back at him, while cocking her head to one side.

"I suppose it would come in handy," Horace said, "and it would also act as a guard dog when we are not there, and a dog would be more useful than that crazy cat."

"Oh," Delia said, "I thought we might take the crazy cat as well, she's around here somewhere; she will be needing a home also."

Chapter 31

By the time early December arrived, the new house was ready for Horace and Delia to move into. The big dog, now called Patsy, and the cat, Miss Tibbles, had already been living there for some time and were settled in very nicely.

In addition, there were also some chickens living there by the time that Horace and Delia arrived. The builders had built them a chicken coop, recycling all of the wood from the pallets that had been used for bringing all the building materials to the site originally. They had constructed it in the shape of a Swiss-style chalet and had painted the outside with a water-based light blue wood preserver.

Thiago spent all of his time up in the hills, tending the goats, although nothing had been discussed. After he had very successfully delivered the whole heard unscathed, he had stayed on, spending all his days wandering around in the Andalusian countryside.

Horace, as previously agreed with Ron and Maria, transferred all the money for the goats into their bank account, leaving their joint account practically empty with hardly any money left over to buy furniture for the new house.

Delia had found herself a job at the English college, a forty-minute drive from the house. As soon as she had arrived for the interview, they gave her the job instantly, purely based on her poise and eloquent use of the English language.

Horace, on the other hand, said for the time being, he was done with all that shit and was quite happy spending most of his time wandering around the local countryside. He had stumbled across a very well-organised English-speaking walking group and they had welcomed him to join them with open arms. Mostly consisting of all retired professional people, who had retired to Spain for the better life with more outdoor living.

Everyone had been given a nickname and there was a lot of humorous banter on the walks, for the very first time Horace felt like he was part of a club, and he was affectionately christened the ginger-haired goat guy.

Christmas day arrived, it seemed to spring up on Horace and Delia without any prior warning. Up to that point they had not had an English TV installed, so they hadn't been constantly reminded by commercials, selling chocolate logs and all the plastic toys that were manufactured in China. One other thing that had taken a fair-sized lump from their savings was the purchase of the new six-seater people carrier.

Horace had set his mind on a small four-door run-around, but Delia had insisted on buying a huge six-seater people carrier. Something big enough to accommodate Patsy, so she could also enjoy days out to the beach and all the surrounding national parks.

Patsy didn't show any interest at all in helping Thiago manage the goat herd, and spent most of her days lying down in the garden next to Miss Tibbles, both taking in the warm winter sun together.

By the time that mid-January had arrived, the days were already getting slightly longer, with eleven hours of daylight. The big house was still quite empty lacking a lot furniture in most of the rooms, and Horace was becoming more and more worried about their finances. He had twisted his ankle on some loose rocks, out on the latest walking trip and the following morning it had swollen up like a balloon. With Patsy safety harnessed in the back of the car, Horace set off to the village, first stopping at the local garage to fill the car up with petrol and then on to the chemist for some painkillers.

Horace managed to park the car close enough to walk to the chemist, with Patsy inside on guard, leaving all the car windows wide open, he hobbled off to the chemist. It didn't come as a complete shock to Horace when his bank card was declined for the payment of two boxes of paracetamol.

Delia's salary was nothing like what she was used to earning back in England and he still hadn't gotten around to entering all the outgoing and incomings onto his laptop and making an accurate cash flow forecast.

Horace hobbled back to the car, feeling very annoyed with himself. His ankle seemed to hurt even more and his palms of his hands felt all hot and sweaty as he opened the car door. Patsy seemed to sense something was wrong, and even though she was securely harnessed at the back of the car, she could still stretch her neck far enough forward to lick Horace's left ear for most of the journey on the way home.

Horace parked the car around the back of the house. He needed to speak with Thiago about the running costs of maintaining all the goats.

Horace opened the rear door, letting Patsy out. "Find Thiago," he said.

Patsy took up the challenge, beginning the walk up the incline to the rear of the property and into the countryside, Miss Tibbles also took an interest in what was happening and joined in with the hunt. After a good half an hour had passed of steady walking, Horace could see Thiago sitting under a huge tree on an elevated level of flat ground.

Thiago spotted Horace hobbling towards him and stood up, he still wasn't very comfortable with Horace's brief visits and talking with him. Unlike the more frequent visits from Delia, who had made a lot of progress with her Spanish and between them they were getting along just fine.

Patsy flopped over on her side, lying under the tree, wagging her tail, acknowledging what Thiago was saying to her. Miss Tibbles was still full of energy and set about dragging her claws of her front paws up and then down the huge trunk of the tree.

Thiago watched Horace struggling with the last part of the incline, he was leaning forward, stooped and slightly twisted like a hunchback, and was now limping even more than before. Thiago tightened the grip on his huge stick, wondering if Horace had gone crazy with heat stroke or something, his face was also very pink and sweaty and he was mumbling to himself.

"Thiago," Horace called out, "we are all buggered, all the money has gone!" Horace put his hands deep inside his pockets, pulling out the mesh linings, so they hung down by his sides.

Thiago over the years had self-taught himself a lot of English and he had become very good at recognising the key words of a sentence and understanding what people were saying to him, more or less.

On this occasion he only caught a couple of words, buggered, and the word money, he wrapped his fingers further around his stick, tightening his grip even more. He had always had his doubts about Horace and his sexual preferences, right from the start when he first set his eyes on him at Ron and Maria's finca, what with his milky white skin and light ginger hair.

"I don't know what we are going to do," Horace panted, "everything has spiralled out of control! It all started with a raffle ticket and a dream holiday home in the sun," Horace whined. "But it all went horribly wrong, and then with Covid and Brexit and all these goats," Horace mumbled.

Thiago looked at Horace, he didn't have a clue what he was ranting about, he didn't think he was there for sex, so luckily for Horace, he didn't have to bash him one over the head with his huge stick.

"We will have to sell the house in England and use the money from that; I can't think of any other option," Horace said, looking towards Thiago, waiting for his opinion.

At last Thiago understood enough key words from the last sentence that Horace had delivered. Sell the house in England, and money, this was good, the goats would have a secure future and he could stay on and do what he loved doing the most. Thiago dropped down his stick and grabbed hold of Horace, very firmly, by one of his turned inside out pocket linings, and pulled him over to the edge off the raised platformed area of ground.

Then turned Horace around in the direction of facing North and still holding onto him very firmly by his pocket lining stood next to Horace and raised his right hand and spoke three words in perfect English, while waving his hand from side to side.

"Bye-bye, Inglaterra," he said, smiling.

Ingram Content Group UK Ltd.
Milton Keynes UK
UKHW020612070423
419773UK00007B/639